Voices of the South

THE KEEPERS OF THE HOUSE

Other Books by Shirley Ann Grau

The Black Prince and Other Stories

The Hard Blue Sky

The House on Coliseum Street

The Condor Passes

The Wind Shifting West

Evidence of Love

Nine Women

Roadwalkers

THE KEEPERS OF THE HOUSE

Shirley Ann Grau

Louisiana State University Press
Baton Rouge

The quotation on page 32 is from "The Land of Heart's Desire" in *The Collected Plays of W. B. Yeats.* Reprinted with permission of The Macmillan Company, Mrs. W. B. Yeats, and Macmillan & Co. Ltd. Copyright 1934, 1952 by The Macmillan Company.

Lines from "Johnny Cuckoo" by Bessie Jones appear on page 114. Copyright © 1960 by Progressive Music Publishing Co., Inc., 1619 Broadway, New York 19, N.Y. Used by permission.

A condensation of this novel appeared in *Ladies' Home Journal.*

Originally published by Alfred A. Knopf, Inc.
LSU Press edition published 1995 by arrangement with Alfred A. Knopf, Inc.

Manufactured in the United States of America
ISBN: 0-8071-2031-6 (pbk.)
04 03 02 01 00 99 98 97 96 95 5 4 3 2 1

Library of Congress Catalog Card No. 64-12306

The paper in this book meets the guidelines for permanence and durability of the Committee on Production Guidelines for Book Longevity of the Council on Library Resources ♾

IN the day when the keepers of the house shall tremble, and the strong men shall bow themselves, and the grinders cease because they are few, and those that look out of the windows be darkened,

AND the doors shall be shut in the streets, when the sound of the grinding is low, and he shall rise up at the voice of the bird, and all the daughters of musick shall be brought low;

ALSO when they shall be afraid of that which is high, and fears shall be in the way, and the almond tree shall flourish, and the grasshopper shall be a burden, and desire shall fail: because man goeth to his long home, and the mourners go about the streets.

ECCLESIASTES 12:3–5

CONTENTS

ABIGAIL

November evenings are quiet and still and dry. The frost-stripped trees and the bleached grasses glisten and shine in the small light. In the winter-emptied fields granite outcroppings gleam white and stark. The bones of the earth, old people call them. In the deepest fold of the land—to the southwest where the sun went down solid and red not long ago—the Providence River reflects a little grey light. The river is small this time of year, drought-shrunken. It turns back the sky, dully, like an old mirror.

November evenings are so quiet, so final. This one now. It is mist-free; you see for miles in all directions. East and north, up the rising ridges, each tree is sharp and clear. There isn't even a trace of smoke up there, though earlier, in October, there were ugly smears of drifting ashes from forest fires in the Smokies. And there is no trace of fog along the fold that holds the Providence River. Everything is crisp and clear. There is only the quiet steadily fading light.

Last month there were two whippoorwills crying all night around the house. I did not think I would miss their shrieking, but I do. Now.

Behind me the house is quiet as my children get ready for supper—an early supper because only the two youngest are here. My oldest girls have gone to school in New Orleans. The county does not know of that yet, but they will, they always know everything. "Just like a Howland," they will say. "Always doing crazy things, high and mighty, the way they are. Broke their neck last time, though, broke it clean. . . ."

I have the illusion that I am sitting here, dead. That I am like the granite outcroppings, the bones of the earth, fleshless and eternal.

I turn on the porch light. Since I have come out to water the geraniums, I do just that. With the great tin watering can in my hand I sprinkle the dense line of sprawling red-and-white flowers. I was taught that a geranium will stand the cold of the night better if the roots are wet. These now, growing under the porch roof and back against the warm house wall, last until the very worst of the winter.

I pour carelessly and the water splashes across the porch boards. I am looking out at the yard, at the front yard. Even in this dim light you can see that the turf has been broken and torn. It looks a bit like a choppy sea. The paling fence is completely gone; all you see is the gentle fountain-like rise of the branches of the cherokee rose that grew on it once.

I shall not replace that fence. I want to remember.

As I stand there in the immaculate evening I do not find it strange to be fighting an entire town, a whole county. I am alone, yes, of course I am, but I am not particularly afraid. The house was empty and lonely before—I just did not realize it—it's no worse now. I know that I shall hurt as much as I have been hurt. I shall destroy as much as I have lost.

It's a way to live, you know. It's a way to keep your heart ticking under the sheltering arches of your ribs. And that's enough for now.

There are some big white moths fluttering around the porch light; and a few fat-bellied beetles flip over on their backs and squirm helplessly on the boards. I wonder how they have survived the frost. They must have hatched under the house, in the warmth there, or between the clapboards. A screech owl pumps silently past the corner of the porch, avoiding the light.

I wrap my sweater tighter around me, I lean on the porch rail and watch the night come. Not from any particular quarter—it's not that sort of night—it creeps in from all over, like stain up a sponge. There is no wind yet; it will rise later on. It always does.

I hear the brief scream of a rabbit; the owl has found supper.

I stand on the porch of the house my great-great-great-great-grandfather built, and through the open door I hear my children clatter along the hall to their supper. Marge, the baby, is laughing as Johnny teases her: "You are, you are, you are!" The words carry on the quiet motionless air until a door cuts them short.

I was a child in this house once too, rushing through those halls and up and down those stairs. It was not as nice as it is now—that was before the war, before my grandfather made his money—but it was the same house. For them, for me. I feel the pressure of generations behind me, pushing me along the recurring cycles of birth and death. I was once the child going to bed upstairs, whispering to reassure myself against the creatures of the night. My mother slept in the great tester bed in the south bedroom. And my grandfather stood, where I am standing, this same spot. . . . And those before him too. They sat on this porch and looked out across the fields, resting from the heat of the day, letting their eyes run over the soft turns of the land until they reached the dark woods. In those days the woods were much closer.

They are dead, all of them. I am caught and tangled around by their doings. It is as if their lives left a weaving of invisible threads in the air of this house, of this town, of this county. And I stumbled and fell into them.

The owl gives his quivering descending call, far off now. For a minute I think I see his sweeping shape against the sky over the Providence River. I stand in the pitch darkness and listen to the sounds of voices that roar around in my head and watch the parade of figures that come and jostle for attention before my eyes. My grandfather. My mother. Margaret. Margaret's children: Robert and Nina and Crissy.

It's been several years since I've heard from either Crissy or Nina. I don't know where they are now. I don't know what they are doing. I don't even know if they are still alive. But Robert, now, Robert came back. And how long ago?—three months, no more. He came back jeering and hating. He drifts out of the crowd of people inside my head and stands next to me on the porch. Not the boy I grew up with, not the child I knew, but the man I saw just three months ago.

He is my age, almost exactly, though he carries himself like an old man, rubbing at his mouth, batting his eyes rapidly. But he is alive. And when I am being honest with myself, as I am tonight, I know that I wish he were not.

WILLIAM

I want to tell you the story of my grandfather, and Margaret Carmichael, and me. It's hard to know where to begin, everything leading back and weaving into everything else the way it does. My grandfather was William Howland. Margaret was a Freejack from over by New Church. But it didn't exactly start there either.

When you think about it, you see that it started way back, a long long time ago, in the early 1800's, when Andrew Jackson and his army marched north from New Orleans. It had been a fine war, good and brisk, and it didn't even take a man away from his place too long—there was plenty of time for spring planting work. It was a dull winter's worth of war, and they'd have something to tell about now for the rest of their lives. How they'd chased the British army in the fields and swamps of Chalmette. How they'd had a hero's welcome in the city afterwards. A city bigger than any they'd ever seen. A fine rich city with great sailing ships moored in the river, and a Pope's cathedral and priests in long black dresses. And women like they'd never seen before either, round-faced, smoothly fleshed, dark-eyed; softer, gentler than their own gaunt wives. All dressed in bright silks, even the mothers, all jabbering away in a language they couldn't understand.

The army went home heroes, and even the slaves felt pretty good. There were quite a few of them—Andrew Jackson had taken them along when he marched south, nervous and worried, not knowing the kind of British army he'd be facing. Those slaves went down with the army, served with it, and came back with it. As each man left, he got a bit of paper signed by Andrew Jackson giving him his freedom. Now, the General had a poor hand and he signed carelessly, with only the first four letters of his name showing clearly. On those pieces of paper there was just the word "Free" and a scrawl that looked like "Jack." So these new freemen and their children for all the years after were called Freejacks.

They were proud of their station and they kept apart from other Negroes. In the generations that followed they got themselves some Choctaw blood, and kept even more to themselves, taking on many of the Indian ways and customs. They were scattered all across the state, little communities of them. In particular they settled the pine uplands and the swampy bottomlands between the east and west branches of the Providence River. That was good fertile land, though it had considerable malaria. There were at least fifty families scattered through there, and you could be born and marry and die in the triangle of land between the forks of that river, a community they called New Church. And that's where Margaret Carmichael was born.

Now in the same army that straggled north during the spring of 1815 there was a man named William Marshall Howland. He was from Tennessee, a young man, sixteen or seventeen or eighteen, he wasn't quite sure; his mother had died when he was a baby and other people—his aunts and such—hadn't bothered keeping count. He was tall and thin and brown-haired and blue-eyed. When he took the road with his friends, marching home after the war was over, his head was aching from the liquor he had drunk and his brain spinning with the things he had seen. After a day or so he felt better and began to look around him. He saw the roll and pitch of the land and the soft sandy soil. He saw endless stretches of trees, the pines and hickories, big-leafed magnolias and huge live oaks. He saw how plants bloomed in the warmer soil, how they grew double their usual size with no wind to cut them down: dogwood and redbud, flame azalea and laurel. And he remembered the hill country he was going back to—razorback ridges, and valleys so narrow the sun never shone into them and little patches of tobacco on slopes so steep a man reached up to tend the plants. He remembered the balds too, flower-flecked and open, and the great blue-green distances seen from them. But his eyes were tired of reaches, he wanted a friendlier country, cut to the measure of a man, where the hills could be walked over, and the land turned easily under his plow.

His friends told him that if he wanted to turn farmer, he should go on to the fat black delta land that lay just a bit to the north. But William Marshall Howland shook his head and said he was tired. He dropped out to make his own way. He hadn't nearly done walking though, because it took him weeks to find a spot that he liked. He finally settled in the almost empty country toward the east, by a bluff that stuck red sides straight up in the air over a deep fast-running little river. Since it had no name he called it the Providence River, which was his mother's name, and just about all he knew about her. The land was heavily wooded and he could see very little. So he walked slowly back and forth across the surface, mapping it in his mind. From the river bluffs the land rose gently in a series of long waves, lifting gradually to the higher ridges in the east. He put his house on the fourth of the rises from the riverbank, halfway between river and ridge.

That William Howland was murdered by five raiding Indians one April while he was clearing his fields. They took his ax and his rifle and his powder horn and the shot pouch of groundhog hide, but they didn't bother the house up on the hill. They were drunk and careless and maybe they just didn't notice. The Howland boys went racing off to their nearest neighbors—there were six or seven families in the area by then. In little more than a day nine men set out, and William Howland's oldest son, who was fourteen, went with them. They trailed the Indians to the Black Warrior River, and they killed them—all but one—on the banks there. They took that single survivor back, along with the half-dry scalp. They called the Howland family out to watch while they hanged the Indian to a white oak in front of the house. They buried William Howland's scalp decently at the edge of his grave.

That was how the first William Howland died, a youngish man still, but not before he had left a wife and six children to fill his house.

All in all the Howlands thrived. They farmed and hunted; they made whiskey and rum and took it to market down the Providence River to Mobile. Pretty soon they bought a couple of slaves, and then a couple more. By the middle of the century they had twenty-five, so it wasn't a big plantation; it wasn't ever anything more than a prosperous farm, run pretty much along the lines of the Carolina farms the first William Howland had seen. There was cotton, blooming its pinkish flower and lifting its heavy white boll under the summer sun; there was corn, soft-tasseled and then rusty as the winter cattle grazed over it; there was sorghum to give its thin sweet taste to the watery syrup; there were hogs whose blood steamed on the frozen ground in November; there were little patches of tobacco, moved each two years to fresh clean virgin ground. The house grew larger; there was a barn and a stable, and four smokehouses, and a curing shed for the tobacco. There was a grist mill with a cypress wheel and granite stones. In the prosperous days before the Civil War even the interior began to have touches of elegance—harmoniums, and inlaid tables and shelves full of china figures. By then the county had a proper name—Wade—and the little boat landing that the first William Howland cleared had turned into Madison City, a tight neat town with a brick courthouse and a square and a single street lined with stores and houses.

And every generation had a William Howland. Sometimes he had his mother's maiden name for a middle initial and sometimes he didn't. There was William Marshall Howland, who'd come first from Tennessee. His son was just plain William Howland, his mother having come from ordinary people with no feeling for their name. His son was William Carter Howland. He was killed in the Civil War, maimed and burned to death in the thickets of the Wilderness—a young man without a wife or even a bastard son to carry his name. Within three years, his brother's son was named William Legendre Howland, and the name was back. That particular Mrs. Howland, whose name had been Aimée Legendre, caused quite a commotion in the county. First of all she was a Catholic from New Orleans, had married before a priest, and never once set foot in either the Baptist or the Methodist church of the town where she lived her entire married life. That was one thing. And then there was her father. Mr. Legendre dealt in cotton; and during the last days of the Civil War, cotton sold at fabulous prices both to the mills of the North and those of England. A man who wasn't troubled by Confederate loyalty could make a fortune in no time at all. Mr. Legendre did, and he continued to prosper all through the Reconstruction. He was a very wealthy man when he dropped dead on the steps of the St. Louis Cathedral, as he left mass on a rainy Sunday morning. His money went to his daughter, and with it the Howland place prospered and grew. Aimée Legendre Howland had a craving for land, perhaps because she was city-bred herself, and as other farms were sold (in the poverty-ridden '70's and '80's) she began buying. All sorts of land. Bottoms, for cotton. Sandy pine ridges that weren't used for anything in those days except woodlots.

After her son, there was one more William Howland. He was my grandfather.

When I knew my grandfather he was an old man, a big heavy man, with faded blue eyes, and a shiny bald head fringed by dark hair. His beard had gone so white that there was no longer any shadow on his cheeks and they shone bright pink at you like a child's. That was the man I knew. But there was another, an earlier one—I had seen him in pictures and I knew him from stories.

Everyone tells stories around here. Every place, every person has a ring of stories around them, like a halo almost. People have told me tales ever since I was a tiny girl squatting in the front dooryard, in mud-caked overalls, digging for doodlebugs. They have talked to me, and talked to me. Some I've forgotten, but most I remember. And so my memory goes back before my birth.

When I want to, I can see my grandfather William Howland as a young man, tall and heavy already, but with fair hair and a fair mustache that curled over his lips. A handsome, gentle man. He went to Atlanta to study law in his cousin Michael Campbell's office. He was there for two years, not working very hard, not even interested in the law. He stayed that long only because his father wanted it—he never liked cities and this one was still bleak and new; it hadn't quite lost the burned, gutted look.

He was bored but he wasn't really miserable. His studies did not interest him, but his holidays did; he was very much in demand among his cousin's younger friends. The women thought him handsome in a rugged, unfashionable way. They took him on long drives to visit the burned-out hulls of buildings and plantation houses fired during the war. There was a perfect craze for moonlight picnics among ruined houses, on battlefields. They told him long stories of raiding and valor and courage; he nodded solemnly, sadly, though he didn't believe a word, because he had come from a part of the country that had been burned out too, and he knew how stories grew. Still, he had to admit ruins made a nice spot for a picnic. Enough time had passed so that the brick and rubble were mostly covered by smilax and creepers, softening their outlines. On a gentle summer night, you could forget the fire and the killing and see only the soft forms of the young women, vague and floating and romantic in the diffused light.

He liked hunting with their brothers and their fathers, and every house party invariably included a hunt. Coonshine, they sometimes called it.

No women ever went with them. It was a man's hunt. On foot, back-country style. (Now and then the women talked about the mounted English hunts and wondered how becoming a formal black habit would be. But none of them could ride well enough, and the country was too broken anyway.)

The hunt began about midnight. First the Negro handlers arrived with the dogs in a wagon; a squirming yelping pack. Then the hunters and their servants crowded into other wagons and bumped their way to a likely spot. The handlers released the pack; they scattered and circled, yelping, looking for a trail. The hunters lounged around the wagons, talking, laughing, listening to the hounds work, waiting for them to pick up a scent. When they did, the men trotted after them. They went for miles sometimes following the hounds, crashing through underbrush, resting on fallen logs. If they found they had treed a bobcat (a painter some people called them) the Negroes shook it down from the tree, and let the pack finish it. When that happened, William walked quickly away from the brief scrawling tussle; afterwards he avoided passing that particular spot of torn ground and scattered bits of fur. (He could stick a hog and he often worked in the slaughter pens in the early-winter killing, but he did not like to kill wild things. He never had since the day he went dove shooting with his father in the pasture lots at home, and the matted bloody feathers made him vomit.)

Most times they did not even see any game, and anyway white men almost never killed on a hunt. They had bearers for their guns, and these usually dropped behind early in the chase—so the hunters could not have fired, had they wanted to. (Sometimes William wondered why they bothered bringing guns along at all.) The Negroes clubbed the game to death . . . coon or possum for the pot, the fox's tail to decorate the side of a cabin. After all, no white man ate possum or coon, unless he counted himself trash. Once a possum was cooked in the house, people said, twenty years later you could smell it. . . .

After a couple of hours the hunters tired. They built a fire and waited for their gun bearers to catch up with them. With the bearers came several boys carrying jugs of whiskey, panting under the awkward load, staggering over the broken ground.

William Howland, back against a pine, legs aching with the unaccustomed exercise, lungs aching with the effort of scrambling up and down the razorback ridges, drank the warm whiskey and stared into the blazing fire, listening to the pack work in circles around him. And even before the whiskey, he felt drunk. It was the race through the night, with the bright moon whirling around your head as you went, and the dogs on after something, calling to you. It was the smell of the night, of leaf mold, of bark. It was the feel of the night earth, of the sleeping ground.

He was in Atlanta two years; he left when he married. Her name was Lorena Hale Adams.

(There are no pictures of her. No pictures at all. He burned them one summer afternoon.)

He was not supposed to have married her. He was not even supposed to have met her. She was not at any of the house parties and dances. She was not at the concerts or the assemblies or the memorials. She was not at the teas, or the receptions, or the Sunday dinners. That he met her at all was an accident.

Soon after he came to Atlanta he acquired a mistress, Selma Morrisey, the widow of a contractor. She was Irish-born—she kept a faint touch of the brogue—nearly forty, with two children in their teens. She rented rooms, and William Howland saw her pleasant pecan-shaded yard and wide, gingerbread-fretted porch, and moved in. In a couple of weeks he had left his small upstairs room for the larger and far more comfortable one downstairs, the one that held the enormous double bed her mother had brought from Ireland.

Selma Morrisey was a pleasant comfortable woman, and they were very happy. Now, William never came back to her house at noon. Each day he had dinner with his cousin Michael Campbell and his wife, a long slow heavy meal, in their huge dark dining room. Afterwards the two men went back to the office. This particular day, Michael Campbell had been trying a case, and William as his clerk scurried back and forth, carrying notes, running errands. It was May and very hot. Heavy morning rains gouged ruts in the streets and turned to steam in the heavy air. William's face was red and streaked with dirt, his mustache was ruffled and wispy. His linen coat showed huge blotches of sweat across the back. The starch in his shirt stuck to his body in dabs and gave out a strange sweet smell in the heat. At the noon recess, Michael Campbell sent him off to change his clothes.

For the first time in two years William went home, walking the few blocks rapidly so that he could feel the currents of air moving about his body. He swung through the front gate, bounced up the steps, and burst into the parlor, whistling loudly. He had expected Selma. Or no one. But there were two women sitting over their teacups at the dining-room table. He bowed politely, apologizing.

"This is my cousin," Selma Morrisey said, "Miss Lorena Hale Adams."

He bowed again, as his eyes accustomed themselves to the soft gloom of the drawn shutters. He looked, and then looked again.

She stood up, politely, still having the manners of a child. She was very young; her cheeks were smooth and round and bright pink. Her nose and mouth were very small and her eyes were very large, and a luminous grey. She was also extremely tall for a woman, the face that looked across at him was almost at his own level.

"We'll go into the parlor," Selma Morrisey said. "William, would you like some tea?"

"I have to go back," he said.

But he went into the parlor. They sat on the linen covers of the horsehair furniture, and he studied Lorena Adams carefully. Her face was round, her skin very white. Her hair, which she had pulled back over her ears into a crisp bun at her neck, was straight and heavy and black. William thought he could see her glowing, and all the verses of Poe, of which he was so fond, began running through his head.

In half an hour or so, he left, because he had to, and changed and went back to work. All the rest of the long hot day he was conscious of a silly smile quivering the ends of his mustache. They lost the case, and he did not care. As he was pushing his way through the crowded corridors, an old man hawked and spat, and the slimy white wad hit William's shoe. He wiped it clean with a clump of rain-washed grass. And that was when he decided that he could never manage the law. That he was a farmer and nothing more.

Much later that evening—when it had gotten cooler, with a little breeze blowing down off the hills to the north—he lay in bed and waited for Selma. The room was dim. They had only one very small lamp burning, because of the heat. Nothing so stifling as the smell of kerosene, Selma said.

She had been making her nightly round of the house, opening the shutters on the west side, closing them on the east against the rising sun. William could hear her moving about, and he folded his arms under his head and stretched contentedly. She came finally, closing the door behind her, stopping at the dresser to take the last of the pins from her hair, and do its regular brushing. William, for the first time, noticed the nightgown she wore—the long plain gown of lawn, drawn tight to the neck with a drawstring, falling loosely to the wrists, falling straight to the floor. A shapeless proper night gown . . . a wifely motherly gown . . . he would have supposed that a mistress would have something more fancy, more seductive . . . He chuckled; it had never been like that for them.

"You are laughing," she told him through the mirror.

"I've never noticed your gown before."

"They are all alike," she said.

He chuckled again, and she smiled back at him.

"Selma," he said, in a bit, "I'm going home."

"I have been wondering when."

"I'm no lawyer."

She brushed regularly, slowly. "You have been thinking of this?"

"Just today."

"Oh," she said.

"I'd rather go home." He lay silent staring at the faintly lit ceiling, thinking how it would be there. Then he said: "You won't mind, will you? There wasn't anything between us, nothing to keep us."

She turned around now, finished with her brushing, tying the hair into the wide pink ribbon she used every night. "No," she said. "No, I imagine not."

He sat up at her tone, surprised. "But there wasn't. I haven't taken advantage of you."

"You are a gentleman," she said, "and so formal. No, of course not."

She had forgotten the bedroom shutters; he got up and began closing them. "And your cousin," he said, "do you think I could call on her?"

She walked slowly to bed, bringing the lamp, setting it on the small table. "She is seventeen," Selma said. "I think so."

"You'll tell me where she lives?"

"Yes." Selma stretched herself out on the bed. It was so hot that they slept without even a sheet to cover them, and she lay on the open bed, staring at her toes.

"What sort of cousin is she of yours?"

Selma said: "Her mother and my husband were first cousins. Their mothers were twins."

"She's the most beautiful girl I've ever seen."

Selma reached over and blew out the lamp, so that he had to find his way to bed in darkness.

He courted Lorena Hale Adams, quickly, impatiently, because he wanted to leave Atlanta. He scarcely noticed her family; he neither liked nor disliked them, though he realized that his own parents would have called them trash. Mrs. Adams was a thin plain woman, with wiry black hair and loose-hanging arms; she kept a bottle of gin in the kitchen safe, and sipped at it all day long. There was a brother too—William forgot to ask his name—who had run off to a ship at Savannah and disappeared. He had written once, from Marseille, over a year ago. They thought he must be dead. Only his mother insisted stubbornly that he was fine—that he was hiding from them all in Turkey. "Why there?" William asked and started to add: "Do you even know where it is?"

"He was always an aggravating child. . . . Sharper than a serpent's tooth. . . . I forget the rest." Mrs. Adams got up. "I think the cat's come inside." She slipped out into the kitchen to have another drink.

There was an older sister, married to a railroad engineer. They lived next door, in a neat white house with four red-headed children, and raised fighting cocks in the back yard.

Mr. Adams was a railroad telegrapher, a slight gentle man. He carved bits of soft yellow pine, and the surface of every table and every mantel was covered with the grotesque results of his enterprise. His people had been storekeepers at Mobile before they drifted north during the hard days right after the Civil War. His mild grey eyes, large, luminous, with their look of infinite tenderness, of grief for all things living, never changed. His daughter Lorena had them too.

In two weeks William was engaged. In four weeks he was married and on his way home.

They lived with William's parents in the old house by the Providence River. They added another wing, and a broad gallery, which Lorena planted with white wisteria. It was finished just in time for the birth of their first child, a girl. They called her Abigail.

Within a year, in the following August, Lorena delivered again, a boy, called William.

He was a strapping child, heavy and fat. Lorena lay in her bed and smiled, her large grey eyes gleamed. "That wasn't bad at all," she told her husband. "They get easier all the time. This one was easy."

Three days later the colored nurse noticed that her eyes glittered too much and too wildly. She felt her cheek, then her neck. Lorena said: "This is a hot day, but in August they always are." And the nurse smiled, and slipped down the hall to call William's mother. She went for her son. "The fever," she said simply. "Fetch the doctor."

William went; his horse was so worn that he had to leave it and come back in the doctor's surrey. By then it was almost sunset. Lorena's skin was dry and rough to the touch; her lips were split and blistered. "It is such a hot day," she said, "I hope the baby doesn't get covered with rash."

She fretted about that. Finally they brought in the child to show her. She opened the cotton blanket and searched all over his body before she would believe that he did not have a heat rash. As the fever rose, she laughed and talked, calling on people William did not recognize. She sang bits of songs too, particularly that one whose title was her own name: Lorena.

They covered her with wet sheets sprinkled with camphor. They gave her the spoons of whiskey and quinine the doctor ordered. They even sent for the Negro voodoo woman. She hung her snakeskin bags in the four corners of the room, and then went outside to the corner of the yard just off the new porch—she stayed there all night, over the little fire she had built in spite of the heat, praying to her gods for them.

The fever lasted through the night and into the next day. William slept in a corner of the room under one of the voodoo bags. His parents went to bed, old people, frightened and afraid. The doctor dozed upright in a chair. Only Lorena seemed happy. In the very early morning when William woke, he found her luminous eyes on him. She was humming gently, and he took a chair and sat by her. He was no longer frantic with fear. That had passed. He was numb with exhaustion; his head was a great ball that bobbed about at the end of his neck. The color of her round smooth face, the pinched look about her nose, and the vague faint smell that rose from the bed—he understood with quiet icy finality.

Lorena waved her hand weakly at invisible people, smiled at them, and kept humming, tunelessly now. All the rest of his life William remembered sitting and watching those great grey eyes, watching the light fade from them, gradually, bit by bit, until he was not sure when it had happened exactly, when it was gone. Until it was gone completely—the humming, the movement, and he sat looking into a pair of open dead eyes. Not grey, not any color, only lightless. He closed them himself.

The doctor still slept, but the colored nurse was coming down the hall as William stepped through the door. He heard the rattling of her starched white skirts; he smelled the odor of sun and hot iron. He noticed these things detachedly, as if they had nothing to do with him. He saw that the nurse was hurrying toward him, her fat black legs pumping under the starched cloth. With a single jerk of his head he motioned her into the room. Then he walked through the hall to the gallery and along its length, noticing as he did the smell of the new boards and the new paint in the hot sun. He crossed the yard and was swinging himself through the rail fence, when he heard the nurse's sobbing scream, muffled by the walls of the house. William walked through the pasture lot, vaguely aware that behind him other voices answered the nurse and a tangle of sound spilled out across the sun-scorched fields. He climbed the fence on the other side of the pasture and entered the woods. He walked slowly, naming the things that passed before his eyes, naming them to himself as if he had never seen them before. He looked into the sandy ground, mostly bare under the fall of pine needles, and he saw how grainy it was. And he saw the ants and the doodlebugs and the other little things that tunneled through it. He stood for the longest time in front of a dense clump of white titi, studying its shape and its thickness, noticing how the white flowers had given way to the beginnings of yellow berries. He saw that the wild azaleas, past their bloom, looked brown and dry. He moved slowly, as if he were in a park, looking. Looking at the bushes and the flowers he had seen his whole life long. Bayberry, fragrant in the sun, sparkleberry, the poisonous coral bean. Catbriar, where the shrikes stored their prey, white jasmine. He named them to himself silently. And the flowers too—the cherokee rose, blooming now; the grass pinks, and the gentians; the milkworts and the live-forevers; the railroad vine and the truehearts and the greenfly orchids. He found a fallen pine and he rested on that, sitting quietly so that the squirrels ran down the trees and looked into his face and chattered and screamed at him.

In a while, more than two hours, but less than three, he got up and started back. He walked lightly, easily, as if his body was no weight to him. He did not feel that he was within it any more.

He came out of the woods and saw the house lying against its green flower-fringed yard. He heard the mourning from the kitchen, the rising and falling wails that had no pattern beyond the movement of the singer's body. There was a Negro boy sitting on the back porch, a small boy, no more than four. William did not remember seeing him before. *I must ask about him*, he thought. *He must be somebody's child and I just haven't noticed him.* The child sat perfectly still on the top step, turning his head slightly to follow William as he went past. William nodded to him. The child nodded back.

William went around the house, passing the new wing he'd built for his wife and for his children. The broad gallery was edged by the white wisteria vines Lorena had planted two years before. Those vines had grown and spread; their blooming past, they were covered with feathery leaves. William circled around the house, listening to the heavy tromp of his shoes on the soft sun-baked grass. When he found himself at the front door, he went inside, sniffing the sudden odor of furniture polish. They would be opening the parlors, cleaning them for the wake.

Where are my parents? he asked the maids, and was surprised to find that he hadn't spoken aloud. They were so busy at their work that they did not turn or notice him.

He found his parents in the dining room. Two old people sitting in the big rockers by the bay window. They were just sitting, looking out through the open window at the slope of the grass down to the orderly green rows of the fields, where the cotton was making. He stood across the dining-room table from them, his thumb rubbing the smooth mahogany surface in little arcs. "I will need the tomb," he said. "After all."

His parents had built it, five years before, when they hired a regular tomb builder to come from Mobile. It stood on the highest slope of the Methodist graveyard in Madison City. It was brick, whitewashed, with a curving arch of a roof and a cross on the very top. There were two marble steps, and two urns flanking them, and the smooth unmarked sheet of marble over the front where names would go.

It had been built for the old people. But when William came back from the woods and saw the great black ribbon on the front door, and the maids cleaning out the summer-closed parlor, he knew what he had to do.

"I don't want a grave for her," he told his parents. "I want the tomb."

They nodded, agreeing silently. Behind him, there was the scrape of a chair as the maids began to turn the mirrors to the wall.

William had his name carved across the top of the tomb—in the long days after the funeral, when the stonecutter came from Mobile. Lorena's name was there, no other inscription besides the two words that preceded it: My Wife.

A year later William carved another set of dates and the words: My Son.

Then there was a war, and William went off to Camp Martin in New Orleans. That was as close as he got to the trenches of France, though he did almost die there—in the flu epidemic. He came home finally, thin and spindly and shaky. He went back to his parents' house and to his only daughter, and he almost never left the county again, except for business trips every four or five months to Chattanooga.

Now, William Howland had a younger sister, whose name was Ann. She married a second cousin, Howland Campbell, the son of the man in whose office William had read for the law. (Howlands often married cousins. It was a way they had, there was no plan to it; it just happened.) Ann was a tall, noisy, capable woman, who worried about her brother, widowed at thirty. She wrote him endless letters, in purple ink, begging him to come spend some time with her. "A change of scene would be so good for you," she always said.

William always answered her letters politely, though he hated to write and even his account books were trouble for him. Year after year he explained patiently why he could not come. Weevils were in the cotton; he had a new red clover he was trying in his pasture lot; he was working on a new variety of field corn.

Ann Howland Campbell sat in her big white house on the tree-lined Atlanta street and read the letters and showed them to her jolly fat husband.

He chuckled and tossed them aside. "Honey," he told her, "you can plain right now stop trying to match him up."

"I didn't say anything about that."

"He knows well as I do what's going to happen if he ever sets foot in here."

Ann looked out at her house filling up with children, at her own belly swollen with the newest one, and she folded her hands protectively across it. "He needs a wife. The first one he had wasn't at all suitable for him, and he'd found that out pretty soon."

"Well," her husband said, "seems he don't agree."

Years—many years—later when he took his granddaughter for a picnic in the cemetery with a Negro gardener or two along to clean up, William Howland talked about his wife Lorena. "There was such a light to her," he said, "all over her. I used to think she'd glow in the night.

He hadn't mourned for her, not the way a widower is supposed to. It seemed that part of him had died with her and in a way it was a mercy that it hadn't been left behind to grieve.

On that sunny morning he looked at the tomb that had his name carved across the top and he said: "She might have turned into the same sort of drunk her mother was. And maybe all that gentleness would have gone like her father's. . . ." He shrugged and smiled. "But it didn't."

He went on living a widower. He may not have been very happy, but he certainly wasn't unhappy either. There was a lot for him to do, what with the cotton and the cattle and the new demand for lumber and pulp. And he had his daughter to raise and his parents to bury. (They never got around to building another tomb. They were dropped into the sandy red earth with a blob of grey granite at their heads.) The days passed imperceptibly: short cold winter, long hot summer. He wasn't a hermit, and he wasn't unfriendly. He went to church when he wasn't too busy, and to parties all over the county. He was a fine dancer, he played the mandolin and sang all the popular songs in his pleasant light baritone. He just didn't seem interested in the daughters or the widows. Not at all. If he had a mistress, she didn't live in town. Perhaps he had some sort of arrangement in Chattanooga, but no one ever knew for sure. It just gave them something to talk about.

Maybe if he'd lived in a city, things would have been different. Maybe if he'd met more people, he would have found somebody. But the farms in this part of the country were far apart, with nothing but sharecropper cabins in between. People worked hard spring and summer, with only that couple of weeks' rest in August while the cotton was making. Once the fields were ready, once picking started, until the last of the crop was gone to the gin, William didn't leave the place, not even on Sundays. After that there was the corn and the tobacco and the syrup making in the cool days of fall. Finally there was the slaughtering. When the kids all had their pig bladders to play with and the smokehouses put out their flavor on the cold air, the year's work was over. Winters were party time, when there was only lumbering to be looked to, but winters are a short time, and William Howland did not find a wife.

Throughout all these slowly revolving years, William's daughter Abigail grew. She had no resemblance to her mother at all—she might not have had one, she was so much like her father. She was not a very pretty girl, but she was bright and gay and cheerful. And interested in the world. In high school she made her father subscribe for the *New York Tribune*, though he grumbled a good deal that he already had three papers coming to the house every week: the *Wade County Ledger*, the *Mobile Clarion*, and the *Atlanta Constitution.*

He gave in of course, as he always did. "Abigail," he told her, "I hope they have sense to wrap that paper up tight or we won't never hear the end of this."

The *Tribune* came the way newspapers always came, open for anyone to read. In those days there was no delivery and William always went in to Madison City twice a week for his mail. He got quite a lot of it, because he liked to read: *The Saturday Evening Post, Collier's, National Geographic*, and all the farm papers. The first time the *Tribune* arrived, Roger Ainsworth, the postmaster, leaned on the counter and said: "William, I am plain afraid you have lost your mind."

Now the post office was half of Ainsworth's Feed and Grain Store without so much as a wall between. That particular morning there were five or six people inside, there always were about that many. They came in to play checkers, or to pass the time of day, munching on the platter of parched corn and peanuts that stood on top the iron stove. From the way they sat, expressionless and waiting, you could tell they knew all about it, and had been talking it over already.

"How come, Roger?" William asked.

Roger Ainsworth dumped a pile of magazines on the counter. "These here's yours." He reached over to a special spot where he had put the *Tribune*. He held it up, silently.

"That?" William asked.

Ainsworth nodded. The people in the store shifted expectantly. A cane chair creaked, and a board. And somebody snapped a hard corn kernel between his teeth.

"What about it?" William asked.

Ainsworth said: "Didn't used to be like you to go reading the Yankee press."

"My daughter wanted that," William said, and then because he didn't want to seem to be hiding behind a girl, he said more loudly: "but I reckon I'll be reading some of it too."

There was a stir behind him, as if they were all taking a breath together. William picked up his mail. "Roger," he said quietly, "you are more of a jackass than I thought."

Mariah Peters, a short fat brisk woman, popped in the front door, and bustled over to the counter. "Three postcards, Roger," she said. Then: "You look like you could plain eat on nails."

"The way some people turn traitors," Roger said grimly, "you wouldn't think their granddaddies got killed in the war."

William chuckled and dragged the newspaper from under Roger Ainsworth's protesting fingers. "Wasn't my granddaddy; 'twas my granduncle and I don't reckon anybody'll know whether he was glad to give his life for a cause or not." He shuffled the papers in his hands, reflectively. "I always kind of felt he wasn't so happy," William Howland said. "He burned to death in the Wilderness, and from what I seen of brush fires I don't believe nobody wants any part of 'em."

As he was leaving he saw Ernest Franklin slip out the door ahead of him, and go hurrying off down the street to spread the news. He was an old, arthritic man and he scuttled like a frightened crab up to the front veranda of the Washington Hotel. He scrambled up the steps there, yanking himself along by the brass railing, and disappeared behind the sheltering lattice of morning glory vine.

William Howland, they say, just stood in the middle of the main street, the hot dry dust coming up to touch the cuffs of his trousers, and laughed. People popped their heads out the front door of Ainsworth's Feed Store and thought he had a touch of sunstroke or had gone out of his mind for being a secret drinker. When he finally wiped away the last of the tears with his big blue handkerchief and scrubbed dry his cheeks and his chin, he looked at them solemnly. He looked at the line of heads and the shifting and jostling as those caught back in the store tried to push their way up to see too, and he said very loudly and very clearly: "You old bastards!" He didn't even sound very angry when he said it.

It took the town a while to get over that. Lucy Whittemore, who'd been one of the heads in the Feed Store doorway, even considered not asking him to her daughter's wedding. When William met her on the street, a week or so later, Lucy was a bit stiff, because he ought to have known that she was thinking of not sending him an invitation and that would make him just about the only one in town she had left out, excepting the youngest Lykes girl, who had married a Catholic in his church and wasn't spoken to by anybody any more, even though they all liked her parents, with whom she lived while waiting for her first child. William only seemed amused by her formal answers. His blue eyes were bright and laughing as he asked after her daughter: "How is she? And how is her new husband?" Lucy answered stiffly: "They are not married yet." "Oh," William said gently, "first things first and all in good time." And he bowed his way off. Lucy Whittemore went on with her shopping, quivering with anger at her daughter and telling herself fiercely that people who had to have shotgun weddings shouldn't be too surprised at what they got. And she decided that she couldn't not ask William Howland, in spite of his crude references.

The town's anger never lasted long—especially at William Howland. The Frasers didn't ask him to supper on the first Sunday of the month as they always had done. And the Patersons didn't ask him over to meet their visiting cousin from Lafayette. But he didn't seem to care and the visiting cousin had gotten in poison ivy the very first picnic and berry-picking party they had taken her to, and that happened in a corner of the Howland land.

In a couple of weeks things were back to normal. Not that they had forgotten the business of the *Tribune* or the way that laughing word "Bastard" had sounded in the still heat of a dusty morning. . . . But there wasn't anything they could do besides adding it to their stories about him. He was still the most eligible man around, and they couldn't understand why he seemed content to raise his daughter all alone. Every person in the county had thought about that problem, and a good many of them had tried to find a solution to it. By then of course William Howland was well into middle age, but he might have had any of the widows, grass and sod, and even quite a few of the younger girls too, the ones just coming to marriageable age. He was still a strong-looking man, though his hair was thinning and he had shaved off his mustache. And he was a Howland, the real Howland, best blood in the county, best land, and most of the money.

His sister Ann—who came to visit him every year (since he had refused to stay with her), bringing the last of her children for his inspection—she was the only one who dared to speak of it openly. She often did, those afternoons when she sat in a cane rocker on the screened front porch of one of her girlhood friends, busy with sewing or knitting, or coloring Christmas cards for the Ladies' Evangelical League. She would purse her lips and say: "It's indecent. He needs a wife and he ought to have one, with her dead these sixteen years and him acting like she was only off on a trip."

And the other ladies nodded their heads and agreed that that was just exactly the way he did behave.

William's daughter Abigail finished high school, a tall thin girl, with long blond-white hair. Though most of the girls at her age had at least one serious caller, she had none. She did not seem interested. She was too shy to enjoy parties, and she did not dance at all. She spent her evenings in the big upholstered rocker in the living room, reading, steadily reading. After the first week or two, she found the *Tribune* too difficult for her. The copies kept coming, year after year, but she almost never opened one any more. She read nothing but poetry. Shelley in a fancy morocco binding with her great-grandmother's name in it. Yeats for reciting aloud. She sat looking out at the screening wisteria and the glittering day beyond and she would say to the soft greenness:

The wind blows out of the gates of the day
The wind blows over the lonely of heart
And the lonely of heart is withered away.
While the fairies dance in a place apart. . . .

The people in the house, the servants and her father, soon got used to her singsong sounds. They were even rather proud of her. It was very elegant to have a young girl murmuring verse to herself of an afternoon, quite alone with only her wide bright eyes showing the excitement and the aching of seventeen.

She went away to college, to Mary Baldwin in Virginia. Her father took her there, and that was the first time she had ever left the state. She was not even particularly eager to go. But since her father expected it, she packed dutifully.

When she was gone, the town settled down to think of her future. Most thought of her as an old maid, sitting up in the big house, turning the pages of her books with papery dry hands. And they shook their heads sadly that the real Howlands were not only going to disappear in name but in fact also.

That first summer she came home thinner than ever, with only a slight flush to her cheeks from the cold mountain winter. She immediately got her father to buy her a horse, an elderly and gentle grey mare, and she took long early-morning rides, always alone. People wondered and clucked about that, but the talk soon died down, because she still spent her afternoons in the little gazebo in the corner of the lawn. Her father had built that for her as a homecoming surprise. It was a very special gazebo, and everyone in town knew all about it, though few of them had actually seen it. It had trellis work delicate as lace and gingerbread hung from the rafters and eaves in great swirls and grape-like clusters. The benches built around its octagonal walls were cushioned in blue-and-white-striped cotton, and there was an octagonal table in the center of the room. It had been made specially to match the shape of the house. Abigail Howland spent her summer afternoons there; she wrote poetry now. And letters too—Roger Ainsworth at the post office soon noticed that she got at least one letter a week. He also noticed that the handwriting was the same, though the postmarks were different. So Mr. Ainsworth decided that Abigail Howland had at last gotten a beau and that he was a traveling salesman. What else, he argued to the people clustered in the back of the Feed Store, crunching their parched peanuts and corn, could explain the different postmarks on the letters?

So all that summer the town watched and waited to see who would come. No one did. Not even William's sister, whose last child was too young to travel. Just the letters. By the end of the summer when Abigail went back to college the town had forgotten all about her. They were busy watching the doings of Calvin and John Robertson. They'd made likker for years, like their father before them. Ridge runners, people called them, because they stayed off the roads and brought their produce directly across the ridges. The Robertsons had been supplying two counties around for almost a generation; they ran an honest still and had a fine reputation. As prohibition extended year after year, and good likker began to be harder and more expensive to get, the Robertsons found that they had far too many orders, from all over the state. Their yard (Calvin had moved to a little white house in town, to be more available) was always crowded with horses and buggies, and even a few cars. . . .

Business was so good that the Robertsons built a new still. People said they built it right in the middle of the Honey Island Swamp. Nobody knew too much about that place; nobody bothered finding out. Some said there was a great spring-fed lake in the middle and only the edges were swamp. Others said there wasn't anything in the middle but more swamp. Old people sometimes talked about an island of solid ground out there, where the fishing was so good blue gill sunfish ran to two pounds or so. Where every other tree was a honey tree and the bears and gators fought and roared all night long. Nobody believed them.

Honey Island Swamp was a huge area; on maps you could see that it took up about a quarter of the county, in the southeast corner. It began abruptly in a sharp dip of the sandy ground, a wide irregular stretch of swamp—of river birch and water oak, of black gum and dahoon bushes grown into full-sized trees. And cypress, mile after mile of dreary moss-hung cypress and oily thick water. Boys played around its margins, crawfishing in the spring, gigging frogs at night, chasing the big sirens, the eel-like animals that flashed along the water. But nobody dared go very far inside—until the Robertsons hinted that they did. They said they had a great fine still boiling away—and everybody knew it must be mighty big by the quantity of whiskey that came out. The Robertsons had no trouble because they worked so quietly. People suspected that they brought the likker out in skiffs and packed it on mules for the rest of the trip to the places where they left it. They were careful never to come across anybody, anybody at all, even if it meant extra miles walking up and down the ridges. There were lots of ways a man could go, if he knew the country and wasn't in a hurry.

William Howland had been buying from the Robertsons for years; he'd always had a taste for corn likker. At first he paid no attention to the talk of a new still. Gossip, he thought. Then as the summer wore on, he began to wonder more and more about its exact location. They must have found an island in the swamp, much bigger than the usual hummock. It couldn't be any other way. He'd been to the swamp a lot when he was a boy. He'd found deep clear lakes with sandy bottoms, and that was passing strange, but he'd never found any island large enough and high and dry enough to hold a still. And where would it be?

Those long summer evenings, after supper when he sat in the new gazebo with his daughter, fanning gently at the gathering mosquitoes, he wondered about it. Abigail was reading to him. She had come home from school with a passionate desire to read poetry aloud to someone; alone would not do any more. She had a teacher, she told her father, who said it was absolutely the only way to appreciate the full quality of the sound. This particular evening she was reading *Paradise Lost,* and he was not listening. He never listened. He heard the gentle tones of her voice in the same way he heard the buzzing of the mosquitoes and the louder thumping of the beetles as they bumbled their way along, the whizzing sound of the swifts' wings as they fed on them, the deeper pumping of the owls' wings as they began to move. The tree frogs and the bullfrogs. The locusts and the crickets. He heard them all and he heard none of them. They were as vague and misty, as remote as the western sky with its evening star swimming into view through the pink haze. Did they still tell children, he wondered, that if they looked up a chimney they could see stars in daylight? He would have to ask Abigail if her nurse had told her that. There was so much he hadn't asked her, that he never seemed to get around to asking. . . . Now, that much color in the sunset might mean something toward rain and that wouldn't do the cotton any good. And wasn't it a peculiar thing, good summer for cotton made a bad one for corn. Seemed you couldn't get the two together.

Her soft gentle voice went on, blurring into the dusk. There was the smell of cut grass from the house lot, of dust from the road. The dry clean smells. . . . William began to remember how a swamp smelled, thick and sweet. And how the water bubbled with rising gases when you stirred it with a stick, how the crawfish hung on the underside of a log, and you picked them off like fruit. The sharp angle a swimming moccasin made—the jut of the neck and the V of waves fluttering out behind. The close smell of unmoving water, of decay. The roar of gators mating, and their wobbling waddle as they launched themselves into the water. The sweet sick odor of the nest banks, the wallows.

I'll find it, William said silently to the bright dry dusk. If the still is there, I'll find it.

And Abigail wondered why, all of a sudden, her father raised himself upright and began to pay particular attention to the details of the battle of the angels.

Later on, a few weeks later, she wondered why he was so cheerful at her going. Usually she felt a great twinge at leaving him, he was so plainly distressed. This time, he waved her off with a real smile and a secret satisfaction that glared out of his face at the passing world.

He stayed overnight in town, because the next day was market Saturday and he wanted to hire some extra hands for the cotton picking. It was the busiest day of all, it always was, the streets lined with wagons, the sidewalks and the town square full of people walking about, or just standing, watching the passing. The porch of the Washington Hotel was lined solid with chairs, but you had to be early to get one of them. There was even a line of men, chairless, hunkered down against the front of the building. They were spitting tobacco juice at big greenbottle flies. Now and then a winner would stick out his hand and collect the bets. The still hot air smelled of dust and sweat. If you listened, over the chatter of people you could hear the sounds of the animals in the back lots. The town was only one street wide; their racket like their smell carried clearly.

William Howland finished his business and began to think of going home. Crowded streets always made him a little restless anyway. He was walking to where he had left his buggy, wondering if the little Negro boy he had brought in with him had remembered to get the horse from the livery stable, when he passed Calvin Robertson. William stopped dead still, grinning suddenly. "I been thinking about you, Cal."

"You needing anything this week?" Calvin asked politely.

"Maybe not this week," William said, "but I'll come fetch it."

"I reckon I can bring you whatever you have a mind for."

"What I have a mind for," William said, "is something else." And he reached out and caught the arm of Dr. Armstrong, who was just passing, carrying a wooden crate full of chickens.

"Harry," he said, "I want you to listen to this."

Harry Armstrong put down his crate, wearily. "What, Will?"

"A sporting proposition."

Harry Armstrong took out his large brown handkerchief and wiped his face. "You figuring to outproduce Calvin?"

"No," William said, "I'm figuring to locate his still."

Harry Armstrong just looked at him. "You going chasing around Honey Island Swamp?"

"That's where I hear tell it is."

Perspiration beaded Harry Armstrong's face again. He rubbed at it with the back of his hand, shook his wrist dry, and got out the handkerchief again. "My mother was a Howland," he said into the handkerchief, "so I reckon I can't be blamed for speaking, but that whole family always was crazy."

William chuckled. "This here is a sporting proposition, Harry."

"No, it ain't," Calvin said.

"Don't be a sour bugger," William said, "I'm betting you a gallon of your likker I can find out where you are."

Armstrong sighed gently. "You better take it, Calvin," he said. "Or you never going to hear the end of it."

"No," Calvin said.

"No bet, then," William said. "I'll do it for free."

Armstrong said: "The whole family been like that for years."

"Just to make it come out right," William said, "if I ain't been seen for a couple of days I'll be in the swamp. If it's more than four, I'm in trouble. If it's a week, Dr. Harry Howland Armstrong goes and fetches the rest of my cousins and tells them that my blood is all over Mr. Calvin Robertson's hands."

"Aw, Will," Calvin said.

"Games," Armstrong said. "The Howlands never did grow up either." He picked up the crate, resting it on his round belly. "A man's got to work."

"You going in the chicken business?"

"Ours died," Harry Armstrong said. "Yesterday morning we went out and the whole yard of 'em was laying there, upside down, dead and stinking."

"A doctor ought to do better with chickens. Makes you wonder about his human patients."

Harry Armstrong sighed. The sweat was back, trickling down his face, but he had no free hand to wipe it. So he sighed again, bowed his good-bye with a quick jerk of the head, and trudged off.

"You be looking for me, now," William told Calvin Robertson, who just grunted, spun on his heel, and walked away.

That afternoon, as they sat down to a late lunch, Harry Armstrong told his wife: "Guess what Will Howland is going to do now?"

She did not ask. She did not need to. After thirty-five years she knew that her husband would tell his story just the way he wanted.

"He's going still-hunting," he chuckled. "Told me about it to keep Calvin Robertson from shotgunning him in the swamp."

Mrs. Armstrong clucked her tongue sympathetically. "He's not for turning them in?"

Harry was startled. "Will Howland, best blood in the county?"

She looked ashamed. "I just was asking."

"He won't be figuring on nothing like that," Harry said flatly. "He's just making up games to amuse himself."

Will Howland set about his game carefully. First he went to see Peter Washburn, the Negro who built skiffs. He found him planing away, outside his shed on the riverbank, the willows all around him whistling and rattling their thin dust-caked leaves. Will bought a skiff, one that was just begun, and waited impatiently for it. Washburn worked slowly—William Howland made two special trips to town to check. When everything was finished finally, he and Peter Washburn put the skiff on the river, to let the wood swell and tighten. They moored it to a river birch and swamped it, leaving just the gunwales showing—to age and ripen in the muddy water.

Then William had no more time, for the cotton was ready. He put a sack on his shoulder and did a few rows himself, because he liked to keep his hand in. It wasn't hard work, picking, all the small children did it. And in a way it was easier for them: a man his size had to stoop considerably. Picking did give you a very muscular hand: you yanked the cotton out of the prongs of the boll with the tips of your fingers. William Howland's right hand was much bigger than his left. He was rather proud of that fact.

The pickers worked until the fields were stripped, seven days a week, under skies that were brilliant blue and edged with huge black thunderheads. There was almost never rain this time of year. Though the clouds piled themselves higher and higher, they never moved from the horizon. They seemed fixed there, like mountains. The first sun picked them up in the mornings, and they turned purple red with the last of its light. Sometimes the pickers worked by moonlight, and when they stood up to stretch and rest their backs, they would see those same clouds rising at the edges of the world, silvery and shining white.

William fell into bed at night, not bothering to take off his clothes. Sometimes in the very few minutes before he fell asleep, he would think of his new skiff and the swamp, and what he would do when the picking was over and the roar of the gins had ceased. . . . He and Peter Washburn would drag the skiff from the muddy shallows and slosh it clean with fresh water. Then they would put it on a wagon and haul it across the Howland roads, ones that generations had cut into the red sandy hills, following their own pursuits, lumbering or hunting, or just for the pleasure of marking a new way. Finally they would set the skiff down in the little stream that was called Deer Run. From there he would have to find the way into the swamp alone. He was sure he could.

William Howland found himself remembering more and more as the picking season moved to a close. "I'll be going soon," he sent word to Peter Washburn.

But he didn't. The very afternoon he had decided that he was ready to leave, he got a letter from his daughter. She wrote as she read, slanting, ornate, vague. She had dashed off this note quickly and folded it before the ink dried. William studied it, the beautiful shapes of the letters, the soft perfume that lifted from the paper, the smeared unintelligible words. About the only thing he understood was that she was coming home.

He met the train.

She was as always tall, thin, and blond. But this time her vagueness seemed to have disappeared. She rushed up to him and—something she had never done in public—hugged him. "Papa!" She giggled in his ear: "And weren't you surprised, and wasn't it wonderful, it just couldn't be better, it just was perfect."

Patiently William Howland explained: "The letter was smeared, lamb. There wasn't much I could make out."

He saw her face fall, her underlip quiver. "You folded the paper too soon," he said gently, "but tell me now."

She stepped back and said loudly, spacing the words carefully, the way you would for a deaf person or a foreigner. (And William suddenly wondered if he were not.) "I am going to be married."

He looked at her, conscious only that Rufus Matthews, the stationmaster, grabbed for his broom and began sweeping the dusty dry platform, to pretend he hadn't heard.

"You're surprised, aren't you, Papa?" Abigail giggled. "Isn't it lovely? I know you thought you'd never get me off your hands."

"No," William said, "I can't say I was bothered about that."

"Not being pretty . . . it worries a girl."

Had it? he thought. She seemed not to have noticed, seemed never to have given it a wisp of consideration. . . . He saw endless unknown stretches opening up before him. She thought, she worried. Behind that bland smooth face, those gentle eyes. . . . He had never before imagined her as having thoughts or feelings of her own. She had always seemed so content. . . .

"Aren't you going to say something, Papa?"

"I wasn't worried about your finding a husband when you're not twenty."

She took his arm and they started for the waiting buggy. William Howland was in no hurry to own a car. The roads were too bad for them most of the year.

"He is the most wonderful man." She hugged her father's arm, remembering.

"He from town?"

She stopped, and laughed. "Mercy sakes, no!"

Rufus Matthews dropped his broom. Served him right, William thought grimly. People who listen got to take their chances.

"I met him at Mary Baldwin," she said.

"I might could've guessed that," William said.

"He teaches there. English."

All those poems, William thought. All of them, and all that reading aloud.

When he did speak, he surprised himself by asking: "So he wrote those letters you got last summer?" The amusement showed in his voice.

Abigail looked at him sharply. "How could you know?"

"Whole town knew," William said. And he lifted his voice for Rufus's waiting ears. "Old Ainsworth spent most of the summer speculating on it."

As they drove home, Abigail told him: "His name is Mason, Gregory Edward Mason."

"He come from Virginia?"

"Mercy no!" (William wondered why she used that word so often when she never had before.) "He's from England, from London. He's just teaching there."

William said: "Your great-great-great grandaddy'd be spinning in his grave and he knew you were marrying an Englishman."

She answered complacently. "I know."

The wheels wiggled and jolted in the ruts in the road. Six or eight quail scuttled across the gravel and disappeared into a stripped-bare corn field. William said: "I reckon I should know more about weddings, but what do we do now?"

"Oh, Papa," she said, "*you* don't do anything. I'll write Aunt Annie and ask her to come down. If you can stand having her in the house."

"I've stood her my whole life," William said to the horse's back. "I can manage a bit more."

"Well, that's all there is to it. Really."

William said: "I'm right glad to hear it."

As they were turning into the drive that led to the front door, Abigail said: "And I nearly forgot. . . . Greg is coming down next Friday."

"For the wedding?"

"Oh, Papa. . . ." She clucked her tongue at him and he thought for a fraction of a second that she sounded just like her grandmother, the slatternly drunkard who kept a bottle of gin hidden in the kitchen safe and clucked her way to and from it.

"Well, what?"

Abigail giggled, the smug contented giggle of that same woman. "Greg is so proper that he's coming all this way just to ask you for my hand."

"Oh," William said. "Well, I've never known it done at such long distance before."

"Nobody marries from their home town any more," she told him confidentially. "Really."

William did not have to flip the reins; the horse stopped at his proper place. "Tell me what to do, lamb."

"Absolutely nothing," she said. "I'll write to Aunt Annie and you won't have to do a thing."

She danced a little step in the dust of the drive, her long blond hair spinning around her eyes. "There's just such a lot to be done, Papa. I haven't got a single thing for a trousseau. It came up so sudden."

"How sudden?"

"The day before I wrote you. But you couldn't read that either, could you?"

William shook his head.

"Do you think I could go to Atlanta for a trousseau? Aunt Annie would know all about it."

He just nodded silently. He followed her inside, not bothering to call the servants, carrying her single bag himself, feeling for the first time old and solid and tired. She was a baby he had held, a baby who had wet his pants and vomited across the front of his shirt. And she wasn't. . . . His feet felt rooted to the earth. The round hoops of his ribs seemed awkward and stiff like barrel staves. I am forty-eight, he thought, and that is old.

Abigail was talking to him, and he nodded his head, not listening, just agreeing.

Our children grow up, he thought, echoing something he had heard long ago and had not remembered for the years since. "Our children grow old and elbow us into the grave."

William went to the dining room and poured himself a whiskey. Looking at the light yellow liquid, he thought of the still in the swamp and how he had planned to hunt for it. He didn't seem to want to any more. He didn't seem to have the energy for it now.

He took the drink and went back to the porch. He sat in his rocker, and put the drink on its arm. He looked out across the road to his fields and his woods beyond them.

At least, he thought, the ground was solid. The sandy ground you knew so well you got to thinking of it as a person. Tricky, hard, not particularly agreeable. But the same, still the same, for you, for your father, for your children. And that helped. That was a comfort.

ANNIE HOWLAND CAMPBELL sent a long effusive telegram from Atlanta. William held the yellow sheet in his hand, and said to Rufus Matthews, who was the telegrapher as well as the stationmaster: "Cost her a lot of good money. . . ." Rufus nodded. "Seeing that," William went on, "a person would think you'd get more sense out of it."

"I took it off just the way it come in," Rufus said, miffed.

Most of the message was not understandable, but the meaning was clear—the wedding had her approval and she was delighted.

William sighed. "Least I can tell the thought of the whole."

He was having an awful lot of trouble with messages lately, he thought. Even telegrams. . . . He hadn't got one of those since the time his wife died. . . .

"Wedding here?" Rufus asked.

"I suppose," William said. "You ask my sister and Abigail."

Gregory Edward Mason came, as he had said he would, and had the proper talk with his future father-in-law. William was vague and polite; he did not think very much of him—this tall, thin, sandy-haired man with very bad teeth—but said nothing beyond commenting that he sat a horse with unusual grace and ease.

Abigail and Greg rode almost constantly for the two days he was there. William watched them dashing about, the calm certain elegance against Abigail's hesitant amateurishness.

And William remembered something else. Abigail had not liked horses as a child, had refused all offers of a pony. Only the past summer had she wanted one. So it was like the poetry read aloud. . . . It hadn't been his doing at all. William began to wonder if he had given her a single thing besides her blood.

He took her to Atlanta to buy her trousseau, to have her wedding dress cut and fitted. Abigail stayed for four weeks. William came home the very next day, over his sister's squeals of protest.

That single day had been enough. He had not recognized the city. A few landmarks were vaguely familiar, but distorted in a new setting. Even his sister's house—it had been painted and added to—was different, as was she, older and heavier. There were strange infants playing in the front hall, the first of her grandchildren. . . . And Howland Campbell, his brother-in-law, whom he had not seen in ten years—William shuddered. Always fat, he was now surrounded by tiers of flesh. His eyes peered out from a face that had run, the way icing runs on a cake. His neck was enormous, scallops of fat overhanging his collar. When he took off his coat, his extralong tie dangled midway down his arch of stomach; his trousers were pasted on beneath the curve, like the egg dolls children make at Christmas and call Humpty Dumptys. William found only the shadow of the man he had known, the man who had come courting his sister.

The whole city was like that. Just enough resemblance to confuse him. The one afternoon he was there, he went looking for the house in which he had been married, the house where his wife's parents had lived, with his wife's sister next door. The old people were dead, the sister moved away to Florida, but still he went. He could not find the house. He could not even find the neighborhood. He might have asked, but he did not. He simply walked and walked, down streets he did not recognize, hunting for what had been there. He kept looking all through the summer evening, kept at it so long that he missed supper.

"Honestly, Willie, honey," Annie said, "we were worried to death about you. Let me fix you an egg, right now."

"No," he said, "I'm tired and I reckon I'll go straight to bed."

"Now, Willie," she began, but he simply ignored her. In the softness of an unfamiliar bed, he solved the whole confusing problem by falling fast asleep. His tired body decided him. And he dreamed confusing dreams about not being young any more, of things lost and of endless searches.

He slept late. Only his sister was waiting for him at breakfast.

"We're not young any more, Annie." He was ashamed of how silly that sentence sounded in the hard light of the morning.

"Willie." She put a pudgy hand on his arm. "It's the first wedding. It gets you down, but everything's all right with the first grandchild. You'll see."

He brushed her aside. "It isn't so much that. It's more like where did it go? It moved off while I was looking at it, and I didn't even see it."

"Willie, lamb," she said, "you best go back to bed, and take some tea. You look bone tired to me."

He shook his head. "I've got a ticket, and there's work to do at the mill. You know there ain't nobody but me can touch those wheels."

"Willie, lamb," she said, "you are killing yourself dead."

He kissed her good-bye, smelled the old-woman smell of her, was appalled and shivered inside his shirt. He patted her grandchildren good-bye, took up his little suitcase.

Way down in the pit of his stomach there was a soft tugging, as if he were straining toward the earth. And though it was a very hot October day, and his shirt was drenched with sweat, he kept believing that he was cold. On the train he had a couple of quick drinks from the bottle he always carried, but they didn't seem to do much good. He had a couple more, and the straining lessened.

It had frightened him, this feeling of wanting to crawl into the earth. He had a few more drinks and leaned his head back against the seat and felt the hot air pour in the window and run over him like warm water.

When Abigail came back to Madison City, Annie came with her, and trunks and boxes began to clutter the front hall. "Willie," Annie told him abruptly, "this house is a mess."

He shrugged. "Fix it to suit yourself."

"Do you know there's a bat hanging from the tester in Mama's room?"

"Somebody left the window open," William said.

"Colored girls, Willie," Annie said, "they are sinfully careless. You got to watch them."

He only shrugged.

"You look like a Dago doing that," she said sharply. "And where are the people going to sleep? The bedrooms are terrible."

"What people?"

"Oh, Papa, don't be so silly," Abigail said. "All the people who'll come for the wedding."

He gave up then. "Suit yourself," he said.

They did. Annie and Abigail together. My God, William thought, they look alike too. . . .

They hired six maids and got all the silver out and polished it on the back porch; the strong ammonia smell drifted through the house. They washed all the glassware and polished it carefully and scrubbed the cabinets and the buffets, trying to remove the old old smell of sweet fruitcake. They washed down the walls, and they polished the floors by hand, creeping across them like some sort of beetles, swirling rags ahead. They opened up all the wings of the house, wings that had been closed for years. They brought in painters, and those bedrooms were done quickly, just one coat, because there was no time. All the sheets and spreads were washed and boiled in a big tub over a charcoal pot in the back yard, left spread out on the grass for the dews to bleach out the brown age spots. And the curtains were washed and starched. The wooden frames of stretchers with their lines of tiny nails crowded the open sunny spaces—with a child left there to keep the birds away. When those curtains finally were finished, they stood stiffly by themselves and had little decorations of browned blood in the corners from the sharp tiny nails. Abigail showed them to William. "Aunt Annie says there's got to be blood on a curtain or it's not clean."

"Your aunt," William said, "knows a great many things."

He was annoyed. He had never been able to get on with her, not from the days when they were children together. It was something about her voice. She made him nervous. . . .

"I'm not used to women in my house," he said. "And when I got two of them tearing it apart, I just plain got to get out."

He left the house to them finally, and moved down to the mill his grandfather had built on Wilcox Run. In the old days, long before William could remember, a miller lived there, a Scotch bachelor who was first hired as a builder. He had traveled all over the South, building mills on one creek or another. He'd just happened to be at work for the Howlands when he'd felt the first stings of age come on him. So the journeyman turned miller and lived out his days in the last of his mills. He'd made two small rooms for himself in the building and they were still there—dirty and grimy, unused except for storage for fifty years. William Howland brought a cot down from the main house and took a couple of blankets under his arm and lived there.

He liked the cool watery sound of the mill, and the constant all-night scurrying of the little animals that came to feed on the scattered grain. He looked at the corn that sprouted below the mill—the second toll, his father would have called it: fee for grinding, fallen kernels to sprout. Most of the grinding was over now, but there was still a bit to do now and then. At times like that, William himself would go up behind the mill and open the gates and start the water into the race. He would watch it run its way through, talking like a thing alive, and fall into the cups of the cypress wheel. Then he would go inside and throw the gears that started the sheller and the great granite grist wheels, and the floor would rattle and shake with their motion. He always stood there and watched carefully, because a wheel the least bit out of line would be apt to crack and turn useless.

Water mills were out of date; there weren't even many of them left. I like it, William told himself, I reckon I'll keep it.

In a few weeks, the grinding was finished—completely this time; and the mill was swept clean and its roof tightened against the winter. William had seen to that, and to his other work. The tobacco hung in its small curing shed. The sorghum cane had been cut and crushed and boiled into syrup and the bottles sent up to the big cellar under the main house. The hogs were fattening on acorns and molasses, waiting for slaughtering time.

Annie sent her brother a note by a passing Negro child. It had one line: "You can come back now. P.S. Give this child a nickel."

William left his dirty quiet room, which was getting rather chilly at night, and went back to his house.

He was startled at the change. The porches were painted, the big front one, and the kitchen one and all the other little ones that different generations had hung on the building. There were screens at all the windows—William had never gotten around to doing that himself—and they glistened coppery in the light. Inside, the house reeked of paint and Octagon soap powder. William felt his eyes smart at the unaccustomed fumes.

Annie bustled out of the back hall leading to the kitchen. "There you are, Willie. I just replaced your pump."

Her fat figure was wrapped in a huge white apron, and she had a wad of cheesecloth wound around her head. "You look kind of like a sausage. . . . What pump?"

"The well pump, and we'll be getting a big new pressure tank too. It's down in Madison City waiting for you to send and fetch it."

"We needed more water, Papa." Abigail floated down the stairs in a long whispery silk robe and kissed him gently. "Aunt Annie's done a wonderful job around here, don't you think?"

Annie looked at her brother and chuckled. "Liars' tongues drop off, William."

"It looks lovely," Abigail insisted.

"Oliver," Annie said abruptly, "if you're going to meet that train you got to leave."

Oliver Brandon was short and stocky and middle-aged. Chucklehead Negro, people called him, from the way his round head sat on his thick neck. He had worked for William Howland for twenty-five years as a handyman and helper. He was really manager for the place, though being a Negro he didn't have that title. This particular afternoon, he was wearing polished shoes and black pants, a white shirt and a black tie. He had parted his thin kinky hair, and plastered it down with brilliantine.

"What you dressed up for?" William demanded. And of Annie he asked: "What train?"

"There's only two a day, William, and Oliver's got to meet each one every day until the wedding."

"For God's sake, why?"

"Now, Willie," Annie said, "be sensible. You've got a lot of people coming down, and it's getting to be about time to start looking for them." She wiped her perspiring face on the corner of her apron. "Even if they telegraph just exactly when they're arriving, Rufus Matthews is likely to lose the messages or get them wrong."

William had to admit that was true. "Leastways," he said, "I don't like the idea of my man asking everybody that gets off the train at Madison City if they're coming to Miss Abigail Howland's wedding."

Annie darted him a look of disgust. "Are so many people going to get off the train that he's likely to make a mistake?"

So William gave up and went to fix himself a drink. The strange odors of the house no longer bothered him; he seemed to be getting used to them already. He stopped in front of the hall table and studied its great silver bowl, glistening dully in the light. With his finger he touched the tracing of grapes and leaves on the top edge. "Where'd this come from?"

Abigail giggled delightedly. "The attic. . . . I bet you didn't even know that there was a box of silver up there."

William shook his head. "No. . . ."

"I used to look at it sometimes and swear to myself that I'd have it at my wedding."

"You went up to the attic?" There was rat poison up there and it was strictly forbidden.

"Oh, Papa," Abigail said, "I'm not a child any more. I don't have to be afraid of saying what I did."

"No," William said, "I guess not."

"It's lovely, from the initials it must be Grandma Legendre's."

"I wasn't saying anything about that," William said, "I was just remarking on the number of things that I didn't know about, even while I was living with them."

"Oh, Papa," Abigail said.

In the following days, William watched his house fill up with cousins and second cousins and great-uncles and -aunts by marriage.

People he hadn't seen for thirty years, old people, crusty and fragile with age. Their stolid children. And their grandchildren, scurrying around, stumbled underfoot, slammed by doors, scratched by brambles, blotched by poison ivy whose unknown clumps they wandered into.

One afternoon he noticed a line of Negro children, small ones, nine or younger, straggling across the yard, carrying huge armfuls of smilax. "What in God's name is that?"

"We needed it," Annie said calmly, "for decorations."

"I went down to the school," Abigail said, "and told them all that you'd pay them ten cents an armload."

William did. Some of the children were so badly scratched from the thorns of the catbriar and blackberry bushes that he gave them double. As they dumped their greens on the porch on the shady side of the house and fetched buckets of water to pour over them, William noticed some poison ivy in the lot.

He said nothing, wondering idly if his sister was susceptible. She must not have been, because she hung the loops of green with her own gloveless hands, and he heard no more about it.

The day of the wedding, he met Gregory Mason on the early train. Mason looked tired—William saw that at once. His thin face was gaunt, his tall lanky body seemed stretched and fragile in the chill winter light.

William shook hands with him, marveling again that this was the man his daughter had picked for a husband. "Hard trip?"

"I believe so."

There were dozens of people getting off the train, milling about on the small platform. "Will," they called to him, "here we are!"

And William saw that they were his cousins from Jackson. He was surprised. He thought they'd arrived yesterday—but no, now that he thought about it, the ones at his house were from Montgomery. A different branch altogether. As he moved across the platform to greet them, he thought how stupid he'd been to mix them up. But then the various branches of his family had always seemed a good deal alike to him.

As he began shaking hands, he had a sudden thought. White men often said all niggers looked alike, but to him now, niggers looked different. . . .

He covered his chuckle with a bland welcoming smile and went about dutifully pumping arms and kissing cheeks. When he was done, he and Gregory Mason walked off toward the Washington Hotel.

"You got the Groom's Breakfast," William told him abruptly. "Abigail tell you?"

"I don't believe she did."

"Expect she was scared to. . . . Every man that's come for the wedding'll be there, blood and in-law and friend. I reckon you'll see."

"It's customary, I suppose," Gregory Mason said.

"Hereabouts, it is. Hotel's right there." As William pointed, a man stepped out on the lattice-trimmed porch and waved to them. "That's Harry Armstrong," William said. "He'll be best man, seeing how you don't have any family here."

"A cousin?"

William looked for mockery, found none. "His mother was my father's sister. Harry's a great man with the bottle, but I reckon you'll see that too."

By the middle of the afternoon William Howland found himself sitting alone in the dining room of the Washington Hotel. His elbow was propped on the long glass-littered table, his hand was holding his head up, and the walls were singing and zooming around his ears. He was watching Gregory Mason stagger through the door, guided by Oliver's black arm.

"Careful with him," he shouted to Oliver. And then softer, to no one in particular: "Holds his likker right well, that fella. And who'd thought it?"

William Howland took his fist from under his chin and turned his head carefully and slowly. He discovered that he wasn't alone at all. Almost hidden by a row of bottles and jugs, Harry Armstrong dozed, head down on the table. "You poor son of a bitch," William said aloud, "wake up."

Harry Armstrong did not even move or mumble. "Son of a bitch," William said again as he looked around the room. The guests were gone, helped to their beds by teams of servants directed by Oliver. Except for one—William finally noticed him. In the far corner of the room someone slept on the floor. Face to the wall, he was covered with a grey blanket and there was a pillow under his head.

Good for Oliver, William thought, Oliver and his boys. . . .

William stood up carefully, holding the room steady around him. He walked slowly over and shook Harry Armstrong's arm. "They gone," he said.

"Who?" Harry Armstrong pushed himself up, using both hands. "Who was here."

Armstrong looked at his watch. "Can't see a damn thing." He rubbed his eyes and squinted harder. "Past two. I'm going to bed."

"Harry," William said, "who's that on the floor there?"

Harry Armstrong looked. "Can't see his face."

Oliver came back. His white jacket was rumpled and stained. A button was pulled off, and the pocket ripped. The too heavy brilliantine on his hair had run down on his forehead and his neck. He scrubbed at it with a large blue handkerchief but he couldn't seem to get it off.

"You put the groom to bed?" William asked him.

Oliver nodded. "I reckon everybody gone now."

Harry Armstrong chuckled and pointed. "You forgot him, Oliver."

Oliver looked at the sleeping huddled form with the pillow tucked neatly under its head. "You want me to move him?"

Harry Armstrong stood up, gingerly. "See who it is."

Oliver walked over and peeped into the face. "Mr. Bannister."

William said: "He's comfortable, let him be. I'm going for a swim."

Harry Armstrong thought a minute. "Me too."

So Oliver put an overcoat over his white jacket and followed them down to the foot of the street. He watched them shed their clothes and slide into the icy water of the Providence River. He turned up his collar and found a log to sit on, waiting patiently. A group of black children gathered around him, giggling.

That evening, bathed and shaved and aching, they rode—all the men together, thirty-odd of them—to the Howland place for the wedding.

In his crowded parlor, during the ceremony when John Hale, the Methodist minister, was pronouncing the familiar words in his very best manner, William's eye focused on a swatch of green that hung directly over the portrait of his grandfather. He could have sworn that in the massed and twisted leaves he saw the unmistakable shape of poison ivy.

Afterwards, bride and groom gone, Annie said to him: "It was the loveliest wedding I have ever seen."

And he answered: "Do you get poison ivy?"

"For heaven's sake, Willie . . . no."

"I saw some, all bound up with the others."

She gave him a quick smile, the sort of smile that he had not seen on her face since they had been very young children together. She winked at him too, a vague dipping of an eyelid. "It's green like the others," she said, "and we were running short."

That evening Annie giggled like a young girl, had far too much to drink, and sat at the piano and played and sang "Juanita" and "The Rosewood Spinet" and "Kathleen" and "The Letter Edged in Black" until she fell asleep across the keys. Then, because she was such a heavy woman no one dared carry her upstairs (the staff by this time had drunk as much as the guests), they put her to sleep on a sofa in the dining room. Later still when the moon came up, most of the men went off on a hunt, stumbling and singing their way across the fields and over the fences, followed by unsteady Negro boys with bottles of whiskey, preceded by the swift brown-and-white flashes of dogs.

William started them off, as was polite, but soon turned back, cut toward the road, and followed it home. He was remembering the wedding parties he'd been to when he was a young man, here in these same woods and ridges, and in the counties around Atlanta. They were all pretty much like this. Drunken men still sounded alike. And the dogs still sounded familiar, and the night wind hadn't changed, nor the ground underfoot.

Bit by bit, day by day, the wedding broke up. By the end of the second week, they were all gone, except for his sister Annie. Her husband left the day after the wedding itself—he had an office to run—and he took his children back with him. Annie stayed on to close up the unused portions of the house.

She did not even ask William if he would like it. She and the six maids hired for the wedding (Ramona, the cook, was old and crotchety and stayed home) were busy for a week. They pulled and fastened shutters, took curtains down and folded them in chests, rolled rugs and sprinkled them with mothballs against the grey mice, covered mattresses with sheets of brown paper. They jammed chimneys with newspapers against the swifts and swallows. They closed doors one by one, doors of rooms, doors of wings. Until it was finished.

On her last evening Annie said: "Do you know there are twenty-two bedrooms in this house, if you count the three upstairs in Grandpapa's wing?"

"I didn't know that," William said.

"We been living here all of our lives and somehow never took it into our heads to count the bedrooms."

"Funny," William said.

"It was all open for my wedding," Annie said, remembering, "but I suppose Mama did that. I know I didn't have a thing to do with it."

To please her William said: "That was quite a wedding you had."

She smiled brightly. "Always meant to ask Father how much it cost, only I never got to it. . . . But it was lively."

While the women squealed their admiration, the men shot all the windows out of the church, and rode their horses in and out of the drugstore, the hotel, and the railroad station. It was July, and the railroad platforms were piled high with watermelons awaiting shipment. Thousands of them. Next morning the whole main street was slippery and slimy with the pulp and seeds of the smashed melons. . . .

She remembered, chuckling.

William patted her shoulder, pleased with himself for having pleased her. She wasn't bad, he thought. It wasn't her fault that she was fat and old and a little dull. . . . Like me, he thought, just like me.

"I don't suppose those rooms'll be opened now, until Abigail's children come to getting married."

"I reckon so," he said shortly.

She leered at him impishly, and said: "Willie, you are jealous."

"Annie," he said, "you are a silly old woman."

She sat grinning at him, not hearing, until he thought he would like to smash something down on her head. Just as he was about to, she got up and poured him a whiskey, and brought it to him, taking one for herself.

Sitting in the old chairs, in the old house, scrubbed unnaturally clean now, and empty of the people who had sheltered in it, they drank to each other.

"Luck!" William Howland toasted his sister.

"The future, Willie!" And again there was that faint ghost of a wink.

"Annie," he said, "go home."

"In the morning, Willie."

She did. And he was left alone, except for Ramona rattling pots in the kitchen or muttering her way through the rooms, flipping a feather duster at the edges of the furniture. The house was no more empty than it had been with Abigail at college. But it felt emptier. One morning toward the end of the first week, William discovered that he was talking to himself. He had just waked up. He was lying in the big tester bed, staring at the glowing square of shaded window, and he said aloud: "Wind's to the west."

He heard himself and jumped. And looked around guiltily, wondering: How long have I done that?

He dressed and went out on the kitchen porch, where the bowl of hot water was waiting for him, as it was every morning. He shaved in front of a little mirror that hung on the post, wiping the foam from the straight blade off on the railing. Later Ramona would come and pitch the contents of the bowl on the railing, so that it would wash clean, in a way. But even so, years at the same spot had left a greasy darkening on the rail.

On that particular day, he planned to see to his cattle. As usual there was some foot rot that needed attention, though he hated that job, hated the scraping and the foul odor. There were some hide sores too, he wondered briefly if the heel flies were not hatching out early this year. Like screw worms they usually came later in the spring. He'd go have a look now and he'd remember to take the benzol and pine-tar oil with him.

He was thinking like that when he started out. Only somehow he took a different turning and found himself going the way to town. He had remembered Peter Washburn and the new skiff. And the game he was going to play in Honey Island Swamp.

HE put his blanket in the bow of the skiff, carefully, in the driest part, with his oilskin folded under it. He put his food on top the blanket. He'd have to find something to eat along the way, or he was going to be pretty hungry. He had brought only a slab of boiled bacon, a good-sized hunk of cornbread, and some of the small greenish apples that grew in his orchard. They were extremely tart and they were good for freshening your mouth and cleaning the bacon fat from your teeth. He also had a small canteen of water, and some barley drops that he had found in the kitchen cupboard. He had not seen them before, but he assumed they had been left by some child visiting for the wedding.

He put his shotgun next to him and shoved off. For an hour or so, he rowed with the sluggish current of the little run, slumping easily over the oars, saving his breath for crossing the Providence River. He felt the water tighten against his oars as he approached. He shipped them—idly noticing the muddy water drip from them to the bottom of the skiff—and got out his pole. The run became quite swift here, taking current from the winter-swollen river. It would be easier to pole the skiff through the narrow break in the tangle of bushes and trees.

From the river, you could not see where the run entered, the willows and the water beeches and black gums and the hackberry bushes and the elderberries grew so low and tangled. Approaching from the run, it was easier. The current marked your way. William swung his pole over the side, noticing with satisfaction that he had selected a good light one, smooth to the hand and balanced nicely, even with the crossbar at its tip. All poles had something like that; it kept them from sinking too deep in the mucky bottoms. He pushed the skiff through the swirling muddy water, avoiding the sawyers and the fallen trees and the densest tangles of vines. He went slowly, handling his pole carefully to avoid brushing or knocking into hanging foliage. He did not want a water moccasin tumbling down on his head.

He came out into the river, and the skiff swung sharply in the full current. He was thrown off balance by a tug on the end of the pole as the crossbar dragged. He heaved it out, cursing his carelessness. It had been so long since he crossed here that he'd forgotten the tricks and he'd almost got a dunking because of his slowness.

Using his oars again, he maneuvered himself across the river, searching for the slough that was the entrance to Honey Island Swamp. He'd not been here since he was a boy, and floods had changed the shape of the banks so completely that he no longer recognized them. He remembered once marking the entrance by a solitary cypress tree that grew there, alone in a clump of water oaks. He would have to look for that.

It was much farther downstream than he thought. He had almost given up when he finally saw it. It had died—years ago—but the brown pole of its trunk still jutted out above the oaks. He swung the skiff around, bow to the current, and rowed steadily forward so that the boat remained stationary, while he looked. He spotted the entrance, swung the bow in, and clumsily knocked against a feathery low-hanging branch. A dark shape tumbled athwart his bow and slithered into the water. He cursed silently with relief and, using a single oar for a paddle, maneuvered himself out of the trees into the clear slough.

He disliked snakes, though as a boy he had hunted them, to grab them by the tail and snap them whip-fashion so that their brains spattered out neatly. He sold the skins to his father for a quarter apiece, until his mother found out and insisted that no bounty be paid for poisonous ones. He'd stopped catching them then. . . .

He rowed for a bit, then changed to the pole. These sloughs were often very deep—he tested and found no bottom—so he used the pole as a sweep. Back and forth, rocking his way along, steadily.

By midmorning he was well into the swamp. The slough twisted and turned between drowned cypress trees and hummocks of hardwoods and palmetto, rustling in the little breeze. There was no current here, he balanced the skiff against a cypress knee and ate half the bacon and a bit of cornbread. He drank the sun-warmed water and watched the birds: ricebirds, mockingbirds, a pelican or two, egrets, and the big blue herons.

He poled steadily along the oily, muddy water. Ahead, in the distance—if he lifted his eyes—that dull water took on the shine of the sky and looked sparkling clear. Gators which had been sunning themselves on the muddy edge of the bank lumbered down into the water and disappeared. Turtles sunning on floating logs pulled in their heads. On one of the hummocks he passed, he noticed a tall gum with splintered bark. That would be a bear's work; it must be a honey tree.

By afternoon he got out his compass, because the sky had turned cloudy, and, except for the wandering twisting sloughs, there were no trails, no markings. Once, when he was a boy, he'd been lost in here for two days, caught under a heavy blanket of clouds and fog that confused his directions. He'd had to wait for the sky to clear. The second night, he dozed fitfully and woke staring straight up into a bright star-freckled sky. He was out of the swamp before daylight and he never went in again without a compass. . . .

He left the slough and made his way through the cypresses. The water was shallower, his pole caught ground and he moved more rapidly. He started to mark his passage—he had the machete ready in his hand to make the first blaze—when he hesitated. If he should find the still, there was no reason to leave a marked path right up to its door. He would use compass alone.

The cypresses were thick and moss-hung. The water among their roots was the opaque impenetrable brown of the swamps. Once as he rested, he picked up a floating stick and scraped the bottom. A string of gas bubbles escaped to the surface.

This water was like that. So much gas formed at the bottom, there was so much plant and animal matter decaying there, that bubbles often rose of their own accord. Sometimes the surface of the water seemed to be boiling with hundreds of tiny exploding bubbles.

Here too, William remembered, ghost fires ran over the water, blue and flickering, dodging in and out of the trees. It must be some of that gas burning. . .

The cypress swamp became a wide stretch of saw grass and alligator grass and duck potatoes. He crossed it, heading for the scattered high hummocks of oak and water hickory he saw on the other side. He spent the night there, in his skiff drawn up on the clear sand beach of the largest hummock. The mosquitoes were not bad, but still he slept fitfully. He had gotten unused to the swamp sounds. The loud whine of insects, the swooshing of bats and owls. He even jerked upright and grabbed his shotgun when a big gator roared. He listened carefully again—it was half a mile away, in the silence it had seemed closer. Even knowing that, he woke to each succeeding roar all night long. And in the morning, before dawn even, the first sounds he heard were those of the gators. The sharp bang—almost like a shot—of their great jaws snapping together on breakfast.

William opened his barley candies, found them soft and spongy, but ate them anyhow. He drained his canteen and tossed it aside. If he got really thirsty, he could always drink swamp water. It made some people sick, made some throw up, but it had never bothered him particularly. It had a very unpleasant taste, but it was water when you needed it.

Along toward noon of the second day he located the large fresh lake he had first found as a boy. A lake in the middle of the stagnant marsh, surrounded by a fringe of bushes and hardwoods and sandy beaches. It was probably fed by underwater springs, its basin a limestone sink. In this country there were lots like that.

William scooped up a handful of water and tasted; it was cool and fresh. He leaned over the side, washed his face and tried to see the bottom. The surface dazzle of the bright sun blinded him, he looked into water as impenetrable as a mirror. When he was here as a boy he had taken a quick swim in those blind depths, dodging among the snapping turtles. . . .

There didn't seem to be any about now. He looked carefully. Had they died off, or were they just hidden under the bright surface of the water? He wouldn't risk a swim—he was too old and the day too cool.

William sat quite still and watched some short white feathers float by on the surface of the water while little fish nibbled at them futilely from beneath.

The swamp had always made him lethargic and dull. He moved slowly, content to watch the animal life that thrived all around him. . . . But he'd come looking for something. There was that bet with Calvin Robertson. No, it wasn't exactly a bet. . . . Harry Armstrong's face, now—William chuckled remembering—while he stood juggling that case of chickens and sweating like a horse. . . . He'd never had much luck in his life, William thought, first his father had gone broke and now his wife was ailing with some female complaint. . . .

On the far side of the lake a black panther emerged from the tangled green of a hummock and padded lazily down to the water. That was upwind, a good quarter mile away, William noticed, so the animal was not aware of him. He kept perfectly still, barely breathing. You didn't see too many of those real panthers any more. There had been bounties on them time and again, and people had just about cleaned them out. You never heard their night shrieks any more—except in the swamp.

William watched the lean dark shape pad along the small sand beach. The panther seemed disturbed. It dabbled its forepaws in the water, reaching for something, then gave up and strolled back into its cover.

William shook himself awake, fitted oars into locks and rowed across the silent empty lake, the noise of his strokes sounding enormous and loud.

He approached cautiously—panthers had been known to attack men, especially if they had a litter nearby. The foliage did not move —there wasn't even a wind in the noonday heat—and he edged right up to the beach. He saw what it was. A small animal carcass lay in the shallow water. William nudged it with his oar and dozens of little water scavengers scurried away. An otter, and skinned. No wonder the panther acted so strangely. The bloody meat attracted him, the scent of man sent him away. . . .

William flipped the stripped red-grey flesh into deep water. Let the fish clean up. As he did, he smiled to himself. The Robertsons couldn't have left him a plainer trail. They had gotten careless. And he'd gotten lucky. The carcass had fallen into the shallows, and the panther had pointed it out to him.

He set himself to thinking. For a still you needed high ground and good water and thick overgrowth to disguise whatever smoke came from your boiling fires.

Now where would that be? To the north, the direction he had just come from, there wasn't enough cover. Those hummocks, all of them, were tiny lumps of shell. Not enough room on them. To the west, there was mostly grass, and cypress stands, hardly any dry ground at all. Going any farther toward the south would bring you too close to the settlements at Cobs Landing and Stilltoe. The

Robertsons must have gone east from here. No other way. But to the eastward was still a huge tract of land.

"Little bit more," he told himself aloud. "It's got to be luck."

It was luck and nothing else. He had only gone a few miles when a little breeze picked up, and on that breeze—clear as day—was the smell of mash. It led like a highway for him to follow, the odor getting stronger and stronger as he pushed his way into a thick patch of swamp. He couldn't see more than fifty feet in front of him, through the maze of cypress trunks and the tangle of buck vines. He didn't even see the island until he was right on it. One minute there was nothing but cypress and brown swamp water and the scurry and splash of little creatures running from his passing. The next minute he found himself staring at the steep, palmetto-covered slope of a shell hummock.

He held the skiff steady and shouted: "Hey, anybody there!"

The swamp all round him burst into activity. Egrets and herons and starlings and robins rose up screeching and frightened. Even the great noisy black bird that people called the Lord God Bird sailed up from the top of a peaked cypress tree.

"Hey," he called again. "It's Will Howland." He waited and no answer so he repeated: "Will Howland."

He waited again. He had no wish to be shot for a stranger. "Hey, you Robertsons here?"

He beached the skiff on a small shell stretch that bore the marks of many previous hulls. The smell of mash was overpowering, but he had trouble finding the actual still, it was so cleverly hidden. When he did, he was disappointed: it was not particularly large. The amount of whiskey the Robertsons were selling could not possibly have come from here. But maybe, William thought, they had several small stills scattered around among the hummocks. Smaller the still, sweeter the whiskey, he'd always heard. And too, he chuckled, the loss of one still wouldn't put them out of business. . . .

This, now, was a nice clean professional job, nothing like the makeshift things you saw around the pine hills. The copper alone would have cost the Robertsons a pretty penny. . . . William checked it over admiringly, and could find no fault. The filters were oak barrels filled with charcoal. The whiskey aged properly in oak kegs. There was a neat line of them over there, half of them seemed to be full. William noticed that the coils were cooled by a trickle of water from a small pipe. He followed it to the center of the hummock—a small spring. Clever, William thought, putting the still just a little lower so the water flowed naturally. As he walked back, the shell ground crunching under his feet, he noticed two neatly stacked piles of wood. It had not been cut on this particular hummock. William chuckled to himself. They'd deliberately left this one unmarked, with nothing to call attention to it. They must bring the wood by skiff from a considerable distance. He picked up a piece: pine, and aged nicely. The Robertsons were careful workers.

Somebody had been tending the still, and not long ago. Perhaps they'd noticed him coming and slipped away. Or perhaps they were making the rounds of the other stills.

In a crate under a palmetto-roofed shelter there were a dozen filled bottles. William took them out and lined them up in a zigzag path that anyone would have to notice. Then he took a bit of charred wood out of the fire and scratched laboriously on a flat board: W. Howland. It was not too clear but it was enough. After all, they had been expecting him. . . .

He was quite tired now, and hungry too. He prowled around the camp, finding two things: A can of beans, which he opened with his knife and ate at once. And four otter skins stretched carefully on a rack of twigs and branches. One was fresh.

He chuckled. The energetic Robertsons were even doing a little illegal trapping while they ran their illegal stills.

He would have to start back now; he'd already taken longer than he'd expected. It had been a greater effort too. He wasn't young any more, he acknowledged wryly to a big oak tree, and he was feeling the strain.

He filled his canteen with water; he also filled a small empty bottle with whiskey. The Robertsons could spare him that. . . .

He stepped wearily into his skiff and picked up his pole with a twinge of back and side muscles. He pushed free of the hummock, and checked his compass. He decided to go straight west. It would be shorter. He should reach the edge of the swamp around New Church, and he could walk home from there, if he found no one to give him a lift.

He poled steadily west, and the falling sun shone straight into his eyes. He jammed his cap way down on his forehead and squinted his eyes tight as he could, but the glare still gave him a headache. He stopped and took a few swallows of whiskey. He poled through miles of moss-hung cypress stands where gators splashed away from his bow and moccasins swam alongside with their bright intelligent stare. He jabbed at these with the pole. Now and then he hit one, but the pole was heavy and he soon gave up that extra effort. At sunset he was crossing a grassy marsh, sweeping his way along a fair-sized slough. As the sun dropped, a cloud of biting gnats rose from the grasses—the saw grass and the oyster grass, and the duck grass—until the sky was dark with them. William felt his whole body begin to tingle. Not just his hands and face and neck, not just the exposed skin, but his whole body burned as the tiny insects slipped inside his clothing. He dropped the pole for the oars and rowed frantically, trying to reach the edge of the cloud. It did not work: either it was a very large cloud, covering the entire marsh, or it was moving along with him. He gave up trying to outrun them, and slammed the skiff into the bank. As rapidly as he could, he stripped off his clothes, grimacing with pain as the needles jabbed harder into his naked body. He scooped up handfuls of black muck and plastered it all over his body and his head, thick as he could. He tied a handkerchief across his nose and mouth and ears. When the mud was partially dry he put back his clothes, fixing them to hang loosely and not disturb the protective caking.

Then he resumed his poling. The mud stank of decay, of stagnant water and dead roots, but it helped with the gnats. William took a few more swallows of whiskey to help him get over the smell.

He chuckled, thinking how he must look. A big heavy bald man, smeared with mud like an Indian, his blue eyes buried in the black smear of his face.

He crossed the open marsh, and then a small lake. This one, now, seemed to be fed by sulphur springs, because the odor lay heavy over its almost still surface. With the last of the dusk the full moon rose, heavy and yellow, behind him. His shadow and the shadow of the skiff stretched out longer and longer like rubber on the water ahead. With the rising moon, cats began to prowl in the distance. He heard a couple of panthers yeowl, and a couple of screeches that he recognized as bobcats. As the water birds settled for the night gators began to prey on them, and he heard the loud snapping of their huge jaws.

Beyond the lake, following the compass, he entered swamp again. The bright moon was reduced to a tiny glow inside the shelter of the tall trees, filtered to nothing by the tangled strings of moss. He kept poling steadily, checking his direction, maneuvering his way around those spots where cypress had fallen on cypress and their knees stuck out so thickly that a skiff could not pass between them. Now and then, disturbed by his passage, tree frogs dropped down and splashed gently into the water. He ate the last of his cornbread and had a bit of bacon. It was beginning to taste strange, spoiling in the sun.

There were millions of mosquitoes now, though he couldn't see them in the dusky moonlight. They sang fiercely around his ears and he felt them brush his face and hands. They did not sting very much—perhaps it was the caked mud, or perhaps it just wasn't their season for needing blood.

He was extremely sleepy, but he did not want to stop here. There were too many snakes overhead and one was sure to drop down unless he could make a fire. He remembered that old-time swamp men had always carried a little brazier in the bow of their skiffs and dugouts. They had the security of a fire whenever they needed it. He had to keep going until he found a hummock.

He did finally. He cleared a little space among the palmettos with his machete and grounded the bow of the skiff firmly. His legs, numbed by the cramped hours in the skiff, stumbled and shook under him as he gathered dead wood. He kicked aside a dry palmetto and uncovered a rattler. He felt the shape slip from under his foot; he heard the quick annoyed shake of rattles; but in the dark he saw nothing until the snake struck. He was wearing high woods boots and the fangs scratched harmlessly against the heavy leather. He killed it with a few quick blows and kicked the twitching shape aside. When he had gathered wood and started his fire he looked down at the smear of milky venom on the side of his boot; he scraped it away with a leaf. He built a big fire and a smoky one, and settled himself down in the skiff. He would not sleep but he would doze a bit until dawn came.

On the afternoon of the following day, across the shimmering wind-marked marsh grass, he saw a line of trees, clearly more than just a hummock. He poled toward them, eagerly. Long before he reached the edge of the grasses he felt the tug of a current on his skiff. Between marsh and trees there must be a strong-flowing river, and that could only be the east branch of the Providence. He had come out of the swamp. . . . He was tired, he let the current move him slowly along. He stared into the thick syrupy oily brown water, resting his eyes from the brilliance of the afternoon. As he did, he remembered his Creole grandmother's name for these narrow channels in a marsh: *trainasse.* He hadn't thought of her in years, that thin silent beaked-nosed woman. Her English had remained stilted and formal all her life, she had never seemed quite at home with it.

But she had not made any effort to teach French to her children or her grandchildren. She hadn't wanted to go to France either, though she had more than enough money for the trip. She simply hadn't seemed to mind not belonging. She hadn't seemed to mind perching uncomfortably on the edge of her world. . . .

William forgot about her again as he concentrated on getting the skiff out into the river, and safely across, avoiding the snags and the sand bars, and keeping a special watch out for whirlpools. This stretch of the river, always swift and deep, was spotted with those swirling circles. They could tear a boat apart in seconds, sucking it down to their depths. And that wasn't all. You had to watch what did get sucked into their swirls. . . . William hesitated at the edge of the marsh, looking up and down the river carefully. He saw only one whirlpool, slightly upriver from his position. It seemed small enough. Then he noticed a log, an old one that rode very low in the muddy water. He jammed his pole into the bottom and held his skiff steady. The log was moving directly toward the whirlpool. As he watched it was caught by the gentle outer rim, swung slowly about. Its speed increased as it moved to the center, faster and faster until it disappeared into the cone, slowly, silently, like a picture without sound. William, leaning on his pole, swung his eyes slowly downriver, waiting. The log reappeared fifty yards below, bursting to the surface, end first. It rose a couple of feet in the air and traveled some ten feet downstream before it splashed back into the water.

William rowed across quickly. There did not seem to be any house nearby, so he decided to pull the skiff up on the bank and leave it there. He took his machete and chopped a series of V's into the gunwales on both sides of the bow. They would make it easy to identify when he sent back for it later.

He looked at the empty bottle in the bottom of the skiff, the bottle that had held whiskey from the still. It seemed a mighty small thing for all the work and ache of the last three days, for the plagues of mosquitoes and gnats. A damn-fool bet to start with, he thought. You'd think I'd plain have better sense. . . .

He'd made a bet, he'd gone on through with it, and he'd won. And it was still a damn-fool thing. That's what came of being a Howland, he thought, they always were kind of crazy.

He picked up the empty bottle and tossed it out into the river.

He did not know precisely where he was—somewhere around New Church, he figured. So it was just a matter of cutting across the ridges until he fetched up in his own back lot. He folded his blanket and slung it across his shoulder. He put the shotgun across the blanket, settled his pants more comfortably on his hips, and made up his mind to a long walk. Some hours later, when he had scrambled up and across two ridges, he realized that it was getting dark, and that he was very tired. He had had only light restless naps in the skiff. He selected a good high spot, a stand of shortleaf pine with a heavy fall of needles; he rolled in his blanket and went to sleep.

He woke with the first dawn, the false dawn. He lay with his hands behind his head, waiting for the true light, listening to the birds, to the insects, to the nervous rustling of pine needles. And—from a long way off—wind-borne, he heard the sound of running water. William stood up and stretched, and the sun swung over the edge of the intervening ridge and flashed in his eyes. He was very thirsty; and in spite of the sour apples, his mouth was foul-tasting and fuzzy. He listened again for the running water, found it, fixed directions before the birds drowned it out.

He swung his shotgun to the pad of blanket and started toward the sound, rubbing his hand briskly over his beard, which made little crackling sounds in the cool morning. He passed a Negro graveyard, its trees dangling with sand-filled blue bottles and martins' nests of gourds; its graves, smooth-worn heaps, decorated with broken cups and glasses and plates, all glass, all turned lavender by years of sun. He passed the faintly outlined foundations of what had been a church, its burned bones picked clean by scavengers. The sound of water came, sharp and distinct, from the other side.

He quickened his steps, came to it. He saw that a baptistry had been built across the stream a hundred yards or so above the church. There was a little natural fall there and pious men had lined and blocked it with bricks to make a pool for their services. There was always a drain in the bottom, William knew, but this one had not been used for a long time (like the burnt church it belonged to) and the plug had gotten clogged. The flow now spilled over the top.

He decided to go above it. The water would be fresher—he did not know what sort of trash was tangled and held there to rot. He saw that there was a kind of footpath, not well-defined but still visible. It followed the easiest natural way, winding as the land went, swinging in a wide arc from the stream. William followed it. When he thought he'd gone far enough he cut back to the stream. He was now well above the baptistry. He drank and hung his head in the cold water, until the ache and weariness of the past day and night were gone. He washed his face and his neck and his arms until all traces of the swamp muck were gone. He dunked his head in and out like a duck, letting the water run down his neck, holding his head under, feeling the soft flow of the water, the soft taste of leaf-filtered water. He sat back on his heels and wiped his face with his hands and combed his hair with his fingers.

Resting, he looked down the stream to the baptistry. He could see it clearly from here—nothing fancy, just a brick widening of the natural bed, to make a small pool. The water there was the opaque brown-grey of leaf-litter, and heaps of dead branches and small tree trunks were snagged against the banks. His eyes followed the stream to the edge of the baptistry, seeing the lean shapes of the willows, the shiny leaves of the sweet bay trees, the dahoons with their red berries, the titi bushes with their yellow fruit. His eyes circled the pool twice before he saw the woman. She was that earth-colored.

She knelt at the side of the creek, just above the baptistry, washing clothes. Her dress was brown, her hair black as her skin. Only a flash of bright yellow from the material in her hand caught William's eye.

She had not heard him. She went on quietly lifting and bending, wringing the clothes and stacking them on a clean stone beside her.

In the sudden noise of fighting mockingbirds the sounds of her splashing disappeared. William wondered for a minute if she were really there at all—if, soundless, she wasn't a part of the morning fog that twisted between the trees behind her.

Watching, William remembered some of the stories he'd heard years and years ago. Stories of Alberta, the great tall black woman who lived up in the hills with her man Stanley Albert Thompson and drank likker all day, while waiting for his huge gold watch to strike the hours. She had nothing at all to do except wash his clothes. Sometimes you would see a kind of froth at the edge of streams, and women would say: "Alberta's been doing her load here."

A great tall woman, free and easy in her movements as if her skin was white. Mostly she and Stanley Albert Thompson wandered around in the high peaks of the Smokies, but sometimes they came down south. Sometimes. During the crackle and sparkle of a blackberry winter their hills would get too cold to suit them and they would drift south for a bit, laughing and drinking. Out in the woods and around, people would hear them, hear their laugh or the sound of the chiming watch. And sure enough they'd find the place where those two had lain down to sleep, pine needles stirred and flattened by the violence of their loving. And thin wisps of smoke way up in the ridges—those were their fires, they were cooking that night. Sometimes too, when they were restless and bored they would toss rocks—you could hear the rattle of the slides for miles—and Alberta slung stones like a man. When they were tired of their game they'd stroll off, leaving the hillside torn and gashed by the falling rocks. Oh yes, Alberta and Stanley Albert Thompson always left their marks in passing, and the next day or the following week people could read them plain.

The Negro woman by the stream stood up, and William saw that she too was tall, very tall. She moved like a young woman, big but lithe. She stretched her cramped back, hands on hips. Moved her shoulders up and down, hands running over buttocks. Tilted up her head, hands smoothing over cheeks and eyes.

The only sounds were the birds' screeching and fussing and feather-tearing fights, the running stream, the rustling shivering leaves. William couldn't get the tales of Alberta out of his mind as he walked downstream toward her. He expected at any moment to hear the chimes of the watch.

She was looking away from him, across the leaf-littered baptistry, out at the trees sliding off down the slope, their green blocking out the sight of the burned church and the graveyard. Wasps came and settled on the little pile of twisted laundry at her feet, humping about on their straddled legs until they settled in the right spot, sucking moisture from the cloth.

She did not hear him. For all his size, he had kept the hunter's ability to move silently, even over broken ground. Finally when he was about ten feet from her, he deliberately put his boot to a twig and snapped it.

She turned around. Not spun around, not jerked around as he expected her to. Turned slowly, curiously. The large brown eyes studied him, not startled, just surprised.

She was not pretty, William saw that at once. The face was too dark, and too long. And she was a Freejack. The Indian showed in her high cheekbones.

"I was up a way," he said finally.

She didn't answer. The mixed-blood face waited patiently.

"I been walking some, and I figured I might be lost. Where's this?"

"New Church," she said.

Her voice was not deep, nor high. It was neither gentle nor harsh. After she stopped speaking, you had to wonder if you really heard anything. You couldn't remember what she had sounded like. As if, when she had done, the space all around her closed in again, tight, and wiped all traces of her from the air.

"I wasn't too far off," he said. "This branch got a name?"

"No," she said.

She did not say no sir. Most Negroes would have. William wondered: "You from around here?"

For the first time she moved her head, Negro-like, self-effacing. "Down there."

"Whose place?"

"Abner Carmichael."

He shook his head. "There's so many people in the county I never heard of."

"He's the one with the floating house."

William nodded, then. "I heard tell of him." An old man who lived in the bottomlands and who had built his house like a boat. Every spring when the flood crests came down the Providence River and all the creeks overflowed their banks, the land where his house stood was flooded. So each year he and his family (large family, not all his, cousins and sisters and brothers scrambled together) moved away to camp on high ground until the water subsided. He had built his house tight and sturdy like a boat, on mud and rock foundations that washed away with the seep and rush of water and left the house floating, half dry even in the flood. He had anchored it too, like a boat. It wasn't a large house and he had circled it with great ropes that he had brought himself from the wharfs of Mobile (he'd once worked there to make a little hard cash). He ran the ropes around the house—directly around as if he were tying it together—and he had fastened other ropes to it, running loosely to the trees on either side. When the water went down, the house would be there. He and his menfolk would build new foundations under it, and lever the house onto them. His women would wash out the inside, getting rid of the mud and whatever drowned animals were caught there. And then they would be set for the next ten months.

"I heard of him," William said. "You his daughter?"

"Granddaughter."

He smiled at her quick correction. "I reckon you don't look old enough to be much else."

"I'm eighteen," she said.

He just smiled again, and nodded.

She added: "My name's Margaret."

That was the way it began. That was how he found Margaret, washing clothes by a creek that didn't have a name. She lived with him all the rest of his life, the next thirty years.

Living with him, she lived with us all, all the Howlands, and her life got mixed up with ours. Her face was black and ours were white, but we were together anyhow. Her life and his. And ours.

MARGARET

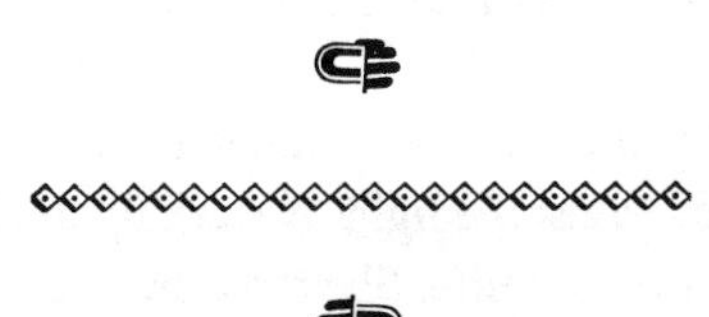

First there was nothing but cold and the noisy rustling crackling nights. Those were the earliest things she remembered.

Then she remembered the shapes of the floor boards and the way the undersides of tables looked, streaked and dirty. And she remembered being stepped on and stumbled over; and pinched by the rockers of rocking chairs. She even remembered the weight of her diaper—hippin, her mother called it—sagging behind.

It was funny though, she could remember all that, and she couldn't remember her mother's face—only a vague black shape and a name. Sometimes Margaret wondered how she had come to forget a face so completely. Why, she even remembered the way her mother's hands looked—holding the rusty, greasy handle of an iron skillet at the stove; skinning and gutting catfish on the back steps. . . . She could even remember one day when her mother stood on the edge of the porch, light behind her. She, the baby Margaret, had been in a corner of the rail-less porch, hemmed in by chairs laid on their sides, and the whole world of woods and the swamps and the shining sky lay beyond her. She had looked up and saw her mother standing on the edge of the porch, black figure against the bright stretching world. And she had never forgotten that. The small neat figure, bare feet jutting out from under the almost ankle-length dress.

That was finally the way her mother stayed in her mind—just hands and a shape against the light. A stark figure, lonely and slight. An outcast, by her own desire. Sheltered by her family because she had no place to go, but part of nothing. Living in the house, the small house that rose like a boat with the spring rains and the floods from the swamp. Living there, but not being there. Waiting. A whole long youth of waiting. Who would have thought a small slight body would have so much determination in it?

The stubborn head, the steady shaking no. He will come back. . . . He said he would come back.

A youth of waiting. With a child, first a baby and then a girl, growing, day after day, like her mother, so like her mother. No trace of white blood showing. No trace at all.

A black baby with kinky hair and knobby arms and legs. . . . A black girl, like the other girls of New Church. . . . A woman, tall and angular and black. Her father's rangy build, but none of his coloring.

By the time she was three or four, her mother was smearing her face with buttermilk, was dampening her hair and sitting her in the blazing sun to bleach, was sending her to the voodoo woman for a charm to bring out her white blood, to bring it to the surface. . . .

When Margaret was eight, her mother left. And they never heard of her again. She went south to Mobile, they thought. She was looking for somebody. She left her daughter Margaret in her grandfather's house, in Abner Carmichael's house, to be raised with all the other children, only more alone.

Margaret was eleven or so before she dared ask about her father. She was afraid. She saw how the other people deferred to her, how they pretended she wasn't there. But in the end, she got up her courage, and her great-grandmother told her all about it. Half a dozen sentences, that was all.

It began when the state decided to run a new highway down from the capital to the Gulf coast. Everything about that highway was bad luck. It came through Wade County the same summer weevils first really destroyed the cotton, the time people went hungry with their whole year's work eaten out. Some thought that cutting and grading for the road brought the weevils out of the earth where they had been sleeping. Some said the damage wasn't weevils at all —that some old, forgotten law had been broken and this was punishment. And it was true that when the road crews blasted their way through McCarren Hill, they turned up an Indian graveyard, so old that nobody knew it was there. For a while every bite of their shovels sent skulls and bowls and arrowheads rolling out into the light of day, the way they weren't supposed to. People said that those dead Indians wandered about and moaned on nights when the moon was down, fretting and cursing how they had been thrown from their beds to walk the damp pine woods. Nobody went abroad at night, not knowing what a strip of fog might be, not knowing what a bullfrog's croak might signify. People jumped at the caw of a tree frog and even the ridge runners, the bootleggers, stayed home at night, and dropped a couple of extra pieces of lightwood on the fire to keep the room from getting too dim. Nobody hunted, dogs ran alone after the foxes and the bobcats and the rabbits. And all around, houses began to show signs of magic—the mark on the porch post, the bottle swung from a tree, the circle of powerful stones. People who thought they had forgotten began to remember ways of working protecting magic.

It was in those days that Margaret was born. Her father was one of the surveyors for the new road. He spent two weeks in New Church that summer. He and another white man lived in a tent, and directed the first crews. After a couple of weeks the line of road moved too far toward the south to be in easy reach, so they took up their tent and packed it in the back of their state truck and went on. One of them told a young Negro girl that he would send back for her.

Most likely he never thought of it again. Most likely he didn't even remember. But she did. Her mother fussed and screamed at her, and called her a fool, but the words washed right over her head. Like the words of the men who would have married her, men she had known all her life, good men from the New Church community. She was small and pretty, and they would have married her together with the baby girl she had borne that terrible season when Indian ghosts walked the hills.

She preferred to wait. When she tired of that, she left. Alone.

That was the story the old woman told Margaret. Told it quickly and flatly. When she was done, she sighed and blew into the lump of snuff under her lip, turned and walked away. She had work to do; it was midsummer and the tomato plants needed her time. It was a pretty poor woman who couldn't grow enough tomatoes to line her pantry shelves for the winter.

Margaret watched her go, watched the horny yellow heels plop up and down in the dust of the swept yard. Then she herself left. Not thinking quite what she was doing, just moving. She got into the skiff, the light one that the smaller boys usually took, poled it out across the river and into the swamp. She put the full strength of her shoulder to the pole, sending the boat scooting through the shallow water, dodging around the cypresses, fish jumping out of her way, birds rising up overhead, furious at her passing. She crossed a wide slough, using the pole as a paddle in the still lead-colored scum-frosted water. Out of breath finally, she stopped with the bow of the skiff resting against the rotten pointed knee of a cypress. She shipped the pole and sat down, her body rocking rhythmically with the spasms of her breathing. The crows settled into the tops of the cypress trees again, and the black-and-red ricebirds came back. The mosquito hawks—mamselles, old people called them—skimmed the surface of the water, chasing the fluttering mosquitoes, while the croakers and the turtles and the frogs lunged after them.

Margaret sat and looked at the cypress knees, naked and slimy, at the still, unmoving swamp water. She peered down into its depths and saw the light spot that marked a place where bream had their bed. Then she looked at her own reflection in the water, distorted and glazed by the bright sky overhead. She looked at her own arms and hands: thin, striped with muscle and sinew. Bones showing clearly, the shell of bone with skin stretched over it.

Black skin. She looked at it, pinched it between her fingers, rubbed it. It was black, and that was all. Her father's blood, where would it be? It had to be somewhere, because it had gone into her. It would be inside maybe. Inside she would be white and blond-haired like him. . . . Her father's blood now, maybe it had given her her liver and her heart and her lights. But none of them was any use. And maybe too he'd left her her bones, the shell over which her mother's skin was stretched. . . .

Margaret watched a water moccasin swim slowly across the water and slither up a dangling branch. Congo, some people called them, because they were black.

She had always thought of her body as solid, one piece. Now she knew it was otherwise. She was black outside, but inside there was her father's blood.

She thought about this carefully. And her body seemed to expand, to swell, growing like a balloon. She thought of all the distance between the two parts of her, the white and the black. And it seemed to her that those two halves would pull away and separate and leave her there in the open, popped out like a kernel from its husk. She bent her head down into her lap and fought against the separating until bitter tears poured off her face and the front of her stained pink dress was soaked with salt. She wrapped her arms tight around her middle to keep herself together, and her ribs quivered and shook under her fingers.

A tree frog fell on her neck. She felt the little pat of his suction-cupped toes. She didn't dare look up.

There was a scab on her knee, an old one, half healed. She released one hand and scratched at it quickly. She wrapped herself up again and set her head so that one eye was close to the welling spot. She studied the dark red liquid that bubbled and finally flowed down the slant of black skin. And that was what white blood looked like. . . . She stuck out her tongue and nudged the edge . . . and that was what white blood tasted like. . . .

She watched until the blood lost its glassy color and clotted into dark streaks. She straightened up, releasing her body carefully, gingerly. The two parts of her seemed to hold together.

She looked around curiously, as if she had never seen this stretch of swamp before, surprised to find it familiar. There, a little way over, turtles lived: a small one was sunning himself on a fallen log. Farther over, across that second slough she saw dimly through the maze of vines and cypress and dead fallen trees, was a gator wallow. If she were closer she could smell the sweet sickish odor of those places.

She remembered. And everything seemed to be in its right place. Only she was different. No, that wasn't even so; she was just as she had been all along, she just hadn't known.

Margaret sat and looked at the rough splintery bow of the skiff. He had never intended to come back, her father. Of course not. Her mother was a fool. And that was why her family had always treated her with a shrug and a turn of the head, and a little gesture that meant moonstruck and sun-dry. . . .

There was Cousin Francine now, married ten years when her husband left to take work on the docks at New Orleans. He'd been gone a year, and no word from him, when she gave him up, and married another man. (That was three years past, and he still hadn't come.) He might have been dead, and nobody thought to tell her.

Or he might have found himself another wife in New Orleans, one he liked better, younger and without those four children.

It was the way things went, like it or not. Her mother ought to have taken another man and forgot the whole thing. After all, she had nothing to stop her. No other blood in her veins.

Margaret looked down at her own hand, at the black skin with the white blood under it.

Not like me, she thought. Not like me. She was all one piece. . . . Not like me.

A water turkey settled in a tree almost overhead. Margaret automatically noted its brown neck: a female. Skinks skittered up and down and over the trunks of fallen trees. . . . Margaret thought: If I'd brought a line I could take back a few bream.

The angle of the sun was different now. It was shining directly into her eyes. A couple of hours must have passed. She'd have to be getting back.

Her great-grandmother was finished with the tomato plants. She was resting in the shady part of the porch, her lip puffed out with a fresh wad of snuff. Little Matthew, who was about four, was watering the garden with a small bucket and a gourd dipper. He went down the rows, from plant to plant, ladling out the water carefully, singing a wordless song. When his two buckets were empty, he trotted off to get the yoke. He settled it across his shoulders, fitted the buckets in place, and started down to the riverbank.

The youngest child always did the watering under the old woman's gleaming black eye from the shade of the porch. Spring was very dry and shallow-rooted plants shriveled quickly. But there were always plenty of children around Abner Carmichael's house, plenty to do the watering.

Margaret remembered when she had done that, remembered the

feel of the smooth greasy yoke over her own shoulders. The yoke was old, old as Abner himself; he had made it when he was a small boy, made it well, and it lasted, darkening with sweat and the greasy hands that lifted and pulled at it.

Margaret waited until little Matthew came out of the willows and the water locusts that lined the river. He moved much slower now, full pails swinging on each side, his thin black legs pushing him up the gentle slope. He stopped at the edge of the garden, bent his knees and swung under the yoke, leaving the buckets safely on the ground. He lifted them one at a time and carried them down the rows to continue his watering.

He was sweating. Margaret saw the glisten of his black skin. She went toward him, stepping carefully between the triple poles of the bean hills. "Matt."

He stuck out his tongue.

"That pink looks plain silly in a black face," she said curtly. "You got no hat. Take mine."

She plopped it down on his head. He was too surprised to object.

She walked back and up the two steps to the porch. The old woman, her great-grandmother, said: "You give him you hat."

Margaret looked at the black old face in the dark cobwebbed corner of the porch. "I can't hardly see you back in there."

Her great-grandmother wobbled her head. The band of Indian beadwork shone briefly in the light. "Why you give it to him?"

"He's working," Margaret said, "I ain't."

"You never done it before."

"That so," Margaret agreed.

The old woman bent her head to cough, holding one hand tight across her mouth so the lipful of snuff wouldn't get away. The headband gleamed again, white and purple.

"Where that come from?" Margaret said. "The band."

The old woman straightened up and carefully arranged her thin figure in the chair again. You could see her stretching and placing every one of her vertebrae. Finally she settled her spine against the straight wood back and gave a little sigh of relief. Her bare yellow-soled feet had shaken apart during the paroxysm of coughing. Now she brought them together again and placed them properly, heels together, toes with their nails like yellow horns pointing slightly out.

Margaret waited.

"Made it," the old woman said.

One autumn when she was a little girl they had gotten the clams and the mussels from Dead Man Shoals, a long way to the north. During the following winter they had ground down and polished the shells into beads.

"Nobody do that any more," she said aloud.

They'd forgotten most of the Indian things that had come to them with their blood. Nobody made beads, not even the old people any more. They kept what they had, wore them, but that was all. They probably didn't remember how to make them any more. And nobody else had learned, none of the younger people at all. The old woman sighed. Even the shoals were gone. Dead Man Shoals, where the river swirled and broadened and the pines were thick on both sides, so thick that it was always dim under the interlocking branches, so thick that nothing could grow in the heavy mat of needles, not even a single blade of grass. At night it was like an enormous bed, without end, one that was soft and sweet-smelling and warm on a gusty fall night.

"You never been up them hills," the old woman said. "Never once."

"No."

The air was cool and light in the summer. Nothing like the steamy denseness of the bottomlands. Even the trees were different. The pines had heavier trunks and longer needles. The sassafras was thicker and better; they always dug the roots there and brought them back for tea and medicine. The hickories were bigger and taller; even the mockernuts promised more. Just before they left for the south, they always gathered hickories and walnuts and beechnuts—cleaned out the woods—after the first hard frost had set their bones to shivering.

Nobody did that any more. And even the shoals were gone. There was a dam below them now; all that region was flooded and the little sand beach was gone twenty feet or more under the water.

She sighed, the windy dry sigh of an old old woman. "You give Matt your hat."

"I'm going inside," Margaret said. "I'm going back to bed."

The old eyes flickered their answer, old black eyes, hooded like a bird's.

"I'll gig me some frogs tonight," Margaret said. "I reckon you like 'em enough to eat a leg or two."

The hoods dropped and opened.

"Old woman," Margaret began. But she forgot the rest and lost interest and instead of standing and trying to remember what it was she had been thinking to say, she turned and went inside. She didn't unroll her pallet from where it lay neatly placed by the wall; she climbed into the iron bed that stood with three others, filling the room, and fell asleep almost at once.

She never again slept on a pallet on the floor like the other children. She never had to because she no longer slept at night. She never again woke to see the lumpy quilt-wrapped shapes huddled on the floor among the round iron posts of the three real beds. She slept her days in the comfort of the bed, and spent her nights outside. Nobody bothered her; nobody noticed.

Only during the coldest nights of the winter she stayed home, when it was way below freezing outside and rain was falling. Then she sat up by the kitchen stove, feeding it little bits of wood, staring into the black iron surface and the red-tinged cracks. Those cold winter nights, all the others got into one bed, all who could get in, body piled on top of body, skinny limb to fat, sucking warmth.

The underside of the mattress was lined with newspapers, and between the covers were more newspapers, and every time a child turned or stirred the whole quiet night was full of the sound of moving papers, crackling like a fire.

There was also the sound of breathing, the sound of moving air, in and out. Quick and rustly like squirrels on a roof. Heavy and slow like a giant dying. Creaky and thin like the turning of a wheel.

It seemed to Margaret that the room rocked and echoed and shook with the noise. How did I sleep before, she thought, and I couldn't now. . . .

She remembered that winter beds were lumpy things, with always an elbow or an arm, strange bodies pressing together for warmth.

All through the winter nights she sat at the stove, while hoarfrost crusted like mold on the ground, and the puddle-filled ruts of the road froze solid, just the way the last passing had shaped them. When the sun came up, Margaret left the house quietly. She had found a hollow tree trunk, up the slope about a mile away. Its hollow, which faced toward the south, was partially covered by another fallen tree. In this shelter she built a small fire and kept it going with bits of moss and twigs until the sun had swung up high enough to give some warmth.

She liked the hours she spent crouched inside the trunk. It was warm, it was alone, and she could listen to the shrunken winter sounds of the woods. She always waited until the steady dripping of the night ice ended, then she stopped feeding her fire and watched it go out. She never once stomped the coals—somewhere in the back of her memory was a warning never to kill a fire on your hearth. Way back, from a story long ago—she did not think about it, did not question or wonder, she merely obeyed. The same way she never put a hat on a bed, nor entered and left a house by anything but the same identical door.

When her fire was gone, died of itself, she would get up, feeling her knees prick and shiver with their long cramping. She would shake herself and smooth down her hair. And she would go back to Abner Carmichael's house for something to eat. Most times there was cornbread and drippings and sorghum syrup, thin and stale. Sometimes there would be fatback or cold bacon. And sometimes there wouldn't be anything. Specially towards the first of spring, when the pantry shelves were stripped bare, and the bottom of the meal sack squirmed with weevils. Margaret did not mind—she was not hungry—and only children fretted when they found nothing to eat until dinner. Margaret did not really care about food. What she wanted most, she now had. Those mornings, the bed and the room were hers. The empty bed, its lumpy moss-filled mattress resting on old-fashioned rope slings, its heap of quilts faded muted splotches of bumpy color. There were no pillows, and the bed smelled faintly of kerosene, with which it was sprinkled every month, against vermin. It smelled of the many bodies that had lain on its bare striped ticking, the stale sweet smell of old sweat and sex. Margaret curled into it, sleeping hard and without the annoyance of dreams.

◇◇◇◇◇◇◇◇◇◇◇◇◇◇◇◇◇◇◇◇◇◇◇◇◇◇

ALONG toward the end of that first winter, her great-grandmother was taken sick, struck down in her chair on the porch—in the thin pale sun this time—so that her head dropped to her chest and her wad of snuff fell out of her lips with a little wet plop on the bare boards of the floor. They moved her inside, her daughters and granddaughters, and sent children running in all directions to tell the men at their work about it. They brought her into the bedroom, an old woman, shriveled red-brown body, small and dry like a husk, dying by inches. Her eyes were open but they weren't seeing; even when it got dark and they lit a lamp close by her head she didn't turn toward it, or even blink at its yellow shine. Her shriveled flat old chest rose and fell, shuddering each time in a deep rasping snore.

Margaret was asleep when they carried her great-grandmother in and laid her down in the narrow bed she had occupied all her old life. Margaret woke to the sound of rattling breathing and hushed whispering and quiet feet scurrying over the boards. She rolled out hastily and went into the kitchen. She stayed there, slumped sleepily in a corner, watching, while the evening dark deepened, and the stars finally began to come out, clear and frosty.

The first of the old woman's children and grandchildren and relatives began arriving: they crowded the porch until the beams sagged.

When it was too chill to stay out there, they jammed themselves into the kitchen, talking in whispers, passing a gallon jug of corn likker from mouth to mouth. The house shook and groaned under their weight.

In a bit, the preacher drove up, a short heavy man, whose name was Robert Stokes. They all hushed and listened to the short mutterings of prayer in the bedroom, giving responses themselves now and then. When Robert Stokes came out and took his place at the table, the muffled conversations began again. Since he was the preacher, they gave him his whiskey mixed with water in one of the few glasses they had. He waited with them, death-watching with them, talking crops and markets and animals with the men. His round black head nodded, solemnly sleepy. He was as tired as any of them, he farmed like them, and preached and watched in his spare time. He wasn't young, everybody remembered him always being there, preaching on Sunday mornings, and visiting the sick and the dying every hour of the night. It had been forty years past that he and his bride built their first house. Not that it was a house really, it was just a lean-to against some big pines, but it was warm and dry and enough for them, and it would do until they got around to building something more. They had the spot picked already, stones marking the ground where the foundations would be. It was a nice spot, on a little rise with two big pecan trees and a spreading dogwood that turned sparkling every March, like moonlight. It was four years before they got to do anything, and then they used the old-fashioned mud-and-moss between lathes. Their grandfathers built houses like that; they brought the method with them when they spread north from the Gulf coast, slaves on the run maybe, or hungry freemen. There had even once been a special name for the way it was done, but that word was long forgotten.

Robert Stokes built his house that way, room after room, year after year.

He'd been lucky in his wife too. He'd taken a young skinny girl, an orphan living in her cousin's house and not welcome there. Kettle cousins, people called them. They got to do most of the work and to lick the kettle when everybody else was done. She couldn't have been more than thirteen when they married; he himself was only fifteen, but he had reached his full height: he had the same square dumpy figure. His skinny small girl grew after her marriage, until she stood almost six feet tall. She had only sons and she bore them—all of them—alone. It did not occur to her to have a woman stay with her as her time approached. Maybe she thought there was no one to ask. The first time she was weeding her garden, seeing that the bugs did not eat up the tomatoes and fastening down the stakes of the beans, when the ammonia-smelling water spurted down her legs and stained the ground by her bare feet. With the first quiver of her belly muscles straining, she went back to the lean-to, stood her hoe carefully against the wall. Inside she spread a quilt on the floor and squatted, shaking with the spasms and panting with relief in between. When her husband came home that evening, late because he worked as long as there was light in the sky, the baby was sucking, the bloody quilt was folded away in the corner.

Even at her present age, she still worked the fields with her husband and her five living sons. Robert Stokes was a lucky man, the Lord had been good to him. He was saying so as he sat at the kitchen table with the family of a dying old woman. He had a deep voice, best voice in the county, and the words of praise for his lot and for the soul of the old woman struggling to leave her body blended together.

"And you hear that now," he said abruptly. They all went silent, listening. Margaret heard nothing but the wind and the stamping and rattling of the tethered mules on the frozen ground. He pointed up to the roof. "Jesus and his angels waiting to carry off the soul of our sister." Everybody looked up, at the soot-stained and water-streaked ceiling. Margaret glanced out the window into the dark cold winter sky. "You hear their wings, children," the preacher said.

"Yes, Lord," somebody answered, and they all fell silent, listening again. This time there were two great strangled snores from the dying woman. They dropped their eyes, cleared their throats, and moved about. Some went on the porch, some fetched the likker jug.

As the crowd shifted and parted, the preacher saw Margaret standing by the corner window, where she had been staring into the sky, looking for the brushing wings. "I don't know you, child," he said kindly. "I ain't never seen you before for all that you look familiar to my eyes."

Somebody bent down and whispered into his ear: "It's nothing but Sara's baby, the only one she had."

"Jesus save us," he said, and looked at her again. This time with curiosity. Margaret stood perfectly still, knowing that he was searching her face and body for some sign of white blood. She stared her great brown eyes directly into his small black ones, shrewd and bright in the folds of his fat face. She stared, daring him to ask her more, daring him to say anything. . . . She held her breath.

He looked away. Other bodies slipped between them, people moved about, and he disappeared.

Margaret began to breathe again. But now the air in the room had gotten too hot for her, it was too full of the smell of whiskey-laden breaths. She had to go outside. She pushed her way through the room, using her elbows.

The night was very cold. The ground glistened with frost. It was marked like snow, with footprints going off in one direction to the privy, in the other around the yard to the small barn where the visitors' mules were sheltered. Margaret stared at the two trails, visible in the dim kerosene light from the window, and wondered where she could go. It was too cold for her hollow tree; even with a fire she was sure to have frostbite by morning. Even the porch was too cold. The snuffling snort of a mule decided her. She went to the barn. It was jammed with animals, but she found an empty feeding trough and climbed in. Here, the steamy reeking air was passably warm—in spite of the cracks and holes in the walls—and Margaret settled down to study the watery dark eyes and the slope of the varicolored flanks that surrounded her. The sharp heavy odor was a kind of anesthetic, and she slept with her eyes open, staring at the pattern of light and dark, lulled by the animals' breathing and their occasional shuffling.

She was aware that time was passing, but she could not see out to gauge the movement of the stars. She heard nothing and noticed nothing until the first shriek from the house.

The animals stirred slightly and backed, their rope halters creaking. There was a second cry, the long descending wail of mourning. The old woman was dead.

Margaret settled back. No need to go in, just an old woman who had died, worn out with the revolving years. No need at all. . . . Then all of a sudden in the dark empty space over the back of the big grey mule that belonged to her cousin Zelda, Margaret saw her great-grandmother. Saw her clearly, just as she used to sit on the porch—shawl around her shoulders, band around her head. Her blackbird eyes under the folds of brown skin glared out, angry as always. She lifted her hand, the one that had the jagged scar of a ceremonial magic cut across the back, and she beckoned.

Margaret stared at the hand, at the design of the scar, at the veins raised like vines on a wall, at the long fingernails, thick and yellow as horn.

"Come into the house," she told Margaret.

Her voice was strong and loud just the way it had been before. But that, Margaret thought, would be because she wasn't more than a minute or so dead, and her soul hadn't had time to fade off, to go wherever it was that dead souls went, off somewhere in the pine hills to the north, where people said they saw them sometimes on warm summer nights, walking around, taking the breeze as if they were alive.

"Plenty people in the house," Margaret told her, "you see that kitchen, there isn't a foot of open space. And your brother's family from over Tchefuncta Creek that still got to get here."

The ghost turned her head, looking over her shoulder, back at the house. The purple and white beads of her headband winked.

"You see," Margaret said. "I been telling you."

The head swung back, and the eyes fastened on her again. "Come to the house," it said, "child of my daughter's daughter. My flesh and blood."

She slipped lower then and faded into the grey of the mule's flank.

Margaret stared at the place where she had been, feeling the tug of the blood in her veins, feeling it pull her out of the stable into the house. The old woman's blood bringing her back into the family group in the kitchen.

Grudgingly Margaret crossed the empty yard, swept clean by a twig broom each week, and frozen now so that it crackled beneath her feet. "Only half my blood," she said aloud into the night.

"Be with my blood," her great-grandmother's voice said emphatically though fainter this time. "Go."

Margaret looked up, into the clear, star-freckled night. "Is that where you are," she asked, "up there?"

She stood and squinted into the depths trying to make out the figure of her great-grandmother drawing farther and farther off, dodging her way among the stars.

Margaret sighed and nodded after her and did her bidding. She went into the house.

The bedroom was noisy and bustling now—Margaret glanced through the door. All the oldest women had crowded themselves into the narrow spaces between the beds to begin the waking. They had brought straight wood chairs with them, lined them up close as possible there. Now they were sitting straight-backed in those close-packed rows, hands folded across their chests, rocking their bodies back and forth from the waist, mourning. It was a descending long nasal wail, repeated over and over again, each one exactly like the one before. It was not a hymn. It had no tune; it did not even have any rhythm. No two voices were together. It was only a raggedy picket line of sound to keep the evil spirits away from the dead.

Three younger women were bent over the bed, washing and preparing the body, putting half-dollars on the eyes. They were singing a familiar hymn: "Will There Be Any Stars in My Crown." They were singing more softly and they kept losing the melody in the noise of the mourners, but they just picked it up again and went on.

Margaret turned back to the kitchen. A few people were leaving—to carry the news—so the room was no longer unbearably full. Robert Stokes still sat at the table, alone now. All the other wooden chairs had been taken into the bedroom for the mourners, and only the preacher was left his. The men squatted on the floor, some hunkered down in the middle, others resting their backs against the walls, talking quietly or just staring out into the center of the room. The children were propped in the corners, sound asleep; now and then one cried or whimpered. The women—all those who weren't actually waking in the bedroom—were jammed into the far corner around the wood range. Pots clattered on the iron top and the sweet odor of squirrel stew mushroomed up with the steam.

All during the following day they came, from twenty-five miles around, the old woman's descendants, jolting along behind the patient rumps of their mules. The house floors sagged and groaned under their weight. The hams and the cold joints and the fowls they brought with them crowded the shady north corner of the porch, hung there out of the way of raiding varmints. The old woman had been washed and laid out in her plain pinewood coffin. Candles stuck in blue bottles were burning in a triangle at her head.

It was so noisy, Margaret thought as she huddled in the farthest corner of the kitchen, it was so very very noisy.

She slept in the barn that night, patiently waiting for the end. In the morning, she stood on the porch in the little pool of cold winter sunlight and waited while they nailed closed the coffin, and carried it outside to the wagon for the five-mile trip to the cemetery.

There was a band now, a five-piece band. They looked pretty tired because they had been playing at a dance over in Mill River, but they took a few quick drinks and swung into place behind the wagon. Their feet crunched on the frozen mud and the mules snorted and grumbled, but they played their saddest marches: "Garlands of Flowers" and "Westlawn Dirge." The trombone and the trumpets lifted clear and sad in the cold morning air, the drums gave a slow dull beat. Everybody walked the whole way along the rutted road. The men had gone out the day before and cut pine branches and spread them across the muddiest parts so the wagon with the coffin and the band and the first of the line of marchers got across dry-shod. But the branches sank farther and farther into the mud, and by the time the end of the procession came, the puddles were as deep as before, only now they had bits of twig and broken stalks of pine sticking up in them. Those in the last of the line had to make their own way, had to jump across or clamber up the low slopes on each side, slipping and sliding on the icy rocks.

Margaret was among the last, with the smallest of the children who could walk on their own. She hitched up her skirts and jumped. The children chattered and clambered around. And all this time the drum kept a steady funeral beat.

The graveyard was only partially fenced by a single strand of barbed wire, but no animals ever wandered in. Under the tall thick pines, no bushes and practically no grass grew. The sandy stretch stayed clean and open with only the gentle drift of pine needles across it. There had been no burials for quite a while; the graves had all sunk into gentle rises, smoothed by the rain. Most had no headstones; a few still had their wooden ones, cut into the rough outline of an hourglass—they would soon fall away. Two or three had been covered with cement poured into wood molds. In the cement, under a pane of glass, was a colored picture of the dead. Margaret remembered one: a young man standing stiffly, hand in coat. A wedding picture for a grave. . . .

It would be over there, the east corner, Margaret thought. I don't have to see, I know it's there, with the name and date scratched under it. . . . But nobody does that any more.

All they did now was outline the grave with white stones, set that wood hourglass marker at the head, and put the dead gifts on the top. . . .

Every grave had them. Cups, and glasses turned purple by the sun, and china animals—dogs and cats, and a broody hen or two. And plates. Lots of plates. Most of these stood on two-inch-high spires of sandy mud, jutting out like mushrooms from the grave. The rain had given them that form, and the plates that sat on that thin rain-carved stem were called Death's Cups. If you touched one, old Death himself would come riding after you on his white horse with a long tail that rattled in the wind because it was made of little finger bones. . . .

There was a black smear around the open grave. To lighten their work, to thaw the first inches of ground, the diggers had built fires there. They had not watched too carefully because the flames had left their bounds, spread through the strand of barbed wire, and run up a young pine tree. Soot and ash lifted and hung in the air as the tramping feet passed through.

The band became silent, only the drum thudded slowly. Margaret felt her skin quiver across the back of her neck. There were the grunts of men bearing the coffin and the squeak of ropes. Abruptly the drum stopped.

For a moment there wasn't even a wind. Then there was a scuffle at the grave and the wailing began again—a dozen or more voices this time, high-pitched, echoing off the tallest of the pines, shaking the buck vines that twisted high overhead. Somebody had jumped into the grave and they were pulling them out. Even women who did not know how to wail the way the old ones did were screaming softly now, with a slow breath-like rhythm. The preacher began a proper hymn as he picked up a handful of mud. He dropped it into the grave, letting the sandy grains trickle between his fingers like sugar, savoring the feel of the earth. He moved aside, gesturing with a swing of his arm. Then there was shuffling as everyone pressed in to drop other handfuls on the pine boards. "Jesus save, Jesus save," the preacher sang at the top of his fine voice. Margaret noticed a couple of black crows circling high up in the clear sky, watching. What do they think? she wondered. Whatever do they think?

A couple of men picked up shovels, and the dirt filled back in with a rush, whispering as it went. The preacher finished his singing and said something, briefly and softly. Margaret did not listen; his grave speeches were all the same. Then everybody shook hands, and kissed cheeks. The oldest women and the musicians got in the wagon for the ride back. The trace chains clanked and the mules plodded out. As they passed, Margaret noticed that Elfetha Harris, the youngest of the dead woman's granddaughters, was covered with mud. She had jumped into the grave. Now she sat wiping her eyes, looking less and less sad with each turn of the wheels of the wagon. She always jumped in, Margaret remembered. When her husband died, and her sister, and her own child that had been born a cripple, and her husband's father—it was part of every funeral, Margaret thought.

They started the walk home. The short winter sun, deep in the south, showed afternoon. The rutted stone-littered road climbed a rise, narrowing as the woods darkened and pressed in at the crest. It was there, lurking in the darkness of a grove of pecan, sweet gum, and persimmon trees that Margaret saw her great-grandmother again. She beckoned but Margaret did not stop. She beckoned again, and Margaret told her: "Quit bothering me. You got your grave to lie in." The ghost stood stock still and watched her. Margaret said:

"We threw in the mud and I threw in my handful and we covered you up and you got to stay there."

"Flesh and blood," the ghost mourned.

"I buried my blood with you," Margaret said recklessly. "I'm using only the other half now."

The ghost didn't answer, just got fainter against the bare tree trunks.

"Go back to your grave," Margaret said, "and quit pestering me."

She turned and walked on, hearing nothing from the trees on top of the hill behind her, not even the stirring of a breeze.

The rest of the funeral lasted for the next three days, but then funerals for the oldest people usually did. It was as if the old people had left more to mourn, despite it being in the course of things that they should die. Infants and children were buried quickly and it was all over.

Margaret wondered about that. A mother mourned a child, for sure, and a father too. And maybe a brother or a sister, but not many more. It seemed strange . . . when they were the ones who weren't supposed to die.

Margaret shrugged. Things came in a certain form and that was all there was to it. . . .

She had gone for a walk, leaving the crowded house and the noisy people. She had walked straight north, climbing the slopes until she got to the open stretches of clear pine and hickory, vineless and brambleless.

There was another funny thing about funerals, she thought. They let you see people you wouldn't otherwise see one year to the next . . . people who only came for important funerals. Cousin Mary's family, for instance, from over Twin Fawns way. That was twenty-five miles of bad roads straight north, toward the rising hills. But they were cousins, first and second and third, and so on, and they had a duty. So they came, just the way they had this time. And there were always new people with them, not counting the babies. Men who'd gone North to work and come back, not finding a job or not liking the living there. Families who'd been in Mobile and had finally come home, cash in the sock. New wives and husbands that the cousins had gathered.

This time there were five people she had never seen before. There was Jack Tobias and his wife Kate. They came back from Cincinnati and went to farming again with his father because cotton was bringing near a dollar a pound and it was worth your work. (Margaret recognized them easily: Tobiases all looked alike.) There was Grover Kent too—she remembered him as the boy who'd bummed his way over to Port Gibson and joined up with a circus there. He'd come back with a hernia that gurgled and bulged when he took off his truss—he did that to make the children laugh. And there was Roger Ellis, a short thin man who'd married Elfetha Harris's widowed daughter. He'd broken his hip working at a gin in Memphis two years before and it mended crooked. He was the one carried a banjo with him. Could he play it now? . . .

Margaret shrugged. It was getting cold and she turned to walk back.

Roger Ellis was sitting on the porch when Margaret got home, in the warm corner where the thin sun reached, the same corner where the old woman was struck dead. Nobody had dared to go there before. *Like there was a fence around it,* Margaret thought. But now there was this little man, grey-haired, with a tiny mustache, chair tipped back against the wall, playing his banjo. He was singing too, very softly, an old blues. Margaret didn't know its name, if it had one, but she recognized the one line that repeated in it, and she liked its soft sad sound: long lonesome home. She stopped on the edge of the porch by the steps and listened. She shivered and it wasn't so much from the cold as from the sad turn of the melody: "Who chop you cotton when I'm gone?"

One or two people looked out the door, some came on the porch to listen to him.

"Roll me a pallet on your floor, oh yes.
I'm leaving for that long lonesome home."

Margaret shivered again. She saw it all. The generations of weeping that had been done, the generations of weeping that were to come. She could feel it all, feel the pulse and the heartbeat in the banjo chords and in the gentle light voice that sang across them. "Going where those chilly winds don't blow, oh yes."

Margaret felt herself grow big and bigger until she stood way above the house. So tall she could look down the chimney and see the soot-blackened inside. So tall she could look down on the pine trees growing at the very top of the ridge that sheltered the house from the north. So tall that she could see way up and down the river, following it in its twists and turns, through its willows and its birches. Following it southward, looking down on even the huge river birches and the water oaks, following it all the way to the Gulf. . . . She could feel too, great like her size. She could feel the earth move under her feet, breathing slowly as it passed from season to season. She could hear the sound the stars made in their rounds, as they passed by her hair.

Her body grew great and full, and she thought, I'll never be put in a box and lowered into the earth. I'll never grow old and watch the veins on my hands begin to work their way out of my skin. . . . It was funny, now, the way all the inner workings of old people moved to the outside. Their muscles and their sinews got hard and ropy and hung on the outside of their skins. Their veins rose up, so where you hadn't been able to see them before you could see them now. There were little blue ones that appeared on the forehead, jagged like a saw blade, where the skin had once been smooth. There were others like cords wrapping their way across the backs of hands, and along legs. And pulses turned up where they never had been before. The throat one now, you didn't even know it was there, until one day you saw it, naked and exposed, pumping your blood for everybody to see. . . . I won't be like that, Margaret thought. I won't ever get old and I won't ever die. I couldn't. . . .

She saw that the women had come out of the kitchen to listen to the singing. They crowded out and stood in a raggedy line across the porch, all of them wiping their damp or greasy hands on their aprons. They were all wearing print dresses, their best ones, the ones kept specially for funerals and weddings.

Those always come together, Margaret thought. Why would that be? One was life and one was death and nothing could be more different, but they always seem to fall together. . . . There was Cousin Hilda now, and the youngest of Robert Stokes's boys. They had slipped out to the barn just last night, and Margaret had huddled back and pretended she wasn't there and pretended that she hadn't seen or heard. It was then, in the dark ammonia-clouded barn, that she felt the first real tug of longing, and way back in her mind she wished that she had been Hilda. It was the tug, the pull, the first time. . . . She cursed herself and men, and hated her body for what it would do to her. . . . She ached all over with the effort and the struggle. And in the morning she felt like she had chopped cotton for days. . . .

Margaret looked at Hilda now, standing on the porch among the women, and she saw how slight and shapely her figure was, even under the two long raggedy sweaters. How she carried her hands in front of her, a gentle manner, almost pleading. How soft and unmarked her face was in the harsh winter daylight. Except for the dark circles and the sleepy eyes.

Margaret glanced down at her own hard angular body. Fit for the wood lot or the fields. Clumsy and out of place in a kitchen. With a man. She turned away, near to crying.

• • •

The following day people began leaving, the Twin Fawns group first, because they had the longest way. Margaret stood in the littered, rutted yard and watched them load up.

Roger Ellis, who was driving one of the two wagons—a bright blue one with a small young mule in the shafts—looked down suddenly, directly at her. "Morning."

She did not answer. The mule twitched its ears at the circling deer flies.

"You favor you mammy," he said.

"Might be," she said.

"She was a right pretty woman."

Margaret felt herself blushing with pleasure and hated it. "I got no mammy," she said. "Leastways, I always heard I took after my daddy."

She spun on her heel and went into the house, carrying her tall broad body defiantly.

THE short hard winter passed. Fine early-spring rains began, light delicate ones like fog or smoke, that dusted the surfaces of houses and trees and earth—the gentle ones. The sun shone fitfully, the sky was an even light grey, and the ground warmed every hour. The farmers went out and tested it, laying their hands flat on it, seeing whether it gave or took away heat. It was only a thing to do. They knew before they started that the warmth of the ground would pass into their hands. They could almost feel the earth begin to breathe. Those whose fields were high began to break for their cotton and peas and corn. People in the bottomlands waited for the floods to come, to cover their fields with rich black silt brought down from the north. For them, early spring was a time of rest, almost like the winter had been. It was the last bit of slack they would have until the end of summer, those short weeks when the cotton was making and there was nothing to do but wait for it.

Margaret no longer huddled in her hollow tree. She could walk anywhere, warm and comfortable now. She counted off the signs of spring as they passed in front of her eyes: the grass pinks were blooming up in the damp pine woods. Other small nameless pink flowers showed in the bottom of the meadows, and in the deeper bogs pitcher plants raised their greenish heads in search of flies. The swamp azalea appeared, white and pink. And the flame azalea, with tiny flowers like glowing coals. And the sweet shrub, bubby blossoms, whose dark flower was the color of a woman's nipples.

Margaret counted the mild days, waiting. She saw the river, which had been rising steadily all the last month, top its low bluffs and inch across the land. Finally, she saw the thick heavy clouds boil over the horizon and the heavy hail-spotted rains begin. These hard falls—tempests, old people called them—sent the creeks boiling white along their courses, ripping up trees and rolling rocks, tumbling along the drowned bodies of animals under a thick lightning-streaked black sky.

Margaret helped her family move out of the house, load everything on wagons, cover them with torn tarpaulins, mold-spotted, and drive them away. The crates of chickens and the first of the spring calves riding, the stock driven on behind. The squeals of the bound calves and the nervous calling of the cows softened and blended in the steady falling rain.

Margaret waited until last, until Abner Carmichael was ready to leave. He looked over the house carefully, checked the cables that anchored it to the nearest trees. He checked his small barn too. He had knocked almost all the lower planks out of those walls and tied them securely to the rafters. The flood water would flow directly through—across the dirt floor—and unless some very large object smashed into it, the building would stand.

Margaret watched him finish and turn to leave. The water was already at the lower side of the dooryard and this was about as late as they could get mules and wagons out. She watched his grizzled head look from one side to the other, as he plodded away, putting his heels down hard against the ground, as old men will.

She waited for him. Though he seemed surprised to see her, he said nothing, and they walked together along the road, the ground rising steadily under their feet as they climbed out of the river bottoms and overtook the slow-moving wagons and the plodding stock.

It would be three or four weeks before they could go back. They spent the time in different ways, in different places. Sometimes with cousins. Sometimes in abandoned barns or houses that they had located during the winter. Sometimes they all stopped. Sometimes only the women. Most times, though—as this year—they all moved directly to the high pine woods. They turned their cattle to graze in the balds, the little high meadows, flower-covered and lush this time of year. They themselves lived in shelters of pine branches and made fires of the cones. The high sandy ground carried off the water almost before it fell and they were dry and warm. The only things that bothered them were the fierce sudden thunderstorms that ripped the sky and struck into the pine stands, splitting the tallest trees open, singeing their needles into dancing sputtering fires, like a child's sparkler. And sometimes too there would be fire balls, rolling along the ground—fire devils, some people called them—running across the open ground, zigzagging and darting, bright as fire, bright as burning hell, until they smashed into a tree and ran up the trunk and exploded with a puff at the top, leaving nothing but the smell of burning and the charred marks of their course.

After a while the rains stopped, but no one in Abner Carmichael's household moved. The river would continue to rise for many more days, long after the actual fall stopped. Margaret sat at the door of her shelter—she had built one for herself and lived in it alone—and dropped pine cones into the little fire. She did not need it; the weather was very warm. She did it because it gave her something to do when she was thinking about her mother. She was trying to remember what she'd looked like. All she found in her memory were the worn pictures she had seen so often before. They weren't very much better than nothing.

And what was she doing now? . . . And where was she? . . .

Margaret made herself stop thinking of that. Finally, she forced herself to study the pine cones she held in her hands, the tapered cones of the longleaf pine.

She was grown now herself. She was seventeen. Most girls that age were married. Lots of them had a child or two. They wouldn't be crying over a mama.

Margaret looked out across the misty pasture where a single black-and-white cow grazed.

I been coming here ever since I was born, she thought. This spot or another like it. Every year since I been born. But this one here, this is the last....

She stopped, startled. She looked around, half expecting to have discovered somebody else had spoken those words aloud. Now that they were said—or thought, which was the same thing—they seemed true enough. But she was afraid of prophecy, and its connections with the devil; her heart beat much faster and irregularly, and she shivered. But she believed: this would be the last year.

Knowing that, she looked at everything more carefully. The first sweet-smelling tall flowers of the greenfly plant. The pipewort, the moss verbena. The blue flowers of the pickerelweed in moist overgrown beds of ponds. The reddish curled lips of the skunk cabbage. And milkweeds, tall and purple. Jacob's-ladder, poking its way between pine needles. The ginseng with its tiny purple flower, whose root, people said, was good for making love. Yarrow, lacy-leaved and fragrant. The poisonous Indian weed. And the sweet-tasting honeysuckle. Four-o'clocks to string on a child's necklace. And whole fields full of wild pinks, brilliant and glowing in the sun.

And the little animals that rustled among them. The snapping turtle catching flies by the rubbly edge of a pond, splashing into the water at the slightest noise. The box turtle lumbering into its burrow. And the snakes. Kick aside a fallen pine and you were sure to find a bull snake, blotchy grey, and hissing at you. Rattlers too, all kinds and sizes; when you found one, you called the children together and stoned it. And all the others, the milk snakes and the the black runners and the green snakes and the corn snakes and the rat snakes. There were so many, when you thought about it, so very many.

Margaret wondered: There a lot of things I don't have no names for. Plants and varmints both, that I can't call by name.

She was alone the whole day, watching, looking, going wherever she wanted and as far as she could walk.

The stand of pines the family was sheltering in now, it was a kind of narrow strip running up the side of the rising sandy hills. If she went very far in either direction the land changed rapidly. Hickories began to appear, and scrub oak, and soon she was in a dense wood of holly and beech and sweet gum and water oak and dogwood and sweet bay, buck vines lacing them all tight together overhead. Now and then she passed a persimmon and a pecan, and she noticed their location carefully, in case she should come this way in the fall after a hard frost when their fruits would be ripe.

She found streams, too, ones that the flood season hadn't seemed to touch. Most were very small, a trickle over a sand bottom. She drank their leafy-tasting water and ate the wild watercress from their banks. She found a large one, down in a gully, almost out of sight in a clump of sweet bay trees and wild azaleas. This one was older; it had cut its way through the sand and had even channeled its way deep into the rock. She stood looking down into the opaque smooth-flowing water. By the far bank, no more than five feet across, she saw the quick flick of a sunfish.

He would be good fried, she thought automatically. And then: Why am I always eating, always thinking of that? Why does it take so much trouble to keep your stomach full and quiet?

A leaf sailed by, and a long-legged fly walked the quiet water in the lee of a fallen rock. Water bugs twitched their way about the surface. She knelt and looked at her reflection in the water that flowed half an inch below the rock shelving. She studied her face, heavy-lidded large eyes, full mouth, ears that were too long. She spat and the white froth sailed by her cheek. Another water-walker, caught in the flow, spun past, long legs skating feverishly. Margaret cupped some of the water in her hands; it was perfectly clear. She drank, and it was much colder than the other streams. She dipped in her arm, groping for the bottom, found none. She stood up, dragged over the fallen branch of a magnolia and thrust it down, pushing against the little current. It did not touch. Margaret pulled it out, tossed it aside. The creek must not have had a bottom.

She walked on. There were a few very early blackberries, small and sour before their season. She stopped and ate them anyway, face crinkling at their flavor.

And it be right strange, she told herself silently, the way things come in their seasons. The way they appear and go each year at the same time, without never a mistake. . . . And the way people come. And me, I am here now, but I won't be next year. And where will I be? I don't know the answer to that any more than I know why berries have their seasons and the persimmons only ripen after a frost and a rattler is poison and a king snake isn't. And why a milk snake sucks the cows dry and a hoop snake puts its tail in its mouth and rolls down the road when the moon is small. . . . And there be reasons for all of those and causes too, only I don't know them. I don't know anything. . . . I don't know what Mobile looks like, only what Grover Kent tells about the docks and the bananas. And I don't know what New Orleans looks like, only the stories people bring. And I never seen the ocean. . . . All I seen is the cotton fields and the rivers, flood and dry, and the way pines move in the wind, moaning.

She began to walk back to the place where her family was stopping. Thinking: I won't pass here again. Maybe for a long time. Maybe not ever.

Watching carefully, looking carefully. To remember.

She entered the stretch of pine, and passed her way among them, weaving silently, playing that she was a ray of light or a wind. Shapeless, formless, smooth, passing. . . .

She slipped into the shelter she had built for herself, a bit away from all the others, and, tired by her long walk, stretched out under it. And listened to the sounds. The bells of the cows. The games of the children, their reedy voices raised in the singsong chant: "Here come Johnny Cuckoo. . . ."

Whatever did that mean? Margaret thought. . . . Nothing seemed to mean anything clear this morning. . . . Not even words which were supposed to.

The children went on chanting in a raggedy chorus: "I come from being a soljer, a soljer, a soljer, I come from being a soljer on a dark and stormy night."

It was a silly song, Margaret said to herself. As silly as the moaning sounds Katy was making. . . .

Margaret opened her eyes and glanced across the clearing. Katy was walking slowly up and down, arms across the shoulders of two women. She seemed to be laboring in earnest now, Margaret thought. . . .

Margaret closed her eyes again. Katy always labored hard. Her babies were always born with long mashed heads that they kept for the first months of their lives. . . . She was taking on now. Her moans were interrupted by screams. So that was why, Margaret thought, the men had disappeared. It was supposed to be bad luck for a man to be too near a birthing.

I've got to remember this too, Margaret thought. And the way the sounds go right straight up into the open sky.

Then, because she was tired, she fell asleep.

When the ground finally dried a bit, they began moving back to the bottomlands. The men went first, to start the plowing. They were ready to plant by the time Margaret and the other women arrived.

They also had replaced the rock foundations and levered the house back on them. The women had the inside to clean, the mud to scrape and slosh away with buckets of water. When they were done, they brought the beds and the bedding from the wagons. The old men built the mud-and-moss chimney. The children swept the yard, and took the dead animals (possums and rats and squirrels) and carried the bloated bodies down to the river and tossed them in.

The stove went back into the kitchen while they were hammering the lower boards on the barn. They were ready for another year.

Spring passed into summer, shimmering with heat. Endless, work-filled unmarked days, one very like the other. Finally, a rest in the hot days when the cotton was making, when there was nothing more to do until the bolls swelled open and full. Then it was time to start dragging the long sacks up and down the rows in the crouching, sweating weeks of picking. Imperceptively the nights cooled, and the mornings. Margaret noticed the change as she carried the washing over to the baptistry behind the old church—a long walk but the water was clearer than the river. Margaret had never liked the smell of river-washed clothes, and they always took on the muddy color so soon.

It was on one of those cool early mornings—she had left the house long before it was light—washing her clothes in the clear creek water, that she met William Howland.

At first she did not think he was flesh and blood. She had not heard him come, had not heard the crinkle and crunch of the ground under his feet. He just appeared, not far from her.

She often saw things in the woods. Faces and figures. Sometimes they talked to her and sometimes they only stood back and looked. Sometimes they were friendly and sometimes they scowled and warned her away from places they were guarding. Sometimes she recognized them and sometimes they were people she had never seen before. Sometimes, they weren't even people. They were just shapes without a name, like a breeze if you could see it. Or they were animals. There was a chicken, a big red rooster, that she saw everywhere. It seemed to follow her for days at a time.

So when she saw a tall heavy blue-eyed bald man in the morning fog, she was not surprised. He was one of many. . . .

For the first minutes she talked to him, she was sure that if she put out her hand, she could reach right through him. Then she began to realize that he was solid, and she felt disappointed. He was real. . . .

She sat down abruptly. Almost crying.

"You sick?" he asked.

She shook her head, still having trouble with tears.

"What ails you?"

She shook her head again, and he sat beside her, and talked for a while. She heard his words but she did not bother to listen to them. Not for a long time, until she had gotten herself used to this new situation, then she sharpened and focused her ears again.

"So there's one thing sure," he was saying. "I got to get myself a housekeeper."

She looked down at her hands folded in her lap, big hands.

"And I reckon it's got to be somebody young, account of it's no easy job. The house needs lots of work, you can see that from what I been telling you."

I weren't paying any mind, she protested silently.

He was waiting for her to say something.

"Why you tell me?"

"You might want the job, seeing it's open."

She lifted her hands and held them out in front of her, fingers stretched. "I figured to be going away," she said. "I been figuring on that."

Last spring. Spring past. That day she found the persimmon trees and saw the sunfish in the creek that didn't have a bottom. . . .

"I been knowing I would."

"What your family say?"

"Got none."

"Not a mama?" He frowned, unbelieving.

"She been gone."

"A while back?"

"She never come back from looking for my papa."

He chuckled. "I heard tell of things like that."

"My papa was white."

William Howland hesitated. Finally because he had to say something, "I don't mind," he said.

"I got nobody to ask. My grandpappy, he be glad of the room in the house."

William rubbed his face, feeling very tired, hearing the stubble of his beard grate in the quiet morning. "If this here is New Church, I got maybe a twenty-mile walk."

He stood up, and she seemed much smaller, fragile almost. She did not raise her head to look at him, the way a white woman might. She didn't act at all like a white woman. As for her having a white father, he didn't believe it, not with the color of that skin. But lots of gals said so, and you had to let them have the comfort of it, if there was any.

"Look now," he said, "you go back and talk to your people and tell 'em where you going, and then you come over to my place, if you still want to." How could anybody that tall, he wondered, look so delicate just because she was sitting down? Then he saw that she wasn't sitting, she had folded herself into the earth. Her weight and size had passed into it. She perched, suspended on the very crust.

"That's the way to do it," he said, more to hear the sound of his voice and stop another deep feeling that was beginning to bother him, a tensing of muscles he had forgotten about. "It plain wouldn't be right to expect you to go rushing off when it can't help but be a surprise to you."

"No," she said.

"You ain't used to people walking out the woods and offering you a job."

"It don't surprise me," she said quietly, in the light even voice that was so hard to remember. "Nothing that happens surprises me, 'cause I know it ahead of time."

He gave a quick laugh, and reaching down, touched the top of her head, briefly. She still did not look up.

He walked away, feeling her eyes follow him the whole way up the stream, where he picked up his shotgun and coat, all the way until he disappeared into the woods.

Margaret sat and stared at the wasps crawling over the damp surfaces of her laundry. "I knowed you was coming," she said after him.

Only I didn't know what shape you'd have. And maybe that's what the chicken meant, and the shape I saw yesterday in the branches of a hickory tree, the one that was bluish white and made a sound like an old-fashioned harp. They were telling me that something was about to happen. They were telling me and I wasn't understanding what, beyond that there was something coming. . . .

She glanced up at the sun through the pine trees. It had hardly moved. No more than half an hour had passed.

Unless the sun was standing still. . . . No, she thought, it wouldn't do that for me. It would do it for kings, but not for me. . . . It was real time. And it hadn't been very long.

She stood up, put her washing under her arm, and went home. As she walked, she looked carefully, every which way, in every patch of shadow and light, up slopes into the dark shelter of trees, but there were no sounds, there were no movements. Nothing followed her. The signs had been telling her and now they didn't have to any more. There was nothing more to say.

She nodded to herself. As she went, she began to whistle. She no longer had to watch and listen.

That same day she packed her things. She took the fancy apron her mother had left her, and she put all her possessions in it: her combs—the red one and the black one with the fine teeth—the snakeskin bag of Indian charms that she had never dared open, a couple of arrowheads that were lucky, a stone with a hole bored in the middle that was lucky too. She put in her pair of shoes and her good dress, the green silk one.

Then she went looking for her grandfather, to tell him. It took her a couple of hours to find him. He was resting his team of mules in the shade of a tupelo tree. He was a very old man and the heat of the late-fall day bothered him. He was squatting under the light, spattered shade with his chin resting on his knees, and he was breathing heavily.

How much longer has he got, Margaret found herself thinking, before he gets to see that long lonesome home of his? Before there won't be nobody sitting under that tree? Before all there will be of him is a heap of mud in the graveyard, and not even too much of that?

We'll remember him, she thought. For a time, a little time, before it starts slipping away from us, and we won't remember hardly at all. Then we'll be dead too, and that'll be the end of him, for good.

And isn't it funny, she thought, that it takes two generations to kill off a man? . . . First him, and then his memory. . . .

And what would it be like to be dead? To be in the ground, with the Death Cups rising higher and higher over your head. To be a ghost, haunting with the ghosts of your people, drifting through the dark pine woods, drifting between the cypresses of the swamps. . . . And what did you do, and what did you think when you were dead?

She looked down at Abner Carmichael. He was staring with his eyes open but he did not seem to see her. As if he were halfway there already. . . .

She touched his shoulder. He turned his head slowly.

"I come to tell you I was leaving." He did not move; she wondered if he understood. "I got to go."

He nodded. His dark skin was beaded and reamed with sweat.

"If somebody, they ask for me—" And who would that be? Nobody. Nobody, but maybe one. "If somebody comes asking, like my mama, maybe . . ."

The old eyes, hooded like a bird's, slipped open and looked at her.

She held her own face steady. "You got to say that Margaret has gone away from New Church. She gone to work on the Howland place and she don't expect to be coming back."

He didn't look surprised. "Nothing for you to do here," he said slowly. "You got to be moving on." His voice wavered off absently.

When she was littler, Margaret might have hugged and kissed him. But that time was past; that time was gone. She wasn't a child any more and there was nothing for her to do. So she only turned and began to walk away, steadily, unhurriedly, knowing she had a long stretch ahead.

Behind her, her grandfather said abruptly: "It's hot and I'm miseried."

She wasn't little any more. She was a woman grown, and making her own way. So she kept walking, leaving him to his old man's ache, and his old man's dullness.

For a while the landmarks were familiar. Then she passed into country she'd never seen before. She walked steadily, shifting her bundle from hand to hand as she went. Not hurrying, not stopping either. She had brought nothing; at first she did not miss food. She felt light and strong and drifting. When dark came, she slept in the woods along the road, curled up on the leaves and the pine needles, shivering a bit in the night cold. In the morning she felt her hunger, sharp and demanding, so she chewed a few pine needles and a couple of pieces of bitter grass. Once she stopped to ask directions of a woman feeding a flock in her dooryard. Margaret smiled at the funny bobbing walk of the chickens. They'd had their toes smashed to keep them from running away.

The woman, heavy-bellied with child, answered her politely, while she stared at the unfamiliar face. "From New Church," Margaret said, and watched the expression harden. Indian blood wasn't a good thing, and the New Church people had always kept pretty much to themselves. Margaret moved off, not minding. After all she had only asked directions because she wanted to talk to somebody. She wasn't lost. She only needed to follow the road until she came to the white-painted house on the fourth slope up from the river.

She recognized it at once. She turned off the road and climbed the rutted, gravel-crusted footpath that cut across the weedy fields. She found herself in a dusty silent yard. Slowly she looked about her—at the higher ridges to the north, at the Providence River almost hidden behind its thick trees, at the sagging barns and the cluster of sheds off by the pasture lots. She walked around the house, searching. She found a family of cats, yellow and white spotted. And she found the kitchen door under the sheltering frame of the back porch. Without hesitating, she pushed through the sagging torn screen. The kitchen was empty. She walked through the dark rooms of the lower part of the house, as far as she dared, as far as she could without opening any closed doors, afraid to open them, but curious just the same. Then she went back to the kitchen. She waited a little while there, sitting at the big center table. Then she waited outside on the back steps, sitting in the sun, body curled over her legs to stop the aching of her stomach, her black skin sweating gently into the heat of the afternoon.

William Howland came home just before dusk. He left his wagon by the barn, unhitched his mules, turned them into the lot. He closed and fastened the gate—moving slowly, weighted down by a day's dust—and climbed the hill to his house. He'd come half the distance before he even lifted his head. As soon as he caught sight of her, he began to hurry. She sat perfectly still and waited.

"My God," he said. "I plain wasn't looking for you so soon."

She did not answer. She followed him inside.

"You walk here?"

"Not far."

"From New Church?"

She nodded.

"Ramona!" he called. The sound echoed around the house; no one answered.

"You have anything to eat?"

"No."

"Not at all?"

"Not today."

"My God," he said. "Ramona!" And to Margaret: "You got no cause to do that, child."

"I didn't have nothing to take," she said simply. It was true.

"Ramona!" he shouted, out the back door.

"I didn't see nobody," she said, "and I been here a while."

He ruffled his lips in a half whistle. "She be coming by for supper . . . but you can't wait none that long."

He walked over to the great wood range, black and sticky with grease. He opened a couple of pots and looked in. "She cooked it anyhow. . . ."

Margaret sat down in a straight wood chair, her stomach cramps making her weak-kneed all of a sudden. She had thought he wouldn't notice, but in a moment he was standing beside her, and there was a hand on her shoulder.

She laughed, ashamed. "Bitter grass make you lightheaded somehow."

The hand was pulling her to her feet. "Go get a plate—I'll get it—and eat something, whatever that is there."

Outside a man's voice shouted: "Will Howland!"

"You feed yourself, and when the old woman comes in, tell her to come see me."

"Hey, Will," the man outside roared, "where you want your hog molasses?"

"Take you time," William said, "don't fret."

So she sat in the kitchen alone, eating quietly. She listened to the voices of the men outside, and then she heard the trace chains clank as the wagon moved. Her hunger eased, she looked around the kitchen. It was a large room, at one end the greasy black range, with the greasy black skillets on it. At the other was a brick fireplace, tall enough for a half-grown man to stand in, black with years of use. Over it was a heavy scrolled and carved mantel. Over that, a long musket and a powder horn, slung crosswise.

Margaret let her eyes run around the room a few times. Gently, inquiring. She finished her plate and shoved it away. Slowly she got up and poured herself a cup of coffee from the blue enameled pot on the back of the range. Holding the cup in her hand, she looked down the room again, into the black open hole of the fireplace. It was as familiar to her then as if she had always lived here.

When the old woman Ramona came back, Margaret stood up politely, waiting. The old woman looked at her, shifting the wad of snuff from her lower lip to her cheek. "I seen Mr. William already," she said. "And I got to open a bed for you."

Margaret followed her through the house, through doors she

hadn't dared open earlier. They climbed a wide bare stair, its dark rail chipped with years of use; they went along a dark hall that smelled strongly of new paint. At the back of the hall, next to a small low door, was a tall mahogany armoire with mirrored doors and a heavy flaring crest on top. The key was missing and there was no handle; Ramona simply pried it open with her fingernail, yellow and hard as horn. Inside the wardrobe was lined with smooth swirled bird's-eye maple, but someone had put shelves across it, in the space where clothes might once have hung. They were not new shelves, because the unfinished wood was already darkening, but they had been put in crudely. They rested unevenly on strips of wood.

Ramona hunted through the piles of cloth, pulling out one sheet after the other, shaking her head and putting them back. She found one finally. She took it out, and held it up. There was a rip down the middle. She nodded to herself.

It took half an hour to find a pillow and a blanket that were raggedly enough. Then Ramona tucked the lot under her arm and opened the low small door.

It led to the ell at the back of the house, directly over the kitchen. It must have been the oldest part, for the rooms were smaller and the ceilings lower. There were two rooms here, one leading into the other. They were musty and stuffy, and the mattresses on the beds had been rolled up and covered with newspapers.

Ramona put down the sheets and started for another door on the far wall. "Goes to the kitchen," she said. "You come up and down this way. Lights there." She yanked a cord and the single naked bulb hanging from the rafters overhead snapped on. "You get enough supper?"

"Yes'm," Margaret said.

The old woman started down the steps, groaning and wheezing. "Mr. William, he say I got to ask if you have everything."

"Yes'm," she said again.

Margaret did not feel tired, though her legs ached slightly from the long walk. She ran down the stairs, avoiding the eyes of the old woman, who was now warming supper at the stove, and got the broom she had seen in the corner there. She ran back up and opened her windows, all of them, so that the cool evening air came pouring inside. She brushed down the walls and chased out the spiders, and swept the floors. She unrolled the mattress and put the sheet on it.

I got to fix that rip tomorrow, she thought. It was the first sheet she had ever had. At home they always slept on the bare ticking.

She stood in the center of the room, studying it. And it also looked familiar to her, though these two rooms were as large as her grandfather's house. She wondered why she did not miss that more. After all she would be alone up here, and she had never before been alone in a house. But then, she told herself, it wasn't any different from being alone outside, and she had done that lots of times.

All at once she was tired. Very tired. She began having trouble standing up, and she weaved from foot to foot, as she slipped out of her clothes. Downstairs she could hear the old woman rattling pans and dishes in the kitchen, and singing under her breath.

She had forgot the light. She got up slowly and pulled the cord. In the dark she stumbled back to bed, slipped under the unfamiliar blanket. And naked in a strange room, she fell asleep.

William Howland had been busy. First there was the hog molasses, and then he decided to have a look at the new smokehouse that they were just finishing for him. Then, because he was thinking about it, he walked down to where the wallow was, and looked at the hogs, fat and lumbering and filthy. He was satisfied. When it got cold, which couldn't be very long now, they would have the hog sticking. With the great boiling tubs of water set in the yard, and four extra men brought up from town. . . . He liked the smell of a smokehouse.

He liked to take care of the fires himself, just to be sure that they were banked correctly. A slip could ruin a whole season's meat, and he was a particular man.

He turned and began his trip back to the main house, noticing the new light in the window of the ell over the kitchen. That would be the room Ramona had given Margaret.

He wanted to stop, but he didn't let himself. Damn-fool thing for a grown man to stand staring at a light. . . . He kept putting one foot in front of the other, steadily, until he got to the porch. And then it was easy to open the door, call to Ramona, and go to supper.

"Let her help you," William Howland said when the old woman asked about Margaret. "Got to be something the child can do."

He saw the wad of snuff flutter at the word "child" and he chuckled. "She's kind of big, for sure, but she's not old. . . . Anyway seems my sister was telling me just a little while ago that the house needed some extra hands."

"She come out New Church," Ramona said.

William shrugged. Those people had a bad name among Wade County Negroes. As a matter of fact, they didn't usually come down this way—and that made it all the stranger, this girl's coming to work for him.

William remembered again how he had first seen her washing clothes, and how the Alberta story had come popping into his mind. She seemed more like that, somehow, than like somebody who'd come out of the flooded bottoms and the piney uplands of New Church.

She was around the house for a week before he even saw her again. Ramona must have been giving her things outside to do. He was aware that the sprawling Cherokee rose by the dining-room window had been pruned, and that somebody had been working in the herb garden his mother had put in years ago. It hadn't been tended since then. The mint ran out of its bed and spread its roots across the adjacent yard. The thyme, once planted along the walk, had crawled over the stones and eaten them up. The rosemary formed large stiff bushes bristly with spiky shoots. A single enormous clump of chives lifted its seed globes through the crushing weight of the creepers. Margaret's fingers pulled out the weeds inch by inch, the red earth lay torn and startled under the sun.

When the garden was finished—ripped naked, forced back to its proper bounds—and there was no more, Margaret went hunting for fruit to preserve. She did not know these woods and fields, but she learned quickly. She was used to finding and taking whatever the country had to offer. At New Church foraging was something that older children taught younger. So now, Margaret came home with her sacks full of quinces and persimmons and apples and pears. And lines of glasses cooled on the window sills. One afternoon she rooted in the tangle of the vegetable garden, and she brought out pumpkins and acorn squashes, sturdy things that had survived their neglect.

William saw them heaped on the back porch, glistening yellow even in the shade, and he wondered why he had not thought about them for all these years, them growing out there under the tangle of grass and creepers, year after year, season after season, with only deer to nibble them.

They looked right pretty piled there, he thought, pumpkins and squash and the bumpy ornamental gourds that somebody had planted —somebody forgotten now.

Toward the end of the first week, he came across her, sitting at the kitchen table, under the hanging green-shaded lamp.

He'd worked late that day. First at the spring house: the new pump (the one his sister had ordered in time for the wedding) was giving trouble. He'd still been tinkering with it at suppertime, so he sent for Ramona to bring him down his food. When he finished with the pump, he still wasn't through. There was one more thing to do: he had to go to the mill. All that day there had been small tornadoes about, sudden funnels dropping from the low puffy black sky—he'd been watching them. One, he thought, had passed close to the mill. He'd have to see. He'd have to be sure that the winds had not damaged the building or the stones—they were both old and brittle. And so he went, hunched over his horse's back against the blowing rain. He checked the building carefully and thoroughly by the yellow light of his kerosene lantern (only the main house had electricity). The mill was secure. The winds of the afternoon had cracked a window, no more.

William stood for a quiet while looking at the great stones that were getting harder and harder to find these days, when almost nobody ground their own meal any more. He listened to the dropping wind outside, and to the scurry of the mice and the small animals who always lived in any mill. He sat on the floor, tired and thoughtless, resting in the shelter of the roof, waiting for the sky to clear.

So it was near ten o'clock when he finally unsaddled his horse and climbed the slope to his house. He saw the light in the kitchen. It could not be Ramona. She would have left long ago for the house she shared with her husband and her old-maid daughter a quarter of a mile down the road.

William Howland walked across the yard, noticing through a gap in the eastern clouds the outline of the Bear. He saw the bright starry shape clearly. Head down, tail up, it had always looked more like a skunk to him.

So few people watched the stars any more, he thought. His uncle now had been able to tell the names of every constellation as it lifted itself over the shelter of the trees.

He stepped quietly to the back porch, and glanced in the window. It was Margaret (always in his mind he called her Alberta and corrected himself now). She had greased her hair and pulled it straight back, pinning it flat to her head. He saw the twin tendons of her bent neck, the same delicate arch that he had noticed when he stood up to leave her by the creek in New Church.

It was strange, he thought, standing on his porch in the chilly night, how she changed. Sitting she was a child, delicate, uncertain. When she walked, she moved with the stride of a country woman, long steps, arms hanging motionless at her sides. A primitive walk, effortless, unassuming, unconscious, old as the earth under her feet.

She was sewing, William noticed, but not very well. He had seen his sister whip the needle back and forth through the material, quick, deft, sure. Margaret sewed slowly, pulling the thread out to its full length after each stitch.

She did not know how, he thought. But she would never have had the time or the chance to learn over at New Church. . . .

The bend of the neck, the slow clumsy stitching—he caught his breath, aching, as the sight of poverty always hurt him.

If she wants to learn, he told himself, I'll get somebody to teach her. If she wants to learn. . . .

He went inside. She turned her head slowly at the sound of the door.

"Just me," he said. "Go ahead."

She folded her hands over the material. He glanced at it. He had seen that flowered cloth somewhere. . . . Yes. His sister had bought it to make curtains for the hall upstairs. This must be the remnant.

She did not say anything, so he asked: "You're making curtains?"

"No," she said. "No."

"If you want to learn," he said, "I can find somebody to teach you."

"My grandmama showed me," she said softly, and her voice was wispy and dry. "I be all right if I can remember me what she say."

Her voice always vanished like smoke on the air. He felt uncomfortable. "Whatever you want."

He went to bed. And only the aching tiredness of his muscles pushed him to sleep. He kept wanting to stay awake and listen. To be sure she had finished in the kitchen and come safely upstairs to bed.

It was Sunday—its bright warmth carried an edge of winter in the yellow sun and the hard blue of the sky. The fields were deserted and so was the dirt road. Ramona came plodding along early in the morning and fixed dinner and left it on the back of the range. She was the last person to pass by. Sundays were like that, empty. No one moved about. Some of them—the good people—had been to church and were now home resting after their heavy Sunday dinners. They sat on their sunny porches in big cane rockers, bobbing gently to ease the distention of their bellies, on the porch boards beside them were sweating highball glasses with their slivers of ice.

And the other people, well, some of them would still be out on Saturday-night hunts, shacked up back in the woods, beside a fire, drinking corn likker straight from the jug. And some others would be fishing, dozing over their poles among the willows.

William Howland sat alone on his front porch and mended traces, a glass of bourbon and water by his side. When he had finished with them, he got out his guns and his cleaning rags and brushes and went over them carefully. He even took down the old long rifle from the kitchen wall, the one that had belonged to his great-great-grandfather who'd drifted down from the Tennessee hills with it over his shoulder. William Howland always kept it clear and clean and oiled. He didn't dare fire it. He didn't have the ball and he wasn't sure of the charge and he didn't believe the old barrel would hold together anyway. But he kept it clean just the same.

When he finished that—and it was just like any other Sunday—it was time to go down for the milking. Oliver Brandon was alone at the barn—nobody else around on a Sunday. William helped whenever he wasn't going out to supper. He enjoyed it, even the three-times-a-day milking schedule of full summer. He liked the smell of the cow's flanks pressing against his cheek. He liked the way the teats felt under his hand, the way the milk pulsed under his fingers, he liked the feeling that his hands had a life apart from his body. When he was through in the barn, he got himself supper in the kitchen, walking up and down, prowling around among the cupboards.

This particular Sunday he found a mouse's nest in the large china tureen at the top of the deepest closet. (He remembered the tureen, though it hadn't been on a table since his mother was alive and only rarely then. It belonged to the Lowestoft service his Creole grandmother brought with her as a bride.) He clapped the cover on and carried nest and mice to the back yard and flung them out. As he came back inside, he heard the wooshing swoop of an owl's wings, and he nodded to himself, satisfied. He hated animals and vermin in the house. He would have to talk to Ramona, he thought. She was getting unusually careless.

He went into the living room, and under the light of the gooseneck lamp he began the newspapers and the magazines he had been too tired to read during the week. He still kept glass and bottle close at hand, and as usual at Sunday bedtime, he was quite drunk. He had been drinking steadily most of the day.

He put down the last magazine, snapped off the lamp, picked up the liquor, and began his trip upstairs in the dark. He did not need a light. He knew the rooms so well. No piece of furniture had been shifted in all the years he had been living here alone. And almost none had been shifted since the time his parents were alive. . . .

His parents. He stopped for a minute and thought about them, the way he hadn't for years.

He stood in the dark hall and looked across the living room to the bright squares of moonlit windows. It seemed he could see them sitting in the humps of maple rocking chairs by the big fireplace.

They always had sat there. . . . His mother. Crocheting by the hour, filling all the tables with centerpieces, all the beds with spreads. There were even crocheted curtains at the bathroom window. His mother had stopped everything else and done them especially for that room, when they first got inside plumbing. She crocheted capes and gowns for all the babies in the county, white and black—and William smiled to himself in the dark—the same pattern over and over, only the ones for black babies did not have the three tiny ribbon bows stitched on top. . . . William took another swallow from his glass. Poor old lady, he thought, with everything hanging on those three bows of ribbon. You had them. . . . You did not. . . . And that was your whole place in life.

William was not the first to notice the significance of the ribbons. His father pointed it out to him one day, shortly before he went off to Atlanta to read for the law. "Damn silly thing, but just plain like her. . . . And you was to tell her, she'd throw a fit right at you." His father chuckled, contentedly. "Should have your women spoiled," he told his son. "Leastways Howland women is always spoiled." It had been his mark of manhood, his wife's soprano giggles, her great penchant for collecting cut-glass and rose-flowered Haviland china. . . .

William turned away from the dark parlor. But across the hall, on the other side, the door to the dining room was open, and he saw his parents again, in there. Saw them sitting in the little bay window, where plants used to be kept but which was bare and empty and dusty now. They were sitting right where they had been the day of his wife's death, that afternoon when he had come and told them he would need to have the tomb. The laughter was gone; they were two old people, shivering, paralyzed with fear.

And it ends like that, William thought. The gaiety and the pride in fear and death.

William closed the dining-room door, shutting them in there. He would work again tomorrow and be too tired for such thoughts.

He began his slow drunken climb up the steps. He dragged his hand heavily along the rail, and his fingers passed over the charred spot that dated from his great-grandfather's time. One evening bandits came upon the house (there were a lot of them on the trace at that time). They caught and killed the youngest daughter—found her asleep in bed, in the room that was now the kitchen—kicked her to death on the brick floor. They lit a bonfire in the center of the big main hall, and were cooking their supper when that William Howland and his four grown sons and their slaves came back. The old man stayed behind to put out the fire and tend the broken body of his youngest. The rest of them drove the robbers into the cane-brake in the dark and killed them there, one by one as they wallowed hip deep in the swamp. . . . The railing had been one of the things that the fire had charred. They kept it to remember by. Generation after generation. When they enlarged the house, they added the old railing to the new stairway. . . . To remember by. . . .

Killing and death, William thought as he rubbed his fingers across the charred rail, those were the things you set yourself up to remember. And the others went to their graves unmarked.

He'd told Abigail the stories, all the stories he knew. She'd listened of course, but how much would she remember? Women never took those things too seriously. His sister Annie now, she hadn't remembered, hadn't even tried. She'd simply forgotten everything before the time she married and moved to Atlanta. Even the long days of their childhood. How they'd hunted tupelo honey and found the bobcat's young in an old eagle's nest. . . .

His lips were numb. He must have had more to drink than he thought. He put his knees firmly into the business of lifting him upstairs.

Sometimes he felt the age of the house, felt the people who had lived in it peer over his shoulder, wondering and watching what he was doing. He felt them now, like mice in the walls, voiceless and rustling. It seemed to him too—tonight especially—that he could hear their breathing, all of them, dozens of them, breathing together, deep and steady, the way they had when they were alive. . . .

He dropped down on the bed, not bothering to take off his clothes. And he chuckled to himself. He had been listening to his own rasping breath. No more.

He rested a few minutes, before he crooked one leg and pulled off the heavy boot and tossed it into the far corner of the room. It made so much noise that he stopped and listened, startled.

He was thinking about the other boot when Margaret came in.

He'd left his door open. By the moon which slanted bright and low through his east windows, he noticed her standing just inside the room. She was wearing a nightgown of a familiar flowered material, high neck and long sleeves, a bit like a choir gown, he thought.

"I scare you with that noise?" He was surprised at the huskiness of his voice.

"I can take the other one off," she said. And she did, standing it carefully by the side of the bed.

"If you wasn't so young," he said, "I'd offer you a drink."

"What you read down in the parlor?"

"Huh?" he said. "The papers."

She sat on the side of the bed and the moonlight picked out the pattern of her nightgown. He recognized it. "That's what you were sewing on, the other day in the kitchen."

"I found it," she said.

"It was right clever of you," he said. "Reach me my drink, child."

She handed him the glass. He shook his head, and reached across her to get the bottle. His unsteady hand brushed her breast. It wasn't until the hand had come back with the bottle in it that he realized her nipple was hard and erect.

He put the bottle down on the floor beside the bed carefully, in case he should want it later.

He wondered if she'd been waiting all these nights to come because she hadn't had a nightgown. He started to ask her. But there was something—she had her hair pinned back and she was studying her own hands—that changed his mind. She seemed small and fragile again, and for the first time in his life he wanted to hit a woman. It was the bend of the neck that did it. It was so exposed and patient.

She bore him five children, all told. Three of them lived, two girls and a boy.

ABIGAIL

I came ten years later, my mother and I. The two Abigails. Mrs. Abigail Howland Mason and Miss Abigail Howland Mason. Coming back home.

We came on the overnight train from Lexington, Virginia, to Atlanta, and we had to wait around a couple of hours there. For some reason or other—I suppose she just felt too awful—my mother hadn't told her Aunt Annie, so there was nobody to meet us. It was just us two waiting in the station, which was stifling in the summer heat, just two of us sitting on the hard benches not far from the stand where a man sold oranges and newspapers.

Like I said, we had to wait around for a couple or three hours for the local—Number 8—to Madison City. You could see that waiting was hard on my mother. You could see her getting tireder and tireder. I guess she hadn't slept very much on the Pullman the night before, and it even looked like she wouldn't make it down the long flight of steps to the tracks. But once we got on and settled in our seats—in the dirty coaches that still carried spittoons in the far corners of them, where luggage was always falling out of the sagging racks high over your head—she took off her hat and put her head back and dozed a bit.

I hung out the open windows and chattered to myself. First I talked about getting my head cut off by passing poles and an occasional boxcar on a siding. Then I tried to see how much I could remember from the last time I came this way. (We had visited my grandfather every Christmas since I was old enough to travel.)

"I came here when I was three months old," I told a cotton field full of pinkish blooms.

I have been here all along, the field told me back.

"But I remember more." And to prove it I chanted out the names of towns along the way.

Actually, I didn't remember much more than the string of names. Because a year is a long time at eight and from one to the next was an immense distance. I couldn't even have told you what my grandfather looked like.

I suppose my talking bothered her, because my mother opened her eyes and patted the bun of hair at the nape of her neck back into place and looked at her watch and looked out the window and sent me down the car to ask the conductor exactly where we were. We were then three and a half hours late and we got steadily later. It annoyed my mother, though she should have known better. That train was always late. There was some trouble with a switch just out of Opelika, and then we waited for a fast freight. There was trouble with a hot box that took an hour to fix. And the signals were wrong for the bridge crossing over the Red River.

All she said to me finally was: "Please, child . . . you'll have to be good if I'm to travel with you alone."

I fell silent after that, remembering all the things I had been told. That my mother wasn't well, that I must not disturb her. That my father was gone, for years anyhow, and I must help her just as he had.

When we got near our stop, the conductor woke my mother.

"Thank you, Mr. Edwards," she said. He took our baggage and piled it ready on the platform. When we felt the grating as the brakes began to take hold, he shook hands with my mother. "I am right proud to have Will Howland's daughter home again."

She smiled at him. She wasn't a pretty woman, but she always looked radiant when she smiled. "I've been gone too long, Mr. Edwards," she said, "but I'll be staying now."

Then the train stopped and I found I did recognize my grandfather, after all.

Right then and there the first part of my life ended. And the second began. Sometimes as the years passed, the hot dusty country years, I found myself thinking back to the first part, to the smooth green college town. And wondering if it had happened at all. I remembered so little. The clean light mountain air, evenings when your nose would just shiver with the sparkle in it. The smooth roll of the campus and the columned buildings. My father walking off to teach his class in the mornings, leaving a thin line of pipe smoke behind. The way leaves fell in the fall until there were great bright heaps on the ground (they don't do that this far south). I remember a small town, all brick and narrow streets, shabby-looking. It had been burned in '63 when the whole Valley was fired. There was only one house left standing, way on top of the highest hill in town. Not a pretty house—it was too squat for its row of white columns—but a real old one. It had been used as headquarters during the war because of its great view. They were supposed to burn it when they left, but they must have forgotten. . . . There was also a river, down between sharp banks, a trash-littered river. I saw them pull a body from it one day, when I had gone to fetch something from the grocery. A couple of fishermen dragged it out, one by an arm, one by a leg. I remember it was a Negro, I saw the dark skin clearly, and it was naked.

I remember too that my parents weren't getting along. You could feel how stiff they were to each other sometimes. Often as I lay in bed, I'd hear their angry voices through the closed doors. And her eyes were red for days on end.

Maybe that was the reason my father was so anxious to go back to England when the war started in 1939. I remember him going around quoting Rupert Brooke over and over to my mother, until she dabbed at her eyes openly. It was about going to meet Armageddon.

He went of course. The week before he left there was a great deal of partying—for him, I guess. I had never known them to go out so much. Then he was gone, and my mother, silent and red-eyed again, went about the business of moving home to her father.

Once I was back in Madison City, it seemed I'd never been away—the flat cotton fields, the tangled pine uplands, the stretching swamps were home. I had no personal memory of the place—not very much anyway, but everybody assumed that I would have an atavistic one. And maybe I did. Within a single day I felt that I had always lived there. My father was gone; I never even had a letter from him. (My mother did, but she didn't talk about them or show them to me.) He just disappeared from my life, and that was all. People always called me the Howland girl, and it was hard to remember sometimes that my real name was Mason. Whenever I'd go calling with my mother, making a little procession up somebody's front walk—my mother first, then me—all the ladies greeted us the same way: "Why, my dear, it's the two Howland girls!"

We were Howlands and we were living where the Howlands always lived. I forgot my father, there were so many other things. He hadn't forgotten, though; he tried to see me once after the war, he came back to the country just for that, I guess—but by then it was too late. And now, today, I don't even know where he is. I don't have any address. I don't even know what country. He is gone as completely as if he never existed.

Sometimes I feel that my grandfather was my father. And that

Margaret, black Margaret, was my mother. Living in a house like this you got your feelings all mixed up.

She was his wife, only she wasn't. She kept house for him and the law said they couldn't marry, couldn't ever. Their children took their mother's last name, so though they were Howlands they all had the last name Carmichael.

The oldest was Robert. He was a year older than I, tall for his age, very tall (he'd gotten his mother's height). He had red hair, and his freckled skin was fair. At first glance you would not have thought he had any Negro blood. But if you looked sharper—and if you were used to looking—you could see the signs. It was the planes of the face mostly, the way the skin sloped from cheekbone to jaw. It was also the way the eyelids fell. You had to look close, yes. But southern women do. It was a thing they prided themselves on, this ability to tell Negro blood. And to detect pregnancies before a formal announcement, and to guess the exact length of gestation. Blood and birth—these were their two concerns.

In the South, most people could tell that Robert was a Negro. In the North, he would have been white.

After Robert there was Nina, a couple of months younger than I, so she would have been almost eight that summer we came back to Madison City. Then there was a gap of three years: that child had died. Then there was Crissy, Christine. Both girls were fair, with red hair like their brother's. Their other blood showed in the shape and color of their eyes, in the waxy pallor of their skins, in the color of their fingernails.

And how did I know? Because I've spent my time sitting on porches on a sunny dusty afternoon, listening to the ladies talk, learning to see what they saw. . . .

They taught me my Bible lessons the exact same way. And to this day I am very good at spotting signs of Negro blood and at reciting the endless lists of genealogies in the Bible. It's a southern talent, you might say.

. . .

Funny how memory is. There are places—months and years even—when I cannot recall a thing. There are simply blank spots with nothing to fill them.

And I have tried. Because somehow or other I convinced myself that if I could just remember—could have all the parts—I would understand. And even so I can't. I've lost it somewhere.

I can remember coming to my grandfather's house. I can remember that one particular train ride, out of all the others. But I can't remember what I thought of the house. And of that first night there. I can't remember what I thought of Margaret and her children. Maybe I didn't think of them at all.

I don't remember when I figured out that Margaret's children were also my grandfather's children. Not even that. I suppose it just came to me slowly, the way things seem to do. I never have any great revelation—I'm too dull for that. But bit by bit, fraction by fraction, a thing impinges on me, inches its way into my mind, until by the time it is full-grown I am quite used to it. I suppose that was the way with the children my grandfather and Margaret had together. By the time I knew, by the time I understood, it was as if I always had.

No one told me. I'm sure of that. I don't know what my mother thought, but she never said a word. She always pretended to believe that Margaret's children had just come.

Maybe that was what she had in mind when she told me all the old Negro stories about Alberta. Her children, now, had just come to her, without a father. They had just come sneaking into her body when she was asleep in the soon of a foggy morning, come sneaking as gently as the dew that dripped off the tips of the pine needles. Her children had no father, and they were born alone too, in the tops of the highest ridges where there was nobody but some noisy jaybirds to hear her panting in labor.

There were no more children for Margaret. The last had been born—and died—two years before we came, so it wasn't until much later, when I was a grown woman, that I found out Margaret, unlike Alberta, didn't go away up on the ridges to bear alone. She got on the train and went to Cleveland and bore them in a hospital there. That way their birth certificates didn't have the word "Negro" on them.

The first time I ever heard any talk about Margaret's children, it was a little girl in my class at school—third grade or so—a blue-eyed girl with frizzy blond hair that her mother put up in papers every afternoon. It was a sniggering remark, and all I could think of was: Sure, I know. But I couldn't let her get away with it, it wouldn't have done my standing as a Howland any good. A couple of days later, I poured a half bottle of India ink into that fuzzy scalp. And a week later I managed to work a large blob of nail polish into it too. It had dried before she noticed. You could see it shining through the thin hair.

I wasn't startled, I wasn't hurt. Somebody had just put into words what I had known for a long while.

Margaret's children didn't go to school with us, of course. They went to the Negro school four of five blocks away. We didn't even go in together. Some mornings my grandfather drove me—if he had business in town—and sometimes Oliver Brandon did. Oliver had worked for my grandfather from the time he was twelve, at one job or another. He was in his forties now, and he could do just about anything, from doctoring sick animals to tinkering with the cars, and in those days cars needed a lot of tinkering. It wasn't too unusual for them to break an axle on the ruts in the road.

Cars weren't common in our part of the country. Not with the depression thick and heavy still. I suppose there were a dozen of them in town, no more. The horses were still scared of them.

But every morning I drove into town to school—barely two miles by the direct road, but nearly five the way a car had to go, keeping to the best of the graded roads. It took me almost as long as it did Margaret and her children. They went by wagon, a new one that handled easily and wouldn't tire the mule. Margaret drove them every day, along with any of the other Negro children who wanted to go. In bad weather she'd be bundled up in an old waterproof of my grandfather's and the children would be crouched down in the bed of the wagon under their tarpaulins. In fine weather they'd ride up on the seat beside her. But they went. Every day. She was strict about that. I could fake colds and sore throats and general aches, and spend long lazy days in bed, playing tent with the quilt. My mother didn't object. But if Margaret's kids complained, she paid no attention. Robert whined for days about being sick, before he broke out in flat blotches of chicken pox. Margaret let him stay in bed then, but she'd pushed him too hard, because he caught pneumonia and almost died. You could hear his strangled wheezy breathing through half the house. You could even hear it over the noisy gusty spring storm that was roaring outside.

My grandfather, with Oliver Brandon, went to fetch Dr. Harry Armstrong. They stomped into his hall, rain pouring off them both, and my grandfather shouting for him at the top of his voice.

"My gracious, Cousin Will," Miss Linda Armstrong said from the parlor, "he's only just stepped down to the cellar to see about the rats." She was a pretty girl, and a bold one, and she smiled directly at him, something no lady was supposed to do. "Would you like to talk to me for a while?"

"Go fetch him," my grandfather said to Oliver. "Cellar door's off the kitchen."

"Why, Cousin Will, you are in a hurry, for sure. You got somebody sick?"

"I wouldn't be likely to come yelling for a doctor if I hadn't."

"Oh my now." She had straw-colored hair and large brown eyes and fine-shaped breasts.

He looked unimpressed. "You grown up, Linda," he said. "I can remember you in pigtails."

Oliver came back with Harry Armstrong. The three of them bundled into raincoats and went off, and Linda scurried down to the drugstore during the next pause in the storm and told everybody there that the Howlands were all crazy. She often spent evenings talking in the drugstore, after she gave her father his supper. She liked company, and somebody always brought her home.

My grandfather didn't tell Harry Armstrong who was sick until they were on the road out of town, and driving steadily on.

Harry Armstrong just shook his head, unbelieving. "God damn it, Will, you get me out on a night like this for a nigger kid?"

"Looks like," my grandfather said.

"You said it was little Abby."

"No I never," my grandfather told him. "You figured that yourself."

"Jesus Christ," Harry Armstrong said. "I got to be thinking of my practice."

They hit a washed-out rut and yellow water sprayed out like sheets on all sides of them and ran through cracks in the windows. The car rocked and skidded, but stayed on the road, and they spun their way through a patch of loose gravel to a hard surface again. Oliver Brandon pulled out a cloth and began to wipe up all the water he could find inside the car.

Harry Armstrong rubbed a splash off his face and went right on. "God damn it, Will, with your money you got no cause to worry, but I got to figure what your damn-fool trick's going to cost me."

"I'll pay you," Will said flatly.

"When people find out I treated a nigger kid, what kind of a practice do you reckon I have left?"

"To hell with them," my grandfather said.

They were still squabbling when they got to the house and went inside. Harry Armstrong took a look at Robert, and gave him some codeine to make him feel better, and aspirin to bring his fever down, and whiskey to keep him from sinking too low. Since he didn't know much else to do, he left Margaret there and came back to the kitchen.

We were waiting, my grandfather, my mother, and me. "I reckon I'll be going home," he said.

"Have some supper," my grandfather said.

Harry Armstrong shook his head. "Thanks."

"You didn't have none at home," my grandfather said.

"I'll get some right enough."

"I'm telling you you're staying the night."

Harry Armstrong stared at him. He might have had a lot to say if my mother hadn't been right there. He finally just sat down with a whistling sigh. "What I ever do to you, Will?" He turned to my mother. "Abigail, your father has plain done me in tonight."

She looked at her father and said nothing.

"Staying all night to treat a nigger kid—ain't a patient I got will stand for that."

My mother's delicate face got hard and worried. "He's right, Papa," she said. "We should have thought of that. . . . Cousin Harry, it's little Abby that's got chicken pox." She looked at me, thoughtfully. "I can see the spots, child, go to bed and the doctor will come right up."

I gaped at her. My grandfather chuckled.

"Cousin Harry," she said, "you're spending the night because your little cousin is so sick. Nobody would mind that."

"No," he said, slowly.

"We'll keep her in bed for a few days or a week."

"Hey," I said.

"In your room, then, missy."

My grandfather chuckled again. "Have some supper, Harry."

"Anyway," my mother said quietly, "Margaret will be very glad to have you here. She's worried frantic over the boy."

And that was another thing. My mother liked Margaret. Maybe because Margaret had everything she hadn't: size and strength and physical endurance. Maybe my mother was so sure of her own position that she couldn't be challenged by her father's Negro mistress. And maybe too, maybe as simple as this: my mother was a lady and a lady is unfailingly polite and gentle to everyone. . . .

Before I went to bed that night, Harry Armstrong had settled down to a glass of whiskey and water by the kitchen fire. He'd stopped complaining, even. He looked in on Robert every hour or so all night long, drinking steadily in between times with my grandfather. In the morning Robert was better, so maybe some little trick of his had made the difference.

I spent the next week in my room, and my grandfather got me all the books I had been wanting: *The Swiss Family Robinson* and *Kidnapped* and *Jo's Boys*. I had a fine time, reading and watching the rain on the window glass. I never had liked school.

Though a lot of people knew about it, that story never got out. When I really did get chicken pox, we called it a second case of measles.

Robert got up after three weeks in bed, and walked around on shivery uncertain legs. He was so pale and thin you kept thinking that you could see right through him if he stood in the sunlight.

By the time he was able to go back to school, it was too late: summer vacation had started. The next September he went off to boarding school in Cincinnati. He was eleven then, and he never came home again, not until he was long past a man. But that's another part of the story.

Money was tight those depression days, but my grandfather managed to keep Robert away at school and at camp, and off on one visit or another. It must have been very expensive for him then, but he did it, because the boy was his son, the only one he had, and because Margaret wanted it so.

Margaret never visited him, and he never came South. She wanted it that way too. Once every year, usually during the slack in the middle of the winter, my grandfather would get on the train and go North to see how he was making out. And of course Robert wrote to his mother—the one letter a week that the school required.

I remember other letters too. I remember my grandfather padding stocking-footed (he had left his dirt-crusted boots on the back porch) into the living room with the mail. My mother selected one particular envelope and held it up to him. "You see, Papa, unopened." She tossed it into the fire. "That's what I think."

I noticed it then, and noted it, but didn't think about it. Now I wonder how many letters from my father went unread, that flared and shriveled and turned to crinkly ash in the living-room fireplace.

The days went rattling by at a good fast pace. There weren't many people around but there were lots of things to watch and see. Lots of them.

Like the great canebrake below the house, down by the edge of the river. I remember the enormous rattler some men found down there, thick around as my arm, head smashed by an ax. The man who'd killed it brought it up to the house to show, and there was still some life to it, some movement. All the dogs slunk off howling.

I remember the way the branches of the pecan rubbed against the boards of the house. Faint squeaky brushings, the ghost noises that peopled my dreams. . . . The way a hunting pack sounded, the carefully picked voices. And the men's faces flushed and red in the light of the pine knots. Back-country hunting, on foot, with lots of whiskey. . . . The way cattle sounded when they were turned into a dry corn field. . . . The sweet-bitter smell from the windrows of the first haying; the crisp clean odor of the later stacks when you slid down them. . . . How the land looked under the moon, soft and sweet like water, even the rocks gentle and tender in the light. The bones of the earth, old people called those chalk white outcroppings. Where the giants were buried, where earthquakes had thrown up their bones. . . . How the frost looked lying heavy and blue as mold at night on the roof, on the ground. . . . A chicken hawk caught by a shotgun blast, spun to the ground. . . . My pet coon torn by the dogs into bits of bloodied fur. . . . And over and over again, animals straining in birth. Cows in the pasture lots, an occasional mare in the shelter of the barn. Cats under the porch, backs arched and crouching. And the hounds—they whelped in the kitchen with Oliver watching over them, and my grandfather puttering around the house doing all the things that had needed doing for months and that he hadn't ever got to until then.

His heart was in the dogs. He did not really like cattle; he raised them only because there was money in it. He had good stock, he took good care of them, and he never enjoyed a minute of it. When, now and then, an animal died, he and Oliver checked to see what happened. Sometimes it was a fall. A few of the pastures had sharp rocky drops down a slope: cattle lost their balance and tumbled over, and they starved with a broken leg. You could tell that in a glance: their skin hung loosely on their bodies. You could tell too when they died of snake bite: just that leg was swollen while the rest of them was perfectly normal. When they were swollen all over, why, then they had died of poison: lambkill, or sheepbane, or Jisson weed, or one of the poisonous creepers. My grandfather would give the hide a kick, wrinkling his nose at the smell. "Damn-fool creatures," he'd say, "know what's poison and they still eat it."

He thought the cows and steers were stupid. But he really hated his bull. He had a fine one, a beautiful monstrous ring-nosed creature, who lived in a special lot down below the peach orchard. He was injured when a bolt of lightning struck a pine under which he was sheltering during a storm, and he had to be destroyed. My grandfather looked almost pleased, in spite of the money that was going to be lost. He went to the cabinet where he kept his ammunition, and took out a handful of .303 cartridges grimly. He never kept another bull, because by then the Department of Agriculture was supplying the artificial ones.

The cattle business was good, and little by little he let his cotton acreage go, and increased his herds. But—excepting his hounds—he never got to like any animal. Though he could have afforded it, he never kept horses for pleasure. And he had as little to do with his mules as he could manage. Unless something was very wrong, he never went down to the lot when the hands were hitching up in the early mornings as I did. I liked sitting on the rail fence, above the reeking hoof-torn mud. There was hardly a blade of grass that their long yellow teeth hadn't destroyed. The trees had been stripped of their leaves too, high as the animals could reach. Even the trunks had a blotched look: their bark had all been rubbed off. The mules scratched themselves against those trees every chance they got. Though they were sprayed and dipped and treated, and though they never had those great harness sores, like white-rimmed welts across their backs and forequarters, the way a lot of work animals did, they never did seem to get over being itchy. They were stupid and mean, and they would bite. A lot of times I had to tumble off the fence because one was coming for me.

When the men began getting them into harness and between the shafts of the wagons (maybe it was picking time and every animal on the place had to work), it got noisy. The mules snorted and screeched, and the men yelled back at them, and whacked them with sticks and palms and fists, and twisted ears and twisted tails. By then the sun was up and the whole place warmed, and your nose began to wrinkle with the thick sweetish odors of sweat and animals and mud.

My grandfather eventually got rid of them all, and had a flock of tractors to take their place. First time they were ready, he sniffed the clear sharp gas odor and told me: "Smells one hell of a lot better than a mule."

He was a strange man, and decided in his tastes. The only animals he liked were his hounds. Though he himself wasn't too fond of hunting, he kept a very fine pack. And when—three or four times a year—he held a hunt, every man in the county was there. It was a pleasure to watch a pack like that work, they said. Now, a hunting dog doesn't live too long what with accidents and heart worms and just plain exhaustion, and William Howland had to put a lot of money in that pack. He didn't seem to mind, though he was pretty close with money as a rule. I've known him to pay five hundred dollars for a likely Blue Tick bitch. And whenever a whelping was finished, he would come quickly and look over the litter as they scrabbled for their mother's teats. He always believed you could tell a lot about a brand-new pup—that you could actually see how it would look full-grown—while it was still wet and ruffled, before it took on the lumpy butterball shape of a puppy. He and Oliver would talk it over; then they would select the pup they wanted to keep, and they would mark it, because within a day it would look no different from the rest of the litter.

To this day I believe in that method. I believe I can see the future in a brand-new pup. . . .

As I remember it, there were more animals than people on the Howland place. And I guess they were more important too, because animals were business and cost money, and people, well unless they were your own family, you just didn't see them often enough. Winters were school, but that hardly counted because I lived out of town and didn't see too much of those children; and summers I hardly saw anybody who didn't live on the place. I didn't go to Sunday school—I think both my grandfather and my mother forgot that I ought to. And we never went to church unless it was for a wedding or a christening or a funeral. There wasn't much to choose between them, really. They each had the same cakes and Cokes for the children and whiskey for the adults.

I didn't think much about the ways people arrived and departed. In fact I hardly thought about them when they were around.

For all I cared, there was just me and Margaret's Crissy and Nina. I never had very much to do with Robert. Even when he was living here, he didn't play with us. He was older, of course, and a boy; and he was a serious child. He spent all his free time reading in a sunny corner of the back porch. His mother had taught him to be that way.

So it was just three little girls. In all those acres. By this time the place was very large. My great-great-grandmother, the one from New Orleans, had gone land-crazy during the Reconstruction . . . because she was city-born, the stories went, she wanted more and more room in the country. It was she who looked up the old letters and found that the Howland farm had once been called Shirley. She tried to bring back the name; all her papers and diaries referred to it that way. But it hadn't worked, and after her death it went right back to being called the Howland Place the way it had always been. She hadn't changed its name but she had changed its shape and its size. And she had also bought most of the timber lands that were going to be so valuable.

When I was a child they were beginning to look to those stretches, and my grandfather was just beginning to realize what he owned. He was in no hurry. When he went into lumbering he would go in right, not just with one silly little coffeepot mill sawing away. . . . He told us that, us three little girls, when he took us with him on those rides up to the timber lands.

Once we found a still, smelled it cooking quite a ways off. He only laughed and said: "I plain ought to charge them rent," and he wrote that message on a piece of paper and left it there. A couple of nights later there was a bottle of white lightning standing on the kitchen table. He said it was awful stuff, that they hadn't any idea how to make likker, and he gave it to Oliver.

Crissy and Nina and me. . . . That was all. My grandfather didn't like visitors. My mother preferred—more and more—to stay quietly at home and read or rest, she wasn't very strong. And we were too far from town to walk in. Of course there were plenty of other children living on the place, Negro children from the tenant and the cropper cabins scattered around the farm. We didn't seem to play with them. I don't know why. Most times we didn't even see them; now and then we found them in the middle of a game, but they simply moved off. They wouldn't play—no matter we wanted to—they pulled away from us. They wouldn't have us, and after a while we stopped trying and forgot that they had ever been there. I never quite knew why. In town they played with white children. Maybe it was Margaret's children, the half-bloods, that they didn't want. They understood about me, even if they didn't like me, but they didn't know about them.

Almost the only time I went out was with some distant cousins from town. (I went alone. Crissy and Nina stayed home.) Once or twice a month my mother sent me in the car with Oliver to pick them up. I never much liked the outing, nor those children. They were younger than I, the last was just a baby still in diapers, and their names were Clara, Reggie, and Maxim Bannister. They would come out with their nurse, a great fat black woman who kept a bottle of gin hidden in the front of her dress, and we would go for a ride. We always went the same way and to the same place—I suppose Oliver took the best road. We drove up the paved state highway for half an hour, the engine sputtering on the slopes but making it anyhow. At the top of Norton's Hill we stopped at the old cemetery, the one that wasn't used any more, right by the spring-fed lake where lots of people came to fish. We got out there and I did what my mother told me to do—breathe the air. There was supposed to be something especially good about it at that spot. As my mother explained it, it had something to do with ozone, but I forget just how it went. So I breathed in and out, played tag around the old graves, looked for skulls and bits of bones, and drank the Thermos jug of lemonade that we always brought along. Oliver, who was pretty much bored with the whole thing, sat on the running board of the car and whittled peach stones into fantastic figures. He never worked with wood, only the peach pits. And he did the same thing over and over again, a funny little animal that might have been a monkey. Sometimes when he'd gotten an unusually large pit, he'd cut two animals facing each other.

"What's that?" I asked him practically every time we went out.

"Lay-overs to catch meddlers, missy," he'd tell me quietly and that was that.

I never did find out what they were, or what they were for, or what he did with them. I never saw any of them around, so I guess he didn't give them away; but if he didn't then he must have had roomfuls of them in the house he shared with his old-maid sister down by the big spring that was called the Sobbing Woman.

It was a good, cleaned-out spring. Somebody, my grandfather or his father, had taken a great pipe four feet across and sunk it there, so that when you knelt to draw your water you knelt on clean solid terra cotta. Beyond that rim somebody had laid other stones, so carefully that they were almost smooth and even as a sidewalk or a street. It was a big spring; the water flowed out of its gap at a great rate and down across the stones into the run. As it went over those stones it gave the peculiar sound that had got it its name, the Sobbing Woman. I always went and looked straight down, the bottom of any spring seemed wonderful and mysterious to me, though I was never sure what I expected to find. This one particular time, as I was staring down into it, I saw two rats. They were near the bottom, they were a little off it because they seemed to be bobbing slightly, which meant that they had been there awhile and were beginning to rise. I never told Oliver or his sister, but I suppose they scooped them out when they came to the surface, and anyway the water from there didn't seem to hurt them.

I thought about it afterwards and I began to wonder if maybe there wasn't always a rat in the spring and if that wasn't the carving Oliver made.

"That a rat?" I asked him the next time we went for a drive.

He studied the little piece of dried pit between his fingers. "Look like a rat?"

"No," I said. "Not any I ever saw."

"Then," he said, "I don't reckon it is a rat."

"Looks like a monkey."

He looked again, turning it around and around in his black fingers. "You seen a monkey like that?"

I had to admit: "No."

"Then I reckon it ain't a monkey." That was all he'd say besides telling me to go away and play because it was almost time for us to be starting back or my mama'd worry.

On the way back, somebody would be sure to have to go real bad, so bad they couldn't wait. Since Oliver was in a hurry to get home, and the nurse was too, they didn't stop. I suppose with four kids they'd have spent most of the trip back stopping. But they didn't have to. The nurse pushed aside the piece of old carpeting in the back, and she lifted the thin flat piece of tin that covered a hole in the floor. Then, propping both carpet and cover back with her foot, she motioned us to come on. If it was the baby, she'd pull down his diaper herself and hold him over the raggedy hole. If it was any of us, we could do it ourselves. It was kind of fun to squint out the hole, when you got finished, and watch the uneven tar-lined concrete whiz by underneath you. But the nurse never let us do that very long. She got tired holding up the rug and the piece of tin.

I remember things like that.

About that time too, the drifters arrived.

They came to our kitchen door, the two of them, one Sunday

afternoon. They walked up the path from the woods by the river, the girl leading the way, the boy following, but not too closely. They seemed about six and seven, ordinary-looking Negro children, more raggedy than most. They moved slowly—not hurrying, but not uncertain either—right up to the door. They turned around and sat down on the steps there, silently. And tucked their heads in their laps, like ducks, dozing.

My mother lifted her eyebrows. "Drifters?"

My grandfather nodded. "Looks like we be having these two for a while."

We did. They stayed for almost a month. Everyone was very kind to them because there was a saying that if you chased off a drifter you yourself would be hungry before the year was out.

In those depression times there was a lot of moving about. My grandfather said that there were streams of people on the main roads, in little trucks with all their furniture and bedding piled around them, traveling. They were moving into towns, looking for work, they were moving out of towns looking for places to settle. And with all that going on, some children lost their families. Maybe they died (there was a bad winter in '36 when a lot of people died, whole housefuls); and maybe they just moved on and forgot to take all the children. And sometimes they didn't forget, they intended to lose them. It was that sort of time.

Those left-over children became the drifters. They went about in little bands, like stray dogs, two and three and four. Sometimes they were brother and sister and sometimes they had just found each other out on the roads. They traveled amazingly far, when you think how small some of them were. They didn't know who they were—most times they had only first names—and they didn't have any place to go. They lived out in the fields and the deep woods, and sometimes they found a cave and stayed there awhile. The older children could slip about like shadows at night, stealing what they needed. Winters they came into the barns for shelter, sleeping with the same cattle they had been milking on the sly all summer.

And sometimes they would come straight up to a house and wait for food, as those two did. At suppertime Margaret filled two pie plates and brought them to the porch. They ate, without forks or spoons, steadily and daintily, like cats. When they were finished, they disappeared. They came back once or twice a day, as if they couldn't remember when it was that we ate.

"You've got to do something about them, Papa," my mother insisted.

"I'm feeding 'em."

"You know what I mean."

He shook his head. "You want me to put 'em in a cage?"

"Really, now."

"World's got a lot of troubles," he said slowly, "and you can't worry over them all. . . . Those little ones won't stay. Even food won't keep 'em."

He was right, of course. One day they were gone. They hadn't said a single word to anybody all that month, and they didn't give any sign that they were leaving. Just one day they didn't come any more. . . .

We didn't know who they were, nor where they'd come from. Drifters were like that.

And I remember when the war began. We hadn't turned on the radio that Sunday, because we'd worked straight through the day. It was hog-sticking time. Lots of the girls at school said they couldn't bear to watch, but it never bothered me, and anyway my grandfather expected me to learn. Work really started the day before when the knives, the two-sided slaughtering knives, were honed on the back porch. By then the hogs had been brought to the slaughter pen;

they hadn't eaten for two days, but they kept Oliver and a couple of boys busy filling the water troughs. Early, before dawn on sticking day, those boys began putting shovelfuls of hardwood ash into barrels of boiling water—to scald the hair away. The butchers came, three men hired specially from town. They'd test the knives and stick their fingers into the water (if it was too hot the hair got stiff and difficult to scrape). And then, just as it was getting light, they'd start to work. They tried not to excite the hogs, tried to move them out of the pen one or two at a time; but somehow it didn't ever work. The last ones got wild, and had to be knocked on the head or shot with a rifle. Oliver did the shooting; he stood on the edge of the pen, pumping his shots into the grunting squealing heads below him. My grandfather always hated to tell him to start. "Pity to do that, child," he'd tell me, "the meat ain't going to taste right done that way. Their hearts bound to stop before we can get to them."

The proper way was to stick them, to jab the knife over the heart and cut all those veins and arteries and let the heart pump out its own blood. . . .

Soon as Oliver finished his shooting, the pen was full of men dragging at the hogs, to wash and scrape them, to slit them open and hang them. All the time my grandfather bustled around saying something like "Cool it fast. Prop 'em open. . . ." It was late evening before the meat was finally cut and salted in barrels waiting for the smoking. By then my grandfather was staggering tired, and I had a couple of new bladders to make balls with.

We went straight to bed, while my mother clucked and fussed over us. "Papa, you'll wear that child out."

My grandfather was so stooped with weariness that he seemed short. "She's got to know the way of the place."

Since my mother hadn't listened to the radio (she never did turn it on; she preferred to read), she knew nothing about Pearl Harbor. I found out the next day at school.

We all left our classrooms in the middle of the morning and crowded into the downstairs hall to listen to the President asking for a declaration of war. The school had only one small radio, and they turned it on top volume so that everybody could hear. The words were blurry and not at all clear, and I remember wondering what everybody was so excited about. I didn't understand. For me the war had started when my father went off to fight, and that was over two years before.

There was one immediate difference—planes. Before, you almost never saw any—we weren't on any of the regular air runs. Now there were lots of them, zooming up and down and buzzing houses and scaring the cattle worse than ox-warble flies.

There were accidents too. You'd hear about them occasionally. My third cousin Hester, who lived on her father's place a little to the north of town, woke up one night thinking the house was falling down. A trainer shot by overhead, trying to land in a cotton field. It missed in the dark, tore through the field into the wood lot, exploding as it went. It started a brushfire that ate its way up the back ridges, running fast before a rising wind. Troops worked for two days, hundreds of them, before they got it in the right place and could dynamite it. My cousin Hester kept a piece of the plane's glass. It was broken into a sort of heart shape, and polished by the fire. Her father drilled a tiny hole in it for her, and she wore it around her neck on the same little chain that held her gold cross.

That piece of broken melted glass was just about all the war we had. There were a few uniforms around and a navy poster in front of the post office. And the town looked empty. The young men had been drafted. The older men and the young women had gone down to Mobile and Pascagoula and New Orleans for jobs in the shipyards there. That left nobody except women with small children, and those who wouldn't leave their homes to go job hunting with their husbands.

Most all of the hands were gone. Kids chopped cotton, and

brought it in too, and the way they picked made my grandfather sick at heart. But the prices were so high he could afford to waste, and anyway he wasn't nearly as bad off as some of his neighbors. He didn't have much in cotton any more. Cattle and hogs didn't take nearly the manpower. He was also doing a lot more lumbering than he ever had before. Way on the other side of the ridge there was a big new sawmill that went day and night, and a new railroad spur leading to it.

My grandfather and my mother listened to the radio every night and every morning, and he kept marking the war map he'd pinned up on the dining-room wall. But that was all. Or it was all I noticed. I was busy trying to catch a hoop snake.

Nina and I were doing that. It was Margaret who'd first told us the story of the hoop snake, the long black snake that has a smile on his face, and a taste for fun and games. When the moon was new, he'd crawl out on dirt roads and roll himself into a hoop, holding his tail in his mouth. It was lots of fun for him, so he'd sing a song as he went along. And the song was so jolly that all the animals would come out and listen, the coons and possums, and the other snakes, and the deer, and the bobcats. The mice and the rabbits came to the edge of their burrows. And even the birds woke up and listened.

Nina and I, soon as the moon was new, we'd sneak out of bed and meet behind the chicken yard. We looked and looked, for miles in all directions, and stayed up most of the nights that way. (I used to fall asleep over my desk at school every single afternoon. Though the teacher must have noticed, she didn't say anything. She was an old lady and happy to have one child really quiet.) For all our work we never found a single hoop snake, not one. Though we did see lots of tracks.

And while we hunted the road, we were on the lookout for Johnny Cuckoo too. He was the crippled soldier who marched up and down the empty roads, and all the little kids sang about him. We didn't really expect to find him, because he mostly came out and walked on dark and stormy nights, when it was raining hard and blowing and he was sure to be covered with mud. But we kept an eye out for him anyway. There was no telling.

In those days I was far more at home outside the house than in it. The house was shivery and strange and there were things going on that I didn't understand. Nobody told me—you just learn to find out things—but I knew that my mother was dying. I'd heard the word "tuberculosis" whispered about, but a fair number of people around our way had it, and it didn't seem to do them too much harm, and it certainly didn't kill them, so I didn't know what to think.

One day Margaret packed my clothes and pushed me in the car and Oliver drove me into town to stay with my cousins, the Bannisters. On the way over he told us that Margaret's children were going to stay with him. I don't think he was very happy about that, he and his old-maid sister, with children in the house for the first time—but there wasn't anybody else.

Margaret and my grandfather took my mother to a sanitarium near Santa Fe. They were there the best part of a year. And only my grandfather and Margaret came back, my mother was buried out there.

But all this was still in the future that cloudy gusty day in June when Oliver drove me to my cousins' house and carried my suitcases inside. Clara and Reggie and Maxie were lined up on the porch waiting for me. Maxie was chewing the top of the porch railing.

"You'll get lead poisoning," I told him, and he stopped. "Don't you take care of him?" I asked Clara. "Don't you know anything?"

I wasn't particularly happy to stay with them, and I really didn't like being in town where you never could get away from people's eyes. They knew when you walked down the street, whether you went to the drugstore or the dentist, whether you had a cherry Coke or a root beer. The only secrets you had were the ones inside your head. . . .

These particular grown-up cousins (they were Peter and Betsy Bannister; he ran the Pyrofax office in town) were just about the only ones my family was on good terms with. There were others I liked a lot more (I had dozens of them all around), but these were the only ones my family approved of.

It went back beyond the turn of the century, to the time of the Catholic Mrs. Howland from New Orleans. What with her religion and the way her father made his money, the Howland family had not treated her very well; they split into those who would accept her and those who wouldn't. Now she was long dead, but the different cousins went on being cool to each other. I once asked my grandfather why we didn't see some cousins who lived only a little way out of town and who had four sons and the oldest was the star basketball player on the high school team. He shrugged. "Damn-fool thing, child, but they were right mean to my grandmother." He didn't try to change it though, maybe because he didn't want to have to deal with more family than he already had.

And that was why I found myself staying with the Bannisters. Cousin Peter traveled a great deal—I forget why—and he was supposed to have a mistress in Birmingham. He was a diabetic, so he didn't smoke or drink and he carried cans of special diet food with him. He always seemed to be eating fruit of some kind, and when he did sit down at the table with us, his plate was never like ours. Years later, on one of those trips to Birmingham, he happened to go to a revival meeting, and he was converted. Now, this preacher was a healer who told him that he didn't need insulin if he believed in God's Grace and Healing Power. He sent Cousin Peter home with God's Holy Words rolled up in a little wad and tied around his neck with thread. Cousin Peter did believe, so he threw out his syringes and he sat on the porch (it was a hot day) praying for a miracle, until he passed into a coma. Cousin Betsy hesitated to call a doctor because she didn't think Peter would like it if she interrupted a miracle or anything like that; and by the time she got him to the hospital it was too late and he died.

But the time when I lived in his house was long before he got religion and killed himself. In those days he was just a kind pleasant man, who didn't seem to be around very much.

Cousin Betsy was a short stout woman, quiet and easygoing. She had two or three servants but the house was always dirty. "All this town dust," she would cluck, "it just comes in all the cracks." It also came in all the windows, because nobody ever bothered to shut them, even if it was raining or blowing. They closed them for warmth in the winter, but not before. And the heavy greasy cooking that you could smell from the minute you began climbing the front steps came from a black wood range (Aunt Betsy had never gotten around to changing and the cook liked this one) that had grease and soot a quarter inch thick all over it.

Like the windows, the doors were always open and the screens sagged partially ajar, and animals wandered through. A cat dropped her litter in the hall closet—it was a stray cat and I don't know why she picked that spot—but Cousin Betsy fed her until she decided to leave. And of course birds flew in and out of the upstairs windows. It was an old house and they had never got around to screening the second story. We all slept in tester beds hung with mosquito netting. (And that probably wasn't such a bad idea because in those days there was considerable malaria in this part of the country.) Once wasps built a great nest in the upstairs hall, right over the picture of Cousin Betsy's father, the one who'd been Senator from South Carolina. She didn't seem to notice, though the rest of us used to dash along that part of the hall for fear of them. They finally bit Jeff, the cook's husband, while he was changing the bulb in the overhead light. He almost fell off the ladder and he did drop the glass cover with a great crash. He and his wife went after the wasps then, wrapping themselves up in layers of mosquito netting, and got rid of them. Afterwards the upstairs hall was lighted by a bare bulb because the glass shade was broken, and things like that didn't bother Cousin Betsy.

There was only one thing that did, as far as I remember. That was underwear. Everybody in that house always had new or almost-new and very fancy underwear. She kept careful check. "Now, honey," she explained to me, "if you were walking downtown and you were run over by a truck and they took you to the hospital and they saw that your panties were all torn and ragged and your slip was pinned at the shoulder by a safety, you'd be so ashamed you'd have to die."

"And just think how people would talk after," I tried to joke with her.

She didn't see it. "And think of that," she said seriously. "Yes, indeed."

But it really wasn't bad living with them, not bad at all. Aunt Annie, my grandfather's sister, came down to see me every month or so, I suppose it was her way of checking up on the Bannisters. (She was such a neat woman that house must have made her sick.) The rest of my life was almost the same. I went to school, the same one, only I could walk, and it was rather nice not having to make that long drive every day. Once you got used to it, there were lots of things to do in town. There were even lots of things to do in the house, though it never seemed to occur to Clara, Reggie, and Maxie to do any of them. I had to show them. Maybe it was because they lived there, and just didn't see any more.

Take their house itself. It was one of the funny old town houses built and rebuilt so many times that nobody was sure exactly where anything was. It had a narrow front, but it was very long, extending almost the length of the entire lot. There were halls and wings and different levels. Lots of people had added to the house but they hadn't bothered to attach their different wings very carefully. I once broke my arm because I forgot and sprawled down the step that went from the breakfast room to the kitchen behind it.

The farthest back rooms of the house, the ones behind even the second kitchen, were used for nothing but storage. They were full of wrapped and lumpy things, an occasional dead bird, rat poison, old trunks, and hat racks. Clara, Reggie, Maxie, and I would open the trunks sometimes, the ones that weren't locked. It was a way to spend a rainy day. A lot of the trunks were full of dresses, of wedding dresses mostly. In some the cloth was so delicate that it tore when you picked up the bead ornaments. The egret feathers fluttered into dust when we lifted them out. There were musky furs too; we had to tear open the cloth bags they were stitched into. There were diaries and journals and letters. And one of the trunks had half a dozen old pistols, two cavalry sabers, and four dress swords. We played soldiers with them all one long afternoon.

I suppose we destroyed quite a bit of the stuff we handled. But I didn't think of it then, and I don't feel badly about it now, because it was just lying there, in storage, and the moths and the roaches were doing more slowly what we did rapidly.

They were lovely rooms, stuffy and hot; dust hung in the air like smoke, and the motes drifted back and forth in the panels of light from the dirty windows.

As you went through the line of storage rooms, you noticed that they got smaller and smaller toward the rear. Those must once have been slaves' or servants' quarters. The very end of the house wasn't even a room really, but a kind of last-minute addition. It was painted the same color as the house, and at first glance looked the same, but it hadn't been built for an all-weather room at all. It was more of a tool shed. There were no inside walls—just the studs and the outside boards—and the floor had been laid any old way, with great gaping cracks in it. There was a door leading to the outside yard, but it had been nailed shut years before, probably to keep out burglars. The nails were bleeding streaks of rust down the wood.

The room itself was completely empty. There was just the dusty uneven floor and the dirty unfinished walls, and that was all. The walls weren't even very solid. Unlike the rest of the house, which was clapboard, the boards of these walls ran straight up and down; there were cracks between all of them and large knotholes in some of them.

It wasn't the room. It was what you could see from there. We found out by accident, but once we knew we kept coming back. Just to see.

The room wasn't more than three feet from the board fence that marked the property line. Now this fence had been built seven boards high, but it sagged a great deal until part of it was actually leaning against the house. If you stood in the Bannister yard, it looked like a good solid fence and it really was way over your head. But when you were inside you stood on the foundations of the house —and because it was an old house, its foundations were very high. (They thought it gave them good circulation in the old days and kept down the fevers.)

The other house, the house on the next street, also extended almost to the property line. Though it was an old house too (there were few new ones in town at that time), the additions had been done recently. They had been done very cheaply too, and so they sat almost right on the ground. Because they were so low and the board fence was so high, people over there seemed to think they couldn't be seen. They never bothered pulling the shades. Through the corner crack of that tool room—if we stood on a crate to give a little more height—we could see right in.

We saw a dresser, of some dark wood, mahogany or walnut. It had a lace scarf hanging across the front in scallops and down the sides in long fringes. There was a line of china ornaments too, but we couldn't make out exactly what they were. I thought elephants, but Clara said no, they were china dolls. There was a bed with a pink spread and a couple of bright blue pillows. There was also a brown-haired lady whom we caught sight of now and then. She always seemed to be wearing a pink ruffly robe. The material seemed a bit stiff and shiny, so maybe it was taffeta. We never did see her face, because the head of the bed was out of sight around the corner of the window. And she didn't seem to be home very much unless she was expecting a caller.

All that long vacation the first thing we did every morning was to take a peep through the crack into the room. If it was empty we went outside to play in the yard. Usually we stayed near the back fence, so when we heard feet on the cinder walk, and a knock on the door that led into that back addition, we could go tearing into our tool house and start squabbling over who would get to stand on the box.

She took the pink spread off the bed first, so it wouldn't get spoiled. She always did it quickly, right after they'd first come in. With her long brown hair swinging around the sides of her face, she'd turn the spread back and hang it over the foot of the bed. Then she'd step to the other side of the room, out of our sight. There seemed to be something else over there, chairs maybe and a table, I don't know. The two of them stayed over there quite a while sometimes, and we'd get pretty tired waiting. Once Reggie didn't believe that nothing was happening for so long and he yanked the box out from under me, and I tore my leg on the head of a nail as I fell.

Sooner or later they'd get to the bed. Their heads were completely out of sight under the window ledge. All we ever saw was the tangle of moving bodies. Sometimes they were dressed and sometimes they were naked—it was pretty much the same heaving lump, wrapping and unwrapping, pumping and jerking.

We watched all through that one summer. Even when we had to go to school we kept it up—until the late afternoons got too cold to be standing by a crack in a tool shed. And by the time winter was over, we'd almost forgotten. It wasn't the thing to do any longer.

We didn't care who she was. It wasn't who that interested us. It was what. Years later, when I thought of it again, I remembered that Dr. Harry Armstrong, who was my grandfather's cousin, lived there, and his daughter Linda had brown hair. Her mother was dead and her father was pretty poor, so they only had one servant, who fixed them dinner in the middle of the day and left them a cold supper on the stove. I don't remember Linda Armstrong very clearly. She was much older and she went to Chicago to find a job, after a while. She married there and moved to Des Moines, and never came back. When her father got very old and had a stroke and was kind of silly and half crippled too, he sold the house and moved out with her.

I suppose we left the boxes in place under the crack of that tool house, and eventually somebody found them, and figured out what had been going on. Because, that following spring when I proposed that we go back there, my cousins got a funny expression and said no, they weren't allowed in that room any more. Their little pudgy pasty faces looked scared, but I didn't think anything of their mother—I figured she wouldn't dare do anything to me. I went swaggering back to the shed, but both doors had new hasps and padlocks. . . .

In May my mother died at the hospital in New Mexico. She was buried there.

When they heard, the whole family was terribly upset. They thought she should have been brought home, all the Howlands had been buried in Wade County since the first one had wandered in here. They'd even brought home the bones of the boy who'd died in the Wilderness and the one who'd died of yellow fever in Cuba.

They were always gathered together. Until now. "Just what I expected of Will Howland," Cousin Betsy said, "and imagine her lying all alone way out there. All by herself."

Now it didn't seem to me to matter much where you were when you were dead. One place was as roomy and fine as another. I might have said so too, only nobody asked me. Every time they saw me, they'd hush up whatever they were saying and get a sick look of consolation on their faces. "Poor child," they would say.

At first when I heard, when the phone call came, I got a hard frightened lump in my stomach and it stayed for a couple of days while I felt lonesome and confused. But it didn't last. I hadn't seen too much of my mother since we'd moved back; even when she was living in the house with us, she was mostly lying down or reading in the summerhouse. It was Margaret who took care of us. And it was Margaret I missed when they left. But that passed too. After all they'd been gone a year, and that's a long time to a child. You miss them and you wonder about them and you hurt—hard, for a while. But it eases and it's over.

I met my grandfather and Margaret at the station and went home with them. We sat down on the front porch, while Margaret went inside to see to the housekeeping. My grandfather looked tired, and he was a good deal thinner. You could see the muscles in his neck and count them. We just sat for a while and watched a big black-and-yellow spider with thick furry legs.

"I didn't bring her home," my grandfather said as if I hadn't heard. "It didn't seem the thing to do."

There were two spiders just about this time every year. They would come and live in that same bush with the yellow flowers—great heavy creatures.

My grandfather noticed them. "They come in their season," he said, "everything does."

I thought about the Biblical passage my cousin had given me to read the day we first heard my mother was dead. Something about the wind blowing over the grass and the seasons of things, but I couldn't quite remember it.

"People around here," my grandfather said, "they won't like it, and they'll talk, way they always do. Talk about the Howlands been their favorite sport for a hundred years. More fun than cards even for religious folk. . . ."

I picked up a stone that happened to be on the porch boards and tossed it at one spider. I hit it; the spider dropped down and disappeared.

"It was this way," my grandfather said, not appearing to notice. "She hated to travel so, got so tired on the trip out, it didn't seem right to make her come back. Hating a thing that much you're bound to hate it still, even dead."

The spider climbed back. I started to throw another rock, but I scowled myself into keeping quiet.

"Earth's the same anywhere, I figured, and with her hating to travel. . . ."

His voice kind of trailed off and in a minute he got up and went inside.

"Now you can chuck at the spider," I told myself.

That was all. Living back on the place again, I lost track of town. I didn't hear any talk. I didn't have anybody to hear it from. But they talked, I'm sure. It's the way they are.

There was a memorial service, later, when my grandfather gave a stained-glass window to the Methodist church in town, with a memorial to Abigail Howland Mason spelled out at the bottom.

Some folks didn't like that either, they thought it made the church look too Popish. Maybe they all felt that way, but they didn't feel they could say no, not with the way Will Howland always paid the largest bills.

It took a year to get the window made. By that time the death was so far off nobody felt very sad any more. I even sort of liked going to church because I didn't go very often. After the service, my Aunt Annie (who'd come down from Atlanta especially) gave a big supper. Like most of those things, there was a lot of likker and some of the men passed out on the grass, and some of the women went inside to pass out more properly. The boys got to drag racing on the mill road, and smashed their cars up and had to be taken to the county hospital (Dr. Armstrong was one of the ones who had passed out) to be sewed back together again.

That was the way my mother's life ended, with a grave in New Mexico and a stained-glass window in the Methodist church in Madison City.

That fall Margaret's second child, Nina, went off to school. Money was a lot easier now and so she went to an expensive girls' school in Vermont (she eventually won the school's prize for figure skating, though she'd never had a pair of skates on before she went North). She wrote, more often than Robert, and she sent pictures. But she never saw her mother again. And Margaret didn't write. My grandfather answered her letters and Robert's, and though he must have given them news of their mother, it was as if she were dead or a million miles away. He went to see both Robert and Nina now, and he went twice a year. Margaret never went at all.

She stayed with the last one, the baby, Crissy.

It seemed to me that Margaret was a lot more affectionate with her. I noticed that whenever she passed, she'd scoop her up and give her a hug—something I don't ever remember her doing with either Robert or Nina. And in a way Crissy was the nicest of the lot. Her red hair was sort of curly and it was always sticking out in wisps around her head; her eyes were more green than blue, and she had a string of freckles across her nose and her chin. She was even-tempered and happy and almost never sick. She was also the brightest, a lot brighter than Robert, though everybody encouraged him more. She'd learned to read from the old magazines my grandfather gave her, and long before she was ready to go to school she was reading from my old story books. She'd curl herself up in the crotch of a tree with a book and she'd be settled for the whole morning. I liked her. She was just the sort of child you couldn't help liking.

My grandfather liked her too, and evenings he would play with her by the hour. He'd never done that with the other children. Maybe he'd never had chance before. With my mother dead, he seemed to find more time for the last baby in the house.

Still—when I was sixteen and in high school—and Crissy was eleven, she went away, like the others. And like them, she never came back. Not even on vacation.

This time, because I was older, I asked about it. One day when my grandfather was repairing the pickets of the fence that enclosed the dooryard, I asked him straight out: "Don't you miss Crissy some?"

He had a couple of nails in his mouth and he took them out slowly. "You could say I do."

He had gained back the weight he lost during my mother's illness, and he was a big heavy man again. His face was smooth and pink and unlined; his eyes were the same bright light blue. I was always surprised at how bright their color was—exactly like a winter sky in the soon of a morning.

"Why didn't you let her go to school here," I asked, "if you miss her?"

He yanked up a rotten picket and tossed it aside. "You know as well as I do, lady."

"No," I persisted, "I want to know why."

He wasn't bothering to look at me. "I reckon you want me to put it in words for you. . . . Seems I can remember when I was little I hated to put a thing in words. . . . Scared of the words somehow."

He took the new picket and fitted it against the railing with the others. "You know what it's like for a nigger here. And those kids, they fall right in the middle, they ain't white and they ain't black. . . ." He put a nail in place, gave it a few whacks with his hammer. "And what they go to do around here? The war don't last forever. The plants'll close and the shipyards. We'll all go back to sleep again."

Another nail and the picket was in place. He moved down the fence, shaking each as he went, looking for the rotted-out ones.

"There's hardly a living for the people we got here now," he said. "And they're bright kids, they got a way to go." He found one, knocked it free with the side of his hammer, and twisted it clear of the fence. "Since I got no place here, I'm sending 'em where they got room."

"Oh," I said.

"Seems I got the money to do it." He stopped working and looked straight at me. "Happens you're all that interested . . . Robert goes to Carnegie Tech this September."

"That's Pittsburgh," I said, just to show I knew something.

"That what you wanted me to say for you, lady?"

"Well," I said, "I can't help wondering."

"No," he said, "I reckon you can't."

"What does Margaret think with all her kids gone?"

He was looking at me levelly, the bright blue eyes light and clear. "Our kids," he said quietly.

It was the first time he had ever said that. It was as if my mother's death had made things more open to him.

"Matter of fact," he said, "it was Margaret's idea."

At the time I didn't understand. I just thought it was odd. I thought all mothers always wanted to keep their children around them until the children themselves wandered off. I didn't see what Margaret was doing.

I was sixteen and I was in love. It was a boy in my class. His name was Stanley Carter and he had great luminous brown eyes—mostly because he was very nearsighted. His father was the new druggist and they came from Memphis. I didn't really get to see too much of him, because he lived in town, while I lived out on my grandfather's place. So I spent most of the long afternoons and evenings—when I ought to have been studying—writing long letters to him, which I tore up afterwards. I wrote long poems too, about stars for eyes and clover breath and so forth. I pulled the curtains in my room and turned on one very small light and stretched out on the bed and wrote on a clipboard I held up—as if I were writing on the ceiling. Since I couldn't write for long that way—my arms would start to ache and I'd have to let down the board—I spent most of the time staring at the cracked ceiling and the stained strips of wallpaper.

"Let her be," my grandfather told Margaret, "it's love and she's pining."

I tried to glare at him, but it's hard when the other person is grinning right straight at you. "Nobody in this house," I told him, "understands a single thing. Not a single thing." And I flounced upstairs and started to write an epic poem about unrequited love and star-crossed lovers and all that. Pretty soon I got tired of fitting words into meter, so I read *Romeo and Juliet* straight through again, crying at the saddest passages.

Sometimes I'd climb to the top of the scuppernong trellis by the back door. I'd lie there for hours, staring into the sky and eating the soft yellow grapes. I'd try to see straight on up and through the sky, I'd try to see what was beyond the blue shell. Sometimes I'd think I could, that I was just about to. And then sometimes I knew I couldn't and the sky was a hard china teacup clamped down on the world.

I was busy with things like that and I wasn't paying attention to anything else. So it was only by accident I saw something one day.

That was one of the times I had not come down to supper. Margaret knocked on my door and I yelled that I was busy writing poetry and couldn't possibly stop. (My grandfather never argued.) By nine o'clock, long after supper, I got hungry. I padded downstairs in my socks, the boards smooth and cool and silent to my feet. I remember hearing the faint crackle of wood in the living-room fireplace—it was late fall and the nights were sharp and damp. I came down the stairs carefully, silently. (I was still young enough to get a thrill out of moving without a sound, a hang-over from my days of playing Indian.) The hall was dark; the lamp that usually burned beside the mercury-spotted pier glass had been turned off. The only lights were in the living room, where Margaret and my grandfather were. They couldn't see me in the dark hall and they hadn't heard me. He was reading one of his papers, and she was sewing. I recognized the material—my dress. The whole room looked like a set, or a picture. Margaret stopped sewing, her hands fell into her lap. Her head lifted and she stared across the room into the fire. He must have felt her move because he folded his paper and laid it aside. She did not turn. Her masculine head on its thin neck held perfectly still. The wood of his chair creaked as he got up, the boards of the floor sighed under his weight as he walked over to her and bent down. Then because he was still too tall, because she was sitting in the low rocker with the swan-head legs, he knelt down and put his arms around her. She turned her head then, dropping it to his shoulder, pressing it into his neck.

I backed away and ran upstairs, still keeping perfectly silent. I was afraid. No, it was more than that. I was just plain scared.

That was the only gesture I ever saw pass between them.

I finished high school, and my Aunt Annie took me and her grandchildren on a driving tour of the West. The whole thing was decided quickly. "You should go," my grandfather said firmly. "Good for you." And the very next day, Aunt Annie and four grandchildren drove over from Atlanta in a big new black Cadillac and picked me up. I was absolutely delighted. Her oldest grandson, the one who would help with the driving, was extremely handsome. Six weeks touring around the country with him sounded pretty terrific.

Later, much later, I found out why they had been in such a hurry to spirit me away. That was the summer my father came to see me. My grandfather found out his plans somehow, and off I went to the Grand Canyon and the Painted Desert. I wonder what they had to say to each other, when my father came to Madison City and found that I had been spirited away.

In a way I'm sorry I didn't meet him, at least to see what he looked like—I had long since forgotten. (My mother angrily had not kept any pictures.) But on the other hand I wouldn't have known quite what to say to him; you can't very well talk about blood. Or maybe you can. . . . But I didn't. I was away traveling.

All I remember of the tour is a jumble of mountains and snow peaks, ice-cold lakes and endless deserts, strange flowers and an ocean that didn't look real. On the way home, I stopped in Atlanta. I was to buy things for my first year at college.

"Child," Aunt Annie said, "your clothes are appalling. How could Willie let you go around looking like that?"

"I bought my own clothes, with Margaret."

Her face went blank. "This time I think I'll take Margaret's place with you."

We took Ellen, her oldest granddaughter, along—she'd been to the state university for three years and had just quit to get married. We were doing a trousseau for her, and a college wardrobe for me—it was all very wholesale and grand, like the West we had seen a few weeks before, and just as confused. My Aunt Annie was an energetic woman and she enjoyed every minute. Once when I hesitated over a sleek black suit, she bristled with annoyance. "What's the matter now?" she said. "What are you waiting for?"

"It's kind of expensive," I told her.

"Child, child . . ." she hissed her exasperation, the way so many fat women do, "he can afford it. . . . But it would be just like Willie not to tell you anything. . . . If he complains about the bills, just you ask him about his lumber business and he'll hush up."

That night after dinner, she decided that I must have a car. "Living way out there, you have to have an easy way to get back and forth."

"I can't drive," I told her.

"Well, learn," she said emphatically. "Really now!" And I was quiet, because nothing like this had happened, ever before. "I'm going to call Will about it right now." She went directly into the hall to telephone.

My Uncle Howland said quietly from his chair: "Annie is a driving woman."

"I just never thought about it like that."

He lifted his brandy glass. "Taste—no? You can't hide down on that farm all your life, honey, and Willie can't keep you there."

"I live there."

He waved the glass at me. The light danced on the bubble caught in the stem. "You got to be what you are, the granddaughter of one of the richest men in that state."

I looked shocked. And he chuckled. "War money, maybe, but money all the same."

Annie came back beaming. "Willie is such a tight stubborn man you just have to talk him down."

Later that evening, when she too was a little flushed with brandy, she told her husband: "I asked Willie if he were fixing to come to Ellen's wedding."

"He said no, I reckon."

"Too busy. . . . You know, Howie, I just worry about him. He doesn't ever want to come off that place. He doesn't want to leave that Margaret."

"Shush," my uncle said.

So I went to college. I had a new blue-and-white Ford convertible and a mink stole and a terrible quaking fear that woke me up in the middle of the night. I would often lie in my bed in the cheerful chintzy sorority house and shiver with longing to get in that new car and drive home. I never liked college. I just got to dislike it less the longer I was there.

When I came home for my first vacation—at Christmas that year—my grandfather said: "You're not beholden here, if there's any place you'd sooner go."

"Stay away for good like Margaret's children?"

His eyes didn't even flicker. "No," he said, "you can come back. . . . You can but you might not want to, someday."

I hugged him then, because I was sorry I'd reminded him about his other children, and because he'd begun to look old in the hard morning light. I'd been up all night driving and I felt fine.

"I'd like to live here," I told him, "all the rest of my life."

He was pleased and I could see it, but since he wasn't demonstrative he only rubbed his chin and said: "Depend where your man'll live."

"I haven't got a beau."

"You will," he said. "You will."

It was crispy cool and I was wearing the new mink. I rubbed my fingers up and down the long fur. "Maybe we could live here."

"Maybe," he said, "if you found the right kind of fellow."

"Won't marry any other kind."

"You got to be careful," he said heavily, "your mama married for love and it ran out on her and she was left with nothing to hold her heart together."

"Not me," I said, "not me."

"Well," he said, "you need a cup of coffee. Come inside and we'll see what Margaret's got."

I spent four blurred vague years at college. Green lawns, white-columned buildings, and flowerbeds. Fingers that ached with note-taking, head that ached with cigarette smoke, legs that ached with long hours in spike heels. The unfamiliar singing of alcohol in my ears, and lips that went suddenly numb. And parties.

There was a place on a TVA lake, a pretty spot with woods close all around except for the single road that led to the landing. It was called Harris Pier and it had rowboats moored in lines on each side. At the very end was a large float with a diving board. It was where you went on Saturday nights after the restaurants and cafés and clubs had all closed. It was always jammed—not that anybody particularly wanted a big group, but there was only one float and everybody crowded on it. Sometimes there'd be a guitar and we'd sing. Once Ted Anderson brought a harmonica. He didn't play too well, not nearly like I've heard Negroes play. But it was good enough. And the soft sad reedy sounds drifting out over the still water and softening their edges on the pines—well, you remember things like that.

And you remember how warm bourbon tasted, in a paper cup with water dipped out of the lake at your feet. How the nights were so unbearably, hauntingly beautiful that you wanted to cry How every patch of light and shadow from the moon seemed deep and lovely. Calm or storm, it didn't matter. It was exquisite and mysterious, just because it was night.

I wonder now how I lost it, the mysteriousness, the wonder. It faded steadily until one day it was entirely gone, and night became just dark, and the moon was only something that waxed and waned and heralded a changing in the weather. And rain just washed out graveled roads. The glitter was gone.

And the worst part was that you didn't know exactly at what point it disappeared. There was nothing you could point to and say: now, there. One day you saw that it was missing and had been missing for a long time. It wasn't even anything to grieve over, it had been such a long time passing.

That glitter and hush-breath quality just slipped away. The way most things do, I've found out. The way my mother's life did, gently, bit by bit, until it was gone and I didn't even have the satisfaction of mourning. And my love too. There isn't even a scene—not for me, nothing so definite—just the seepage, the worms of time. Like those wedding dresses my cousins and I found so long ago in the old storage trunks. They looked all right. But when you picked them up, they fell of their own weight, without even a breath touching them, and even the bits of pieces you held in your fingers crumpled.

That's the way it happened with me, during the years. Things that I thought surrounded me have pulled back. Sometimes I wonder if I am not like an island the tide has left, leaving only some sea wrack on the beaches, useless things.

I look at my children now and I think: how long before they slip away, before I am disappointed in them. . . .

But it doesn't matter. Not really. Not to me. Not any more. I have come to expect no more than this. At least I am not disappointed. . . .

But in those days at college, everything glittered and gleamed and my nerves quivered at the slightest breeze, and I still trembled with delight when I had a chance to wear my date's coat. After my first real dance, I didn't sleep at all. I lay in my bed and shivered and remembered until I saw dawn break and sun pour in the window.

It was all part of it, it all went together: the slight bobbing movement of the float, the sad sobbing strains of the harmonica, the dark moon-crusted trees. Ted Anderson only brought that harmonica once. Maybe that was why it sounded so good.

I nearly died, too, one of those lovely nights.

We had been drinking on the float when somebody said: "Throw 'em in." And they did, all the girls in their best dresses went over the edge of the float. I don't think they'd have heard me in all the squealing and screaming, even if I had remembered to tell them. But I didn't—until I felt the cold of the water I didn't remember that I couldn't swim. They had assumed everybody could. With the splashing and laughing, my yells weren't any good. I had a great full skirt on, I remember, and lots of petticoats; they were fashionable then. For half a minute they kept me up, and that was all.

I held my breath when I sank and fought my way up to the surface, got a new breath and went down again. It seemed forever, up and down—and then I made a mistake. I broke water so briefly that I hadn't filled my lungs and I couldn't resist the impulse to take a breath going down. Once you have water in your mouth, once you start coughing under water, it doesn't take long. I remember only a couple of coughs and then I passed out.

They said later that they found me a couple of feet under the surface, floating face down, and that they had a devil of a time hauling me up on the float with all my wet petticoats getting in the way.

I remember coming to, noticing that water was pouring out of my mouth and that an awful pressure on my back was jamming my breast into the canvas-covered deck of the float.

I struggled to turn over. "Stop pushing me," I said. "The floor's hard. It hurts."

Somebody said: "She's all right."

"My God," somebody else said, "I need a drink. Scared me sober."

"Take your time," the first voice said. "I'll take care of her." And then somebody picked me up. I could have opened my eyes to see, but it seemed like too great an effort.

I did, finally. I was lying on the back seat of a car, and there was only a little tiny glow from the light that went on when you opened the door. The people who had brought me—I heard them begin to walk away, heard them talking: "Where'd you leave the bottle?" "Out on the float." "Harry had it."

I didn't want to be left alone. I jerked up, reaching for the door. The first thing I touched was a dripping-wet shirt that had a warm body inside it. And a pair of wet arms grabbed me hard.

I recognized him: Tom Stanley. "Where the hell do you think you're going now?" He held out a cup of whiskey. I drank it quickly, noticing for the first time the cold in my body, the cold of near-death. I shivered, hard. "Take another one." He poured it. "What happened, for God's sake?"

"I can't swim," I said, and my voice was hoarse and broken.

He was silent for just a moment. Then he sucked his teeth softly. "We never thought of that," he said. "We just plain never thought of that."

I drank his whiskey. My mouth tasted awful, as if I'd been throwing up. I wondered if I had, but I didn't dare ask.

"You never learned to swim?" he repeated. "Where the hell'd you grow up?"

"Why the hell'd you throw me in?"

I put my face into the wet front of his shirt and began to cry. The more I cried the harder I held on to him, and by the time I felt better, I had crawled all over him, and had my face jammed into his Adam's apple and my arms wrapped around his neck. When I finished and started scrubbing at my face with my hands, he gave me his handkerchief.

"I'll drive you home," he said. "I'll go tell them we're leaving."

He walked back to the float, and I decided to move to the front seat. I got out all right, but then I nearly fell, my legs were so shaky.

I had to hold on to the back door and fumble with the front latch. When I finally did get into the seat, I felt like I'd really done something. I wasn't even able to close the other door. Tom slammed it when he came back.

It was a long drive back, seven or eight miles over dirt roads that wound and twisted across the very top of the ridge. After a mile or so, he stopped—right in the middle of the road, there wasn't a car anywhere around—and said: "I want a drink. You?"

"Yes," I said, and my voice was getting less hoarse. "I sound better."

"You'll live," he said.

He offered me the bottle and I hunted around on the floor until I found the paper cup that I had dropped earlier. I poured the whiskey in that. He drank directly from the bottle. We hadn't any water or ice; that was all back at the float with the party. But still, liquor helped. I stopped shivering. Soon there was a nice warm alcohol glow out along my fingers.

"I'm sorry I crawled all over you," I said. "I was pretty scared and you were the only thing around and I just had to grab hold."

"Any time." He started the car and we drove slowly and carefully along, the engine laboring in low gear on the steepest places.

The slopes of these hills were heavily wooded on both sides, but the crest was natural open meadow. The road ran directly across it for about half a mile. Behind us you could see dark thick woods and the sharp metallic glint of the lake. On the other side, there were the same trees and beyond them, far beyond them, the town and the college. You could see house lights—a few people were still up. You could see neon signs, red mostly with a bit of green in them. You could see street lights, straight rows of yellowish lamps, obscured by their own trees.

"Let's stop a minute," I said.

"If you won't freeze in that wet dress."

"Just a minute."

I got out (with the whiskey inside me I found I could move lightly), and walked a little away from the car into the stiff sharp grass of the bald and looked around. There wasn't even a wind. I looked at it all, at the ridiculous blotchy lights of the town, at the few moon-faded stars in the sky, and at the magnificent dark heavy slopes of trees. The moonlight was bright and blue and the color of mold on their tops. Just touching them, just brushing them. Underneath their lightened branches the night looked immense, and soft, and as deep as could be. As deep as the water in which I had sunk. I looked at the grass at my feet, at the stubbly grass, at the scattered stones, at the sprinkle of gravel. Each of these things had a shadow, sharp, distinct, a shadow trailing behind.

It was so clear, it was so bright, and the alcohol was singing in my ears, a steady clear humming. . . . There'd never been a night like that, there'd never been such a clear clear night. And silent. Not a night bird, not a wind. It was a night for eyes. Brightness, undisturbed.

It would never seem like that again. I went back to the car, wet skirt dragging between my legs. "I think I would like another drink."

"Wait a minute." He kissed me. And that was like the night, too, hard and clear. I could hear him breathing, I could feel his heart beating under the wet cotton of his shirt. My hand slipped up his arm and my fingers found a tear in the cloth near the shoulder.

"It's ripped," I said.

"I know."

Through the tear I tasted his skin with my tongue. It was faintly salty and faintly metallic, like some oysters. It must have been the lake water which was drying on him. And the moon was shining right in the car window, right straight into my eyes.

In a bit we had another drink and stretched out on the front seat, and it was as quiet as if we weren't there, just the thump of an arm or leg hitting the steering wheel now and then, hardly enough to disturb the night. And the moon still shone in one window and straight out the other, passing uninterrupted right over our heads. Like a river, but flowing across on top of us. And I found that it wasn't so hard to lose your virginity, nor painful either. I hadn't been told about that, I hadn't been taught about that, but then I hadn't even been taught to swim.

There's only one night like that—ever—where you're filled with wonder and excitement for no other reason but the earth is beautiful and mysterious and your body is young and strong.

I can remember him, now, remember just exactly how he looked, though that was over fifteen years ago, and he died in Korea a couple of years later.

That night none of us knew. He took me home and I slipped inside without being seen. I didn't even notice if my roommate was back. I stripped off my clothes, tearing them because they were still damp and sticking to my body. I fell asleep naked on top the bed. In the morning I put my ruined dress into a paper bag and dropped it into the garbage.

I didn't see too much of Tom after that—we hadn't really been friends before. It just sort of happened that we found ourselves together. It was the night and the time and the peculiar quality of things. It wasn't anything personal. It would have been the same with any man.

He did take me to a couple of football games and the big fraternity parties that followed them, but we never were alone again. And then we just sort of forgot.

It happens like that and it's not the less precious. It's the thing you value and not the man. It happened that way with me.

I had no trouble at college. I passed my classes and went to my parties, drank the forbidden bourbon, and held my breath during the drunken rides home. Once we were chased by the state police (we had a trunkful of whiskey that time; we were bringing it from the next county for a party) but we outran them. I had no trouble, until early in my final year. Then I got expelled—because of a wedding. The bride was from New Orleans, though she was in college with us. The groom was a jockey she met when she was home for Thanksgiving vacation. One Tuesday morning, nine of us—two cars full—drove with her to the nearest town in Mississippi. He met us there, a tiny leathery man who said nothing. It didn't seem possible that he had been married three times before. But when the clerk asked him, he produced copies of three separate divorce statements—it was really true.

Now, in those days you could get married in ten minutes; they even rushed out to meet you and be assured of your business. So we all crowded, giggling and pushing, into the office to hear the ceremony. Then we drank their health in champagne—we had brought four bottles neatly packed in ice. They got into his big white Cadillac convertible and drove away, waving. We finished the champagne and drove slowly back to the campus, feeling daring and romantic. None of us had ever been to an elopement before.

And then the trouble started. Her family nearly went out of their minds. They were Catholic—and very serious about it—so the whole thing was a horrible sin. They tried to get to the girl, but she was of age and had gone off to a Florida track somewhere and she didn't even bother to write after that first wire with the news of her marriage.

All of us were shipped back home. I called and told Margaret I was coming. I didn't say why and she didn't ask. She didn't have to. She knew that she would find out.

Of course my grandfather was waiting on the porch when I drove up. He didn't bother getting out of his chair. He let me walk up the steps toward him. "What did you do?" he said.

"You could say hello."

"I reckon I'm more interested in finding out what happened."

"Well," I said airily, "I went to a wedding."

When I finished, he got to his feet, and walked inside. I followed him. "Go take a bath or change your dress or something," he said, "I got to start telephoning."

"For what?"

"To get you back in, Miss Jackass."

"Maybe I don't want to go back. You think of that?"

I had started up the stairs when he called out to me: "You say her people's Catholic?"

"Yessir."

He chuckled, not happily. "That's going to be some help to you in a state that's mostly Baptist."

He stomped off to the phone. I changed and went out. I took one of the horses (there only were three; they belonged to me) and went for a ride until it was too late and too cold and I had to come back. I heard the phone ringing as I walked up from the barn, and went in the kitchen door.

Margaret said: "Mud on your shoes."

"I forgot." I went back and cleaned them on the boot scraper that was in the shape of two friendly rabbits with perky ears.

"You hungry?" Margaret asked.

"No."

"Didn't have lunch?"

"I'm not hungry."

"Soup," she said. "Take some."

She was sitting by the kitchen table. She'd been waiting for me.

"Is he here?"

She smiled. "Where else he going?"

"On the phone?"

"Since you flounced out the house."

"Well, I got reason to flounce," I told her. "The old bastards at school . . ."

"He don't like you talking like that," she said quietly.

"Okay. Okay." I went and looked into the soup pot.

"Abby." I jumped. She almost never called me by name. "You ought called to him this morning, not just leave a message with me."

"I didn't want to talk to him. I couldn't think of a damn thing to say."

"You hurt his feelings."

"Well, they hurt mine."

She chuckled. "Maybe you better stay out here with me, till the both of you quiet down some."

I took the ladle and stirred the soup, not answering.

"He been on the phone all day," Margaret said. "He'll fix it for you."

There was a pride and satisfaction in her tone that I hadn't heard before. "I don't want it fixed."

"Keep out his way tonight, child," she said. "And take youself some soup. All that temper's nothing but empty insides."

I had supper with Margaret, while my grandfather stayed by the telephone in the living room. In a little while she brought him a sandwich and sat there to keep him company. Since there was nothing for me to do, I went to bed and read.

I don't know who he called exactly. I didn't even realize he knew that many people. He was always so quiet and reserved, never talked about himself or his business with me. As for me, I was used to that manner of his, and I didn't mind it at all—after all, there are lots of southern men who treat their ladies that way. It's quite pleasant, really. But still, I couldn't help being shocked when this kind slow-moving grandfather of mine became somebody else. I'd never seen this side before; there hadn't been any reason for him to show it. Until then I had no idea of his influence and the extent of it. I had absolutely no idea of what he could do.

He called a great many people, I know. I only answered once, and that was the following morning. I happened to be passing the phone when it rang, so I picked it up: it was the governor's office calling.

And it all blew over. The next week, I went back. My grandfather drove up with me. "What about the others," I asked him, "will they get back?"

"They got to fight their own battles, honey."

"But it was my idea," I said. "I can't go back without them."

"Child," he said, "you going to get nowhere carrying the world. This whole thing is crooked as a cedar tree with a honeysuckle vine. But you got back, so forget it."

I was furious with him, and I sulked all the long drive. When we got there, my grandfather said abruptly: "Let's us go calling on the president."

I didn't believe him. "You're kidding."

"His brother's done some lawyering work for me."

"Not like this," I said. "I've got to change my dress."

He grinned, and it wasn't pleasant either. "If you'd said a word to me on the way up, I might have had it cross my memory. . . . But I'd just as soon they saw the wicked woman in bobby socks."

I almost died, of course, and after the president we went calling at the dean's house. Both of them were expecting us, and they had their wives there. It seemed some sort of state visit. My grandfather instantly became old-fashioned and formal. He even referred to me as Miss Abigail. He was as courtly as a planter out of a novel.

When we left, he told me to drive him to the hotel. All the way he chuckled softly to himself—I don't know that he was pleased, but he was mighty satisfied.

The only thing he said to me was: "Stop by the cab stand." He got out and went over to talk to the two drivers who were waiting there. One of them got inside his cab and drove off, and my grandfather came back.

"Gone for a spare tire and some more gas," he said. "He's driving me back."

"All that way?" I said. "That's expensive."

He stared at me hard for a moment, and then he chuckled. "Guess I plain better not tell you how much getting you back in school cost me. But seeing I managed that; I reckon I can afford the cab. I'm an old man and I want to go home. I'll be there something past midnight."

"You miss Margaret," I said.

His bright blue eyes went cold as I've ever seen them. His face got set and hard, and almost grey.

"I'm sorry," I said hastily. "I was being funny."

"You're a child," he said, "and like your mother you have very little sense." He got out of the car as if he couldn't stand sitting next to me any more, and he let his eyes wander up and down the street.

I got out too, and ran around the car, because I didn't want him to think whatever it was that he was thinking. In the couple of seconds it took me to get there, he found somebody he knew. He was shaking hands with a stocky young man who had the shortest crew cut I had ever seen. His black hair was like a bruise on his skull.

"John Tolliver," my grandfather said casually, his elaborate manner of the afternoon was completely gone, "my granddaughter."

He had bright blue eyes, startling blue, and long black lashes.

"What are you doing here?" my grandfather demanded.

"Law school, sir," he said.

My grandfather nodded as if that was just what he expected. He turned to me. "Knew his father and his grandfather for that matter, and cousins I can't keep count of."

"Yes, sir," John Tolliver said.

"His father's the district judge out there." The way he said it made it seem like the end of the world. "Matter of fact, got so many out there they call it Tolliver Nation." He waved his hand at me and I noticed suddenly how creased and knotted and old it was.

"Get my granddaughter to tell you how she was thrown out of school."

He flicked his finger against my face and got into his cab and drove off.

John Tolliver said: "What about that?"

"It wasn't very much fun."

"I'd like to hear about it," he said, and his smile was white and perfect. "How about tonight?"

"I didn't even expect to be here," I told him, "so I haven't got a thing to do, but don't you have a date?"

There was just a little flash before he said: "No. I don't."

So he did have one. But he had taken my grandfather's words as an order. I didn't think any more about it, beyond the little shiver of satisfaction at cutting into somebody else's date.

He didn't have a car, so I drove him to the sorority house and he carried my suitcase inside. "I'll be back for you in half an hour."

I raced upstairs and watched from the front-hall window. He went directly to the corner pay phone. I hurried through a shower and looked again. He was still there, he had opened the door for air. I knew that he was canceling his date. I wondered who she was.

My roommate sat on her bed and smoked while I dressed. "I didn't even expect to see you again," she said, "and now you not only turn up, but you've got a gorgeous man in tow. What goes on?"

"He's a friend of my grandfather's," I said.

She made a face.

"You know," I said, "that's really true."

"Where's he from?"

"Out there."

"What?"

"That's all my grandfather said."

"Hell," she said, "he's not all that good-looking."

"I suppose he isn't."

. . .

We went to the Chicken Shack & Roof Garden. Its name made no sense. It was just a one-story building with the usual peaked roof: you couldn't have put a garden up there if you wanted to. And there wasn't even one blade of grass outside. The building was surrounded by black asphalt right up to the edges of the walls.

The Chicken Shack had a bar, a long red leather one stretching the length of the building—though the county was dry. (You'd see state police cars parked in back now and then, half hidden by the high fence. They'd be stopping by for a drink or a payoff.)

I ordered bourbon and water, as I always did. John Tolliver said: "They've got a real good bar here so let's use it. Two martinis."

I didn't mind the correction. I would have to remember that, I thought. And the next time I would order properly.

"My grandfather mentioned Tolliver Nation," I said. "Where's that?"

He shrugged. "Just another name for Somerset County."

"You're the Somerset County Tollivers?"

He nodded.

Somerset was the northernmost county with the darkest, bloodiest past in the state. The breeding plantations had been up there, during the first half of the nineteenth century. They bred slaves and sold them, like stock. There was money in it, but not much else. Even in those days people didn't think too much of the slave runner and the slave breeder. They bought from them, but—as they did with Jew traders—they spat into the dirt to clean out the taste when they were gone. Those breed stations were always discontented and seething. Slave uprisings often began there. Mostly they were stopped before they left the county. But sometimes they weren't and they spread down into the rest of the state. There'd been a big one in the forties, one that left a wide trail of burned houses and bodies hanging on trees. As for the white people of Somerset County, well, they were violent too. Travelers in the old days used to shiver and keep their guns ready when they passed along that section of the

North Trace . . . it was robbers' country. During the Reconstruction they'd gone in for family feuds and for twenty years they killed each other. When it was over, just about the only families left bore the name Tolliver. They settled down peacefully enough—about this time the railroad came through there—and cleared their fat black land and raised huge crops of cotton. The new railroad hauled it off.

Nothing dramatic had happened up there for a long time, but the name remained, somehow, and whenever you said Somerset County, people would think a minute, remembering. It was that sort of name.

John Tolliver was different, too. He carried himself confidently, and that dark head of his was very handsome.

I didn't see too much of him—we were out only that once before it was time for the Christmas vacation. After that came the flurry of exams, and I sort of forgot about him. When he did call, it was almost February.

"Where would you like to go? Harris Pier?"

"No," I said abruptly, and then explained. "I nearly drowned there year before last."

We drove over to the next county, to a café that was supposed to have terrific pizzas. Like all places near the university it was jammed with students and the jukebox was far too loud. We got the last of the empty booths, back in a corner by the kitchen door.

"It'll take all night to get supper," John Tolliver said.

"I don't mind. Anyway, noisy places are kind of friendly."

The jukebox hesitated for two seconds, whirred, and began King Cole's "Mona Lisa." "That's such a pretty song," I said. "I love it."

"I'm sorry I can't ask you to dance," John Tolliver said. "I never learned."

"I don't really care for it."

"I'm glad."

"But how could you avoid it?" I said. "I thought everybody was forced into dancing school."

His blue eyes were level. "You don't know Tolliver Nation."

"No," I said, "no, I don't."

"There's nobody to teach dancing. If there was, they'd only have the babies. By the time you're seven, you've got your chores to do."

"Oh," I said, "I see."

"It's not like Wade County, you know. It's just cotton and more cotton. No timber lands like your grandfather's got."

"Yes," I said, not wishing to appear too ignorant, "I guess timber is valuable."

He laughed at me. And I found that I didn't mind that at all, because his laugh was friendly and intimate.

"Can I have a bourbon and soda?" I said. "It's what I really do prefer."

He had to get up and go over to the bar for the order. It was that kind of place. When he came back, he put the glasses carefully on the table. "I haven't called you before this," he said abruptly, "because I wanted to get myself free from another entanglement."

I didn't know what to say, so I said: "Oh."

"I've never dated more than one girl at a time. Does that sound silly to you?"

"No."

"I work at the library every week night until it closes at ten," he said. "I'll pick you up then."

So every evening after work he met me at the sorority house. Every evening the same time: ten minutes past ten. Mostly we went for a drive and parked and played the radio and talked. He had very little money, and he wouldn't let me pay. So we drove to a different spot every night, and smoked cigarettes, and watched the silly little coals burn red in the dark. The first time he kissed me good night, it was polite but firm. His skin smelled like clover grass. "Now," he said, "that's enough for now. Go on inside."

He sounded like a man with a plan. And that was sort of nice. Most people I knew just drifted and let things happen to them—not John Tolliver. He ordered and directed events himself. Since no one had ever told me what to do before, I liked it immensely.

One evening, my roommate said: "Honey child, if you don't be careful, you are going to be in trouble."

"What?" I was too vague and too happy to understand.

She picked up the green plastic case that contained my diaphragm. "I was looking to see if you had a Band-Aid in your dresser—damn shoe slashed my heel to ribbons—and I found this." She waved it at me. "That's pretty careless."

"I don't need it. I'm not sleeping with him."

She tossed the box back into the drawer, shrugging. "Have it your own way."

"I'm not—I'm going to marry him." I hadn't dared to think like that before, but as I said it I knew it was true.

When he proposed a month later, it was in the same matter-of-fact tone. "I would like to marry you," he said. "Would you?"

"Yes," I said, "I think I would."

Rather than tell my grandfather by phone or write him, I decided to go home during the short Easter holiday.

I drove down overnight, so excited and happy I didn't need sleep. I walked in just as he was having breakfast with Margaret in the kitchen. Without a word she got up and laid another place for me. "Well," my grandfather said, "looks like you got good news this time."

"I'm going to get married."

"I been expecting that." He calmly poured himself a cup of coffee from the old-fashioned flowered pot.

"Don't you want to know who?"

"I expect I do," he said. "But I figured to find out sooner or later."

"John Tolliver."

He went on drinking his coffee slowly.

Margaret said: "You want breakfast?"

"I'm starving."

My grandfather said: "He'll do all right. There's some of his family that's bums, but there's some of ours we can't look too hard at. We could start listing with your father."

"John has one more year at law school."

"That family's had things pretty much their own way up in that county past three or four generations. Tollivers everywhere you look. Having things that way kind of gives a man a strange cast."

"No more than being a Howland," I said.

He smiled and shrugged that one off. "I reckon not."

"Anyway," I said, ashamed that I had snapped at him, "John doesn't want to go back."

"Back?"

"To Tolliver Nation."

"Got too small for him," he said easily. "Eat your breakfast."

When we were done, I went with him to the back porch, while he put on the heavy boots he used for working. "Near stepped on a copperhead yesterday," he told me as he laced them up.

"You don't like John."

He went on lacing. "Don't know him."

"You introduced us."

"I recognized him by the family face that he's carrying, same way I'd know any Tolliver."

"But you don't like him anyhow."

"Know some things about his family I can't give much room to."

"But that's not him."

"No," he said. "I reckon it ain't. You in love with him?"

I felt myself blushing. "I'm not ashamed of it. Yes, I am."

"Didn't say you had cause to be ashamed."

He finished with his boots and straightened his legs out, the way old men will, and he looked across the back yard—muddy as it always was in the spring—down to the barns and the silos and the smokehouses and the other buildings, behind them the fenced lots, and behind them the woods.

"You don't seem happy about it."

He had begun to fill his pipe. "Honey, I'm just too old to get excited. Seems like all I can remember is how many times the same thing has happened to me. Right now you're telling me this. And seems all I can remember is your mother and me, just the two of us driving back from the station in a buggy and coming up that front drive there, same drive, same plants, same everything, and her telling me she was in love and getting married."

"John's not like my father."

"And seems I can remember me coming home to tell my parents I was in love and getting married. And they didn't look surprised either, nor very happy."

"It's not the same with me," I said, "it's different."

"When you're as old as me," he said, "you'll see that there ain't very much that's different or separate or unusual." He stood up. "I'm so old I can remember back before there was any such thing as a boll weevil in this country. . . . You better call your Aunt Annie. Seems like she runs all my weddings for me."

"Okay," I said.

He started off across the yards; he always began the day with a quick look at the barns and the stock there. He hadn't gone more than two feet before he turned and said: "Robert's finished his M.S. and he's got himself a job."

"I didn't know that," I said. "That's wonderful. Where?"

"San Francisco," he said. "They need engineers there."

"I bet Margaret is happy."

He looked at me, that same level surprised look, as if he hadn't seen me before. Not ever. "That's a mighty proper and polite thing to say. And I do think she is."

On my way to bed, because I was terribly sleepy now, I passed Margaret, taking the dead flowers out of the vases on the hall table.

"I just heard about Robert," I said. "That's terrific."

"He's a good boy," she said quietly.

"He ought to be getting married soon."

"Yes," she said. "He will soon."

Then I went to bed, and before I fell asleep, I thought how much older Margaret looked. She'd always been tall and rawboned, and she still was, but now there was a thickening around her hips, and the smooth black skin of her cheeks was lined and there were crinkles around her eyes. She had a little smattering of grey in her hair too, her white blood had given her that. While I was trying to figure out her age—she was about as old as my mother and that would have been in the middle or late forties—I fell asleep.

We had a big June wedding, as everyone expected. The biggest wedding of the year. My grandfather took over the Washington Hotel in town for the extra guests. Even that wasn't enough, and the Bannister cousins (Peter Bannister was dead by this time) opened their huge house.

It seemed to me that I drove over the whole state going to receptions, to cocktail parties, to showers, to dances. Old-fashioned week-long house parties on the Gulf coast. Hunts in the woods of the northern counties. And more dances: black tie, square dance, masquerade. . . . Two weeks before the wedding I went up to Somerset County to meet John's people. They gave no parties—weddings were nothing so special for them—they were serious religious folk. We spent only one day there, and they were polite and kind, after their fashion, but I was very relieved to go. "You see," John said on the way back, "what I mean. It isn't like Wade County."

I nodded. "Did they like me?"

"They approve of you." He flashed that bright smile dryly. "That's a lot better in their books than liking you."

"Your parents say anything at all?"

"Said you'd make a good wife."

"Oh." I sounded doubtful.

"It's their way," he said. "Don't fuss with it."

On the day of the wedding, I was so tired that I stumbled and almost fell coming down the stairs on my grandfather's arm. When the ceremony was done and the reception over, and we drove off in the new Thunderbird convertible that my grandfather had given us, I fell asleep almost the moment we left and slept half the way to New Orleans. I woke to find the car had stopped and it was way past midnight; we were parked on the Gulf coast (you could see the water shining under the moon) and John was sleeping behind the wheel. I settled back and let him sleep. It was dawn before we drove the rest of the way to New Orleans.

Two weeks later we were home; two months later we were back at the university and John was finishing his last year of law school. I was shocked at how hard he worked. I'd never known anyone to do that. My grandfather certainly hadn't; I'd never seen anybody work with such fierce intensity. We had a tiny bright apartment right by the campus, and that whole last year we were there I almost never saw him. I met him for lunch, a quick dash through the university cafeteria, and then I saw him again at night when the library closed, when he came home and pounded on the typewriter for an hour or so. He corresponded with a great many people; the letters were carefully written and carefully thought out. "They could help me someday," he said when I complained. "When you start at the bottom you've got to use everything."

He was away so much—and because I had nothing else to do, I began to suspect. Finally one evening after supper, I followed him to the library. He was working in one of the rooms on the lower floor and from a seat on the front steps I could watch him. He stayed there hour after hour, hunched over, reading. He did not speak to anybody; he did not seem to notice that there were other people in the room. He didn't even stop for a cigarette; he hardly shifted in his uncomfortable wood chair. I sat on the concrete steps for three hours, feeling lonely and sick, and when it was closing time, I scurried home at a run to be there before him.

"Your hands are cold," he said when he came in.

"I went for a walk around the block."

"Do you think that's all right?"

"You just want to get out sometimes. And what could happen?"

"Don't blame me if some of the guys make a pass."

"Do you worry about that?" I asked. "Do you worry if I have a lover?"

He was taking his typewriter out. (Every day I put it back in its case because I didn't want to look at it.)

"A lover? I don't think you do," he said. "I trust you."

Then because I felt so awful, I said I had a headache and went to bed, and cried silent hot tears into the pillow. It was that night, I think, that I decided to let myself get pregnant.

When I was sure, I told him.

"It's too soon," he said softly, "but I should have been more careful too."

"Do you want me to get rid of it?"

"No," he said emphatically. "That's too risky. You might die." There was a minute while he thought it all out. "It'll be all right," he said. "A child will be company for you."

"I'm not lonesome," I said.

"No?" He picked up the evening paper and began to read it. "I thought that was why."

He knew. And that always amazed me—how much he knew, how much he noticed behind his abstracted busy front. . . .

He finished school all right, with all the honors, but there was one thing he hadn't counted on—Korea. Since he'd kept his army commission, he was called up immediately. He was desperate and furious and raging impotently. His face flushed a blotchy grey and red, and he tore a great hunk out of the upholstered arm of a living-room chair. I just sat there, behind my thickening belly, and watched him wrench the chair to pieces. "Two years in Germany," he yelled. "Why the hell don't they take the others? Let them see what its like, freezing in the mud."

He said a lot more, and he didn't sleep for two nights, and he scarcely told me good-bye when he finally left. But it didn't turn out badly for him after all—not at all. But then very few things did. He was adaptable. No matter what happened, he could turn it to his advantage. It was that way with his Korean service. He went to Washington and spent three years in the dim dismal barracks of a purchasing unit's offices. But he saw something else in Washington and he liked it. He saw a size and a scope of things that his family sitting up in Tolliver Nation had never dreamed about. He also saw a place for himself.

He told me about it just before I got on the train to come home. Washington was crowded, the hospitals were jammed, and everything was horrid. I was going back to my grandfather's house to have the baby. On the way down to the station, he told me what he wanted and how he proposed to go about it. It started with governor and it ended with senator. "There isn't a chance of my being president." He patted my taut belly gently. "Too small a state and a southerner couldn't anyway. . . . I've been forgetting to tell you, I joined the Citizens Council and the Klan before I left."

"Oh," I said. "Oh, for heaven's sake."

"Your grandfather belonged to the Klan."

"It was different then."

"Justice Black belonged too."

"But not any more."

"Honey," he said, "when I get where he is, I'll quit too."

So I went back to my grandfather's house during those bright crisp days of early winter. I sat in the sun on the back porch in the morning and the front porch in the evening and passed the time of day with people who came visiting. There were a lot of them too, ladies in the daytime, couples at night. I could tell from their way of inquiring after my husband that John had impressed them.

One evening my grandfather asked me: "He going into politics?"

"Yes."

He chuckled. "Too many old men in politics in this state. You just plain get tired looking at their ugly faces. Seems like we're about ready for a brave young soldier back from a war. And you get to move into the governor's mansion—I reckon that's what he's after."

"He thinks so."

"No reason why not."

"You still don't like him, do you?"

"Don't have much taste for politics, child, and never did. . . . You still like him?"

And I told him the truth. "Not as much as I did. But I love him."

"Makes a difference," my grandfather said.

One cold December morning, when there were a million speckles of frost glistening on the porch railing, and the sky was a bright hard winter blue, I sat down to breakfast. Without warning, I flooded green-flecked ammonia-smelling water down my legs, through my robe, and into a puddle on the floor.

Foolish and dull and heavy in my state, I just stared at it thinking: How nasty it smells. How horrid it looks. I kept staring at it, wrinkling my lips; I almost didn't notice Margaret, who had jumped up and was dialing quickly at the wall phone. While it rang, she turned to me. "You feel anything?"

I shook my head. "Who're you calling?"

"The barn. He's down there."

My grandfather, of course. She never called him by name. At least to me.

Nobody answered. Margaret let it ring for quite a while, then she called Harry Armstrong, the doctor in town. He wasn't there, and she left a message. She went out on the porch and looked up and down, but the winter-swept yards were empty. She came back, bringing the sharp cold wind on her dress.

"You feel anything?"

"Feel queer." I was sleepy all of a sudden. And I had trouble pronouncing my words.

She put her hand to my stomach, right where the swelling of child began, and pressed it tight. She held it for a moment. Then she got me by the arm and stood me on my feet. "We got to get you to bed."

She helped me up the stairs and into my bed. She went into the hall to call the barn again; still no answer. My grandfather would be out somewhere, and he had the only car. I had left mine in Washington with John.

So I would have to have it at home. I thought: How silly. I can't do anything right. I can't even get to the hospital in time for a baby. . . .

Margaret came back. "How long has it been?" I asked her.

"Not five minutes, child."

I was terribly groggy, my eyes couldn't seem to stay open. All of a sudden, my body shivered and shook like a gigantic sneeze. At the end of it I screamed.

Margaret was pulling me out of bed. She had gotten my clothes off. Naked and sweating in the chilly room, I leaned against the side of the bed, swaying and wanting so to go to sleep. "Squat down," she told me. There was a sheet spread on the floor—I hadn't noticed that before. I squatted on it. She slipped behind me, sitting on the bed, her legs around my body, her hands holding my shoulders firmly. "Now," she said, "go on."

Two more tearing pains and the white sheet held a puddle of blood and a baby and some slimy cord.

Margaret was kneeling beside me now, my head rested against her shoulder. She was wiping out the baby's mouth with a corner of the sheet. It was making small chirping sounds. For a minute I thought that the window was open and I was hearing the sounds of birds outside. But it was the blood-smeared ammonia-smelling bit of flesh I had delivered.

We crouched, the two of us, until delivery was finished. Then Margaret helped me back into bed. I forgot about the baby and I fell asleep.

When I woke there was a fire burning and the room was warm, and Margaret was sitting rocking by the fire and there was a basket right beside her. She saw my eyes open and she came over at once.

"They be having a drink downstairs, your grandpa and Dr. Armstrong. They been having quite a few drinks." She smiled gently, but the smile faded and she said with a little hesitation: "I got to call them. . . . Might be better if you was to say the baby birthed in the bed."

"Oh," I said.

"White ladies don't squat down to drop on the floor."

I didn't know if she was mocking me, but I didn't take a chance. I never said a word and everybody assumed that the baby had been born on a mattress, proper and decent.

Anyway it was a girl. And I was sick with disappointment. We named her Abigail.

The next one—just thirteen months later—was born in a hospital, properly. Even the doctor was different. It was Otto Holloway. By then Harry Armstrong had had a stroke and retired. But this baby was a girl too. Mary Lee. I put my head down on the coarse hospital sheets and cried bitterly. I had wanted a boy so much, so very much. John, who'd managed to come down this time, hung around the bed, looking worried and wondering. "Don't take on so," he kept saying. "It isn't serious, it isn't that serious."

I had been a girl and the only child; so had my mother. I had assumed I would do better. I'd always pictured myself with a great family of sons.

John didn't understand. He couldn't. "Oh go away," I told him. "Please go away."

"It isn't just the baby, is it?" he asked sharply. "It's something else."

I hardly bothered to listen. "Go away."

"I know it is. Who's been carrying stories to you?"

His tone was sharp and angry; there was even a little rasp of fear in it.

"Everything you do, innocent as all hell, people read their way, with their dirty little minds."

Numbly, I lay back on my pillows and looked indifferent while he told me how innocent his life in Washington had been, but how open to misinterpretation. I listened, and everything he said, I understood the opposite.

I went back with him though, and we stayed in Washington until his tour was over. (He asked me to come. "People will stop talking if you're there.") Every party we went to, I found myself looking and wondering: Was that the one? Was it she? But I was in love with him, and as my grandfather said, that made a difference.

Korea ended. We came back to Wade County and John set up his office right on the main street in Madison City next to the Rexall Drugstore. He worked, hard as he had in college. He was building his practice, and he was making his political debut. Every week, practically, he'd be off on a speaking trip somewhere in the state. He'd talk on anything from conservation and the boll weevil to the godlessness of youth—always perfectly serious and sincere. One particular weekend he was scheduled to talk to a farmers' group about the state's role in reducing anthrax. I had to say something.

"For heaven's sakes, John," I asked, "what do you know about anthrax?"

He grinned the bright happy smile that was beginning to look like it was adjusted for photographers. "Asked your grandfather at dinner last night," he said. "Bacteria, live in the soil, dormant for as long as thirty years. . . . That's all I need."

"Oh my."

"I'm not telling them about anthrax, honey. I'm telling them about John Tolliver."

He was also an extremely successful lawyer, who had a way with judges and juries all over the state. Of course he was in a good position. He was a Tolliver and that meant he could call on practically all the north part of the state. His wife was a Howland, and that meant kinship with practically all the central counties. As for the three or four southern counties, they didn't interest him. As a matter of fact he usually refused to even speak there, claiming that their Catholic majority was hostile to him. I don't know that there was any truth to his charge. But he often used it to enlist a lot of Protestants who wouldn't have been with him otherwise.

I sat back in my house in Madison City and watched.

We had a new house, we had built it. At first John wanted to take over one of the old empty houses around town (there were quite a few of them). "It looks better for me to live in an old house," he told me. "Substantial, like a wool suit in the summertime."

"I want a new house," I said, fearfully, because if I got in an argument with him I always lost. I just didn't want to have him talk me out of this, so I said something I'd never said before. "It's my money."

For a minute there was a terribly mixed-up look on his face. It wasn't angry, it wasn't hurt. I don't know what it was. Maybe it was just surprised.

"Anyway," I added quickly because I was afraid I'd said too much, "the only old house I ever want to live in is my grandfather's."

He flashed the smile again. "When he leaves that to you, sure. It'll make a great place with some money spent on it."

"All right," I said, though I felt a little tremor in the pit of my stomach—disposing of a man's things while he was still alive.

I built my shiny new house, and my children slept in shiny ruffled bedrooms. The whole town buzzed when I had a contractor from Mobile do the kitchen and the bathrooms. The master bath had a sunken tub and a tiny sun-bathing patio. The kitchen was right out of *House and Garden*: it had everything, every gadget that could be installed. I found out what the town thought of that from Margaret. She had brought us some quail from my grandfather, not more than a week after we moved in. She stared around the kitchen, hands on thickening hips; she pursed her lips and said nothing.

"Like it?"

"Mighty fancy kitchen for a nigger to work in."

She said it flatly. She might have been sarcastic. Or it might have only been a simple statement of fact. Or it might have been her father's blood talking.

I never knew when she was serious and when she was mocking. I think she intended it that way.

Maybe by that time she'd noticed some of the references to John that had been appearing in papers round and about. The first one I saw was a little clipping from an Atlanta paper my cousin Clara Hood sent me. (She was a Bannister cousin from Madison City. She'd married a young Methodist minister named Samuel Hood and moved to Atlanta. He was a plain sandy-haired man, very earnest and devout, and a strong defender of Negro rights. Since she'd met him, Clara Bannister had abandoned all her early White Citizens Council training and become, among other things, a member of the NAACP. Even her vague bewildered mother was shocked. My grandfather found it very amusing.) The clipping was an interview with John. It was on a back page somewhere and it wasn't long and it wasn't particularly interesting. It was full of folksy talk about being glad to come to town and see my wife's people, and always being happy to be in Atlanta. It ended with a phrase that stuck in my mind: "Mr. Tolliver is a rising young lawyer and is considered to be the brightest hope of the southern segregationists."

I showed it to John. "I saw it, honey," he said.

"You don't read the Atlanta papers, do you?"

"My clipping bureau."

"I didn't even know you had one."

"You didn't ask."

"Did you really look up your cousins-in-law?"

He grinned. "I had so damn many appointments that I didn't even get to call them . . . but it looked good in the paper."

That evening—the first he had home in six weeks—he spent patiently crawling around the living-room floor with two small girls on his back. He'd also given them each a large picture and set it up in their rooms. "So they won't forget what I look like," he said. He loved them and they adored him. Our lives moved peacefully along, the girls and I, dull and uneventful until he came home. And he brought excitement with him—he always had been able to do that.

John must have thought my question about the clipping was some sort of criticism, because after that he brought them to me. All of them. I put them carefully in a box—I found it the other day—but I never read them. Sometimes when he handed them to me words would jump out of the print. Racist. Staunch segregationist. Strong friend of states' rights.

I asked about that once, and wished I hadn't. We were driving to the university where the student body had invited him to speak. It was one of those silvery grey winter evenings when everything is soft and delicate and the sky is a kind of pink and the ground shimmery and indistinct with fog. The car was new and shiny and smelled wonderful; the heater poured out a steady stream of warmth on our legs. It's like nothing else, this feeling of a powerful car on good roads in hilly country. We were riding the rises and the falls of the land like the swells of the sea. I was glad to leave the children, too—I'd been home a lot. I was proud to be the wife of the invited speaker. And John had come home yesterday with a sapphire ring in his coat pocket. "Matches your eyes, old duck," he said casually. I wasn't deceived. I knew what money meant to him, and that ring had cost a lot. He'd been a good husband and a hard-working one, but this was the first time he had brought anything like that, a tribute. I thought how lovely it would be, as we went roaring over those hills, us growing old together and seeing our children grow to women and our grandchildren come home. All long sentimental thoughts, like the long grey hills. . . .

Lulled by that gentle light, I asked him something I'd been wondering, something the words in those clippings had reminded me of.

"John," I said, "what do you really think about the Negroes? Not what you're going to say tonight, but what you really think?"

He chuckled and swerved around a stock truck with a blast of his horn. "Love 'em dearly," he said. "Like your grandfather."

The silvery light went out of the evening, and the unborn grandchildren disappeared. It was just bleak winter country and a man driving too fast.

A few more years, pleasant, uneventful, broken only by the holidays that John had begun to afford. I remember the years by the vacations—the Jamaica year, the Bermuda year, the Sun Valley year. We went twice a year, summer and winter. The girls grew up. Crib to bed, stroller to bike, nursery school to first grade. They were handsome children, dark and blue-eyed like their father. He wanted more, I know. He asked about it once. I only said: "Let me get these launched. They're so close it's been a lot of trouble." He was waiting; he would be too proud to ask again.

. . .

And my grandfather died. It was in January, a couple of days after the big snow. Now, we never have a fall of any size in this part of the country—just a few sprinklings like hoarfrost on the ground. But this time a level grey-green sky sifted down fifteen inches, and everybody was caught. The stock in their far-spread pastures went into a panic. They broke their fences, tore through the wire, leaving bloody gobs of hide on the barbs, and wandered into the wood lots and beyond. They were going to have to be gathered up again, a few at a time. Every man my grandfather employed was out working—looking for injured stock, mending fences.

For four mornings my grandfather left early in his truck, bouncing over the rutted frozen lumber roads that thawed slowly into puddles of mud. For three evenings he came home staggering tired, gulped supper, and went straight to bed. On the fourth evening he did not come back.

On that fourth day too, my grandfather was working alone. Oliver Brandon, who usually worked with him, had driven to town for some extra sets of wire clippers and a few things like that. He took Margaret's car, the one that my grandfather had given her the past year, and was back by noon, when my grandfather was supposed to pick him up. When he didn't come, neither Margaret nor Oliver worried. He'd gotten rather forgetful lately, as old men do, and it wasn't in his usual habit of things to come back to the house at noon. Since he hadn't said where he would be, Oliver could not look for him; instead he replaced the cracked boards in the porch floor.

Neither worried until dark fell, and then they found each other staring out the shadowy opaque windows. "Might could be working by headlights," Oliver suggested.

Margaret shook her head.

"Didn't rightly think so," Oliver said.

Margaret went and stood by the window, head leaning against the cold glass, staring out where she couldn't possibly see anything.

At ten o'clock Margaret called me. John happened to be home that evening, and the children were asleep—it was quiet and neat and enclosed and peaceful—until the phone rang. John answered; his face got more and more strained as he listened. "He didn't come back." He told me the story briefly.

"Where'd he go?"

John shook his head. "She didn't know and there's been too many trucks up and down those roads to follow tracks."

We drove over at once. Margaret was alone. Oliver had gone home; he was an old man and tired. John talked to her briefly. Then went to the phone. He was on it almost an hour arranging for a state police helicopter. He wanted them to begin at once; they insisted on waiting for daylight. They settled finally on an immediate ground search.

He joined Margaret and me. The three of us sat in the living room and waited. By eleven o'clock we could hear the cars going by on the road, we could see their lights turn at the big hackberry tree where the trail led up to the wood lots and the timber stands behind that.

"There're a lot of people," I said.

"Better be," John told me. "I promised five thousand dollars whoever finds him."

I just stared at him. I would never have thought of that, but then I never thought of anything.

And the telephone began ringing. The whole county seemed to be waking up. By midnight I even had a call from my cousin Clara in Atlanta wanting to know if what she heard was true. I didn't know it traveled that fast, even bad news. Margaret made the first pot of coffee and I made the next. At one o'clock John got out a bottle of my grandfather's whiskey. I managed the first drink, but after the second I went straight to the bathroom and threw up. When I came back Margaret and John were sitting silent as mannequins, still drinking, waiting for me.

He said: "You better not try that again, honey."

Margaret said: "No stomach for alcohol, Mr. John says."

There was something in the way she said "Mr. John." It was polite enough, but at the same time it was mocking. And knowing. Weary and amused all at once. Every now and then you'll find a Negro who can do that. It's always made me very nervous. I don't want to be understood that much.

It didn't seem to bother John. She may not have been completely at ease with him (and she wasn't a woman who went around being easy in the presence of people) but he was certainly comfortable with her. He liked her and he got on very well with her. Much better than he did with my grandfather. Whenever he came in a room, John tensed up and got that flashy newspaper smile on his face. But he was at ease with Margaret, as he was that night. We were worried, all of us, worried sick. We waited there, just three people together.

While we sat in his parlor my grandfather sat dead in his truck.

The ground search found nothing that night. At daylight the police helicopter arrived, and began a methodical search, chopping its noisy way back and forth across the sky. They spotted the truck in half an hour, though it took much longer to get through the broken roads. You see, he wasn't where anybody expected him to be. He must not have gone to tend stock or mend fences after all. He went down into the cotton bottoms, the old land, it was called. He drove across the open fields, and into a dense stretch of wood that climbed sharply up a razorback ridge. This was the land the first William Howland had claimed for himself. Stories had it that his fields were here, his first fields. But these weren't fields any more; these were woods, thick and dense. There weren't even roads through them, only narrow tracks. In this particular place, there wasn't even room for a helicopter to land.

They got to him finally. He'd driven off the track, just a bit, and parked and turned off his engine and set his brake. So he must have had some warning of what was coming. He was still sitting there, hands on the wheel. Forehead touching the knuckles of his hands. As if he were waiting for something. As if he had stopped and was waiting for something.

The police didn't telephone; they sent a trooper with the news. He came and told us awkwardly enough and then stood around, twirling his cap in his fingers, not being sure what else was required of him, not knowing what you have to say when you've found an old man dead in the woods. I remember looking at him and thinking how much he resembled John. A little heavier, maybe, but the same black hair and close-set blue eyes, the same jaw and the same thin mouth. John looked like everybody from the north part of the state. . . .

The plain bare statement the trooper brought didn't hurt me much. I'd had all night to prepare for it. But it rocked John. His face drained white and then turned a kind of light green. He hadn't shaved and the heavy beard, uneven and thicker in some spots than others, made his face look bruised. "Jesus God!" he said. "I've been thinking all night he must be hurt or sick, a heart attack or something like that because of his age." He began to bite his nails nervously, something I'd never seen him do before. "I never thought he could die like that."

He walked back to the patrol car with the trooper, and then he kept on walking down the muddy side of the state highway. I saw him through the window and started out after him.

"Let him be," Margaret said emphatically.

I hadn't thought of her—neither of us had. I had looked at the trooper and then at John. But I'd forgotten Margaret.

"Margaret," I said, "I'm so sorry."

She didn't seem to hear. Maybe because she wouldn't take anything from me, not even sympathy. "Let him be," she said after John.

"He hasn't got a coat," I said, "and it's cold."

"He be coming back," Margaret said, "when he feel the cold."

Her smooth round black face was unmoved. It was just the face of a middle-aged Negro woman who looked older than her years, and who wasn't particularly concerned by whatever was happening around her. The black skin helped, of course—its color looked so silent, so impenetrable. It hid the blood and bone under it.

"He'll come back with pneumonia."

"He respected him," Margaret said quietly. "Let him grieve."

And she went into the kitchen to cook breakfast. Happiness or death, you had to eat, and she had to fix it.

Her feet were a little heavy as she walked away, and she shuffled a bit, as if the hold the earth had on her had gotten stronger, all of a sudden.

She was right of course. John respected him. And he grieved for him. Not that he loved him. No, it wasn't like that. William Howland had not liked him and John knew it, so that left out love. But respect now, that was something else. A man was due that by reason of what he was. Will Howland had earned it; and it came naturally to John Tolliver to give it.

For me it was the other way around. I loved my grandfather but I didn't respect him. That was why all that long night I had faced up to the fact that he was dead. And John hadn't; he hadn't been able to.

Margaret began to sing as she got breakfast. She never had before, she'd always been the silent dark woman. But she was singing now and her voice was light and high, delicate and gentle. "Cold thing here I can't see, rubbing itself all over me. . . ."

I'd never heard that song before. I listened to the words and shivered. It was death creeping up and killing.

"Stretch my jaw, jerk my legs, break my bones until I'm dead. . . .

Margaret sang it as a kind of chant, monotonous and wailing. "Death spare me for another year." She wasn't talking about herself. She was mourning Will Howland, that he hadn't had just another year. Just one more year.

We left her moaning that dirge, John and I, and went back into town. As we walked out the front door, the telephone began ringing. We hesitated. Margaret didn't answer, didn't seem to hear it. So we didn't answer it either. It would have been like interrupting a funeral.

All the doors of the house were open in spite of the cold and her singing followed us out to the car. I'm not sure, but I think John was crying.

Funerals are a good deal like weddings this part of the country. Only they're a bit quicker and a bit smaller. And that's the only way you get through them at all. But they do end, and people leave, and rooms are empty, and there is only the heaviness in your chest and the nasty taste in your mouth.

A couple of days after the funeral, I put the children in the car and went out to see Margaret—I was going to ask her what her plans were. I felt terrible. I almost threw up on the way over. And my girls, for some reason or other, had taken this time to sing over and over: "We shall meet, we shall meet, we shall meet on that bee-utiful sh--o--ore. . . ."

The front door was locked. I went to the back. That was locked too. I knocked and waited. Oliver came plodding slowly up from the barns: he had seen my car. He handed me a key. "That for the back door. Didn't seem to be none for the front."

I looked at the key, an ordinary Yale key to the night lock on the kitchen door. "Where's Margaret?"

"Been gone."

"Where?"

"New Church."

My children were chasing the big grey cat around the yard. "I didn't know she had any family there to go to. I didn't know she even thought about going back."

Oliver looked at me, patiently. "She got a house there, five, six years ago."

"Oh," I said. "I didn't know."

"Mr. William give it to her."

"Well, Oliver," I told him, "I didn't know that either."

He smiled, a tiny curl of the black lips. "I reckon you didn't."

"Tell me where it is and I'll go see her."

He said: "She come to you." He walked away then, leaving me to stand on the empty porch with a small key in my hand. I started to go in but changed my mind. I would only cry, and I did not want to do that in front of the children. So I gathered them up again and we drove back home.

We saw the will, a few days later, and there wasn't a mention of Margaret in it. "John," I said, "we can't let it go like that. It isn't right."

The mottled look hadn't quite gone from his face. It made him look sick. "Don't be a pea brain, honey," he said. "Can't you figure it out?"

"Margaret's got to live."

"God save me from well-meaning people and idiots."

"You don't have to get nasty."

"Margaret's car, the one she left in—you remember that?"

"Don't be mean, John."

"It was her car. It was in her name."

"Oh," I said.

"That's one thing." He took a deep breath. "I know what you're going to say to this, because I know what you think—but a respectable man just doesn't list a Negro woman in his will as one of the major beneficiaries. Not if he's got children by her. He wouldn't embarrass his white children with his woods colts."

"I didn't know you knew about that."

He flushed impatiently. "Think for once, God damn it. Just don't ooze good will and female charm."

"Well, I didn't know."

"Look, honey, I don't know anything either, except maybe this one thing. He took care of Margaret. He gave it to her, years ago, I bet. He left her plenty to live on, and their kids too. Trust funds when they were in school or something like that."

"He never said anything."

"It's easy enough to do if you want." A tight little flicker of a smile: "And the gift tax is a lot less than the estate tax. That would amuse him too."

In about a month, Margaret sent me a message, as Oliver said she would.

That particular afternoon, I had been shopping. As I turned in our street I noticed a green-and-white Plymouth standing in front of the house. It was Margaret's car, license and all. I hurried into the kitchen, packages spilling out of my arms, expecting to see Margaret's heavy greying head. But there was only a slender dark boy, fifteen or so. I tumbled the packages to the counter.

"Didn't Margaret come?"

"No'm."

"Oh." I was disappointed. "It's her car."

"She sent me."

He was a handsome boy, and he looked familiar. "You related to her?"

"Her ma and my granny was sisters."

"You look like her."

"She sent me to carry a message to you."

"Fine," I said.

"She say to tell you that she is living at New Church, if you ever have need to find her."

"Where, exactly?"

He looked puzzled. "You can't say hardly, but anybody there'll show you. It's kind of back by the baptizing place on the river, sort of."

Automatically I began to unwrap the things I had bought. Two pairs of sneakers, a wad of blue cloth for a gym suit. They looked silly and forlorn on the bright yellow formica counter top.

"What else did she tell you?"

"That I got to make sure Mr. John ain't home before I come in."

That was Margaret, self-effacing, discreet. Margaret, dark and bitter. Except to my grandfather. And what had he seen that was hidden to everybody else?

"Is she living alone?" I asked the boy. "But she wouldn't be."

"No'm. My ma's there and me."

"Just three?"

"Well," he remembered, "when she first built the house, the old lady, her aunt, lived there."

"Not any more?"

"She swelled up and died."

"When Margaret first built the house, when was that?"

He scratched his head. "I wasn't nothing but a kid then. Six, seven years ago."

So that was how long ago my grandfather had given it to her. Oliver had known; he'd told me the truth.

"Well," I said, "tell her if she needs anything let me know."

"No'm," he said, "she don't have to work."

"Tell her anyway." John had been right, too. It had all been settled long long ago.

"She don't want nothing." His eyes flicked over me, curiously. After all, we were related in a way.

"Tell her something else." He turned around in the door. On his face the patient mocking mask of the Negro. "Tell her that I'll be coming up to see her. That there are some things I want to ask her."

There were so many things. . . . All the time we'd been in the same house, and not able to talk. So many things about her. About my grandfather. . . . How she'd met him, and how she'd come to move into his house, and how it had been during the thirty years she was there. And what it was like to send your children away, one after the other, when they were still so young. And never let them come back, so they wouldn't feel the blame of being a Negro. And never go see them, so they wouldn't have the weight of their mother's black face. They were white and she had made them that way.

Margaret's house in New Church was easy to find. I asked once at the gas station and then managed the dirt roads without a single mistake. It was a new house, four or five rooms and a wide lattice-covered porch. It was painted and neat, with a clean-swept dirt yard, and beds of petunias and lantanas growing at the front.

Even when we didn't talk (she was still a silent woman) we communicated. It was just in the air of that house, in the musky Negro-smelling air. I felt at home and comfortable. This was my mother, she had raised me, my grandmother too. . . . When I finally had to leave, she asked me quietly: "You tell Mr. John you was coming?"

For a second I considered lying, but then I couldn't. "No."

She didn't seem hurt or even surprised. "He's not like us." And as she said it, there were suddenly three of us, the other was my grandfather.

On the drive back, he rode right along beside me, telling me how it had been when he had lost his way in the swamp, and had to walk home from New Church. Not on the road (there was no paved road then), but on the trails over the ridges, through pines not touched by the lumberman, with fallen needles so thick there was no sound as you walked.

He was sitting beside me. I could see him. If I looked straight ahead at the road, he was there, right in the corner of my eye. Once I turned to look at him directly and he disappeared. The car swerved and the tires spun up yellow dust from the shoulder. *Watch the road, child,* he said. I didn't look at him directly any more after that, only peeped with the corner of my eye. And he stayed there. I could even smell the metallic odor his sweat had always had, a farmer's sweat, sun-dried on skin and cotton cloth.

I could talk to him too. *Why didn't you tell me anything? You didn't. Not one thing. You should have, you should have.*

By the time I got home that evening, I did understand. As if he'd explained to me at last. He'd protected and cared for so many females in his life, that he just looked on us as responsibilities and burdens. Loved, but still burdens. There'd been his wife, the vague little bumbling girl, who'd been so lovely and who'd died so young. There'd been my mother, who'd read poetry in a summerhouse and married a handsome Englishman, who'd come scurrying home, heartbroken, with another girl. She'd lingered around the house and around the bed until she died. And there was me, the orphan, and my two daughters.

Sometimes he must have felt that he was being smothered in dependents. There hadn't been a man of his blood in so long. And that must have worried him too.

All those clinging female arms. . . . And then there was Margaret.

Who was tall as he was. Who could work like a man in the fields. Who bore him a son. Margaret, who'd asked him for nothing. Margaret, who reminded him of the free-roving Alberta of the old tales. Margaret, who was strong and black. And who had no claim on him.

IN the years that followed, John worked harder than ever, building a solid foundation for his political career, building himself a statewide machine. "Going to be better than the one the Longs have in Louisiana," he told me once.

Of course, he was away more than ever. And once again, the year after my grandfather's death, I found myself suspecting, checking on him. I couldn't help it. I had to. Sometimes I fought with myself for hours. I would work frantically on the napkins I was monogramming and I would try not to look at the telephone, so squat and round and white there on the table. But the end was always the same. Biting my lip and shivering with disgust, I would call long distance and nervously tell them the number he'd left with me. The girls in the telephone office soon got to recognize my voice: "How you, Mrs. Tolliver? This is Jenny Martin." I knew them, of course I did. I knew all the girls—operators, secretaries, clerks—who worked in the white-shingled building across the square from the courthouse. I could see them gossiping between calls: "She keeps up with him, for sure. You suppose she's got reason?" I hated that. Hated to set them talking about me, to give them grounds for suspicion. But I couldn't help it. My arm always went weak, and my will betrayed me.

John didn't say anything for months. Finally, late one night, I reached him at his hotel in New Orleans. I had less to say than usual, even, and he was very tired and you could hear the rasp of irritation in his voice. "Honey, why'd you call?"

You could hear the annoyance and the nervousness and the waspishness in mine too. "Because I get lonesome and afraid when I'm pregnant."

In the silence my thoughts ran around my head, rattling like marbles: You're not sure, you're not sure. . . .

"I'll be damned," he said.

When he came home, he brought me a pearl necklace. "It's not the best," he said, "but it'll do for a while."

I needn't have worried. Soon there was the soft bland feeling of gestation, as my body and I settled down to the comfortable work of building another shape, bone by bone, little flecks of calcium forming, tissue growing, cell by cell, life pouring in through the cord.

I was placid and lazy, and John took charge of the remodeling of my grandfather's house. He brought an architect from New Orleans and the two of them worked for months over the plans. There was plenty of money now, and John used it well. I'd never known it was such an imposing house. John had been clever enough to go back to the original style, the massive solid farmhouse—of the sort that preceded the rage for Greek Revival. It was heavy and rather African, but it was beautiful. They'd also taken off most of the wings and sheds that had grown on it like mushrooms or barnacles over the generations. And they had cleared away the woods that pressed on it and crept up to it. You could see the river now, you could see the outline and the shape of the crest the house stood on.

Before we moved there, our son was born, and his name was John Howland Tolliver. He was a dark ugly baby, jolly and healthy. John sent me a diamond broach from Cartier. "A wonderful wife," the card said.

I was happy; I'd had a son at last. There seemed to be no more problems. Just a happy procession of days leading straight to the capital and that hideous governor's mansion with its ugly red brick walls, and its squat white columns.

I didn't tell John—I didn't want to bother him—when I had a message from Margaret saying Nina was dead. And I didn't tell him when I found out—later—that the news was wrong. I didn't understand what had begun to happen. That Margaret's children had finally grown up and were beginning to have a force and an effect of their own.

One afternoon—we were still living in town then—I took Johnny into the side yard. He was waving his absurdly thin arms and legs in the sun and giggling at the lights and shadows. I was twisting his thick black hair around my finger and making faces at him when I heard heels on the stepping stones behind me. I saw a tall, very tall, red-haired woman, well-dressed, as a northerner is well-dressed. She seemed familiar—yes, very—but I did not know her. So I handed the baby a rattle and went to meet her, wondering who she was. She stopped, waiting for me; she expected me to recognize her. "Yes," I said, "can I . . ." And I recognized her at the very time she said softly: "I'm Nina."

The girl I had played with, who'd run the pasture and chased the cattle, had hunted lamb's-tongue lettuce and pulled dandelion greens for supper, found thickets where deer had lain, sniffed the musky odor of snakes—the girl came back a woman. She stood smiling at me eagerly; she was very beautiful. She looked—somehow—Greek. I blurted the first thing I thought: "Your mother said you were dead."

Her face emptied out, like a glass, quickly and smoothly. "I know she did."

"Who could have told her that? . . . Who'd be so mean? . . . But come inside. I'll take the baby."

Nina shook her head. "We've just come from New Church, and we'll go along. My husband's never seen the South and we thought he should."

I said apologetically: "Margaret didn't mention your marriage. She really didn't."

"I sent her a wedding picture—when we were married a few months ago." She started to say something more. But she shrugged and let the words flutter off her tongue unsaid.

"When I was in New Church—I brought the baby to see her—she seemed fine."

"Did you see her?" Nina asked politely. "The door was locked and the shades were pulled the very minute we came in sight."

In his stroller the baby chirped and waved his fist at a beam of light. And what was wrong? . . . "I can't imagine why," I said truthfully.

"Come to the car, and meet my husband," Nina said.

We walked on the carefully placed stepping stones through the side yard, past the thick hydrangeas with their heavy sagging blue flowerheads. We came around the house and cut across the front lawn. Nina's husband saw us coming and he opened the door and stepped out to meet us.

And then I saw what had happened, then I knew why Margaret called Nina dead.

Nina's husband was a Negro. Tall, strikingly handsome, but very dark and unmistakably a Negro.

It made sense, then, it all made sense. I shook hands with him mechanically, not even hearing his name.

Nina said with a harsh laugh: "You look just the way my mother must have looked when she got our wedding picture."

"Really," I tried not to show that I was annoyed by the sharp edge in her voice, "I *am* dumbfounded. How could I know? I heard you were dead, and now it seems you're alive and married too."

"And you think she might as well be dead as married to me," he added quickly.

I looked at that handsome dark face and I thought: I don't like him, I should pity him, but I don't even like him. "Well," I told him evenly, "you said it, I didn't."

They both got into the car. Nina leaned across her husband: "Tell my mother you saw us."

"No," I said. "I won't. I won't do that."

She lifted her carefully shaped eyebrows.

"I never could stand self-pity." I was furious now; my voice was shaking and that made me even more angry. I did not want them to know that they had the power to make me that upset, to disturb me that much. "And I'm not going to pester an old lady just to give you a thrill."

Nina's pecan-colored eyes flickered a moment. "We shouldn't have come."

"Margaret didn't ask you to come. Nobody sent for you."

They would call me a white bigot. Let them, I thought. To hell with them and all their problems. I marched back into the yard. I yanked the baby out of his stroller and stomped into the house. I went straight to the bar in the corner of the living room. I plunked the baby down on the rug without a word and poured myself a stiff drink. He watched me, too amazed even to cry.

I soon forgot about Nina. I had my own life, my own excitements. We moved to the Howland place that summer when the house was finally finished. It was so elegant now, quiet and dignified and obviously very expensive. It was a magnificent house for entertaining, the house of a man who knows what his future is. I worked hard on the decorating, and John was pleased. "Looks great, old girl," he said lightly. "You've got good taste."

He so seldom complimented me that I felt myself blushing.

"You look prettier when you do that," he joked. "You should always be doing a house. Agrees with you."

My grandfather wouldn't have recognized his place and he wouldn't have recognized the life that went on inside it. He'd never kept any servants to speak of. He didn't like people around his house, so he didn't have them—though everyone in town was shocked. The matter of servants is so very important around this county, this state—kind of like stripes on a uniform sleeve. When John and I were living in town, we kept two, a cook and a nurse for the children—and people clucked and thought that awfully stingy of us. Out at the Howland place, we had a proper staff, and people were finally content. My Aunt Annie, who was now a very very old woman, her fat jolly flesh all melted away with age, paid one duty visit to us and nodded her pleasure. "First time this house has looked like anything since your great-grandmother's time. Where'd you find a trained butler out in this wilderness?"

"John hired him in Atlanta."

"Stole him from one of my friends?" she wheezed with amusement. "He's a love."

She could have meant John and she could have meant the butler. I didn't ask.

She sat on the front porch and had bourbon and three lumps of sugar in an old-fashioned glass. She was at it steadily all day, so she was quite drunk by the time we put her on the plane home. Her great-grandson, who was with her, steered her to the steps very carefully, winking at me as he went. Aunt Annie looked at me too, her thin emaciated face still holding something of the Howland look. And she stopped with one foot on the ramp, puffing, and said loudly: "This boy's something of a prick, but he's the only one I got home now. He still winking over my shoulder?" She didn't expect an answer. "Of course he is."

She heaved herself up the steps and disappeared into the plane. She died a month later and that was the last of my close family.

Even John's parents, dour and silent, visited us for two days. "They don't like it," he reported. "Smells too lush to be godly. Anything nice got to be sinful." He chuckled and kissed me. "Leastways they still think you're a good wife."

"It doesn't look like I'll be bothered with visiting in-law trouble."

"It's a long way to Tolliver Nation," he said. "And they don't take to traveling."

We were peaceful and smug and contented. Things went on smoothly, with only minor changes. Take John, for example. His plan was to run for governor when old Herbert Dade finished his term, and then go for the Senate. It didn't work quite like that. Things weren't changed, but they were delayed. Herbert Dade, who was a political power the like of which people had never seen and whom most people compared to Huey Long in Louisiana, got the state constitution changed, so he could—and he intended to—succeed himself. I thought John would be annoyed, but he only laughed. "Honey baby, the old boy has ulcers and high blood pressure and he's started having strokes already. He can get himself this new term but he sure as hell can't get himself to finish it."

And there was another reason that he didn't mention. Dade was naming John his political heir. Day after day in the papers you saw pictures of them together. I can even remember Governor Dade's flat drawling old man's voice saying: "This young fellow here thinks more like me than I do myself."

John changed his plans slightly. He ran for the state senate and old Dade campaigned for him. That fall, Dade was re-elected by something like three to one. John was elected by something like eight to one.

About a week after the elections, late one night, after all the fuss had died down, I found John working at his desk. He had made one wing of the house into an office. In those four rooms, he kept two clerks and four secretaries. Officially his office was in town, but most of the work was done here. He wanted to keep the business and the clatter out of sight—to keep his official office carefully sparse and simple. Country fashion, he would say. He had even found a beat-up desk that belonged to his grandfather and moved it in. It brooded over the office, a hideous carved yellow oak thing. . . .

On this particular night, the children were asleep, and I was reading. All of a sudden the house seemed so empty and so lonesome that I went looking for John. I found him studying a breakdown of the election returns. He was doing it very carefully, polling place by polling place. He took off his glasses, and rubbed at his eyes. They were red with strain. "I was just coming in, honey."

"How does it look?"

He grinned, and it was the good, slightly lopsided real grin that he gave to the children and not to the photographers. "They came through fine all right, white and black together."

"You did as well in the Negro precincts?"

"You shouldn't sound so surprised, honey, it isn't flattering."

"But the Citizens Council and that sort of thing."

He chuckled again, the wise and knowing chuckle of a politician. "I'm just behaving the way a white man is supposed to behave. White and black both know it."

"Did they count the votes? Really count them honestly?"

"Mostly, I think; they're machines, honey child." He turned serious. "Long as you've been in this state, you haven't figured it out, have you?" He folded his glasses and put them in the leather case he always carried in his breast pocket. "The Negroes figure I'm not old Judge Lynch himself—and I've tried my damndest to see that they get that message straight. And everybody in the district pretty much knows about your grandpa's bastards. That counts for something, I guess. As for the white people, well, they think I'm for just about whatever they're for. And I've told 'em that myself."

He popped up from his chair, grinning happily, and he looked an awful lot like the man I married fourteen years before. "Woman," he said, "let's go to bed."

He was still the most attractive man I'd ever known. I remember that night, even now. I always think of it as the end of the happy times. And in a way it was—though there were some quiet months left to us.

Once I saw the boy who had brought me the first message from Margaret. He was standing outside the Woolworth store on Main Street. He had bought a couple of things, neckties and a baseball cap, and he was checking their colors in the daylight. He didn't see me, he was so busy, and he jumped when I spoke to him. "How's Margaret?" I asked.

He looked so very surprised that I wondered if I had the wrong boy. But I couldn't have.

"You're the boy she sent," I told him. "Aren't you living with her any more?"

"Yes'm."

"How is she?"

"She didn't give me no message this time."

His dark eyes had gone opaque like mirrors. "Don't be the impenetrable African," I said. "I just asked you how she is. . . . Do you know what impenetrable is?"

He shook his head, and I felt silly for snapping at him. He was only a boy after all, and I had pretty much jumped on him. "I didn't mean to startle you. I just want to know if she's well."

The eyes didn't change character at all. "She's an old lady, Miss Margaret is, and they got their aches and pains."

"You mean she's sick."

"No'm." I could almost feel the evasion, his mind rolling away like a drop of water on oil.

"What do you mean?"

"She been low in her mind, you might say."

"Well," I said, "it can't be easy for her." And then I saw my two daughters running across the town square. They had been to the dentist and they each had a huge yellow balloon with the black lettering: "Dr. Marks Happy Friends."

"Tell Margaret hello for me," I said, and walked toward my own children, who were waiting impatiently at the corner for the light to change. It was the only traffic light in the whole town, and they always went to cross at that corner. They enjoyed it more.

Half an hour later as we walked toward the car to drive home, me holding the balloons and feeling the queer live tug of their strings in my hand, Abby asked: "Who was the boy you were talking to?"

"I don't know, honey. I didn't ask him."

I had done what most white people around here did—knew a Negro and dealt with him for years, and never found out his name. Never got curious about who he was, and what he was called. As if Negroes didn't need identities. . . .

Margaret died. Four years after my grandfather, on the very day when he had collapsed over the wheel of his truck and died in the woods. The anniversary of that day was bleak and cold and wintry, with everyone huddled inside by their fires. Margaret had not gone out all day. She never did any more, not even into the yard; she didn't seem to care. In the late afternoon, just after the watery winter sun slipped behind the southwest ridge, she put aside her tatting and got up from her rocker. "Somebody calling outside," she said. And she went, without a coat or a shawl, though the ground was already lightly frozen and crackled under her heavy steps.

Her cousin and the boy waited patiently. At midnight, the boy bundled up and took a flashlight and looked for footprints in the frosty ground. He found them at once. They led straight down the slope toward the trees and the winter-slowed creek. He followed them across the open places, but he hesitated at the dark of the trees —the beam of his flash seemed too small. He turned and scurried back to the house, his hands shaking and his face grey. He refused to go back again. He smelled death, he said.

He and his mother together—because neither of them would stay alone in the house—got into Margaret's car and drove down the road to their family. They spent the night there, and in the morning, they got seven or eight people together and came back to hunt for her. It did not take long. Her steps were plain for everybody to see. They followed them through the trees to the creek and down the creek to the crumbling old brick baptistry. In the morning light the pool had the leaden look of water about to freeze. There, in the leaf-littered, twig-crusted, leaden-green depths they found her. She was bobbing gently to the flow a couple of inches below the surface. She was face down and her arms were spread as if she were flying. Since the baptistry was so deep and they didn't know how to swim very well, any of them, they poked and dragged at her body until they maneuvered it close to shore. Then they lifted her out. She was a big heavy-boned woman and even heavier in the stiffness of frozen death—and the ground was uneven and broken with chunks of rock and bits of branches, and covered and slippery with ice—so they stumbled and dropped her. It seemed to them at that moment she was twisting away from them, was twisting back toward the pool.

Margaret's cousin screamed and ran, her son right behind her. The others, grown men and women that they were, murmured a little rush of words and hurried after them. Even the preacher ran, though he wasn't supposed to be afraid. (His name was Boyd Stokes and his father and his grandfather had preached in New Church in their time.) They all waited an hour or more, standing in the bare empty field, stamping their feet on the frozen ground, and watching toward the wall of trees, as if they were waiting for someone to tell them what to do. After a bit they sent for whiskey. The sun warmed their backs; the shadows shortened, the trees didn't look quite so dark any more; and the likker warmed their souls. Boyd Stokes said a quick prayer and they did what decent people had to do: went back and gathered up the muddy, bruised, leaf-plastered body and brought it into the house.

That was all. That was the end of the girl my grandfather had met on a cool morning washing clothes in a little creek that didn't have a name. When she died, she was an old woman—though she wasn't all that along in years—tired and sick, and there wasn't any part of the world that looked familiar or comforting to her. I wonder now what it was like living for four years, not wanting to, only waiting for your hold to weaken so you could finish up and leave.

John was surprised that I didn't cry at the news. I couldn't explain to him, but it wasn't like that. This was the order re-establishing itself. This was the way I'd known all along it would be, without realizing it. It wasn't something you cried over. You didn't even grieve in the ordinary sense of the term. You just curled up where you were, curled up in pain and fear, and you stayed shriveled and shivering.

John didn't say anything, he was only a little more solicitous. He called me twice a day now, when he was away. And he made special plans to be home when the baby was born—I was pregnant again. It was a horrible time. I never knew whether it was the baby moving or my own fear shaking me inside. I didn't sleep, because Margaret lurked around the corners and the dark spots of all my dreams. She even called to me out of the color-streaked ether-filled cold when the child was born.

It was a girl and I called her Margaret. I expected John to object, but he didn't. "Lay her ghost?" he said.

And that was the thing with him. Just when you thought he was stupid and dense, he would come up with the answer, and he would put it in its bare true terms, the way you hadn't been able to phrase it yourself.

Margaret had not kept the addresses of her children. Her cousin (I found out finally that her name was Hilda Stokes; she was the widow of the youngest of the seven Stokes boys) did not know them. I had a couple of old ones from my grandfather's records and I tried them, but the telegrams and the letters came back, unopened.

They—Robert, Nina, and Crissy—got the news some way. I've never known how. In the year that followed Margaret's death, they appeared, one by one, drifted back into my life. First, a letter from Nina, its only address a post-office box in Philadelphia. It was a single line on heavy white formal paper: "How is my mother?"

She had heard then. So I wrote across the bottom of the letter, not even bothering with a sheet of my own: "She killed herself January 30 last year." I didn't sign it; she would know. Also, I didn't tell her that it might have been an accident after all. A stumble on ice-slick rock. I didn't like Nina and I wasn't going to give her a shred of comfort. Even a tiny shred.

When I dropped it into the mailbox, I thought: Carry that now, and see how strong you are. Carry that behind your arrogant handsome face. Guilt for being a Negro, guilt for having a suicide for a mother. . . .

Nina'd come back to flaunt her marriage, to hurt Margaret. But Margaret was even, in their war of hurt and be hurt. I nodded to her wherever she was, and I almost found myself saying out loud to her: You've won one round. . . .

When the florist in town got a telegraphed order for fifty dollars' worth of flowers for Margaret's grave, I knew I had been right. Nina would ache with guilt the rest of her life, wondering how much she had done in her mother's death.

The florist sent the flowers, of course he did. He didn't want to, but he couldn't think of a reason, and he didn't dare not. He finally came out and asked me openly, nervously. "The telegram came from Philadelphia," he said. "I thought you might know if it's one of her children," and then because he felt he had gone too far, he added: "I been remembering that Margaret worked for your grandfather for years on."

"I don't know," I said, "but have you ever had a single fifty-dollar order before?"

He clucked with confusion, that funny little wispy man who had been florist in the shop just across the street from the county jail for as long as I could remember. People in little towns seem to live forever, drying up like crickets, chirping all the time. . . .

As I left him, I couldn't help smiling at Nina, egotistical self-centered Nina. She thought she had killed her mother. . . . And who could tell her otherwise? Who could tell her that my grandfather's dying had killed Margaret. That after his death, she found an earth of brass, and she hadn't been able to stand it. Who could tell Nina that it wasn't any of the children, that they weren't that important to Margaret, who had known from the moment they were born that she would send them away. No, Nina wouldn't be the sort to believe that people died for love, for weariness.

As I walked over to meet John at his office, I wondered: If he died, what then? But I knew he wasn't all I had. There were the children, and a house and land that had been in my family for a hundred and fifty years, and a round of duties, dull and familiar, but saving, if it ever came to that.

I might miss him, but I wouldn't die of him. That was the difference. Neither Nina nor I was like Margaret. Neither of us was as good.

A while after—a few months—Robert called. I was getting ready for bed—John was out again. The state legislature was in session and he had gone to the capital. I had a nasty cold—I was fixing a hot toddy when the phone rang. "Spokane calling Mrs. John Tolliver." I agreed mechanically, wondering who I knew in Spokane. I did not recognize the voice—how should I? "This is Robert Howland." For a moment that did not register either. He got impatient with my heavy breathing silence. "Margaret's son."

"Oh," I said, "for heaven's sake." Here he had always been called Robert Carmichael.

"Can you hear me?" He had a crisp midwestern voice. It came through the line as sharp and clear as a radio announcer's.

"Of course I can. I was just surprised. After all these years, both of you turn up."

"Who else?"

"Nina."

"What did she want?"

"Don't you know? Don't you see her?"

"I don't even know where she's living." I did not believe him, even when he added: "I don't think much of her husband."

"Neither did Margaret."

"I want to ask you about her. Is it all right or would you rather go to another phone?"

"Why?"

He sounded impatient again. "Is your line tapped?"

"Now who would tap my line?"

"Your husband's in politics. I've been seeing his name around one place or the other. His line might be."

I sneezed and my sinuses began a steady aching. "Oh for God's sake, Robert, everybody for miles around knows about Margaret and her children. What is there to hide?"

He hesitated for a moment, not saying something. Then he asked abruptly: "How is she? I heard she died."

"Who told you?"

"I don't remember."

"It was Nina," I said flatly, and he didn't contradict me. "I thought you'd keep in touch with her whether or not you liked her husband."

"Well, answer me," he said.

"She drowned herself on January 30th."

"Last year?"

"Yes."

"Where?"

"The creek by her house—they tell me. I didn't go over to see."

"Of course you couldn't go over."

"I can go wherever I please, and don't be such a fool."

The operator cut in. "Your three minutes are up. Please deposit . . ."

"Okay," he said, cutting across her voice. "I've got the change here." And there was the dull muffled clang of silver dropping into a pay box.

So he hadn't called from his home or his office, or even his hotel, if he was away traveling. He didn't want anyone to know.

In the renewed silence, he asked: "Did she leave a note?"

"Fixing the blame? No," I said. "You'll have to do that yourself."

"Did she leave anything for me?"

"If you mean money"—he didn't of course, but I wanted to be nasty—"she left the house and the land to the cousin who lived with her, and about a quarter of the money too, whatever she had from my grandfather. The other three-quarters she left to me."

"A will?"

Why did Margaret's children make me so angry? "How else could she leave it?"

"Nothing in it about me?" He hesitated, hating to lump himself with the others: "About us?"

"No. Of course not."

"I wondered."

"Don't you remember even that much about her? When you all left here, you were gone forever. She didn't have children any more."

"It's been a long time," he said slowly, "but I can remember that."

"She did it for you." That sounded so silly, but it was true.

"It might have been better if she'd kept us there."

His voice was as bitter as mine when I answered him. "Then you'd be a Negro in the South, grubbing in the mud."

"A quadroon."

"You've been reading books," I told him. "I never did hear anybody use that word here. You'd be a nigger to the white people, and you'd be a nigger to the blacks."

"I've thought of that," he said quietly.

"She did what she could," I told him, "and you wouldn't have the sense nor the courage to do the same." I slammed down the phone, ending his furtive call, and put my head down on the receiver and cried with fury.

I asked John when he came home the following evening: "Do you think our phone is tapped?"

"You've been hearing clicks?"

"I wondered."

He was going through the stack of mail that had collected for him over the past two days. "I wouldn't be surprised."

"You wouldn't?"

He shrugged and kept slitting the tops of letters, methodically. "Politics, honey."

"You mean it's usual?"

He looked up suddenly and grinned, a bright boyish grin that clashed with the streaks of grey at his temples. "Sometimes the people listening on my office phones can't help commenting on what we say. Now that we know they get angry, we always try something to see if we can't get them to join it."

I didn't say anything; I couldn't think of anything to say.

"After a while you get used to three-way conversations, honey."

"You didn't tell me."

He grinned again. "If you're having long passionate love calls, I thought I'd let the opposition gather my divorce evidence for me."

"Oh John, you should have. I might have said something."

"You couldn't, honey."

And I stopped. I couldn't indeed. I didn't know anything.

"After all," John said, "what does it matter if they know who we're going to have dinner with—they could get that much out of the servants for a few bucks. Or what you're going to send to the church fair, or if Mr. Shaughnessy sent you a lousy roast."

"You're right," I said slowly. "But I don't think I like that."

My grandfather had treated me the same way; but then I was a child.

John shrugged. "Why tell you things I know will upset you? Look right now . . . a little thing like a wire tap and you flip." He stood up and went to the bar, kissing me lightly on the ear as he passed. "A drink for you, Mrs. Tolliver."

The girls came home from dancing school. We could hear them tramp in, teasing Johnny and the baby until they roared with frustration.

"To them!" John lifted his glass toward the noise. "Is Miss Greer going to make dancers out of them?"

"No," I said. "She's trying, but they just don't have any sense of rhythm."

And then he asked what he had been wanting to ask: "Why are you worried about wire tapping all of a sudden?"

I sighed and tried to fish the cherry out of my old-fashioned. I kept getting the orange slice instead. "Margaret's son called today to ask about her, and he wanted to know if it was all right to talk."

John gave a short low whistle and relaxed. I wondered what he thought it might have been. "Everybody knows about your grandfather's woods colts."

"I told him that."

Finally I heard from Crissy. This time I wasn't surprised. I knew by now that those three kept in touch, in a manner of speaking. This was a postcard—Bois de Boulogne in spring—and a couple of lines in clear stiff board-like handwriting. (That writing reminded me that Crissy was left-handed.) "I have heard about my mother" (From Robert or Nina? I wondered), "and I wish to send my thanks for your trouble. I now live in Paris, the haven of American Negroes." She had not signed it, and she had started to fill in my address on the right side. When she was half through, she changed her mind, and put the postcard in an envelope. Careful and discreet. She wanted to avoid trouble for me. But then she had always been the gentlest and the nicest of Margaret's children.

There were a few more months, quiet baby-filled months. I could feel myself sinking into the deceptive softness of early middle age, the comforting round of house and four children, the sentimental wifely role in state politics. Sherries in the morning (little giggles because liquor was still illegal in most counties), coffees in the afternoon, weekends with the proper people. Baby showers, wedding showers. I drove up to the capital every week now, had tea with Mrs. Dade, lunch with three or four other women, and then did my hospital calls. It was the biggest hospital in the state and I always went by, always the same routine—John had told me precisely how to do it. A few chatty words with the grey ladies at the reception desk, a quick pass through the director's office, then the visits to the floors. There was even a special order for that: third floor, second floor, fourth floor, fifth and sixth, then the Negro wing. Third floor was surgical, the dramatic cases, they came first and nobody would object; second was the ordinary jumble of illnesses; fourth was obstetrics ("They won't mind being last of the paying group," John said, "because they'll be so delighted with the child"). Fifth and sixth were the ward floors, the charity floors. Finally the Negro wing, all floors. The first time I did it, I felt silly. I held my breath against the odor of sickness, and the look of pain. Finally I began to realize that these people were glad to see me. That my visits, however obvious their purpose, broke the monotony of hospital routine. John was delighted with my success. "What a campaigner you'll make," he said. I didn't like it. No, I never did, but I was able to do it.

I never drove back home the same day. It was too long and too hard; anyway John didn't like me driving alone at night. I stayed in the apartment he kept at the Piedmont Hotel. In the morning I stopped at one of the big department stores (finer than anything in our town) to bring the children something: clothes or new toys. Then I tossed everything in the car and drove home. I suppose I've made the trip two hundred times, but now that it is all over, I find that I only remember one. Out of all that, only one.

I woke up very early that morning, and the hotel bedroom was cheerless and drab. I hadn't slept at all well—I had been dreaming of my mother. I hadn't even thought of her for years and now all of a sudden there she was. It's funny how those things come back. And it's disturbing too. I couldn't remember what the dream was exactly, but it had something to do with her, and something to do with high grass and fireflies in the trees. It was a summer dream and it had some of that oppressive brooding quality summer nights have. Only in a dream it's worse.

Anyhow, I was awake, and I clearly wasn't going back to sleep, so I decided to go home. I woke the desk clerk and the one bellboy to get the car; I was in a hurry and nervous about it. I didn't really feel good until I was behind the wheel and on the way out of town, ignoring traffic lights because it was so early. The car was chilly, and I turned on the heater. Its little monotonous hum made me worry about falling asleep, as I always do when I am alone. So I turned on the radio. I got the usual early-morning program of hymns and yesterday's quotations from various markets. Soon I was out of the city and there wasn't anything but empty road unrolling in front of my headlights. It was still dark. I had no idea of time—I hadn't looked before I left. The dashboard clock never worked. My own wrist watch was stopped; I had forgotten to wind it. It must have been about four o'clock; since it was still early spring, dawn was fairly late. Some of the farmhouses I passed had lights in them, one or two sleepy lights; now and then, if the house was very close to the road, I could catch a whiff of frying through the small crack of my open window. Then those houses ended, and the road swung directly south through empty lumbering country. There was no traffic, no house lights; there wasn't anything except a stretch of concrete and stands of timber. There was just a black pre-dawn sky and two jabs of my headlights, the friendly glow of the dashboard, and the vibration of the heavy engine, straining slightly as I climbed hills without lessening speed.

I've always liked to drive alone at night. There is a sentimental brightness to things—it's a good deal like being drunk. I always see the world perfectly then, see it in all its great pathetic clarity. I become invincible, beyond life and death. With the hum of wheels under me, I can love the human race, as I never can at any other time. I can think great cloudy thoughts, and tremble with the power of life surging in me. I resolve then to have a dozen children and live forever. It seems possible.

I drove very fast. I knew, as everyone else did, that the highway patrols went home at three and didn't come back until seven. I was making very good time. The grades got steeper and I had to push a little on the accelerator to maintain speed—I was crossing the ridge of hills that separated the Great Central Valley from the smaller Providence Valley. The Providence River was the one you saw from the front of our house, the one that the first William Howland had followed when he was looking for a place to settle, the one he had named for his mother. I didn't believe I could have gotten here so fast. I slowed and opened the window and looked out. Pine trees, neat rows, neat fences, then a lumber road. I slowed even more and read the small identifying sign. It was the Eastman-Halsey tract, I was three-quarters of the way home.

I closed the window again, still puzzled by the distance I had come. I really should have looked at the speedometer. John would be furious if he ever found out.

But I didn't slow down. I came out of the mountain ridges and zoomed down the straight level road through Madison City. The courthouse, street lights burning at each of its four corners. Post office, street lights broken in front of it. John's office, shuttered and empty. (And how does the roll-top desk look in there, teetering on its too thin legs in the dark?) I startled a pack of dogs rooting in the garbage pails in front of the Happy Chicken Café. They bolted for the shadows, yelping. I passed Joe's Place, on the outskirts of town, closed and dark, except for the string of small lights burning in its parking lot. Just then the radio went off. Very suddenly, without static, without any warning, its sound stopped. The lights still burned and I pushed all the buttons and worked the dials. It had never happened before—it was a new car—and it was very annoying.

I do not like to drive alone without a radio. What had been fun turns into something mildly threatening. The dark, which had been filled with the pleasant empty-headed chatter of the machine, closed back—and this time it was filled with its own sounds, not with yours. The sounds of empty country and empty roads—depressing, a little frightening. I was happy that I was almost home and that dawn was almost breaking. The sky was already lightening. You could see that the day would be overcast, at least until the ground fog rose and burned away. I came to the bend at Thatcher's Creek and slowed down. No more than a mile now, I should see the house at the next turn. The sky was silvery-colored, fish-colored: the color of a swamp cat. The wild azaleas were blooming. I hadn't realized how many of them there were. Their sweet wet perfume slipped through the crack of the window. The fog had left the road very wet. I felt the wheels skid once, slightly. I slowed down still more. This valley often had fogs when the higher, drier mountains had none. The road curved up to our pastures, edged by a barbed-wire fence covered with tight pink sweetheart roses, not yet in bloom. And then I came to the last turn and looked up the slope of ground toward the house. Somehow I had gotten the idea that it would not be there, would have disappeared like a ghost. (Damn that radio, I thought.) But of course it was there. Vague and indistinct in the fog, but there, just the way it had been for the last five generations. It looked very very large in this light, and empty. Fog covered the fields beneath it, so that it seemed to float without solid ground, just exactly like those fairy castles in a child's story book.

I turned in the drive, through the great mass of azaleas John had planted. (When was that? Only six years ago?) These weren't quite in bloom, their wet leaves shone black in the fog. I drove faster, the gravel rattling off my tires, until I came to the end, and there was the yard familiar and safe, stretching in front of me, full of known things. A power mower, forgotten and left out overnight. A rake leaning against the house. A bicycle. Empty clothes lines, cords frayed and fluttering.

At that moment the radio went on again. Very loud. I listened for a minute, then switched it off. As I walked to the kitchen door, pulling the key from my purse, shivering a little in the morning chill, I began to wonder. And the more I thought, the surer I was. There'd been a message of some sort. Something had brushed right by me—for good or evil I didn't know. Because I hadn't understood.

I had rocketed through the night alone, something traveling with me. And I had come out all right. The empty roads had saved me from a high-speed accident. And my own spiritual denseness hadn't answered whatever it was that had called to me.

I went into my house and closed the door firmly behind me.

IT'S like this, when you live in a place you've always lived in, where your family has always lived. You get to see things not only in space but in time too. When I look at the Providence River, I don't just see a small yellow river that crests into flood every year and spreads its silt over the bottom cotton lands. I see old William Howland, adventuring his way along, fresh from a war, seeking a place to settle. I see him coming along through its canebrakes and its swamps, the thin homely face of the portrait that now hangs in the dining room. . . . I can't ever see the ridge that rises to the east without seeing more than the deep green of thick timber. I see Cousin Ezra Howland, shot through the middle at the battle of Tim's Crossing, fifteen miles away, during the Civil War, who got to the top of that ridge, and no farther. They said he'd left a fifteen-mile trail of blood. He slipped off his horse and died up there, in sight of his home. His mother and his aunt and his sister, who were in the house alone, they saw the hawks and the buzzards circling and went out themselves and found him. . . . When I drive to Madison City itself, I don't just see a small town with mangy dogs slouching about the gutters. I see the time when the bandit Whittaker brothers—all six of them—tied their boat at the river landing and came into town to rob and murder. When they left, to continue their way toward the Gulf coast, they took the daughter of the livery stable owner with them. People said it wasn't kidnapping, that she offered to go, so it was her own fault that she was never heard of again and that a skeleton found way south, beyond the swamps, was said to be hers.

That's the way it is with me. I don't just see things as they are today. I see them as they were. I see them all around in time. And this is bad. Because it makes you think you know a place. Because it makes you think you know the people in it.

Things fell out this way. Old Governor Dade, who lasted four years longer than John expected, finally died after two years of his third term. His lieutenant governor took the oath of office. His name was Homer O'Keefe, and he was a handsome, silver-haired man, who came from the southern part of the state. He looked respectable, as old Dade did not, and he had been put on the ticket to draw the votes of the respectable well-to-do groups. But he was a stupid pompous fool.

When John told me about Governor Dade's death, he said flatly: "Wait till you see the mess old Homer makes now." He chuckled to himself. "Anybody coming after him is going to be swept in like Jesus Christ on Palm Sunday."

He was right of course. I can't remember all of them, but there was a highway scandal, and a welfare scandal. An instructor at the State Teachers College was discovered to be a card-carrying Communist. A school in Plainview burned down and the parents of the dead children and all the rest of the state blamed Governor O'Keefe for that. A hurricane that seemed headed for Yucatán turned right around and smashed into the Gulf coast. And that same summer there was a polio epidemic that closed every swimming pool in the state, and it was an unusually hot summer. That was probably the worst thing of all.

John looked more and more smug as we went on our usual rounds through the passing months. "Isn't there something I can do?" I asked him once.

He winked. "You're doing great."

"I'm not doing a thing."

"Why should I spoil you by telling you how to do things? You're sweet and kind to everybody."

"Don't joke with me, John."

"Honey, you're perfect for the job, and that's why I married you."

I didn't say any more because I wasn't at all sure that he hadn't told the exact truth.

I did nothing extra or special in the last weeks before the primary. John was almost never home, and the house was quiet. I only saw a couple of reporters who wanted to see how a candidate's wife lived, and they were disappointed.

Once I got a phone call from my cousins Clara and Sam Hood. They were furious over the account of one of John's speeches an Atlanta paper had carried.

I talked to both of them at once; they always picked up both ends of an extension.

"Really, honey," Clara said, "he's gone too far this time."

"I haven't seen it," I said, "the papers here haven't carried it."

"I would think not," Sam said. "Did your grandfather own the papers too?"

"You know better."

"Maybe he really didn't say it." Clara asked: "Did he?"

"I don't know what you're talking about," I told them.

"The contents of the average Negro skull is 169 milligrams lighter than the average white skull. His brain casing is on the average some 121 millimeters thicker. He is simply not suited by nature for equality with the white man. . . ."

I interrupted. "I've got the idea."

"Honestly, my dear," Sam said, "this business of not wanting them to marry your sister was enough to get votes, wasn't it?"

Clara said: "I am really ashamed to be related to him. I thought I would die when the papers here carried that story."

"Is that what you called to tell me?"

"We just couldn't believe it," Sam said.

Clara said: "We thought it was somebody else or a mistake."

"I haven't the slightest idea," I said. "But I'll tell John you didn't approve of it."

"You can't be for things like that, not after the way your grandfather behaved."

"I am very busy," I told him. "I will call you back sometime later on."

When I hung up, my stomach was icy stiff. Anger or fear, I didn't know which. I went into the side yard, and stretched out in the sun there, waiting for the bright yellow rays to warm into my cold. I had plenty to do. I had the month's accounts to check out. I was supposed to call a man in Louisiana to say that we would buy his beautiful little roan Shetland for the children. But I did nothing. I lay still in the warmth and waited for it to seep through me. That sort of bodily cold frightens me. It reminds me of death.

John called the following day. "I got quite a spread in the Atlanta papers," he said. "I suppose you've heard from your cousins about it?"

"Yes."

"Those papers are no friends of mine," he said. "I was sure they'd jump on this one."

"Did you say that?"

"Sure," he said. "Did you notice where I was speaking?"

"No."

"The White Citizens Council."

"Oh," I said, "oh."

"Honey," he said, "I hope those bastards of cousins didn't upset you."

"It was what they wanted to hear, wasn't it?"

"Sure," he said. "The newspapers here won't carry it. And there won't be ten Negroes in the whole state who read the Atlanta papers. Anyhow," he chuckled, "my opponent's been saying a lot more rough stuff than that ever came close to being."

"The phone is tapped," I said.

"Honey child, they can hear this...." He laughed. "My esteemed opponent got carried away with his own eloquence yesterday, and came out in favor of lynching." He chuckled again.

"Oh," I said, "oh."

"I'll call you tomorrow, honey...."

"Yes," I said.

"I love you."

"I do too," I said.

"Just think how that's going to sound on their tape.... Just think what they can make of that: man and wife love each other...." He laughed again. He was in an effusive humor. "Whole state can hear me, bye."

I suppose that should have made me feel better, but it didn't. I felt sicker and sicker.

John did come home once during those last days of campaigning. He got a virus infection of some sort, and a very high fever. In fact he was quite giddy when he first came home, bringing with him a doctor and a huge supply of antibiotics. After a day the fever was gone, and he was gone too.

That one night and one day he was home, I brought him cups of hot broth and dishes of ice cream, and when we were alone, I asked him: "John, you don't think that about Negroes, do you?"

His bright blue eyes were sharp. "So your cousins have put the snake into Eden?"

"I want to know."

"That smaller heads and pea brain stuff. . . . I was quoting what's his name at the university. That lunatic biologist they bought themselves."

"But what do you think?"

He was serious now, very serious. "I'm a practical man," he said. "I've got to deal with things as they are. It's hell for them, but my saying so won't help them or me." He took the cup of steaming broth out of my hand and put it down on the bedside table. It left a celery-flavored trail in the air. "You want me to be a knight on a white horse fighting injustice. . . . But if I did, I'd be nothing but a politician without a job and a lawyer without a practice."

"But you don't have to stay here."

"I don't have a chance anywhere else, honey, and you know that. The connections are here, the help is here, your family and mine."

He was right. Of course he was right. Usually he teased me, but he was not teasing now. He had not shaved and his shadowed face looked gaunt and hollow.

"Why do you say things like that?"

"I say it because it's part of the game." He had rarely been this serious with me before. For a minute or two I saw the quiet rational calm man he was. "It's the credo, and though I don't like it, I don't mind it. I'm no worse than anybody else, and I'm maybe even a bit better."

He picked up the cup of broth and sipped at the scalding liquid. "That isn't enough for you, is it? But, honey, you can only work with things you're given." The doctor bounded in then, bringing swirls of fresh air. He'd been amusing himself playing shuffleboard outside with the children. He checked John's chest for the rattle of congestion, and gave him another capsule.

John said to me, over his shoulder: "That speech will win, honey.

I said so little before—and not even recently—that they wanted to know where I stood. That one speech is going to get the primary for me.

It did. He won by a very large margin. We forgot about the report the Atlanta paper had carried. We thought it had gone into the trash with the paper itself. There may have been just one clipping saved, but it was enough.

In our state the primary is the only real election. The one that is held in November against the Republican candidate is a gesture, and an empty one, toward the two-party system. The margin is usually something like thirty to one. John no longer worked so hard, nor traveled so much. It would be a matter of routine from here in.

I sat in the quiet familiarity of my house, the house where I had lived as a child, in a country I had known as a child, and I was happy and content. My children were healthy and my husband successful.

We didn't know. We didn't know.

That fall our daughters went back to school—Abigail to the seventh grade, Mary Lee to the sixth. Johnny began nursery school. Only the baby Marge and I were left. One day, abruptly, John phoned.

"Have you noticed anything amiss?"

"No. I don't think so."

"Any calls?"

"There are always lots of calls, John."

"Anything you'd notice?"

"You mean crank calls, or threats?"

"No. Not like that. Not necessarily."

"But what?"

"The line is tapped," he said shortly.

"But they'd know anyway, wouldn't they?" We always said they, and I was never sure who really listened to the taped transcriptions of our conversations.

"Well," I said, "if you want to make sense to me, I guess I'll have to come down to your office."

"Come on," he said.

He was standing impatiently waiting in the patch of sun on his front doorstep. "Why did you have to bring her?" He meant the baby.

"John, she likes to ride."

"Leave her with Miss Lucy, then, and come inside."

So Marge was left on Miss Lucy's desk, shaking a box of paper clips. We went into John's office, where that hideous roll-top oak desk stood. I sat in the big cool leather chair while John paced up and down.

"There's something wrong," he said. "You can feel it all around."

"I don't know."

"My father called this morning." He let the sentence hang unfinished.

"Did he know anything?"

"He'll find out," John said, "he's always been able to do that."

"Look," I said, "be practical. What could it be?"

"Damned if I know."

"Tax trouble?"

He looked at me scornfully and snorted, not even bothering to answer.

"A mistress?"

"Don't be a silly jackass."

"You haven't killed anybody?"

"As a matter of fact," he said levelly, "it's got something to do with you."

"Did Papa John tell you that?"

"He's not the only one hearing," John said, "that there's something funny about Mrs. Tolliver."

"Well," I said, remembering Papa John and his close-set blue eyes and his leathery wrinkled face, "I don't have a lover and the children have all been normal, and I don't have any close family still alive."

"I've been asked about it four or five times in the last few days. Nobody knows what, but they all know it's something."

"We'll just have to wait and see what it is, if it's anything," I said. "Maybe you've got a bad case of nerves."

John whistled quietly in and out of his front teeth. "It's something," he said, "and they're leaking it out, while they check back to be sure they've got it right."

"If they're going to lie about you, why would they check?"

"It's not going to be a lie this time," John said grimly. "And I wish to God I knew what it was."

The cigarette he had just tossed into the ash tray fell to the rug. I picked it up, ground it out. "It would have to be a lie."

He stopped dead in his tracks, stopped stock still in his pacing. He looked at me as if he had never seen me before, as if I were something under a microscope. We had been married fifteen years and he simply stood there and stared at me, cold blue eyes and strain lines pulling around his mouth. "Are you so sure?" he said.

I didn't believe it. I just sat staring at him, in a bit I opened my mouth and then closed it again. I couldn't think of anything to say.

After a minute, he said: "Go on home, I've got work to do."

Mechanically I got up. As I left, he asked quietly: "What have you done?"

The door was open, Miss Lucy heard. Behind their heavy glasses her eyes jumped toward me.

Why did he do that, I thought, why did he do that?

I only said: "Thank you for keeping the baby. I hope she didn't interrupt your work too seriously."

Her lips smiled and her eyes didn't. She's in love with John, I thought, but there must be a lot of women around the state who are.

"Will you be home for dinner?" I asked him.

"I told you," he said, "I'm speaking in Longview."

"So you did. . . . Wave bye to Daddy." I pumped the fat arm up and down. At our car I looked back. John was standing in the open door watching us leave just as he had watched us come. And he wasn't seeing his wife and his youngest child, he was seeing some dark nameless horror.

Marge settled in her seat beside me. I studied myself in the car mirror. I didn't look different. I always looked this way. I had the sort of face nobody remembered an hour after seeing it. (They remembered John, of course: he was dark and thin and striking. He looks a good bit like a monk, one flower-hatted lady had told me not too long ago.) Though no one had ever bothered telling me, or probably even thought of it, I knew from my pictures that I had been a plain child. And I was still plain. No, I was pleasant-looking. Brown hair, neither light nor dark, just the color of a mouse's coat. Blue eyes, no black-streaked depths (like John's), no brilliant china flash (like my grandfather's), just ordinary eyes, under straight brows. Nice teeth, fine skin tanned lightly by the sun. And my figure, well, breasts that were too small and hips that were too large —a matronly figure: I carried myself that way, and I knew it. And this was why I had got on so well with the women. I was motherly. . . . I knew what John meant: I was the perfect wife for a candidate. He had chosen and trained me well.

I wondered what the rumors were about. Nothing, I told myself furiously. I had done nothing. Nothing anyone could object to. I had chosen the wrong man, but nobody would know that but me. And I had just found out. . . .

I drove home, wondering how many hundreds of times I had gone that same highway. I hardly heard the baby drooling and jabbering beside me, I was busy with my own bitter thoughts.

They all ran more or less in this path. John had married a wife for his career. Had there been anybody else? Was it the girl he'd been dating when he first met me? The date he had broken to take me to dinner that first time. And did he remember her, the girl he had given up because I had been able to offer him more? . . . I had bid for him, all that openly. Those long spring evenings when we sat in my car. Never putting in words, but fighting my unknown competition silently, listing wordlessly the things I would give to him. . . .

I knew it then, of course I did. But I hadn't minded. I really hadn't. It just seemed the way of things. And now I wasn't so sure. Thoughts will do that sometimes. Once they have gotten close to you, you can never push them off to the old comfortable distances again. It wasn't new, but it hurt now. It hadn't ever before.

Are you so sure? What did you do? . . . John would never have said that, had he not been upset and afraid. But they were said, and that was that. The old structure of innocence—childish, it was—disappeared. He was no longer the husband I loved, he was simply the man I had married. I think now that it was amazing that it had lasted those fifteen long years.

Like my mother, I thought, only hers didn't last this long. Everything ends sometime, I told myself as I drove up to the house, and the hounds came running over to plant their muddy feet on the fenders.

There were two more days of waiting. The first day John called, as he always did. "Tell him I'm in the shower," I said. He said he would call back later if he could. He didn't.

On the morning of the second day, quite early, before the children had gone to school, I noticed a car come up the front drive and stop. The butler had not yet got to work, so I answered the door myself. It was a young man, and I had never seen him before. I didn't even recognize the different family strains in his face as I can so often do. He was just a neat young man in a grey suit. The black Chevrolet behind him wasn't familiar either.

"I was to deliver this," he said, and handed me a plain brown envelope, unmarked and very clean.

The children were laughing over breakfast in the dining room. I closed the door on their voices, and stood and watched the black Chevrolet drive down the hill. I sat down in one of the rockers and studied the slopes tending off toward the river, the river the first William Howland had named for his mother. And finally, I looked in the envelope: two pieces of paper, clipped together. One was newsprint. I looked at it first. It was the front page of the capital's evening paper, dated for the coming afternoon. There was a picture of a man getting off a plane, blurred as newspaper pictures always are. The headline was larger than usual: *Negro returns to visit his legal white family.* And then a subhead: *Past of prominent citizen comes to light. Gubernatorial candidate involved.*

I didn't read the fine print. Instead I looked at the second piece of paper. It was a photostat of a certificate of marriage. Between William Howland and Margaret Carmichael. The place was Cleveland. The date was April 1928, two months before Robert's birth.

I sat on the bright sunny porch and heard John's words over and over again: "Are you sure? What have you done?"

I phoned John's office. Miss Lucy sounded like she had been crying. "Will you tell my husband that I have seen the papers." Luckily I had no more to say, because she hung up on me.

I put the clipping and the photostat back in their crisp clean brown envelope and slipped them under the phone, thinking what I had always known: that my grandfather had been a good man. That he had found a woman to fill the last decades of his life and that he had married her. A good man. And when I thought of what would happen now, I felt sick.

I kept the children from school. I sent them down to the barns to amuse themselves with Oliver. I could see them riding their ponies in the near pasture lots, clumsy figures on fat clumsy ponies. The phone rang. "I'm not home," I told the butler. "Unless it's Mr. Tolliver."

Not that I expected him to call. I wasn't even sure that he'd come back. He might, when the hurt and shock had lessened. But not soon.

All around the house things went on as if it were just another day. The gardeners came and mowed the lawn and set out new daffodil bulbs in the azalea beds. They brought up two large drums of gasoline from the pump by the barns—they parked tractor and flat-bed trailer out of sight behind the bathhouse. Tomorrow they would use that gas for their equipment. They would mow the large front field, they would grade the road too. Bringing the gas drums to the work area had been John's idea—save time and trouble, he said. He'd had a lot of good ideas. The greenhouse, for one, that he had built outside the library door. He grew lovely exotic plants, tending and propagating them himself whenever he was home. The glaziers were repairing some cracked panes there now—any cold leak would ruin the plants—their hammers were tapping gently. In the house itself there were the comfortable familiar sounds of vacuum cleaner and floor polisher, the smell of furniture polish and floor wax. I sat in a chair in the living room, the big one by the fireplace, not doing anything, not even thinking. Just waiting. I was cold. I went to the hall closet and took the first coat I saw. It was my fur, and I huddled inside it, one hand holding the mink tight at my throat. I sat quite alone in an empty room, wrapped in the skins of dead animals.

Oliver came up from the barns and peered in the living-room window, tapping the sill. "I reckon I would close the gate."

"Yes," I said. I watched him walk down the graveled road to swing shut the heavy wood gate, locking it. He came back and handed me the key. "Oliver," I asked, "did you know?"

He shook his head.

"Keep the children close enough to the house."

I put the key on the hall table. The phone rang—almost under my hand—and I picked it up without thinking. It was my cousin Clara in Atlanta. "What is going on, Abigail?" she demanded breathlessly. "What is going on? What's all this we've been hearing?"

"Where's Sam?" I asked her. "I thought you all always talked on the phone like Tweedledum and Tweedledee."

"He hasn't heard. He's working on next week's sermon and I haven't dared tell him."

I laughed in her face and hung up. I kept on chuckling, because it really was funny, when you thought about it. She was in for such a bad time. She was jibbering right now.... She hadn't liked John's white supremacy speech. But how would she like having a jet-black Negro for an aunt? . . .

I sat on the fragile little rosewood chair and reached under the table to the telephone box at the baseboard. I pushed down the handle and turned off the bell. I'd had enough.

More cars than usual seemed to be driving by on the state highway. They'd come to see. Of course. When the paper came out at noon, there would be even more.

I wasn't angry or hurt. I wasn't anything except numb. I didn't seem to be in my own body any longer. I was very far off, watching, curious, but not involved.

I had lunch with the children. We talked about horses and about the new Shetland their father had promised them. I said I would order it by phone that very afternoon. Then they went back outside.

I drifted through the afternoon and the evening in the same way, detached and quiet. After dinner, the servants went away, leaving only the children, their nurse, and me. When the doorbell rang, I opened it, and stood blinking in the sputtering flash of bulbs.

I would have recognized him anywhere. He was a red-haired version of William Howland. "You must be Robert," I said. He stood and let me look. "I've been expecting you." When I said it, it seemed true. And I suppose I had, all day in the house, all the long day's waiting. "Come inside."

There were two photographers, standing to either side. Their bulbs had blinded me. "You too," I said. "It will be chilly waiting on the porch."

We went into the living room, the four of us. "It's changed," Robert said.

"We remodeled. Would you like some coffee?" I asked the photographers.

"No," they said.

"There is plenty," I said. "I really expected more people. . . . but then there *were* more out there, weren't there? I think I saw someone dodge back."

"I suppose they've gone back to the car," Robert said.

"The gate was locked. Did you drive through it?"

"We walked," Robert said.

"Would you like a tour of the house? It's so different, I don't think you'll recognize much."

"I didn't come for that," Robert said.

I looked at this child that my grandfather and Margaret had produced. You could see both of them there. The heavy-boned figure was my grandfather, all Howlands had those heavy stooped shoulders, and that same shaped head. And the blue eyes were my grandfather's too. Robert looked like my grandfather, feature by feature, but there was a mist of Margaret spread over everything. There was nothing of hers you could put your finger on and say: that came from Margaret. She was everywhere, in his face, in his movements, intangible but all-present, as much as her blood running in his veins.

He told the photographers bluntly: "I'll meet you at the car." They went quickly. Robert nodded after them. "They're glad to go. Seems they were scared."

"Not scared, Robert," I told him. "Just disgusted. You're a Negro to them."

His skin, which already had a waxy cast to it, went dead white. I think at that minute he wanted to kill me.

I didn't care. All through the long empty day I had been preparing for this, and now that it was here, I wasn't tired, I wasn't afraid. I felt elated and strong—it was something in Robert's face. It was something that told me. . . .

"Killing me wouldn't help," I said. "And your mother and your father are already dead."

"Did she really kill herself?"

"That's what the people say who found her."

It bothered him, the way it bothered Crissy and the way it bothered Nina.

"Do you know why? Was she sick?"

"I expect she got tired of living alone."

"She wasn't alone. You said she was living with a cousin."

"But alone. . . ." I got up and went to the bar. "A drink? Bourbon or Scotch?"

"No," he said.

"For old times' sake." I fixed two bourbon-and-sodas. "In memory of the time your mother gave you pneumonia taking you out in the sleet with chicken pox.

"She didn't."

"Of course she did." I waved the two glasses around, and for some reason I slipped into my best ladies' tea party accent. "She was going to educate you or kill you."

"I know that," he said quietly, and he took the drink I offered.

His tone stopped me. "Robert," I said seriously, "why did you come back?"

My grandfather's face looked up at me, misery-streaked and lined with pain. "I suppose it was a clipping from an Atlanta paper."

"Oh," I said. "Oh God, that one."

"I suppose I couldn't stomach that."

"John said that, sure," I told him, as patiently as if it would make a difference, "but did you see what his opponent said? Did you?"

"No."

"You've been out of the South too long. . . . The papers don't usually pick up what is said at those small rallies."

He just sat staring at his drink.

"You look incredibly like your father," I said.

"I never doubted my mother's word."

"You've even got the marriage certificate to prove it."

"You've seen it?"

"Couldn't you guess? That was the first thing they sent out to me."

"I suppose."

"You married, Robert?"

He nodded.

"Black or white?"

Again the flash of anger under his skin. "Don't provoke me."

"How would I know? Nina married a Negro."

He appeared not to have heard. I went on, innocently, beginning to see already what it was I should do.

"I'm curious," I told him. "I can't help that. After all, we did grow up together, in a way."

A short nod of agreement. He was staring at a small heavy table. "That was in the upstairs hall."

"I remember. It's really quite a fine Seignouret piece, so I had it refinished."

"There were two up there."

"The other one was too far gone. . . . What's your wife like?"

"She's fine."

"What does she look like?"

"Something like you. The same color hair, and light blue eyes. Her name was Mallory and her father is a radiologist in Oakland. She's about your age too."

"I'm a million years old," I said. "Drink your bourbon. It will help."

"Yes."

"John will lose," I said abruptly, "because of you. For the first time in fifty years the results of the Democratic primary will be upset in the election. There's no doubt in the world that the Republican will win by a landslide."

"I suppose."

"You said that before. . . . Do you know the Republican candidate?"

"I don't even know his name."

"That's a pity," I said. "You should."

Again he didn't seem to hear.

"Do you know about the schools in Tickfaw County closing last year."

"I don't even know what you're talking about."

"But you should. . . . They closed the schools rather than integrate under court order."

"Oh."

"They opened private schools for the whites. I don't think there are any schools for the Negroes."

He shrugged. "I heard of something like that in Virginia."

"This is right here. And the moving spirit of that particular bit was Mr. Stuart Albertson."

"Who the hell is that?"

"The man you just made governor."

I allowed myself a chuckle. Things really were funny if you looked at them right. "Child of my heart," I told him, "you have really done it this time. You got rid of John and got something ten times worse. . . ."

He was staring at me, not quite believing.

"But you didn't come back to help the Negroes around here. Or hurt them either." I had another irresistible fit of giggling. "You're doing it for more personal reasons, you're paying off an old grudge. Your mother or your father?"

"They're dead."

"Makes it harder that way." I fixed myself another drink, very slowly, waiting to see what he would do. He seemed frozen or fixed. He was staring at the refinished Seignouret table.

"Does your wife know you're here? But she doesn't, of course. She doesn't know anything about this or you wouldn't have called me from a pay phone."

He shook his head. "Why should I bother her with this mess?"

"She home?"

"Yes. . . . No, she's gone to the hospital to wait for the child. She's Rh negative, and they're all born that way, with transfusions and so forth."

"So she wouldn't be likely to read the papers too closely, if the papers there carried it."

"No."

"Anyhow the papers always call you Robert Carmichael. She wouldn't think anything of that, would she, even if she saw it?"

"Why should she?"

"She married a white man," I said quietly, "what would she do if she found out he was a Negro?"

He just stared at me.

"You won't have told her. . . . No, not you. But when she knows, what sort of a difference will it make?"

He stood up and walked over to me, his face flushed waxy white again. I sat perfectly still and leaned my head back and looked at him. I was not afraid, my heart was pumping steadily, my lungs were pulsing gently.

"You forgot, Robert," I told him, "or you wouldn't have come. We're all together, you and me and Crissy and Nina. You came to ruin me"—I could feel my lips giving a slow smile (and that was another thing, when my lips moved, I felt how cold they were)—"but I can do that too, I think."

Now that he was so close I could see that his face was covered with sweat. The drops had gathered into streams on his neck; they were soaking his coat collar.

"I can find you, wherever you live. I can appear there, just the way you've appeared here. And I can tell my story. . . . How much does your wife love you?"

Upstairs the baby wailed and then fell silent. Robert jumped and glanced toward the sound.

"I'm not saying I will do that," I told him, "I am only saying that I could, if I wanted to. I haven't made up my mind yet." It will depend on how angry I am and how much I want to hurt you in return, I thought. And when you go home you will have to wonder whether I am coming or when I am coming. . . .

That sweaty white face hung there in the air over me. "Sit down, Robert," I said petulantly, "you're making me nervous." He stepped back a bit—I was surprised. I hadn't expected him to listen to me. But then it had been such a long time since anyone had listened to me. If ever before.

And I said something that I didn't mean to say, something that sounded horrible to me even while I was saying it. "Robert, I know what you are, and I know why you came back. And I know something else. Your skin may be the same color as your wife's, but your blood's not—and you believe that. You really believe that."

There was a tiny tremble to his lips. To stop it he swallowed, and I heard the tiny sound of that.

I looked at him, my grandfather's son, his only son. I looked at his face, haggard and old. And I could hear my grandfather saying: Lady, lady, what are you doing?

I answered him back, wherever he was, wherever ghosts go: Why did you have children, for them to tear each other apart?

But it was over for me, this baiting, this swaggering in the face of collapse. I wanted Robert out of my house. I wanted him away from me.

"I'm sick of it," I said. "Go away."

He got to his feet. Again I was surprised that he had obeyed me.

"Look," I said, "I hope you're leaving tonight. My husband's family is wild enough to kill you."

"I'm going directly to New Orleans and then home."

"It was risky coming," I said. "If John had been here there might have been real trouble."

There was a faint sad smile. "I figured you'd be alone."

"And so I am." He had known that. "Go on ahead now."

I went to the porch with him, and watched him walk off down the dark slope of hill toward the waiting car. "Robert," I called after him, "I may be coming to find you. You'll expect me, you won't forget?"

He didn't turn and I wasn't sure whether he'd shaken his head or not. But it didn't matter. He would remember me and he would look for me all the days of his life.

As for my part I would remember too. I would see my grandfather's face, creased, and hurt, and torn with emotion. I didn't sleep that night. I didn't even bother going to bed. At breakfast time the house was still quiet, without its familiar morning sounds. There were no voices downstairs, no sounds outside. Today they had planned to mow the big front field, but the sunny morning was silent and empty: no rattling tractors and clanking mowers. I heard the children's alarm clock ring sharply; I wondered why they bothered to set it, when they knew they would not be going to school. Perhaps they had not believed me. I went downstairs, passing the charred section of banister that Howlands kept to remember by. I walked through the large center hall: the night light was still burning. That was the first thing the butler turned off when he came in the morning—so he was not here. I went into the kitchen; it was empty. The light by the back door was burning too; I snapped it off. No one at all had come this morning. The whole staff was staying away. They expected trouble. . . .

I put on the kettle for coffee, and used the house phone to call the children's nurse, Julia. She would be frightened when she saw the empty house; I had to explain. "I'll see that you get home before there's any trouble," I promised her. And as I dripped the coffee I wondered about that. What if I couldn't. . . .

I went outside briefly and looked around. The winter-stripped land looked the same. The state road below us was empty, except for a passing car that went directly by without slowing or stopping. The sky was bright and clear and windy, filled with crows riding thermals endlessly. The yard and the big front field were completely deserted, not even a cat crouching in the shadows. Like the house staff, the farm hands had not come. Their equipment was still parked behind the bathhouse: their tractors and mowers and graders, and all their attachments. And the gasoline drums were still there.

No one had come to work. No one at all. I went back inside, and called upstairs again. "Whatever you do," I said, "don't alarm the children, Julia. Take them down to the ponies."

The morning passed, quiet and empty. By afternoon I stretched out on the bed, not bothering to undress. At once I fell into a deep heavy sleep. I didn't even hear John come in; he had to shake me. For a moment, muddled and drunk with sleep, I smiled at his familiar shape. Then his cold grim face came into focus, I remembered and sat up. He had a newspaper. Of course. The picture of Robert and me at the front door.

"Why did you let him in?" John asked.

"He rang the doorbell," I said as if that explained everything.

"If I'd been here . . ."

"Well, you weren't. There was nobody to tell me what to do." John looked dirty. He hadn't shaved for a day or so, and the heavy bluish beard line was now a definite crop of whiskers. His eyes were bloodshot and swollen. "Have you been up with your father?"

"Up that way." Somerset County would still take him in, still hide him, fight for him if necessary. All the Tollivers walking around their cotton fields. All the Tollivers with the once-a-year racket of the gins singing in their ears. Where everybody stood together and blood was the answer to anything.

"Where'd he go?" John asked me.

"He said he was going to New Orleans and then home."

"Where?"

"I don't know."

"He told you," John said, "and you're lying to me."

"No, I'm not, but why would you want to know? To go after him?"

John gave his shoulders a little lift.

"I told Robert you would want to do that."

John walked over and glanced out the window. When he lifted the curtain I got a flash of the bright sunny afternoon.

"I will take care of him, John," I said. "I've started already."

He turned back from the window and it was obvious he hadn't heard me, he'd been too busy with his own bitter thoughts.

I pushed down the quilt that I had covered myself with, and I sat up. "If you'd hand me the brush, I could look a little more presentable."

He did not move. "You look like hell."

"It was a bad day."

"Look," he said, "why?"

"Why what?"

"Why'd he marry her? Do you know?"

It was incomprehensible to him. As incomprehensible as trying to chew up a stone. He didn't understand that there were people who might want to try.

"Why'd he do it? To show us?"

"To show himself, I think," I said.

"That doesn't make sense."

"He couldn't let his children be bastards, even if their mother was a Negro."

"There's a lot of bastards around here."

"He knew they weren't going to be kept around here. Even then he knew that they would send them away."

"Christ," John said, "he must have been out of his mind."

I shook my head. "I think maybe I understand."

"Then you're crazy as he is."

"John," I said, "you're so involved and complicated, you forget some people are simple."

"Simple, my God . . . and what about that other one. What'd I ever do to him? Why'd he have to come back?"

"It's hard to explain."

"What did you talk about, for God's sake?"

"His wife and things like that."

"A tea party. Christ!"

"I don't think he knew quite what he was doing."

"I know what he did," John said. "Everybody's pointed it out to me. I'm through in this state. I couldn't get elected garbage man, and I couldn't get a charity case."

"Where will you go?"

"Home. For a while."

And I started to say: This is your home. But I didn't because I knew better. It wasn't. He was a Tolliver and his home was in Somerset County with his blood.

"All right," I said.

"Look," he said, "why don't you take the children and go away for a while?"

I shook my head.

He sat down abruptly on the foot of the bed. "Look," he said, "if you won't, at least send the girls away. Right now."

"Where?"

He pulled a piece of paper from his pocket. "Here. It's a school in New Orleans. Ray Westbury—I've done some work with him, you met him here a couple of times—he has a daughter there."

I took the slip and tucked it carefully under the lamp. To make it extra secure I put an ash tray on top of it. It was comforting, kind of a link. . . .

"I talked to him today—told him what was happening." The thought of that rehearsal seemed to bother him, he hesitated a moment, remembering. "He arranged it . . . they'll be expecting both girls."

"Will you drive them down?"

He shook his head. "Oliver can do it."

I brushed bits of lint from the soft velvet surface of the quilt, thinking, deciding. "Bundle them in a car and rush them off. . . ."

"They'll be safer," he said, "I'm thinking of them."

"I know you are." He was. He loved them, he was doing his best. I glanced at the little white piece of paper. "I'll send them there, but not just now. In a while."

He stood up with a little impatient jerk.

"They mustn't be run out, John."

"You won't?"

"No. We'll stay."

"Oh Jesus," he said.

"Is there going to be trouble?"

"How the hell would I know? I'm just telling you what I think."

"If I left," I said, "they'd probably burn this house."

"I wish it'd been burned to the ground before I ever saw it."

"Yes, I know you do. But I'll stay."

"Oh Christ," he said. And walked toward the door.

"Are you coming back?" I asked him.

"No."

"I didn't think so."

Then he was gone and all the things we hadn't said still hung in the air and buzzed around my ears. I thought: That's that. That's all. I loved him once, but I don't seem to any more, because I'm not too sorry to see him go.

When the children came in, I asked them: "Did you see your father?"

They shook their heads. He hadn't bothered going down, though he must have seen them working their horses. They didn't look upset. He had been home so little that they didn't really miss him now.

After lunch I took the oldest aside. "Abby," I said, "I want to talk to you."

"I know," she said solemnly.

"Who told you?"

"Oliver."

Of course. They had been talking about it down at the barns.

"You won't go back to school for a while," I said, "and then maybe we'll find you another school."

"Oliver said we'd be run out."

"Not run out," I told her. "Just you and Mary Lee and just for school."

"I wouldn't care if I never came back."

"Honey, you think that now, but it takes a while."

Child, I thought, you don't even know it's possible to love a house and land that much. . . .

Abby said: "Nobody's here today except Julia."

"They're staying away because they think there'll be trouble."

"Will there, Mama?"

She did not look frightened, so I told her the truth. "I think so."

"Oliver said there would."

"Oliver seems to know a lot."

"He's got a shotgun down in the harness room."

I said: "Tell Julia to go home. Tell her I'll let her know when I want her back."

Abby trotted off. I looked at her thin legs under their faded blue jeans, and I thought mechanically: they must have some proper riding clothes. . . .

She came back, saying: "She was glad to go."

"Thank you, Abby."

"Is Daddy coming back in case there's trouble?"

And then because she was only thirteen I lied to her. "He can't get back, honey. We'll have to do it ourselves."

"Oliver's been showing me how to aim a shotgun."

Oliver again. "You keep the children here, Abby, I'm going down and talk to him."

I found him tinkering with the latch on the back gate. "I didn't know that needed fixing."

"Wasn't broke," he said. "I'm keeping myself busy."

"Showing Abby how to shoot."

"Come in handy, maybe."

He was an old man, a very old man, and as I looked at him I remembered all those drives to the top of Norton's Hill with my cousins. Those drives where he'd sat waiting and carving strange little animal figures out of peach stones. . . . He still lived in the same house—his old-maid sister had died some five years before—by the big spring called the Sobbing Woman.

"You expecting trouble?"

He kept working on the latch. "We done took the stock from here over to the east lot."

"For safekeeping?"

"Big target," he said; "them animals cost money."

"Go on home, Oliver, and take the children's ponies with you."

He did not seem to hear me. "There's cars parked down the road right now, behind the rise, where you can't see them from the house."

His own calm was contagious. "What will they do?"

He shook his head. "Mr. John been gone?"

"Yes."

"Coming back?"

"No." I suppose I should have been ashamed, but I wasn't. John's leaving was just a fact like the cars down the road.

"I figure to stay."

"Don't be stupid, Oliver. If there's trouble it might be rough on a Negro here."

He didn't lift his head. He just looked up at me, and the gentle old brown eyes were hard and bright. And I thought: There isn't anything going to be harder than it's been already.

"I don't want you staying," I said. "I don't want to have to worry about you." I was shivering with rage and fury. All my life I had been trained to depend on men, now when I needed them they were gone.

Oliver seemed to hear what I was thinking. "Your husband ain't here, and your grandfather ain't here, and your son ain't into school yet. I be up to the house, when I get finished."

The sun went down and the early winter dark began in the hollows and slipped up the hill. Abby kept the children amused and quiet and only now and then I'd feel her large blue eyes watching me. I fixed supper for them myself, fumbling and searching for pans and pots and dishes in my unfamiliar kitchen. I burned my arm on the oven door, smeared the red streak with butter, and put a bandage on top of that.

Then I called the children in. "Aren't you hungry?"

Abby said: "Oliver took the ponies off."

"He'll bring them back."

Her eyes studied me quietly for a very long time. Whatever she saw seemed all right. "Mama," she said, "the butter's making that bandage fall off. You need a new one."

I left them eating, and fixed a new one in the bathroom. On my way back I passed John's gun rack—the one that had been my grandfather's—and I stopped and took down three shotguns. Oliver came to the door and watched me. I found the shells in boxes on the top shelf of the hall closet. I read the labels carefully, and took two boxes out.

I loaded the 20 gauge first. "For somebody that never could shoot, you remembered how to load right well," Oliver said.

"Number four shot," I said.

He padded into the hall, bringing the ammonia smell of the barns with him.

I began loading the two big 12 gauge. "Double naught buckshot," I said. I put the three guns on the hall table, their steel across the polished surface.

And then because I didn't quite believe it, I called John's father's house. No answer. I called the state police, and told them that I thought there was trouble.

Oliver was still standing there, silently. I asked him: "You think they'll come?"

He didn't answer and he didn't have to. They wouldn't until too late.

"Go get some supper, Oliver. No sense you starving while we're waiting."

The children came out of the kitchen; they were finished and looking for me. "Abby, take them to the play room and let them watch television."

"Mary Lee can do that, Mama," she said. "Marge would rather have her anyway. And I'll stay with you."

I looked at her blue eyes and I wondered why southern children learn so early. . . .

There was a sudden flurry of shooting down by the roadside, out of sight. Abby understood before I did. "They mostly always come down to the fence at dusk," she said, and her large eyes blinked a few times.

So they were killing the animals. I glanced at Oliver.

"I ain't had time to move nothing, excepting the dairy cows. There's quite a few steers they got to practice on."

Abby said: "They came down to see what the cars were parked for."

The irregular popping went on. Oliver cocked his head at the window. "Heard but one shotgun. Rest are pistols."

"That's why it's taking so long to kill them," Abby said calmly. I shivered and she saw me. "I'm sorry, Mama."

My baby, I thought. You were born in the bedroom upstairs on the floor and Margaret wiped your face and cleaned your mouth and tied your cord. And Margaret is dead, and you aren't a baby, standing there with your pinched white face, talking about how many shots it takes to kill a steer. . . .

I became very sleepy. I went upstairs and found John's bottle of dexedrine tablets and swallowed two. It made me a bit lightheaded but the cutting edge of weariness was gone.

And it was just as well, because in the next hour they left their cars and their target practice and drifted on up the road toward the house. They smashed through the locked gate, and straggled up the graveled way until they stood in front of the house, just inside the low picket fence that framed the front yard. Some of them sat down, and some of them hunkered down and smoked. Six or eight of them leaned against the little wood fence and fell backward when it collapsed. They all seemed to be waiting.

Then we saw why. They were firing the big barn. You could see it, the steadily growing glow. Johnny cried briefly upstairs and Mary Lee told him: "Hush, now, behave yourself."

I had plenty of time to study the group outside. They were men, all of them, and some of them were men only barely. I saw the Michaels boy, he couldn't have been more than fifteen. His father was there too, the quiet grey-haired pharmacist. Lester Peterson, and his brother Danny—I recognized them. And the Albert brothers. Hugh Edwards from the post office. The small farmers: Wharton Andrews, and Martin Watkins, and Joe Frazer—they scratched out a living on their cotton farms just the other side of town, and shared that scanty living with their sharecroppers. Those three families were dirt poor, all right, their kids had bellies swollen with worms—but the rest of the people out there weren't. They were respectable, they had a house and a car and money in the bank. There was Peter Demos, who kept the café, and Joe Harriman from the feed store; Frank Sargeant from the lumber yard. His son, who was one of the bookkeepers at the new mill. Claude King, who ran the Ford agency. . . . They were the good people out there.

They had trouble firing the barn. One by one, the entire group left the front of the house and drifted down there to help. It was quite a way—a good quarter mile—and the wind was wrong, so you couldn't hear anything much. You could see them milling about, knocking over rail fences and smashing small windows. There were a couple of flat pops. I looked at Oliver. "I reckon they found the cats," he said.

Abby shivered. Her frail young girl's body shook all over. The thought of the cats terrified her. Against the firelight we saw a man swinging something by its tail. He let go and the dark shape sailed through a window and into the blaze.

Abby said: "Oh. Oh!"

She was green. "Don't be silly, Abby," I said sharply, "or you'll have to go back with the children."

Her face straightened out, but it stayed green. "Listen now," I said, "when the bandits killed that Howland girl in the kitchen—right over there, the same room that's the dining room now—her family hunted them into the swamp and found them and killed them. They say her mother went there to watch." The men dragged the bandits out of the swamp and hanged them, living and dead, from the tallest trees to swing until the animals and the birds cleaned their bones. They say that Mrs. Howland stood under those white oak trees, looking up, and laughing. . . . It hadn't been glee at vengeance, I thought, the way the stories had it. She'd been having hysterics at the blood that was wasted. And she'd been seeing her daughter's death agonies repeated over and over in the agonies of her murderers. . . .

I stood thinking about that old tragedy, its violence and its pain, all of it. And all of a sudden I knew what I should do.

"Abby," I said firmly, "go get the children. Don't wake Marge. Mary Lee is to carry a blanket for each of you. Run."

"Oliver," I said, "do you know those big drums of gas back by the tool house? The tractor's still there. Can you hitch up and drive to where the cars are parked?"

His bright eyes glittered and shifted like oil in the light.

"They'll all be watching the burning," I said. "They won't be thinking of that. . . . You go ahead. It'll take you longer."

He went, still carrying his shotgun across his arm. I fixed two bottles of milk for Marge, and picked up a box of cookies for the others. "Abby!" But they were already coming downstairs.

I put Marge on my shoulder. Abby took Johnny's hand—he was staggering with sleep, but quiet and bewildered. Mary Lee carried the blankets. We went out the back door, across the half-lighted yard. There was a little scuffling and a clank of metal as Oliver cleared the tractor. "I'll leave the children up by the spring," I told him as we passed. There were no lights on in the yard, we were all standing in the deep shadows of the building, the flickering fire-lit sky was way over our heads—but my skin crawled. I nodded to the dark hills. "I kind of feel like I'm being watched."

"You'd make a hunter," Oliver said briefly. "There's eyes there."

"Who?"

"People."

"They won't bother the children?"

He snorted. "They come to watch."

We crossed the last of the yard and slipped through the back gate and cut across the corner of a pasture, as fast as we could. The barn was down the slope on the other side of the house, so it wasn't likely anybody would see us, but even so I was glad when we finally reached the path in the deep sheltering woods. There were pines and oaks and hickories and hackberries and it was dark under their branches, darker than night.

We stopped a minute, letting our eyes find their way.

"I know where you want to go," Abby said. "I'll go first."

I held Marge with one hand and got my fingers around Johnny's fat wrist while Abby led. It was much easier following her light shirt than looking for the path itself. We were climbing steeply, and Johnny began to whine. "You take the blankets, Mama," Mary Lee said. "I'll take him." She rolled the blankets tight as she could and I tucked them under my arm. Johnny clambered on her back, and clung there, arms and legs wrapped around her, his sleepy black head dangling on her left shoulder. He looked monstrously large against her tall thin body.

We felt the spring before we actually got there. Abruptly, there was a feel of damp, an odor of wet leaves, of wet earth. The ground underfoot was trampled and soapy-feeling. I remembered a stand of pine, running off at an angle, like a narrow ribbon through the jam of the other trees. That ground would be drier and softer with the heavy load of needles spread on it. "There," I motioned to Abby. You could hear the spring now, its steady sound loud in the quiet night.

"I tasted that water once," Abby said, as she cleared a space of fallen bits of branches and patted the pine needles smooth. "Tastes awful funny."

I spread a blanket and put Marge on it, covering her carefully. She hadn't waked. I went over to check the spring. It flowed gently from between two lip-like folds of rock. It was not a deep spring and the water was almost warm and quite flat.

"It's all right," I told Abby. "It always did taste like that. It's just not a bubbly spring."

I spread the other blankets for them. "Stay till I come back for you."

They didn't say anything. Their eyes followed me for the short distance I was visible in the tree-shaded dark.

I hurried down another way, brushing through tangles of vines and scrambling over rocks. I hadn't been up here in a good many years and the land had changed somewhat. Freezes and thaws had moved the boulders about, sometimes tumbling them far down the hillside. There were berry brambles where there had been none before. Two or three times I had to retrace my steps and go around an impenetrable patch. I was wearing a skirt and low shoes—I hadn't thought about the brush—and my ankles and legs were streaked with blood. But I found a way through the woods and came out on a low clear hummock, some people said it was an Indian mound. Away to my right the sluggish spring ran into a little marshy hollow. You could hear the bullfrogs and the tree frogs and the crickets in there. They were singing at the top of their voices. All those open cold throats, all those horny legs grinding together. . . . It also meant that there was nobody over there.

The children were on the dark slope of the hill behind me. They were so shut in by trees that they couldn't see me—but as I stood on that open mound, I felt eyes again. Negroes, in the dark that matched their skins, were watching. I remembered something my grandfather had said: "When there's anything going on," he said, "the woods gets so full that you can practically see 'em heave and shift with all the goings and comings."

Why don't they help me? I thought bitterly. And I answered myself just as bitterly: "Because I'm white, and anyway there isn't anything they could do that wouldn't make things worse." I started to cry, but in the soft cool night air the tears vanished. Their gentle source dried up and disappeared. And out of the cracks and barrenness of its leaving, I felt the shaky ghost of my pride begin to rise. Poor tired pride, beaten and sick, it came back after all, and in a moment I stopped being ashamed of what my grandfather had done, if only because he was my grandfather. . . . A warm trickle of anger ran along my scalp.

I scurried down the hummock, panting with the unaccustomed exertion, cursing my body for not being young and strong any more, for softening over the child-filled years. . . . Oliver was waiting in the fold of the slope, in the shadow of a rhododendron bush. He was sitting on the tractor seat, small and black and shriveled, for all the world like those figures he carved from peach stones. . . . The gasoline drums were hitched behind. "All right," I said.

The motor sounded frantic. We both looked around, but nothing moved, nothing happened. Oliver shifted gears and slowly edged out of the shadow. The drums were fitted and braced tightly on the wheeled platform, leaving no room for a rider. I trotted along behind; we had barely a hundred yards to go.

There were about a dozen cars. Three had parked on the road, the rest had driven through a light rail fence into a flat field. It made a wonderful parking lot, but it hadn't made good pasture. For some reason or other (maybe because there are just spots where cattle refuse to graze) it had been allowed to run to weeds and trash grasses. We hadn't had rain in weeks, the fall was always like that—Novembers particularly—and the grasses were rustling dry. We had even had one hard frost to bleach them; they gleamed dully with their own light. I looked back once—I couldn't see the house itself, but I could see the glow in the sky from the burning barn beyond it. I didn't look again.

Oliver stopped by the first of the cars parked on the road.

These drums were made exactly like the big cans of kerosene that used to stand on crossed wood legs by every kitchen door: on their lower front edge they had a little spigot. Over the mouth of the spigot we had installed a length of hose. It had worked fine fueling the tractors and the graders and the mowers, and it worked fine now. I opened the spigot, held the hose up high to keep the gas from splattering around and wasting. Oliver waited, the motor clucking in neutral. He wasn't even looking at me. He was the chauffeur again—as he had been on those afternoon rides, so long ago. He might have been taking four little cousins and their nurse for a breath of air.

I opened the first of the car doors, bent inside, and with my hose soaked the seats and walls. I backed out and quickly lifted the hose again. Only a few drops splashed on my coat. I would have to remember to take that off, I thought.

I finished those cars and sprinkled the grass around them. Once I even opened a gas tank and stuffed a handful of dry grass in the top. I don't know if that worked. It was just something I thought I'd try.

Oliver drove the tractor through the broken fence into the field. The hidden burrs of the waist-high dry grasses tore at the already bloody skin of my ankles and my legs. In my excitement, the pain felt warm and comforting as I went from car to car, soaking the grasses beneath them, drenching as much of seat and wall as I could reach. I even began to leave the doors standing open—the little interior lights made it easier to see the next car.

This field was in the narrow pass between two slopes, and

the rising night wind now blew through it strongly. Needlenose, old people call this particular stretch, and it is supposed to hold ghosts. The wind blows harder here than elsewhere—when I was a child this was where we came to fly our kites, because they sailed easier and higher. Every night between midnight and dawn, the wind whimpers and giggles through this pass, the way freak air always does.

It was jabbering like that when we finished and went to the upper side of the field to spread the last gas there. I took off my splashed and splattered coat. We both rubbed our hands with mud to clean them. Then we set the fire. Oliver's match lit at once. My first two went out in the wind. I knelt and sheltered the third match with my body the way I might do an infant, and burned my hand with the cupping protection I gave it—but I got my grass alight. We stood a moment or two and watched the flame grow. A patch, a blob of light, pushed forward like spume by the wind. Then the two blobs, Oliver's and mine, joined and spread into a line, and the line grew from a flat thing on the ground like a child's mark, to a thing with height and width, and a crackling voice.

Hastily, Oliver drove the tractor back the way he had come. I followed, stopping only once to light the grass by the roadside cars. I scrambled up the Indian mound, panting, with the singing of gasoline-fed flames in my ears. I stumbled and fell full length, the breath jarred out of me, my tired body aching and resisting and wanting to stay huddled against an earth that seemed so warm on the chill windy night. But I got up—just a moment to rest—and ran through the sheltering woods, circling back to the house. And all the way, the pistons of my legs pushing me up and down, the pressure of my lungs bursting my ribs, I kept worrying: Will it be there? Will they have gotten to it in the little while it was left alone?

When, through the last fringe of trees, I could see that the house stood white and untouched, I stopped and felt sick with relief. I leaned against a thin pine and rested my head on its bark. Oliver popped out of the dark, on foot this time; he had left the tractor hidden in the trees. I asked: "How long before they can't put out the fire back there? How long will that take?"

"I never done nothing like that before."

He was an old man and he was breathing very hard.

"Oliver," I said, "you go stay with the children, I'll mind the house." I added: "They'll be scared out of their wits up there, and Abby too proud to admit it."

He may have nodded in the dark but I didn't see it. I only saw him walk off in the direction of the path that led to the spring.

I went back into my house and I called the state police again. "There's a barn burning and a dozen cars afire in a field, and the next thing somebody will get killed. You wouldn't come last time, but these aren't Howland cars, and they aren't Howlands that are going to be getting shot, so maybe you'll come now."

I hung up and knew they would come. This time they would come. I took the three shotguns and went to sit on the front porch. The yard was empty. The crowd was all down by the barn.

But now that wasn't the only glow in the sky. There was another one, one that increased steadily, over the low sheltering hill to the right. The wind brought me the smell of burning from that direction, just as it carried away the smell of my own barn going down to ashes. Once I heard a sort of muffled explosion. That was how a gas tank sounded. I had never heard one before, but it wasn't too unlike the shots that had killed the cattle out that way.

One for one. Like it was before. You kill my child in the kitchen and I murder you in the swamp. . . . I was lightheaded, and exhausted, I began to giggle. . . . They were shooting steers and cats. The Howland they wanted was dead. His Negro wife was dead. Their children disappeared. And so they were wrecking the only thing that was left of him, of them. First the barn and then the house. . . .

They had finally gotten the barn to burn satisfactorily. They had struggled with it a long time. But then I guess none of them were used to setting fires of that sort.

And the glow below the hill—mine—got brighter and larger. Always like that. This one piece of ground now, fought over, blood spilled, outlaws and Civil War raiders, and before all of them, the Indians. . . . And modern raiders now, who came in cars instead of on horses, who shot at cats and steers. . . . They had only kept the fire and the fire was real enough. . . .

I heard a car racing up the hill, engine laboring at the steep fast climb. It was a Ford, a blue Ford. It spun off the drive and crashed through the fence, across the front yard; it was taking the shortest possible route to the barn. There were two men in it, I noticed as it passed not fifteen feet from where I sat. They had come late and, passing along the road, they had seen the second burning. The car roared up to the barn, close as it dared, its horn blaring wildly. With the wind standing the way it was, I couldn't hear, but I knew they would be shouting. They were waving their arms, and the whole group was milling about. Some jumped in the car, and some more hopped on the back trunk, before it spun around and raced up the hill again. I saw it bounce slightly as it crossed the edge of the rose bed, smashed over a lawn chair. It would pass directly in front of me again. I picked up the 20 gauge. There was something about adjusting the choke. I had been taught once, but I'd forgotten. . . . For a fraction of a second too I wondered about the load. I seemed to remember that number four shot was what you used for geese and if that was true it wouldn't hurt a man too much. I wasn't at all sure, but I thought about it only for an instant as I swung the barrels up. Even if they had been loaded with rifled slugs, I would not have stopped now. I pulled both triggers. At that range even I couldn't miss. The car swerved away sharply, brushed a fender against the big dogwood, crashed through another section of the fence, bounced down the small drop to the road. It righted itself, and sped off, a bit of white picket fence stuck to its bumper.

The men who had been holding on the rear fell or dropped off at the swerve; they were running over the edge of the hill, looking for cover, and finding none, because John had cleared all that land down to pasture so that we should have a view of the river. And we had it now. Beyond the scurrying crouching men I could see the line of dark trees and the dull glint of lead-colored water.

As for the rest, most of them went racing past. They hadn't quite seen what happened, or they didn't understand, but they went streaming on by, without so much as a glance in my direction. They wanted to find out what had happened to their cars.

A few, five or six or so, stopped in the front yard, staring. I thought of the empty house behind me, the rooms with nobody in them, and I wondered how long it would take them to think of that too. Not soon. They wouldn't be likely to believe I was really alone. But sooner or later they would come to it. And it would be so very easy to sneak up from behind. . . .

They were standing there on the lawn, a little group together, their faces expressionless. There was young Michaels, whose father was the pharmacist. Wharton Andrews, the farmer. Les Matthews, who worked at the gin. Joe Harriman from the feed store. Lester Peterson from the hatchery. Abruptly I stopped looking at them as people, and saw them only as shapes. It would be easier that way. I put down the empty 20 I had been holding, dropped it clattering by the side of my chair. I picked up one of the 12's. I didn't stand up. My legs were so weak and shaky I don't think I could have. I aimed, and hoped my hands were steady. They weren't, so I rested the barrel on the porch railing. Then I swung the other 12 up too, putting it right beside the first. Four round barrels, facing out.

"Get out," I said. My voice was so very faint that I don't think they heard me. I said louder: "It's double naught buckshot, and I'm willing to try it."

They didn't move.

I pushed down with my right hand, lifting the barrels of that gun, pointing it slightly over their heads, and pulled one trigger. They saw the barrel's angle, they knew the charge was going over them, but they winced and yanked up their shoulders, as the shot splattered down well beyond them.

They didn't break and run, even so; they just hesitated. If they come, I thought, I'm going to aim carefully and fire. I'm going to kill some of them. . . . I didn't hunt them down in the swamp, but I'm going to kill them just the same. I switched the guns, put the one with the two loaded barrels at my right hand, the single barrel at my left. The smell of burnt powder tickled my nose; I rubbed it against my shoulder, still keeping my eyes on them. And then we heard the siren. The wind had carried it a long way, but you couldn't mistake it. We all listened; it got louder, it was coming this way, and no mistake. Now they looked really uncertain. I shifted the barrels against the railing, aiming more carefully. Just that little sound of metal on wood seemed to be enough.

They turned and hurried away. I fired the single barrel into the ground at their feet. They broke into a little trot and cut across the road and disappeared down the slope toward the wailing siren and the blazing cars.

I waited a bit to be sure they were gone. Then I left the two empty guns on the porch floor and put the loaded one across my arm, the way my grandfather had taught me years ago. ("Child, if you're as tense as all that you'll never hit anything." And how would he feel if he'd held a gun with a load in it that could kill? Not aiming at birds, not aiming at deer, but aiming at men. . . .) I walked around the house, looking. Just looking, as if I'd never seen it before. The house itself hadn't been touched. They hadn't even come near the back, the lawns there were smooth and clear as ever. They had gotten to the south side, the side toward the barn. John's greenhouse was destroyed. I looked at the shattered panes reflected brokenly in the bright yellow light of the barn and I wondered when that had happened. I hadn't heard anything—it must have been while I was firing the cars. I thought of John's orchids—the stiff ones and the soft climbing ones, all of them dying in the cold night air, their foliage and blossoms tattered by the glass slivers. And how much had that cost? I didn't know, I rarely looked at the bills, but it had been expensive. . . . And it was wasted now. . . . Funny, tired and silly as I was, and not thinking clearly, not thinking at all, I felt sorrier for the orchids than for John.

I wondered how they had shattered so many panes. I supposed they had used a shotgun blast or two. I hadn't heard that either. But then I'd been down under the hill and very busy.

Tomorrow, I thought, I must look in there and see if I can find any pellets, and see what size they are.

That was important. To know exactly what size.

The chairs that stood on the flagstone patio had been tumbled about and broken. There were a couple of dead cats and a hound pup in the bottom of the empty swimming pool, smashed and huddled against the concrete.

I circled the house, slowly, finding nothing else disturbed. When I was sure of that, when I was quite sure that I had checked everything, I stood—with the shotgun held crosswise in my hands and my scratched and torn legs aching feebly under me—and looked across the sheltering hill to the glow of the burning cars. The sirens were very close now; all at once they died away into a strangled yelp as the cars stopped. In the sudden silence there was a lot of shouting, the words too muffled to understand. I looked briefly at the house behind me, lit dimly by those two distant fires; it was white and smooth and lovely and unruffled. It would belong to my children. It would come to them the way it had come to me. Howlands were not run out, nor burned out.

"You didn't think I could do it," I said, looking around in the dark for my grandfather. It seemed I could see him standing in the dim corner of the porch, looking over at me. And he wasn't alone. That corner was crowded with people, only I couldn't exactly make out who they were.

You do what you got to do, he answered me.

"You were right about John," I said. "But I loved him then."

Do what you got to do, he said again. And I began to recognize the people with him. Some women, some men. Some tranquil-looking like their pictures that lined the dining-room walls. Some hurt and bloody. The girl who had been beaten to death against the kitchen floor. Cousin Ezra, who had died up on the ridge during the Civil War. Old Will Howland himself, scalpless and bloody from Indians. The young man who'd burned to death in the brush fires of the Wilderness in Virginia. And their wives: plain-faced and unsmiling, coy and gay.

I said to them all: "I bet you didn't think I could."

Do what come to you to do, my grandfather answered me. Then he and all his kin, like paper dolls drawn from the grave, disappeared.

I wondered why Margaret hadn't been with them. Maybe they wouldn't admit her as belonging with them. After all, she was a Negro. So maybe not. Will Howland and his wives—I wondered how the three were getting on together. No marriage nor giving in marriage, I remembered. Maybe that would solve it. And if not, the gentle little grey-eyed girl who had been his first wife would certainly make no trouble. Wherever they were.

But Margaret hadn't been with them. . . . All of a sudden I realized why. She was not one of my ghosts. She would haunt her own children, not me. She was not part of me.

I stood on that cold windy grass and saw what I had done. I saw that it wasn't bravery or hate. It was, like my grandfather said, necessity. And that's pretty poor comfort but at times it's all you've got.

The oily black smoke from beneath the hill drifted upward on the clear night air and stung my eyes in passing.

EPILOGUE

That was all. The excitement and the fear left me when I saw that people had expended whatever energy and violence they had within them. Leaving only a bitter taste, a nasty taste in the sight of things as they really were. . . . Aimless anger had burned a barn, had killed cats and steers and a couple of hounds. And all my courage had only fired a parking lot and pumped a load of bird-shot into the side of the car.

The very next afternoon I noticed Oliver back at work. He was puttering around the smoldering heap that had been a barn. I watched his old man's figure move back and forth across the scorched and trampled ground. He seemed to be sorting out the ruins; he seemed to be raking them into little piles.

I got a call from Stuart Albertson, the man who would now get the governorship. I warned him abruptly: "This is not a private wire."

"What I say, Mrs. Tolliver, can be heard all over the country."

"Oh," I said, "I see."

"I hope you don't think what happened last night was planned by any political party."

"No."

"Your husband and I were political opponents—of course we were—but that sort of action is as abhorrent to me as it is to any other decent law-abiding citizen."

He's reading, I thought. He's got a statement and he's trying to make it chatty as he goes along.

"Look, Mr. Albertson, I certainly don't think you were involved in the fuss last night."

"I've taken the liberty—in the absence of your husband—to ask the state police to station a car on the road outside your place. Have you noticed?"

"No, I've been mostly looking at the barn."

"Ah, well, it may be some comfort to know that two troopers are just down the hill."

"I'm not afraid," I said, "I know what to do, I can handle things."

"But a little bit of comfort, still. . . ."

I gave up in the face of his persistence. "You're right."

Abruptly he came to the point. "That unfortunate incident did no credit to the people of our state—although it was a very, very small group."

"I suppose."

"The news does not have to be released, of course. It need travel no farther than it has already."

"Can you stop it?"

"The local papers have advised me that they have no report on it at all. As for the, ah, persons directly involved—they would be confessing to arson—do you understand?"

"You'd like me to forget it?"

"Forget—no, of course not. But some things are better not publicized."

"I don't need to make news of this," I said. "If that's what you mean." And then I had another thought: "Has my husband been in touch with you? Is John making some kind of a deal with you?"

"My dear Mrs. Tolliver . . ."

He sounded so shocked that I knew I was right. I wondered what John was gambling for now; I didn't particularly care, but you had to admire him. He was tough. Maybe he was going to pull something out of the ruins of his career, the way old Oliver was pulling things out of the wreck of a barn. John was a politician born and studied. He might just manage it. . . .

"It's none of my affair," I said. "As you know, we've separated."

"You'll divorce, of course?"

Something in the quick way he said that. . . . Something. . . . The fault was not really John's, if you looked at it one way. It was mine, mine alone. John was innocently led into it. . . . Now I could see how he was thinking. But could he sell that story to the voters? It would take years, but John was patient. He would try. Of course he would. Without me this time.

"Tell him something for me, Mr. Albertson, if you happen to see him."

"My dear lady, I don't expect to."

"If you do, tell him I only want what's mine."

"We've gotten so far off the subject. . . ."

"So we have. I was thinking out loud, I'm afraid." And I looked into the receiver as if it was a face. "Thank you for your concern."

I did not wait for him to say good-bye, I hung up.

A few hours later, I got a call from an Atlanta paper.

"Barns burn all the time," I told them. "It's one of the hazards of life."

"How did the fire start?"

"I don't know. It burned, that's all."

"Stock?"

"No, we got them out."

"Any injuries?"

"Of course not."

"There were two cases of shotgun wounds at the county hospital last night."

So my wild shot at the car had been successful. The choke adjustment wasn't important after all.

I smiled at my invisible informant. "There are always shotgun wounds around here, as I remember. Everybody hunts."

"Your fences are broken."

"Oh my," I said, "you have big eyes. . . . I have a few drunken friends, who did a bit of damage."

"And cars burning in a field?"

"Really? I've been inside. I haven't left the house for several days. Probably I've even forgot to look out the windows."

One thing after the other. The servants came back, the braver ones within two days, the more timid I had to send for. I told them all, except the cook, to begin looking for other jobs. I would no longer run such an elaborate house. In the meantime I did not let them repair anything. They only swept up the broken glass. The fences stayed down, the panes stayed missing. Howlands kept such things to remember by.

One thing after the other. Quickly. Abby and Mary Lee went off to school in New Orleans, to the one their father had found. They were glad to leave; they were bored to death with the restricted life of the place. Not even their ponies amused them now. They wanted to go, and I wanted them away. They were old enough to notice and remember, and I did not want that. Now there was Johnny and Marge only; they were too young to notice anything.

One thing after the other. I reached John's father's house and left a message for him. It said only that my lawyer would get in touch with him about a property settlement, and that I wanted him afterwards to go to Alabama for a quick divorce. If he were too busy to go, I would myself. It only took twenty-four hours.

I was sure he would go. His pride would make him.

Then I hired a lawyer. His name was Edward Delatte, and he was the younger brother of the girl whose elopement had almost ended my college career. I remembered him suddenly. And the more I thought about him, the more perfect for me he seemed. He was a Catholic living in the south part of the state, he knew no one in this county and could ignore their dislike. So I called him.

When I gave my name to his secretary, she recognized it with a little surprised gasp. "Yes, Mrs. Tolliver," she said quickly. "Yes ma'am. Right away."

Everybody in the state knew that name, of course. And William Howland's. . . . Although my grandfather had never liked politics and had only wanted to live on his acres undisturbed. . . .

Then Edward Delatte was on the phone, his light precise voice jarring me back to business. "Yes, Mrs. Tolliver," he said. "May I first tell you how sorry I am."

"Mr. Delatte." I no longer bothered about politeness; I only wanted to explain to him as quickly and as plainly as I could. "I need a lawyer. For two reasons. I need a divorce. Then I need help managing my grandfather's estate."

"I see," he said, "I see."

"I would like you to come talk to me."

"Why, yes," he said. "I will indeed."

And two days later he sat in my living room, a slight small man, balding across the crown, pink skin through black hair.

"There's only one thing," I told him. "I want back everything I brought to the marriage. Every bit of it."

"Why yes," he nodded gently. "I'm sure Mr. Tolliver can have no objections."

"John kept our business records at his office in town. But that's about all I know, I'm afraid. I don't think I can help you very much."

Mr. Delatte said quietly: "I'm sure we can manage."

We drove together to Madison City, the first of endless trips. It was a cold day, the first really cold one we'd had, and the streets were empty—people were huddled inside by their stoves. The wind blew hard, and bits of trash and balls of grass raced along between the buildings. The red bricks of the courthouse were blotched with damp; its slate roof looked stained and moldy in the light. The flag in front of the post office had gotten tangled in its halyards; it slapped and fluttered below half-mast.

John's office was warm and comfortable, the heat had come on automatically. "How nice," Mr. Delatte said.

"John did all of the estate business down here," I told him. "Most of his practice, and all of his political work, came from the office at home."

Mr. Delatte said: "That should make it so much easier for us."

"I do know the combination of the safe."

"Splendid. I'll get right to work."

He did. The rest of that day and evening and all the following day, which was a Sunday. That last afternoon I left him there and took the children for a ride. When I came back in the early winter dusk, I found him waiting for me.

"Mrs. Tolliver," he said (and his voice had an edge of real respect in it), "I'm sure you were aware of this, but your grandfather was a very wealthy man."

"I think I saw the inventory of his estate, though I don't remember too much about it."

"If I were a newspaperman with a license for loose talk, I would say that your grandfather owned the whole county—all the best timber lands, half the grazing land, most of the stock. Why he even owned a lot of these buildings in town. The hotel for instance—an uncle left him that some twenty years ago."

"Howlands always did gather things the way squirrels go after nuts."

"I can see that." He smiled gently. "I'm city-born," he added in explanation. "I always forget how a small town can be owned by one man. It always surprises me. . . . Is there something wrong?"

"I'm sorry." I had been staring at him and I hadn't been seeing him at all. "I was thinking."

"Have I said something?"

"Oh no." I smiled back at him. "I think your observations are extremely useful. You've given me a wonderful idea. You really have."

Mr. Delatte worked weekends and one day a week, driving furiously back and forth, managing both his practice and my business. He stayed in our guest room—I suggested that, it was more comfortable than the hotel, and I was glad of the company. It also amused me to think of the town's talk.

It was a long tedious process, the separating of my belongings from John's. Week after week I plodded along after Mr. Delatte, my head aching and spinning with unaccustomed ideas, strange words. But I kept on, because there was something I wanted. Something that neither my grandfather nor John had ever taught me. I wanted to learn precisely what I owned, what the generations of William Howlands had acquired.

Mr. Delatte finished at last. He packed his briefcase with papers and went off to see John. A few more days and there was the statement of divorce. That part was over.

And I waited, not forgetting. I had a plan; it rose to meet me out of the welter of figures I had studied over the last month. I knew now what I would do, and though I could have begun, I didn't. I wanted everyone to know for sure what was happening, and who was responsible. I waited and let the time pass slowly.

Mr. Delatte continued patient and hard-working. He was so gentle, so light, he was like a crisp brown leaf. If he noticed that people in Madison City were sharp or strange or stared at him, he gave no sign.

"The records are in excellent order," he said to me.

"I'm sure John was very careful."

"Mrs. Tolliver," he said, and his dark mild eyes fluttered uncertainly, "if I may, just for a moment, be personal—this will blow over, you know. This whole affair. People will forget."

I just looked at him. "You couldn't be more wrong."

The emphasis in my voice startled him. "I didn't mean to intrude."

"I can't forget."

"Ah," he said, "well . . ."

"I'll have a chance," I said. "Just wait."

At first, when I went into town with Edward Delatte, people turned their backs. In a month they no longer turned away; they only dropped their eyes. A bit more time, and they looked straight at me; "Good morning," I said quietly. They didn't answer. And then they did. They were curious. They were so very very curious. They were attracted by the very thing that repelled them. They pranced and danced around it like fighting cocks. And like the cocks, you knew that sooner or later they could not stand it any more. They would jump.

The town did just that. It took about three months. Mrs. Otto Holloway asked me to tea to meet her granddaughter who was on spring vacation holiday from the university.

The Holloways had lived, ever since I could remember, in the big grey Victorian house around the corner from the town square. (He was the only doctor in town and had been ever since Harry Armstrong retired.) On that morning, a Saturday, I drove in early with Edward Delatte. We parked in back of the office that had been John's and was now mine. Funny, I couldn't seem to remember that it belonged to me alone now. I was free, but I didn't feel so. . . .

The morning was crisp and cool. We went in the back door that John always used and went directly to his inner office, talking about trivial things, bits of business. A good morning for business, for doing things that needed to be done. . . .

"Mr. Delatte," I said abruptly. "I want to close up the Washington Hotel."

"If I remember correctly, it's been quite profitable."

I hesitated, and in the interval I could hear the steady rattle of my new secretary's typewriter in the outer office. "I've got enough money. I want to close it."

"It's your decision of course."

"I want it closed right now. This morning."

He was horrified, but said nothing. He never did.

"As for the people in there, they can stay as long as they planned this time, until they're finished in town."

He had removed any traces of surprise from his face. "Shall I see about that now?"

"Yes, please. And I want them to board up the front. Big boards. Right across the head of the steps."

I stood at the window and watched Mr. Delatte go down the street toward the hotel. I stood and waited a very long time, until I saw the porter drag a very large plank to the front of the building. It was too heavy for him to manage alone, so Mr. Delatte helped him lift it into place and steady it for the nails. I sat down then and listened to the banging of the hammer until they were finished.

It was still a bit early for the Holloway party, so I picked up a new *Reader's Digest* and read it straight through while I waited. Then I put on my coat and walked slowly around the corner to the Holloways'.

There was a great crowd. You could see cars parked all up and down both sides of the street. So much the better, I thought. I need lots of people. I put my feet down firmly one before the other, I tensed and untensed my leg muscles and I kept walking.

I knew what the tea would be like before I got there. A young woman with flowers on her shoulder, whom I did not know, and all the rest of the women, whom I did. The house would smell like fruitcake and pink gladioli, and there would be trays of sandwiches and iced cakes. The strict Baptists would sip their tea; the not-so-religious would turn giggly and confiding over discreet glasses of sherry or hot toddy because the day was cool.

I've been to so many of these, I thought, as I climbed the front steps. John always wanted me to go, and I always did what he wanted. . . .

"Abigail, my dear," Mrs. Holloway called gaily from the front door.

With her, just emerging from her elaborately fur-trimmed coat, was Jean Bannister, my cousin Reggie's wife. I smiled at them both.

"How nice of you to come," Mrs. Holloway said.

"I've been looking forward to coming." I stepped inside and closed the door behind me. "How are you, Jean?"

"But, Abigail," Mrs. Holloway said, "you've lost weight."

"Have I? I really haven't weighed in months, I'm afraid. John had a scale, but I don't know where it is now. Perhaps he took it with him."

"Oh yes, of course, John . . ."

"John, my ex-husband, yes." The sound of that was harsh in the tinkle of laughter and voices.

"You must meet my granddaughter," Mrs. Holloway said. "Oh dear, she seems to have gotten herself way across the room. . . ."

"That's all right," I said. "I'll manage to cross over in a bit."

"The room is just too crowded to move, isn't it?" Mrs. Holloway said. "I really should have kept things smaller."

"But you have a lot of friends. . . ." Together we looked across the room. It was jammed with silk print dresses—straight through the double parlors into the dining room and even out on the sun porch. "I wonder how many are related to me."

Mrs. Holloway laughed. "Most of them are, I imagine."

"Let's see now, just for fun. You aren't, of course, but you moved here after your husband finished medical school, I believe."

"Long before your time, my dear."

"And Jean, now you're from Montgomery, but your husband is my cousin. So let's see how many cousins I can find if I don't count degrees. . . . There's Emily Frazer, and Louise Allen and Clarissa Harding, and Flora Creech . . ."

"Mercy," Mrs. Holloway interrupted me. She seemed to find the list vaguely disquieting. "Mercy!"

"And I'll tell you another strange thing. I haven't seen any of them in months. Strange, isn't it? Even when you're related. . . ."

"Isn't it?" Mrs. Holloway said. "Isn't it strange? Would you like a glass of sherry?"

And with a firm hand on my arm she launched me into the crowded room.

For a while it was like any other tea. With talk about illnesses and weddings and whose child was entering which school and what grade. For a while.

I said nothing. I could wait. I just didn't think they could. And I was right.

It was Mrs. Holloway herself who finally got around to it.

"Dear," she said, "the fire at your barn was terrible news."

"Yes," I said, "it was."

"I mean, it was the very latest thing in barns, wasn't it?"

"It had a lot of expensive equipment inside. I don't think I know exactly how much."

"How terrible." Abruptly the room got very still. Only the granddaughter chattered away in a corner. I recognized her delicate tone, her sorority-trained lilt. In the hushed silence, the young light voice faltered: she looked uncertainly over her shoulder, and stopped, in the middle of her sentence.

"Dreadful," Mrs. Holloway repeated. "Do you have any idea how it started?"

I looked at the smooth pink face perched atop the round shoulders and the heavy breasts, tightly wrapped in flowered silk. "Did I recognize them?" I asked. "They weren't wearing masks. I suppose they were in too much of a hurry to bother with them."

Mrs. Locke, whose husband was a partner in the drugstore, clucked nervously. "White trash will be the death of the South. Dear, dear!"

"It wasn't all trash," I said. "Which of you had husbands home that night?"

A quick breathing silence, and Mrs. Holloway said: "Well, it was dreadful, but it's over."

As she turned back to her silver coffeepot, I interrupted. "It's not over. It's my turn."

For a moment I caught sight of the granddaughter's face. "I'm sorry, honey," I said to her, "I'm ruining your party, but it really wasn't given for you anyway." Her mouth popped open, but nothing came out, no sound at all. I gave her a quick smile. "Your grandmother really should have explained to you. . . ." I took a deep breath. "You listen now, and you tell your husbands. You bring them a message from me. The Howlands were the first ones here, back when it was Indian country, and you set out your dogs at night, and you barred your doors against them, and went about daytimes with a rifle. It's still Howland country. I'm taking it back."

They clucked then, all of them, nervously, and the fruitcake smell of the house was overpowering.

"There's precious little around here that didn't belong to Will Howland, one way or the other. Only you forgot. But watch now, and you'll be seeing it shrink together, you'll be seeing Madison City go back to what it was thirty years ago. Maybe my son will build it back, I won't."

A nervous titter again. Did they understand what I was saying? Had it gotten through the warmth of sherry? Or would it take a while? Would they understand only after I was gone? I would make them. And now.

"I just closed the hotel," I said. "That's a start. Didn't you hear the hammer sealing it up? Did you drive right by without noticing?"

I caught sight of Jean Bannister's face. It looked frozen and stiff. She understands, I thought; she is the brightest and so she understands and she is trying not to let herself believe. Because she has a new expensive coat and her husband's trucking business has just begun to make money.

I watched her face, fascinated. The large wide-set grey eyes. The straight blond hair. She's feeling her insides go cold, I thought, and she's feeling the tips of her fingers start to shiver. She's feeling just the way I did. . . .

"Barn's gone, and the equipment. I won't rebuild. I won't even pay you to haul the ashes away. I've already sold all my stock, excepting the children's ponies, but I expect you know that. Without them what's going to happen to the slaughter yards and the packing plant? Nobody else around here can fill them. And there's the ice-cream plant. . . . Whose milk was that?"

I went to a window and opened it, the room was stifling. Out of the corner of my eye I saw Louise Allen begin to chew her finger nervously. Her husband and his brother owned the slaughter yards.

And your quavering stomach, I thought, that will change to a permanent lump, a millstone to carry. . . .

There was a shuffle and a rustle behind me as Mrs. Holloway pushed her way through the crowd to stand next to me. She seemed to start to say something, but she didn't and all I heard was the creak and stretch of the old-fashioned stays of her corset. I didn't even look at her.

"The lumber business now, that's the big one around here, and half of it is my land." In the street outside a procession of three dogs went by, solemnly. I watched them out of sight. "That's on contract, so I can't do anything about it right now, but contracts run out. . . . Howlands have crazy blood, I used to hear. . . . It'll cost me to do this, but I will. I figure to have enough money to live." I was still holding the glass of sweet sherry that I had been drinking. I put it down carefully on the window sill. "You watch. This town's going to shrivel and shrink back to its real size. . . . It wasn't Will Howland you burned down, it was your own house."

There wasn't a sound as I walked out, not even the rustle of breathing, just my heels tapping across the floor boards. I found my coat among the ones piled on the hall chairs. The maid, a thin mosquito in black dress and frilly white apron, peeped at me through a crack in the kitchen door. I nodded to her and she jerked back out of sight. I could almost hear her buzzing. I left, slowly, majestically. I didn't feel the concrete street under my steps. My feet touched air, I was floating. You bastards, I told them all, you bastards. . . .

And I said to my grandfather, who seemed to be walking right next to me, just a little behind where I couldn't see: "I should think you'd be laughing."

I'm not, he said.

"I can do it."

I reckon I know that.

"I had to do something."

I heard him sigh, just as plain as the little wind that rippled the dry leaves. It had to be done, he said.

"That was for you," I said. "You won't like what I'm going to do now, but this is for me."

I know, he said, and the light winter breeze sighed for him again.

I went into the office that had been John's. Two of the three secretaries' desks were empty. Miss Lucy and Mrs. Carson were gone with John. There was only one typist now, a new one I'd hired—a slight mousy-colored girl with bad skin. Her mother was the town's prostitute, she didn't know her father. She was bitter and ugly and efficient. I trusted her because she had no one else to be loyal to. She did not like me, but since I was paying her, she disliked the others more.

I nodded to her. She bobbed her head slightly, not missing the rhythm of her furious typing. I went on into the inner office. Mr. Delatte was finishing his work; he smiled his neutral colorless smile.

"Will you do me a favor, please?" I asked him. "Will you call a Dr. Mallory in Oakland, California? I don't know his first name, but he's a radiologist, so you can find him without any trouble. And would you ask him for the address and phone number of his son-in-law?"

With a sudden sharp look in his mild rabbity eyes Mr. Delatte asked: "Who is his son-in-law?"

"Robert Howland."

He hesitated, then picked up the phone. While he did that, I opened the back door, and I propped it wide. I turned back to the huge yellow oak desk; I emptied the drawers, all of them, carefully, tossing the papers and the rubber bands, and the clips and the envelopes, into empty chairs. Then I put my shoulder to the desk and began shoving it toward the door. Mr. Delatte looked up from the phone—he had at first tried to pretend not to notice what I was doing. "If you wait a minute, I'll give you a hand."

The desk was not on rollers but it moved easily enough because the polished rugless floor was quite slippery. "No, thank you," I said. "I can manage."

I pushed the desk toward the open door—its passage left long white scratches on the floor boards—until the slight rise of the sill blocked my progress. I checked quickly to be sure that the door was wide enough—it was. I reached as far under one end as I could, and lifted. It was very solid, my back began to ache—but the desk itself was top-heavy, and I managed to heave it high enough to have it topple of its own weight. Out the door, down the two steps, into the concrete yard. I left it there. It would block this door, but we could use the front. And anyway, I couldn't move it again. I seemed to have strained my back. I put both hands to it and rocked gently while I looked at the gouges on each side of the painted door frame. "I seem to have done a bit of damage," I said to Mr. Delatte. "But I've been meaning to do that for such a long time."

The rubbing and the stretching seemed to do my back no good at all—I would just have to get used to the pain. I stopped and closed the door. Mr. Delatte was sitting by the telephone. He did not seem to notice anything strange. "I've got the number," he said. "Would you like to make a private call?"

"No," I told him, "don't bother to leave."

His face had the empty look of people in church as he handed me the slip of paper. There were two Seattle numbers.

Mr. Delatte said: "One is his office, the other's his home."

Saturday—he would be home. It was so simple. So very, very simple. He himself answered the phone, I recognized his voice. "I said I would find you, Robert," I told him. "Do you remember me? Are you waiting for me?"

He didn't say a single word. Just a quick rasp of breath as he hung up. "Oh, Robert," I said to the empty line, "that won't do any good. I'll be calling again. Over and over and over again." I sat back and laughed. Laughed until my insides hurt. Laughed until I put my head down on the smooth top of the telephone and cried. I was conscious that people came and bent over and looked at me, shook their heads and went away again. On tiptoe as a funeral. I no longer cared. I had my own sob-wracked echoing world, and I was locked into it.

Look at the colors, I thought, why are there so many colors? There never were before. Tears make prisms in the light.

I went on crying until I slipped off the chair. And cried on the floor, huddled fetus-like against the cold unyielding boards.

Voices of the South

Doris Betts, *The Astronomer and Other Stories*

Erskine Caldwell, *Poor Fool*

Fred Chappell, *The Gaudy Place*

Ellen Douglas, *A Lifetime Burning*

Ellen Douglas, *The Rock Cried Out*

George Garrett, *Do, Lord, Remember Me*

Shirley Ann Grau, *The Keepers of the House*

Barry Hannah, *The Tennis Handsome*

Mac Hyman, *No Time for Sergeants*

Madison Jones, *A Cry of Absence*

Willie Morris, *The Last of the Southern Girls*

Louis D. Rubin, Jr., *The Golden Weather*

Lee Smith, *The Last Day the Dogbushes Bloomed*

Elizabeth Spencer, *The Salt Line*

Elizabeth Spencer, *The Voice at the Back Door*

Peter Taylor, *The Widows of Thornton*

Robert Penn Warren, *Band of Angels*

Joan Williams, *The Morning and the Evening*